Lisa ... orical and contemporary ... n published in fourteen languages. In 1985, she was named Miss Massachusetts

... have appeared on the *New York Times* bestseller lists. Lisa is married and has two children.

Visit Lisa Kleypas online:

www.lisakleypas.com
www.facebook.com/LisaKleypas
www.twitter.com/LisaKleypas

Praise for Lisa Kleypas:

'Kleypas launches the Friday Harbour trilogy with a delightful portrait of a picturesque town where people know everything about everyone and look out for each other . . . She enchantingly weaves together additional connections with relatives and friends, leaving many dangling threads that will lead the reader straight to book two'
Publishers Weekly

'Flawlessly written . . . Kleypas brings together richly nuanced characters, an emotionally riveting plot, and a subtle touch of the paranormal to create an unforgettable romance that is pure reading magic'
Booklist

'Magical'
RT Book Reviews

By Lisa Kleypas

The Ravenels Series:
Cold-Hearted Rake
Marrying Winterborne
Devil in Spring

Friday Harbour Series:
Christmas Eve at Friday Harbour
Rainshadow Road
Dream Lake
Crystal Cover

Travis Series:
Sugar Daddy
Blue-Eyed Devil
Smooth Talking Stranger
Brown-Eyed Girl

Wallflower Series:
Secrets of a Summer Night
It Happened One Autumn
The Devil in Winter
Scandal in Spring

Hathaway Series:
Mine Till Midnight
Seduce Me at Sunrise
Tempt Me at Twilight
Married by Morning
Love in the Afternoon

Bow Street Series:
Someone to Watch Over Me
Lady Sophia's Lover
Worth Any Price

Available from Piatkus Entice:
Again the Magic
A Wallflower Christmas

Lisa
KLEYPAS

Devil in Spring

piatkus

PIATKUS

First published in the United States in 2017 by Avon Books,
an imprint of HarperCollins Publishers
First published in Great Britain in 2017 by Piatkus

1 3 5 7 9 10 8 6 4 2

A CIP catalogue record for this book
is available from the British Library.

ISBN: 978-0-349-40765-4

Printed and bound by CPI Group (UK) Ltd, Croydon, CR0 4YY

Papers used by Piatkus are from well-managed forests
and other responsible sources.

Piatkus
An imprint of
Little, Brown Book Group
Carmelite House
50 Victoria Embankment
London EC4Y 0DZ

An Hachette UK Company
www.hachette.co.uk

www.littlebrown.co.uk

To Carrie Feron,
for all your incredible kindness, hard work, and insight,
and for making my life and my books more joyful.

Prologue

EVANGELINE, THE DUCHESS OF KINGSTON, lifted her infant grandson from the nursery tub and wrapped him snugly in a soft white towel. Chortling, the baby braced his sturdy legs and attempted to stand in her lap. He explored her face and hair with grasping wet hands, and Evie laughed at his affectionate mauling. "Be gentle, Stephen." She winced as he grabbed the double strand of pearls around her neck. "Oh, I knew I shouldn't have worn those at your bath time. Too much t-temptation." Evie had always spoken with a stammer, although it was now very slight compared to what it had been in her youth.

"Your Grace," the young nursemaid, Ona, exclaimed, hurrying toward her. "I would have lifted Master Stephen out of the tub for you. A fair armful, he is. Solid as a brick."

"He's no trouble at all," Evie assured her, kissing the baby's rosy cheeks and prying his grip from her pearls.

"Your Grace is very kind to help with the children on Nanny's day off." Carefully the nursemaid took the baby from Evie's arms. "Any of the housemaids would be glad to do it, since you have more important things to attend to."

"There's n-nothing more important than my grandchildren. And I enjoy spending time in the nursery—it reminds me of when my children were small."

Ona chuckled as Stephen reached for the white ruffled cap on her head. "I'll powder and dress him now."

"I'll tidy up the bath things," Evie said.

"Your Grace, you *mustn't*." Clearly the nursemaid was trying to strike an effective balance between sternness and pleading. "Not in your fine silk dress—you must sit in the parlor and read a book, or embroider something." As Evie parted her lips to argue, Ona added meaningfully, "Nanny would have my head if she knew I'd let you help as much as I have."

Checkmate.

Knowing that Nanny would have *both* their heads, Evie responded with a resigned nod, although she was unable to resist muttering, "I'm wearing an apron."

The nursemaid left the bathroom with a satisfied smile, carrying Stephen to the nursery.

Still kneeling on the bath rug in front of the tub, Evie reached behind her back for the flannel apron ties. Ruefully she reflected that it was no easy task to satisfy the servants' expectations of how a duchess should behave. They were determined to prevent her from doing anything more strenuous than stirring her tea with a silver spoon. And while she was a grandmother of two, she was still slim and fit—easily able to lift a slippery infant from a washtub, or romp with the children through the orchard. Just last week, she had been lectured by the master gardener for climbing over a stacked stone wall to retrieve a few stray toy arrows.

As she fumbled with the stubborn apron knot, Evie heard a footstep behind her. Although there was no other sound or sign of the visitor's identity, she knew who it was, even before he sank to his knees behind her. Strong fingers brushed hers away, and the knot was freed with a deft tug.

A low, silken murmur caressed the sensitive skin at the back of her neck. "I see we've hired a new nanny. How delightful." Clever masculine hands slipped beneath the loosening apron, moving in a supple caress from her waist to her breasts. "What a buxom little wench. I predict you'll do well here."

Evie closed her eyes, leaning back between his spread thighs. A gentle mouth, designed for sin and sensation, wandered lightly over her neck.

"I should probably warn you," the seductive voice continued, "to keep your distance from the master. He's an infamous lecher."

A smile came to her lips. "So I've heard. Is he as wicked as they say?"

"No. Much worse. Especially when it comes to women with red hair." He plucked a few pins from her coiffure until a long braid fell over her shoulder. "Poor lass—I'm afraid he won't leave you alone."

Evie shivered in reflexive pleasure as she felt him kiss his way along the side of her neck. "H-how should I handle him?"

"Frequently," he said in between kisses.

A helpless giggle escaped her as she twisted in his arms to face him.

Even after three decades of marriage, Evie's heart still skipped a beat at the sight of her husband, formerly Lord St. Vincent, now the Duke of Kingston. Sebastian had matured into a magnificent man with a presence that both intimidated and dazzled. Since ascending to the dukedom ten years ago, he had acquired a veneer of dignity that befitted a man of his considerable power. But no one could look into those remarkable light blue eyes, alive with glints of fire and ice, without recalling that he had once been the most wicked rake in England. He still was—Evie could attest to that.

Time had treated Sebastian lovingly, and always would. He was a beautiful man, lean and elegant, his tawny-golden hair now lightly brushed with silver at the temples. A lion in winter, whom no one would cross except at their peril. Maturity had given him a look of cool, incisive authority, the sense of a man who had seen and experienced enough that he could rarely, if ever, be outmaneuvered. But when something amused or touched him, his smile was both incandescent and irresistible.

"Oh, it's you," Sebastian said in a tone of mild surprise, seeming to ponder how he had ended up kneeling on a bathroom rug with his wife in his arms. "I was prepared to debauch a resisting servant girl, but you're a more difficult case."

"You can debauch me," Evie offered cheerfully.

Her husband smiled, his glowing gaze moving gently over her face. He smoothed back a few escaping curls that had lightened from ruby to soft apricot. "My love, I've tried for thirty years. But despite my dedicated efforts . . ." A sweetly erotic kiss grazed her lips. ". . . you still have the innocent eyes of that shy wallflower I eloped with. Can't you try to look at least a little jaded? Disillusioned?" He laughed quietly at her efforts and kissed her again, this time with a teasing, sensuous pressure that caused her pulse to quicken.

"Why did you come to find me?" Evie asked languidly, her head tilting back as his lips slid to her throat.

"I've just received news about your son."

"Which one?"

"Gabriel. There's been a scandal."

"Why is he your son when you're pleased with him, and my son whenever he's done something wicked?" Evie asked as Sebastian removed her apron and began to unfasten the front of her bodice.

"Since I'm the virtuous parent," he said, "it only stands to reason that his wickedness must come from you."

"You h-have that exactly backward," she informed him.

"Do I?" Sebastian fondled her slowly as he considered her words. "*I'm* the wicked one? No, my pet, that can't be right. I'm sure it's you."

"You," she said decisively, and her breath hastened as his caresses became more intimate.

"Hmm. This must be sorted out at once. I'm taking you straight to bed."

"Wait. Tell me more about Gabriel. Does the scandal have something to do with . . . that woman?" It was more or less public knowledge that Gabriel was having an affair with the American ambassador's wife. Evie had heartily disapproved of the relationship from the beginning, of course, and had hoped it would end soon. That had been two years ago.

Lifting his head, Sebastian looked down at her with a slight frown. He sighed shortly. "He's managed to compromise an earl's daughter. One of the Ravenels."

Evie frowned, pondering the name, which sounded familiar. "Do we know that family?"

"I was acquainted with the old earl, Lord Trenear. His wife was a flighty, shallow sort—you met her once at a garden show and discussed her orchid collection."

"Yes, I remember." Unfortunately, Evie hadn't liked the woman. "They had a daughter?"

"Twins. Out for their first Season this year. It seems that your idiot son was caught *in flagrante delicto* with one of them."

"He takes after his father," Evie said.

Looking highly insulted, Sebastian rose to his feet in a graceful motion and pulled her up with him. "His father was never caught."

"Except by me," Evie said smugly.

Sebastian laughed. "True."

"What does *in flagrante delicto* mean, exactly?"

"The literal translation? 'While the crime is blazing.'" Picking her up easily, he said, "I believe a demonstration is in order."

"But what about the s-scandal? What about Gabriel, and the Ravenel girl, and—"

"The rest of the world can wait," Sebastian said firmly. "I'm going to debauch you for the ten thousandth time, Evie—and for once, I want you to pay attention."

"Yes, sir," she said demurely, and looped her arms around her husband's neck as he carried her to their bedroom.

Chapter 1

London, 1876
Two days earlier . . .

Lady Pandora Ravenel was bored.

Bored stiff.

Bored of being bored.

And the London Season was barely underway. She would have to endure four months of balls, soirées, concerts, and dinners before Parliament closed and the families of the peerage could return to their county seats. There would be at least sixty dinners, fifty balls, and heaven knew how many soirées.

She would never survive.

Letting her shoulders slump, Pandora sat back in the chair and stared at the crowded ballroom scene. There were gentlemen dressed in their formal schemes of black and white, officers in uniform and dress boots, and ladies swathed in silk and tulle. Why were they all there? What could they possibly say to each other that hadn't been said during the last ball?

The worst kind of alone, Pandora thought morosely, was being the only person in a crowd who wasn't having a good time.

Somewhere in the whirling mass of waltzing couples, her twin sister danced gracefully in the arms of a hopeful suitor. So far Cassandra had found the Season nearly as dull and disappointing as Pandora did, but she was far more willing to play the game.

"Wouldn't you rather move about the room and talk to people," Cassandra had asked earlier in the evening, "instead of staying in the corner?"

"No, at least when I'm sitting here, I can think about interesting things. I don't know how you can bear keeping company with tiresome people for hours."

"They're not all tiresome," Cassandra had protested.

Pandora had given her a skeptical glance. "Of the gentlemen you've met so far, have you met even one you would like to see again?"

"Not yet," Cassandra had admitted. "But I won't give up until I've met them all."

"Once you've met one," Pandora had said darkly, "you *have* met them all."

Cassandra had shrugged. "Talking makes the evenings pass by more quickly. You should try it."

Unfortunately, Pandora was abysmal at small talk. She found it impossible to feign interest when some pompous boor began boasting about himself and his accomplishments, and how well his friends liked him, and how much others admired him. She couldn't muster any patience for a peer in his declining years who wanted a young bride to serve as his companion and nurse, or a widower who was obviously searching for potential breeding stock. The thought of being touched by any of them, even with gloved hands, made her skin crawl. And the idea of making conversation with them reminded her of how bored she was.

Staring down at the polished parquet floor, she tried to think of how many words she could make out of the word *bored*. Orbed . . . robed . . . doer . . . rode . . .

"Pandora," came her chaperone's crisp voice. "Why are you sitting in the corner again? Let me see your dance card."

Looking up at Eleanor, Lady Berwick, Pandora reluctantly handed her the small fan-shaped card.

The countess, a tall woman with a majestic presence and a spine like a broomstick, fanned open the dance card's mother-of-pearl covers and surveyed the thin bone pages with a steely gaze.

All blank.

Lady Berwick's lips tightened as if they'd been hemmed with a drawstring. "This should have been filled by now."

"I turned my ankle," Pandora said, not quite meeting her gaze. Faking a minor injury was the only way she could sit safely in the corner and avoid committing a serious social blunder. According to the rules of etiquette, once a lady declined to dance because of fatigue or injury, she couldn't accept any invitations for the rest of the evening.

Disapproval frosted the older woman's voice. "Is this how you repay Lord Trenear's generosity? All your expensive new gowns and accessories—why did you allow him to purchase them for you, if you had already planned to make ill use of your Season?"

As a matter of fact, Pandora did feel bad about that. Her cousin Devon, Lord Trenear, who had assumed the earldom last year after her brother had died, had been remarkably kind to her and Cassandra. Not only had he paid for them to be well dressed for the Season, he had also provided for dowries substantial enough to guarantee the interest of any eligible bachelor. It was certain that her parents, who had passed away several years ago, would have been far less generous.

"I didn't *plan* to make ill use of my Season," she mumbled. "I just didn't realize how difficult it would be."

Especially the dancing.

Certain dances, such as the grand march and the quadrille, were manageable. She could even navigate the *galop*, as long as her partner didn't whirl her too quickly. But the waltz presented dangers at every turn . . . literally. Pandora lost her equilibrium whenever she spun in a sharp circle. For that matter, she was also thrown off-balance in darkness, when she couldn't rely on vision to orient herself. Lady Berwick didn't know about her problem, and for reasons of pride and shame, Pandora would never tell her. Only Cassandra knew her secret and the story behind it, and had helped to conceal it for years.

"It's only difficult because you make it so," Lady Berwick said sternly.

"I don't see why I should go to all this trouble to catch a husband who'll never like me."

"Whether or not your husband likes you is immaterial. Marriage has nothing to do with personal feelings. It is a union of interests."

Pandora held her tongue, although she didn't agree. Approximately a year ago, her older sister Helen had married Mr. Rhys Winterborne, a common-born Welshman, and they were exceedingly happy. So were Cousin Devon and his wife Kathleen. Love matches might be rare, but they certainly weren't impossible.

Even so, Pandora found it impossible to imagine that kind of future for herself. Unlike Cassandra, who was a romantic, she had never dreamed of marrying and having children. She didn't want to belong to anyone, and she especially didn't want anyone to belong to her. No matter how she had tried to make herself want what she *should* want, she knew she would never be happy in a conventional life.

Lady Berwick sighed and sat beside her, her spine a rigid parallel to the back of the chair. "The month of May has just begun. Do you remember what I told you about that?"

"It's the most important month of the Season, when all the great events are held."

"Correct." Lady Berwick handed the dance card back to her. "After tonight, I expect you to make an effort. You owe it to Lord and Lady Trenear, and to yourself. I daresay you owe it to me as well, after all my efforts to improve you."

"You're right," Pandora said quietly. "And I'm sorry—truly sorry—for the trouble I've caused you. But it's become clear to me that I'm not meant for any of this. I don't want to marry anyone. I've made plans to support myself and live independently. With any luck I'll be successful, and no one will have to worry about me any longer."

"You're referring to that parlor game nonsense?" the countess asked, her tone inflected with scorn.

"It's not nonsense. It's real. I've just been granted a patent. Ask Mr. Winterborne."

Last year, Pandora, who had always loved toys and parlor amusements, had designed a board game. With Mr. Winterborne's encouragement, she had filed for a patent and intended to produce and distribute the game. Mr. Winterborne owned the largest department store in the world, and had already agreed to place an order for five hundred copies. The game was a guaranteed success, if for no other reason than that there was hardly any competition: Whereas the board game industry was flourishing in America, thanks to the efforts of the

Milton Bradley company, it was still in its infancy here in Britain. Pandora had already developed two more games and was almost ready to file patents for them. Someday she would earn enough money to make her own way in the world.

"As fond as I am of Mr. Winterborne," Lady Berwick said dourly, "I fault him for encouraging you in this folly."

"He thinks I have the makings of an excellent business woman."

The countess twitched as if she'd been stung by a wasp. "Pandora, you were born an earl's daughter. It would be appalling enough if you married a merchant or manufacturer, but to become one *yourself* is unthinkable. You wouldn't be received anywhere. You would be ostracized."

"Why should any of these people"—Pandora cast a quick, wary glance at the crowd in the ballroom—"care what I choose to do?"

"Because you are one of them. A fact that, assuredly, pleases them no more than it does you." The countess shook her head. "I can't pretend to understand you, my girl. Your brain has always seemed to me like those fireworks—what are the ones that spin so madly?"

"Catherine wheels."

"Yes. Whirling and sparking, all light and noise. You make judgments without bothering to find out the particulars. It's a fine thing to be clever, but too much cleverness usually produces the same result as ignorance. Do you think you can willfully disregard the world's opinion? Do you expect people to admire you for being different?"

"Of course not." Pandora fiddled with her empty

dance card, fanning it open and closing it repeatedly. "But they might at least try to be accepting."

"Foolish, cross-grained girl, why should they? Nonconformity is nothing but self-interest in disguise." Although it was obvious the countess would have liked to deliver a full-blown lecture, she snapped her mouth shut and rose to her feet. "We will continue this discussion later." Turning away, Lady Berwick headed for a brood of sharp-eyed, vinegar-blooded dowagers at the side of the room.

A metallic sound began in Pandora's left ear, like a vibrating copper wire, as it sometimes did when she was in distress. To her horror, the stinging pressure of frustrated tears rose behind her eyes. Oh God, that would be the ultimate humiliation: eccentric, clumsy, Pandora-the-wallflower crying in the corner of the ballroom. No, it would *not* happen. She stood with such haste that her chair nearly toppled backward.

"Pandora," came an urgent voice from nearby. "I need you to help me."

Perplexed, she turned just as Dolly, Lady Colwick, reached her.

Dolly, a vivacious, dark-haired girl, was the younger of Lady Berwick's two daughters. The families had become well acquainted after Lady Berwick had undertaken to teach etiquette and deportment to Pandora and Cassandra. Dolly was pretty and well-liked, and she had been kind to Pandora when other young women had been indifferent or mocking. Last year, during Dolly's first Season, she had been the toast of London, with a crowd of bachelors collecting around her at every social event. Recently she had married Arthur, Lord Colwick, who, although some twenty years older, had the advantage of a sizeable fortune and a marquessate in his future.

"What's the matter?" Pandora asked in concern.

"First promise you won't tell Mama."

Pandora smiled wryly. "You know I never tell her anything if I can help it. What is the problem?"

"I've lost an earring."

"Oh, bother," Pandora said sympathetically. "Well, that could happen to anyone. I lose things all the time."

"No, you don't understand. Lord Colwick had his mother's sapphire earrings fetched from the safe for me to wear tonight." Dolly turned her head to display a heavy sapphire and diamond pendant that dangled from one of her ears. "The problem isn't just that I lost the other one," she continued unhappily. "It's *where* I lost it. You see, I slipped away from the house for a few minutes with one of my former suitors, Mr. Hayhurst. Lord Colwick would be furious with me if he found out."

Pandora's eyes widened. "Why did you do that?"

"Well, Mr. Hayhurst was always my favorite suitor. The poor boy is still heartbroken that I married Lord Colwick, and he insists on pursuing me. So I had to placate him by agreeing to a rendezvous. We went to a summer house beyond the back terraces. I must have lost the earring when we were on the settee." Her eyes glimmered with tears. "I can't go back to look for it. I've already been absent for too long. And if my husband notices the earring is gone . . . I don't even want to think about what might happen."

A moment of expectant silence ensued.

Pandora glanced at the ballroom windows, their panes glittering with coruscating reflected lights. It was dark outside.

Unease slithered down her spine. She didn't like

going anywhere at night, especially alone. But Dolly seemed desperate, and in light of her past kindness, there was no way Pandora could refuse.

"Do you want me to fetch it for you?" she offered reluctantly.

"Would you? You could dash to the summer house, retrieve the earring, and return in a flash. It's easy to find. Just follow the graveled path across the lawn. Please, please, *dear* Pandora, I'll owe you my life."

"There's no need to beg," Pandora said, perturbed and amused. "I'll do my best to find it. But Dolly, now that you're married, I don't think you should rendezvous with Mr. Hayhurst. He can't be worth the risk."

Dolly gave her a regretful glance. "I'm fond of Lord Colwick, but I'll never love him the way I do Mr. Hayhurst."

"Why didn't you marry him, then?"

"Mr. Hayhurst is a third son and will never have a title."

"But if you love him—"

"Don't be silly, Pandora. Love is for middle-class girls." Dolly's gaze chased anxiously around the room. "No one's looking," she said. "You could slip out now if you're quick about it."

Oh, she was going to be as quick as a March hare. She wouldn't spend any more time outside at night than absolutely necessary. If only she could recruit Cassandra, always her willing conspirator, to accompany her. But it was better for Cassandra to continue dancing; it would keep Lady Berwick's attention occupied.

Casually she made her way along the side of the ballroom, past spills of conversation about the opera, the Park, and the latest "new thing." As she slipped behind Lady Berwick's back, she half expected her chaperone to turn and dive at her like an osprey sighting a mullet. Fortunately Lady Berwick continued to watch the dancing couples, who circumnavigated the room in a swift current of colorful skirts and trousered legs.

As far as Pandora could tell, her exit from the ballroom went unnoticed. She hurried down the great staircase and through the great balconied hall, and reached a brightly lit gallery that stretched along the entire length of the house. Rows of portraits covered the gallery, generations of dignified aristocrats glowering down at her as she half-walked, half-ran across the inlaid flooring.

Finding a door that opened to the back terrace, she paused at the threshold, staring out like a passenger at the railing of a ship at sea. The night was deep, cool, and dark. She *hated* to leave the safety of the house. But she was reassured by the procession of oil-burning garden torches, consisting of copper bowls set on tall iron poles that lined the path across the wide lawn.

Focusing on her mission, Pandora skittered across the back terrace toward the lawn. An abundant grove of Scotch firs made the air agreeably pungent. It helped to mask the smell of the Thames, which coursed turgidly at the edge of the estate grounds.

Rough masculine voices and bursts of hammering came from the direction of the river, where workmen reinforced the scaffolding in preparation for a fireworks display. At the end of the evening, the guests would gather on the back terrace and along the upper floor balconies to watch the pyrotechnics.

The graveled path meandered around a giant statue of London's ancient river deity, Father Thames. Long-bearded and stout of build, the massive figure reclined on an enormous stone plinth with a trident clasped negligently in one hand. He was entirely nude except for a cape, which Pandora thought made him look remarkably silly.

"*Au naturel* in public?" she asked flippantly as she passed him. "One might expect it of a classical Greek statue, but *you*, sir, have no excuse."

She continued to the summer house, which was partially shielded by a yew hedge and a profusion of cabbage roses. The open-sided building, with matchboard walls that went halfway up the columns, was constructed on a brick foundation. It was adorned with colored glass panels, and illuminated only by a tiny Moroccan lamp hanging from the ceiling.

Hesitantly she went up two wooden steps and entered the structure. The only furniture was an openwork settee, which appeared to have been bolted to the nearby columns.

As she searched for the missing earring, Pandora tried not to let the hem of her skirts drag the dirty floor. She was wearing her best dress, a ball gown made of iridescent shot silk, which appeared silver from one angle, and lavender from another. The front was simple in design, with a smooth, tight-fitting bodice and a low scooped neckline. A web of intricate tucks in the back flowed into a cascade of silk that fluttered and shimmered whenever she moved.

After looking beneath the loose cushions, Pandora climbed onto the seat. She squinted at the space between the settee and the curved wall. A satisfied grin crossed her face as she saw a rich glitter at the seam of the wall trim and floor.

Now the only question was how to retrieve the earring. If she knelt on the floor, she would return to the ballroom as dirty as a chimney sweep.

The back of the settee had been carved into an ornate pattern of flourishes and curlicues, with spaces wide enough to reach through. Tugging off her gloves, Pandora tucked them into the concealed pocket of her gown. Gamely she hiked up her skirts, knelt on the settee, and inserted her arm into one of the openwork gaps, all the way to the elbow. Her fingertips wouldn't quite touch the floor.

Leaning farther into the space, she pushed her head through and felt a slight tug at her coiffure, followed by the delicate ping of a fallen hairpin. "Drat," she muttered. Angling her body, she twisted to fit her shoulders through the opening, and felt for the earring until her fingers closed around it.

As she tried to pull out, however, she had unexpected difficulty. The settee's carved woodwork seemed to have closed around her like a shark's jaws. Backing away more strongly, she felt her dress hook on something and heard a few stitches pop. She went still. It certainly wouldn't do to return to the ballroom with a rip in her gown.

She strained and struggled to reach the back of her dress, but stopped again as she heard the fragile silk begin to tear. Perhaps if she slid forward a bit and tried to back out at a different angle . . . but the maneuver only trapped her more firmly, the serrated edges of carved wood digging into her skin. After a minute of squirming and floundering, Pandora held motionless except for the fast, anxious jerks of her lungs.

"I'm not stuck," she muttered. "I can't be." She wriggled helplessly. "Oh God, I am, I'm stuck. Blast. *Blast*."

If she was found like this, it would mean lifelong ridicule. She might find a way to live with it. But it would reflect on her family and make them look ridiculous too, and it would ruin Cassandra's Season, and that was unacceptable.

Despairing and frustrated, Pandora tried to think of the worst word she knew. "*Bollocks.*"

In the next moment, she turned cold with horror as she heard a man clearing his throat.

Was it a servant? A gardener? *Please, dear God, please don't let it be one of the guests.*

She heard footsteps as he entered the summer house.

"You seem to be having some difficulty with that settee," the stranger remarked. "As a rule, I don't recommend the headfirst approach, as it tends to complicate the seating process." The voice contained a cool dark resonance that did something pleasant to her nerves. Gooseflesh rose on her bare skin.

"I'm sure this must be amusing," Pandora said cautiously, straining to see him through the carved woodwork. He was dressed in formal evening clothes. Definitely a guest.

"Not at all. Why would I be amused by the sight of a young woman posing upside-down on a piece of furniture?"

"I'm not posing. My dress is caught in the settee. And I would be much obliged if you would help me out of it!"

"The dress or the settee?" the stranger asked, sounding interested.

"The settee," Pandora said irritably. "I'm all tangled up in these dratted—" she hesitated, wondering what to call the elaborate wooden curls and twists carved into the back of the settee. "—swirladingles," she finished.

"Acanthus scrolls," the man said at the same time. A second passed before he asked blankly, "What did you call them?"

"Never mind," Pandora said with chagrin. "I have a bad habit of making up words, and I'm not supposed to say them in public."

"Why not?"

"People might think I'm eccentric."

His quiet laugh awakened a ticklish feeling in her stomach. "At the moment, darling, made-up words are the least of your problems."

Pandora blinked at the casual endearment, and tensed as he sat beside her. He was close enough that she caught his fragrance, a spice of amber or something cedary, wrapped around fresh earthy coolness. He smelled like an expensive forest.

"Are you going to help me?" she asked.

"I might. If you tell me what you were doing on this settee in the first place."

"Is it necessary for you to know?"

"It is," he assured her.

Pandora scowled. "I was reaching for something."

A long arm draped along the back of the settee. "I'm afraid you'll have to be more specific."

He was not being very chivalrous, she thought with annoyance. "An earring."

"How did you lose your earring?"

"It's not mine. It belongs to a friend and I have to return it to her quickly."

"A friend," he repeated skeptically. "What is her name?"

"I can't tell you that."

"A pity. Well, good luck." He made as if to leave.

"*Wait.*" Pandora wriggled, and heard the sound of

more stitches popping. She stopped with a sound of exasperation. "It's Lady Colwick's earring."

"Ah. I suppose she was out here with Hayhurst?"

"How do you know about that?"

"Everyone knows, including Lord Colwick. I don't think he'll mind Dolly's affairs later on, but it's a bit soon before she's produced a legitimate child."

No gentleman had ever spoken so frankly to Pandora before, and it was shocking. It was also the first truly interesting conversation she'd ever had with anyone at a ball.

"She's not having an affair," Pandora said. "It was only a rendezvous."

"Do you know what a rendezvous is?"

"Of course I do," she said with great dignity. "I've had French lessons. It means to have a meeting."

"In context," he said dryly, "it means a great deal more than that."

Pandora squirmed miserably. "I don't give a pickle about what Dolly and Mr. Hayhurst were doing on this settee, I just want to be *out* of it. Will you help me now?"

"I suppose I must. The novelty of talking to an unfamiliar derrière is beginning to wear off."

Pandora stiffened, her heart jolting as she felt him lean over her.

"Don't worry," he said. "I'm not going to molest you. My tastes don't run to young girls."

"I'm twenty-one," she said indignantly.

"Really?"

"Yes, why do you sound skeptical?"

"I wouldn't have expected to find a woman of your age in such a predicament."

"I'm almost always in a predicament." Pandora jerked as she felt a gentle pressure on her back.

"Hold still. You've hooked your dress on three different scroll points." He was pulling deftly at the silk pleats and ruffles. "How did you manage to squeeze through such a small space?"

"It was easy going forward. But I didn't realize all these dratted swirla—that is, scrolls—were set like backward barbs."

"Your dress is free now. Try pulling yourself out."

Pandora began to ease backward, and yelped as the wood dug into her. "I still can't. Oh, *blast*—"

"Don't panic. Twist your shoulders to the . . . no, not that way, the other way. Wait." The stranger sounded reluctantly amused. "This is like trying to open a Japanese puzzle box."

"What's that?"

"A wooden box made of interconnected parts. It can only be opened if one knows the series of moves required to unlock it." A warm palm settled on her bare shoulder, gently angling it.

His touch sent a strange shock through her. She drew in a sharp breath, cool air swirling inside her hot lungs.

"Relax," he said, "and I'll set you free in a moment."

Her voice came out higher-pitched than usual. "I can't relax with your hand there."

"If you cooperate, this will go faster."

"I'm trying, but it's a very awkward position."

"The position was your doing, not mine," he reminded her.

"Yes, but—*ouch*." The point of a scroll had scratched her upper arm. The situation was becoming intolerable. Spurred by the beginnings of alarm, she moved restlessly within the snarls of carved wood. "Oh, this is horriculous."

"Easy. Let me guide your head."

They both froze as a gruff shout came from just outside the summer house. *"What the devil is going on in there?"*

The man leaning over Pandora swore softly beneath his breath. Pandora wasn't certain what the word meant, but it sounded even worse than "bollocks."

The enraged outsider continued. "Scoundrel! I wouldn't have expected this even of you. Forcing yourself on a helpless female, and abusing my hospitality during a charity ball!"

"My lord," Pandora's companion called out brusquely, "you misunderstand the situation."

"I'm sure I understand it quite well. Unhand her this instant."

"But I'm still stuck," Pandora said plaintively.

"For *shame*." The cantankerous old man seemed to be addressing a third party as he remarked, "Caught in the very act, it seems."

Bewildered, Pandora felt the stranger prying her out of the settee, one of his hands briefly shielding the side of her face to protect her from scratches. His touch was gentle but wildly unsettling, sending a warm shiver through her body. As soon as she was free of the woodwork, Pandora stood too quickly. Her head spun after having been held down for too long, and her balance went off-kilter. Reflexively the stranger caught her against him as she staggered. She had a brief, dizzying impression of a hard chest and a wealth of tightly knit muscle before he let go. Her loosened coiffure flopped forward over her forehead as she looked down at herself. Her skirts were dirty and rumpled. Red marks scored her shoulders and upper arms.

"Damn it," the man facing her muttered. "Who are you?"

"Lady Pandora Ravenel. I'll tell them . . ." Her voice trailed away as she found herself looking up at an arrogant young god, tall and big framed, every line of him taut with feline grace. The tiny pendant lamp overhead sent sunstruck golden glints playing among the thick, well-cut layers of his amber hair. His eyes were winter-blue, his cheekbones high and straight, the line of his jaw hard enough to chisel marble. The full, sensuous curves of his lips lent a note of erotic dissonance to his otherwise classic features. One glance at him was enough to make her feel as if she were trying to breathe at high altitude. What would it do to a man's character to be so inhumanly beautiful? It couldn't be anything good.

Shaken, Pandora shoved her hand into the pocket of her gown and dropped the earring inside. "I'll tell them nothing happened. It's the truth, after all."

"The truth isn't going to matter," came his curt reply.

He motioned for her to precede him from the summer house, and they were immediately confronted by Lord Chaworth, the host of the ball and owner of the estate. As a friend of the Berwicks, he was one of the last people Pandora would have wanted to discover her in a compromising situation. He was accompanied by a dark-haired man Pandora had never seen before.

Chaworth was short and stocky, shaped like an apple set on a pair of nut picks. A white nimbus of side whiskers and beard quivered tensely around his face as he spoke. "The earl and I were walking to the river's edge to view the setup for the fireworks, when we happened to hear the young lady's screams for help."

"I didn't scream," Pandora protested.

"I've already walked down there myself to talk to the contractor," the young man beside her said. "As I was returning to the house, I happened to notice that Lady Pandora was in difficulty, having caught part of her dress in the settee. I was only trying to help her."

The snowy puffs of Chaworth's brows ascended to his hairline as he turned to Pandora. "Is that true?"

"It is, my lord."

"Why, pray tell, were you out here in the first place?"

Pandora hesitated, unwilling to turn evidence against Dolly. "I slipped out for a breath of fresh air. I was . . . bored in there."

"Bored?" Chaworth echoed in outrage. "With a twenty-piece orchestra and a ballroom full of eligible bucks to dance with?"

"I wasn't asked to dance," Pandora mumbled.

"You might have been, had you not been out here consorting with a notorious rake!"

"Chaworth," the dark-haired man beside him intervened quietly, "if I may speak."

The speaker was ruggedly attractive, with boldly hewn features and the sun-browned complexion of an avid outdoorsman. Although he was not young—his black locks were liberally shot with steel, and time had deepened the laugh-lines around his eyes and the brackets between his nose and mouth—he certainly couldn't have been called old. Not with that air of robust health, and the presence of a man with considerable authority.

"I've known the lad since the day he was born," he continued, his voice deep and a bit gravelly. "As you know, his father is a close friend. I'll vouch for his character, and his word. For the girl's sake, I suggest that we hold our silence and handle the matter with discretion."

"I am also acquainted with his father," Lord Chaworth snapped, "who plucked many a fair flower in his day. Obviously the son is following in his footsteps. No, Westcliff, I will not remain silent—he must be held accountable for his actions."

Westcliff? Pandora glanced at him with alert interest. She had heard of the Earl of Westcliff, who, after the Duke of Norfolk, held the oldest and most respected peerage title in England. His vast Hampshire estate, Stony Cross Park, was famed for its fishing, hunting, and shooting.

Westcliff met her gaze, seeming neither shocked nor condemning. "Your father was Lord Trenear?" he asked.

"Yes, my lord."

"We were acquainted. He used to hunt at my estate." The earl paused. "I invited him to bring his family, but he always preferred to come alone."

That was hardly a surprise. Pandora's father had considered his three daughters to be parasites. For that matter, her mother had taken little interest in them either. As a result, Pandora, Cassandra, and Helen had sometimes gone for months without seeing their parents. The surprise was that the recollection still had the power to hurt.

"My father wanted as little to do with his daughters as possible," Pandora said bluntly. "He considered us nuisances." Lowering her head, she mumbled, "Obviously I've proven him right."

"I wouldn't say so." A touch of amused sympathy warmed the earl's voice. "My own daughters have assured me—more than once—that any well-meaning girl of high spirits can find herself in hot water now and then."

Lord Chaworth broke in. "This particular 'hot water' must be cooled immediately. I will return Lady Pandora to the care of her chaperone." He turned to the man beside her. "I suggest that you depart for Ravenel House forthwith, to meet with her family and make the appropriate arrangements."

"What arrangements?" Pandora asked.

"He means marriage," the cold-eyed young man said flatly.

A chill of alarm went through her. "*What?* No. No, I wouldn't marry you for any reason." Realizing he might take that personally, Pandora added in a more conciliatory tone, "It has nothing to do with you; it's just that I don't intend to marry at all."

Lord Chaworth interrupted smugly. "I believe it will quell your objections to learn that the man standing before you is Gabriel, Lord St. Vincent—the heir to a dukedom."

Pandora shook her head. "I would rather be a charwoman than a peer's wife."

Lord St. Vincent's cool gaze slid to her scratched shoulders and torn dress, and returned slowly to her strained face. "The fact is," he said quietly, "you've been absent from the ballroom long enough for people to have noticed."

It began to dawn on Pandora that she was in real trouble, the kind that couldn't be solved with facile explanations, or money, or even her family's influence. Her pulse reverberated like a kettledrum in her ears. "Not if you let me go back immediately. No one ever notices whether I'm there or not."

"I find that impossible to believe."

The way he said it didn't sound like a compliment.

"It's true," Pandora said desperately, talking fast, thinking even faster. "I'm a wallflower. I only agreed to take part in the Season to keep my sister Cassandra company. She's my twin, the nicer, prettier one, and you're the kind of husband she's been hoping for. If you'll let me go fetch her, you could compromise her, and then I'll be off the hook." Seeing his blank look, she explained, "People certainly wouldn't expect you to marry both of us."

"I'm afraid I never ruin more than one young woman a night." His tone was a mockery of politeness. "A man has to draw the line somewhere."

Pandora decided to take another tack. "You do *not* want to marry me, my lord. I would be the worst wife imaginable. I'm forgetful and stubborn, and I can never sit still for more than five minutes. I'm always doing things I shouldn't. I eavesdrop on other people, I shout and run in public, and I'm a clumsy dancer. And I've lowered my character with a great deal of unwholesome reading material." Pausing to draw breath, she noticed that Lord St. Vincent didn't appear properly impressed by her list of faults. "Also, my legs are skinny. Like a stork's."

At the indecent mention of body parts, Lord Chaworth gasped audibly, while Lord Westcliff developed a sudden keen interest in the nearby cabbage roses.

Lord St. Vincent's mouth worked against a brief tremor, as if he were amused despite himself. "I appreciate your candor," he said after a moment. He paused to send Lord Chaworth an icy glance. "However, in light of Lord Chaworth's heroic insistence on seeing justice done, I have no choice but to discuss the situation with your family."

"When?" Pandora asked anxiously.

"Tonight." Lord St. Vincent stepped forward, closing the distance between them. His head lowered over hers. "Go with Chaworth," he said. "Tell your chaperone that I'm leaving for Ravenel House immediately. And for God's sake, try not to be seen. I would hate for people to think I did such an incompetent job of molesting someone." After a pause, he added in an undertone, "You still have to return Dolly's earring. Ask a servant to take it to her."

Pandora made the mistake of looking up. No woman would have been unaffected by the sight of that archangel's face above hers. So far, the privileged young men she had met during the Season seemed to be striving for a certain ideal, a kind of cool aristocratic confidence. But none of them came remotely close to this dazzling stranger, who had undoubtedly been indulged and admired his entire life.

"I can't marry you," she said numbly. "I'd lose everything." Turning away, she took Chaworth's arm and accompanied him back toward the house, while the other two stayed behind to talk privately.

Chaworth chortled to himself with infuriating satisfaction. "By Jove, I look forward to seeing Lady Berwick's reaction when I tell her the news."

"She'll murder me on the spot," Pandora managed to say, nearly choking on misery and desperation.

"For what?" the old man asked incredulously.

"For being compromised."

Chaworth let out a guffaw. "Dear girl, I'll be surprised if she doesn't dance a jig. I've just made the match of the year for you!"

Chapter 2

GABRIEL SWORE AND SHOVED his fists in his pockets.

"I'm sorry," Westcliff said sincerely. "Had it not been for Chaworth—"

"I know." Gabriel paced back and forth in front of the summer house like a caged tiger. He couldn't believe it. Of all the clever marital traps he had evaded with ease, he'd finally been caught. Not by a worldly seductress, or a society beauty with finishing-school polish. Instead, his downfall had come in the form of an eccentric wallflower. Pandora was the daughter of an earl, which meant that even if she were a certifiable lunatic—which certainly wasn't outside the realm of possibility—her honor had to be redeemed.

The overwhelming impression she conveyed was of constant nervous energy, like a thoroughbred waiting for the starter's flag. Even her smallest movements seemed to hold the potential for explosive action. The effect had been unsettling, but at the same time, he'd found himself wanting to capture all that undirected fire and put it to good use, until she was limp and exhausted beneath him.

Bedding her wouldn't be a problem.

It was just everything else about her that would be a problem.

Scowling and troubled, Gabriel turned to set his

back against one of the summer house's outer support columns. "What did she mean when she said she would lose everything if she married me?" he asked aloud. "Perhaps she's in love with someone. If so—"

"There are young women," Westcliff pointed out dryly, "who have goals other than finding a husband."

Folding his arms across his chest, Gabriel sent him a sardonic glance. "Are there? I've never met one of those."

"I believe you may have just now." The earl glanced back in the direction Lady Pandora had gone. "A wallflower," he said softly, with a faint, reminiscent smile on his lips.

Aside from his own father, there was no man Gabriel trusted more than Westcliff, who had always been like an uncle to him. The earl was the kind of man who would always make the moral choice, no matter how difficult.

"I already know your opinion about what I should do," Gabriel muttered.

"A girl with a ruined reputation is at the world's mercy," Westcliff said. "You're aware of your obligations as a gentleman."

Gabriel shook his head with an incredulous laugh. "How could I marry a girl like that?" She would never fit into his life. They would end up killing each other. "She's only half-civilized."

"It would seem Lady Pandora hasn't mixed in society long enough to be familiar with its ways," Westcliff admitted.

Gabriel watched a yellow brimstone moth, besotted by the torchlight, fluttering past the summer house. "She doesn't give a damn about society's ways," he said with certainty. The moth flew in ever-smaller circles, glancing repeatedly off the wavering heat in its fatal dance with the torch flame. "What kind of family are the Ravenels?"

"The name is an old and respected one, but their fortune dwindled years ago. Lady Pandora had an older brother, Theo, who inherited the earldom upon their father's passing. Unfortunately he was killed in a riding accident soon afterward."

"I met him," Gabriel said with a pensive frown. "Two—no, three—years ago, at Jenner's."

Gabriel's family owned a private gaming house, ostensibly a gentlemen's club, patronized by royalty, aristocracy, and men of influence. Before inheriting the dukedom, his father, Sebastian, had personally run and managed the club, turning it into one of London's most fashionable gaming establishments.

In the last few years, many of the family's business interests had transferred to Gabriel's shoulders, including Jenner's. He had always kept a close eye on the place, knowing it was one of his father's pet concerns. One night, Theo, Lord Trenear, had visited the club. Theo had been a robust, good-looking man, blond and blue-eyed. Charming on the surface, all explosive force beneath.

"He came to Jenner's with some friends on a night when I happened to be there," Gabriel continued, "and spent most of his time at the hazard table. He didn't play well—he was the kind who chased his losses instead of knowing when to quit. Before leaving, he wanted to apply for membership. The manager came to me, somewhat agitated, and asked me to deal with him because of his privilege and rank."

"You had to turn him down?" Westcliff asked, wincing visibly.

Gabriel nodded. "His credit was bad, and the family estate was drowning in debt. I declined him in private, in as civil a manner as possible. However . . ." He shook his head at the memory.

"He went into a rage," Westcliff guessed.

"Foaming like a bull in clover," Gabriel said ruefully, recalling how Theo had launched at him without warning. "He wouldn't stop swinging until I dropped him to the floor. I've known more than a few men who couldn't control their tempers, especially when they were in their cups. But I've never seen anyone explode quite like that."

"The Ravenels have always been known for their volatile temperaments."

"Thank you," Gabriel said sourly. "Now I won't be surprised when my future offspring emerge with horns and tails."

Westcliff smiled. "In my experience, it's all in how you handle them." The earl was the calm, steady center of his own boisterous family, which included a high-spirited wife and a brood of rambunctious offspring.

And Lady Pandora made them all look like sloths.

Pinching the bridge of his nose with his thumb and forefinger, Gabriel muttered, "I don't have the damned patience, Westcliff." After a moment, he noticed the brimstone moth had finally ventured too close to the beckoning flame. The delicate wings ignited, and the creature was reduced to a smoldering wisp. "Do you know anything about the new Lord Trenear?"

"His name is Devon Ravenel. From all accounts, he's well-liked in Hampshire, and has been managing the estate quite competently." Westcliff paused. "It seems he married the late earl's young widow, which is certainly not unlawful, but it did raise a few brows."

"She must have had a massive jointure," Gabriel said cynically.

"Perhaps. In any event, I wouldn't expect Trenear to object to a match between you and Lady Pandora."

Gabriel's mouth twisted. "Believe me, he'll be overjoyed to have her taken off his hands."

MOST OF THE mansions on South Audley, a smart address in the heart of Mayfair, were of the standard multi-columned Georgian design. Ravenel House, however, was a Jacobean with triple-story balconies and a hipped roof bristling with slender chimneys.

The great hall was lined with richly carved oak paneling, and a white plasterwork ceiling adorned with mythological figures. The walls were softened with an abundance of rich tapestries and French chinoiserie vases filled with bursts of fresh cut flowers. Judging from the quiet atmosphere, Pandora hadn't yet returned.

A butler showed him to a well-appointed parlor and announced him. As Gabriel stepped forward and bowed, Devon Ravenel stood to reciprocate.

The new Earl of Trenear was a lean, broad-shouldered fellow of no more than thirty, with dark hair and a shrewd gaze. There was an alert but friendly air about him, a relaxed confidence that Gabriel immediately liked.

His wife Kathleen, Lady Trenear, remained on the sofa. "Welcome, my lord." One glance was all it took to refute Gabriel's earlier speculation that Trenear had married her for financial gain. Or at least, that couldn't have been the only reason. She was a lovely woman, delicately feline, with tip-tilted brown eyes. The way her ruddy curls tried to spring free of their pins reminded him of his mother and older sister.

"I apologize for intruding on your privacy," Gabriel said.

"No need," Trenear replied easily. "It's a pleasure to make your acquaintance."

"You may not think so after I explain why I'm here." Gabriel felt his color rising as he met their inquiring gazes. Furious and stunned to find himself in a dilemma that smacked of high farce, he continued with stone-faced resolve. "I've just come from the Chaworth ball. An unexpected situation has . . . cropped up . . . and it must be resolved with all due haste. I—" He paused to clear his throat. "I seem to have compromised Lady Pandora."

Utter silence descended on the room.

In other circumstances, Gabriel might have been amused by the couple's blank expressions.

Lady Trenear was the first to respond. "What do you mean by 'compromised,' my lord? Were you overheard flirting with her, or perhaps discussing some inappropriate subject?"

"I was discovered alone with her. At the summer house behind the mansion."

Another all-encompassing silence, before the earl asked bluntly, "What were you doing?"

"Helping her out of a settee."

Lady Trenear looked increasingly bewildered. "That was very courteous of you, but why—"

"By 'helping her out,'" Gabriel continued, "I mean to say that I had to pull her out *through* the settee. Somehow she had managed to wedge the upper half of her body into the middle of the carved open back, and couldn't free herself without tearing off her dress."

Trenear rubbed his forehead and briefly pressed the heels of his hands against his eye sockets. "That would be Pandora," he muttered. "I'm going to ring for brandy."

"Three glasses," his wife told him, her worried gaze returning to Gabriel. "Lord St. Vincent, come sit by me, please, and tell us what happened." As he complied, she gathered up a thimble, a spool of thread, and a few bits of cloth, and distractedly shoved them into a mending basket near her feet.

Gabriel explained the events of the evening as succinctly as possible, omitting the part about Dolly's earring. Although he had no obligation to keep Dolly's secret, he knew Pandora would want him to hold his silence on that point.

Trenear came to sit beside his wife and listened intently. After a footman had appeared with a tray of brandy, he poured the vintage into short-stemmed glasses and handed one to Gabriel.

Taking a bracing swallow, Gabriel felt the biting glow sink deep in his throat. "Even if Chaworth hadn't been determined to hold my feet to the fire," he said, "Lady Pandora's reputation was already in ruins. She shouldn't have left the ballroom."

Lady Trenear's shoulders drooped like a weary schoolgirl's. "This was my fault. I persuaded Pandora to take part in the Season."

"Don't start that, for God's sake," the earl said gently, guiding her to look at him. "Not everything is your fault, much as you would like to believe otherwise. We all urged Pandora to go out in society. The alternative was to let her stay at home while Cassandra went to balls and parties."

"If she's forced to marry, it will break her spirit."

Taking his wife's small hand, Trenear coaxed her fingers to curl around his. "No one will force her to do anything. Come what may, she and Cassandra can always rely on my protection."

His wife's brown eyes were tender and radiant as she smiled at him. "You dear man. You didn't even have to think about it, did you?"

"Of course not."

Gabriel was disconcerted—no, baffled—by the way they discussed the situation as if there were a choice to be made. Good God, was he really going to have to explain that the disgrace would cast a shadow over the entire family? That the Ravenels' friendships and connections would be severed? That Pandora's twin would have no chance of finding a decent match?

Lady Trenear's attention returned to him. Taking in his confounded expression, she said carefully, "My lord, I should explain that Pandora is no ordinary girl. She has a free spirit, and an original mind. And . . . well, obviously, she's a bit impulsive."

The description was so contrary to the ideal of a proper English bride that Gabriel felt his stomach sink like a millstone.

". . . she and her sisters," Lady Trenear was saying, ". . . were raised in extreme seclusion at the family's country estate. They were all educated, but very unworldly. The first time I met them was the day I married their brother Theo. They seemed like a trio of . . . forest sprites, or wood nymphs, something out of a fairy story. Helen, the oldest, was quiet and shy, but the twins had been left to run wild on the estate, unattended, for most of their lives."

"Why would their parents allow that?" Gabriel asked.

The earl answered quietly. "They had no use for daughters. The only child they valued was their son."

"What we're trying to convey," Lady Trenear said earnestly, "is that Pandora would never thrive with a husband who expected her to be . . . well, conventional. She needs someone who will appreciate her unique qualities."

After swirling the brandy in his glass, Gabriel finished it in two expedient gulps, hoping it would ease the chill of dread in his gut.

It didn't.

Nothing was going to make him feel better about the disastrous turn his life had just taken.

He'd never expected to have a marriage like his parents'—few people on earth ever had. But at the very least Gabriel had hoped to marry an accomplished and respectable woman who would run his household efficiently and raise well-behaved children.

Instead, it seemed he was going to marry a forest sprite. With an original mind.

Gabriel couldn't begin to imagine the ramifications for his family's estates, tenants, and servants. Not to mention his offspring. God, she wouldn't have the first idea of how to mother them.

Setting aside his empty glass, he decided to go home and have a bottle to himself. Or better yet, he would visit his mistress, in whose arms he would find temporary oblivion. Anything would be better than sitting here discussing the peculiar young woman who, in the course of ten minutes, had managed to ruin his life.

"Trenear," he said grimly, "if you can find a solution other than marriage, I swear I'll dance a fiddler's jig on the steps of St. Paul's. But the most likely outcome of this is that I'll be performing the wedding march instead." He reached into an inner pocket of his coat for his card. "I'll await your decision at my London residence."

A defiant voice came from the threshold. "It's *my* decision, and I've already said no."

Gabriel stood automatically, as did Trenear, as Pandora strode into the room. She was trailed by her twin, a pretty blonde, and Eleanor, Lady Berwick.

Pandora's dress was disheveled, her bodice askew, and her gloves were missing. A few raised red scratches marred the surface of her shoulder. The pins had been pulled from her ruined coiffure during the carriage ride, allowing a profusion of heavy black-coffee locks to fall to her waist in waves and ripples. Her coltish form quivered like a wild creature held in restraints. She gave off a kind of . . . energy, of . . . there didn't seem to be a word for it, but Gabriel could feel the irresistible voltage eating up the space between them. Every hair on his body individuated as he was flooded with the hot, humming awareness of her.

Holy hell. With effort, he tore his fascinated gaze from her and bowed to Lady Berwick. "Countess," he murmured. "A pleasure, as always."

"Lord St. Vincent." There was no mistaking the gleam of satisfaction in Lady Berwick's eyes as she beheld the formerly elusive bachelor, now caught. "You're acquainted with Lady Pandora, obviously." Bringing forward the blonde girl, she said, "This is her sister, Lady Cassandra."

Cassandra curtsied in a graceful, well-practiced movement. "My lord." She was pretty, demure, every curl and ruffle in place. Her gaze remained modestly downcast, not rising above his collar button. A lovely girl. She didn't interest him in the least.

Pandora approached Gabriel in a direct way no other young woman of her rank would have dared. She had extraordinary eyes, dark blue rimmed with black, like sapphires charred at the edges. A pair of winged black brows stood out sharply against her snowdrop complexion. She smelled like night air, and white flowers, and a hint of feminine sweat. The fragrance aroused him, all his muscles tightening like bowstrings.

"I know you're trying to do the right thing, my lord," she said. "But I don't need you to save me or my reputation. Please go home."

"Hold your tongue," Lady Berwick told Pandora in an ominous undertone. "Have you taken leave of your senses?"

Pandora twisted to glance back at her. "I've done nothing wrong," she insisted. "Or at least nothing dreadful enough to deserve being married for it."

"It is for your elders to decide what will happen next," Lady Berwick snapped.

"But it's my future." Pandora's gaze returned to Gabriel. Her tone became more urgent. "Please leave. *Please*."

She was trying desperately to control the situation. Either she didn't comprehend or wouldn't accept that it would be like trying to arrest the momentum of a runaway locomotive.

Gabriel puzzled over how to reply. Having been raised by a loving mother, and grown up with two sisters, he understood women nearly as well as any man could. This girl, however, was something entirely outside his experience.

"I'll go," he said. "But this situation isn't something either of us can ignore for long." He extended his card to Trenear. "My lord, obviously you and your family have much to discuss. You may rely on my honor—the offer for Lady Pandora stands indefinitely."

Before Trenear could react, however, Pandora had snatched the card from Gabriel's fingers. "I won't marry you, do you understand? I'd rather launch myself from a cannon into the sun." She proceeded to tear the card into tiny pieces.

"*Pandora*," Lady Berwick exclaimed balefully as the flakes of paper stock fluttered downward.

Both Pandora and Gabriel ignored her. As their gazes caught and held, the rest of the room seemed to disappear.

"Look you," Pandora told him in a businesslike tone, "marriage is not on the table."

Look you? *Look you?* Gabriel was simultaneously amused and outraged. Was she really speaking to him as if he were an errand boy?

"I've never wanted to marry," Pandora continued. "Anyone who knows me will tell you that. When I was little, I never liked the stories about princesses waiting to be rescued. I never wished on falling stars, or pulled the petals off daisies while reciting 'he loves me, he loves me not.' At my brother's wedding, they handed out slivers of wedding cake to all the unmarried girls and said if we put it under our pillows, we would dream of our future husbands. I ate my cake instead. Every crumb. I've made plans for my life that don't involve becoming anyone's wife."

"What plans?" Gabriel asked. How could a girl of her position, with her looks, make plans that didn't include any possibility of marriage?

"That's none of your business," she told him smartly.

"Understood," Gabriel assured her. "There's just one thing I'd like to ask: What the bloody hell were you doing at the ball in the first place, if you don't want to marry?"

"Because I thought it would be only slightly less boring than staying at home."

"Anyone as opposed to marriage as you claim to be has no business taking part in the Season."

"Not every girl who attends a ball wants to be Cinderella."

"If it's grouse season," Gabriel pointed out acidly, "and you're keeping company with a flock of grouse on a grouse-moor, it's a bit disingenuous to ask a sportsman to pretend you're not a grouse."

"Is *that* how men think of it? No wonder I hate balls." Pandora looked scornful. "I'm so sorry for intruding on your happy hunting grounds."

"I wasn't wife-hunting," he snapped. "I'm no more interested in marrying than you are."

"Then why were *you* at the ball?"

"To see a fireworks display!"

After a brief, electric silence, Pandora dropped her head swiftly. He saw her shoulders tremble, and for an alarming moment, he thought she had begun to cry. But then he heard a delicate snorting, snickering sound, and he realized she was . . . laughing?

"Well," she muttered, "it seems you succeeded."

Before Gabriel even realized what he was doing, he reached out to lift her chin with his fingers. She struggled to hold back her amusement, but it slipped out nonetheless. Droll, sneaky laughter, punctuated with vole-like squeaks, while sparks danced in her blue eyes like shy emerging stars. Her grin made him lightheaded.

Damn it.

His annoyance drained away, displaced by a rampage of heat and delight. His heart began to thump with the force of his need to be alone with her. To be inside all that energy. Everything in him had just ignited like a bonfire, and he wanted her, *wanted* her, with all the reckless, self-indulgent desire he usually managed to keep contained. But it made no sense. He was a civilized man, an experienced one with sophisticated tastes, and she was . . . holy God, what *was* she?

He wished to hell he didn't want to find out so badly.

Pandora's amusement faded. Whatever she saw in his gaze caused a soft scald of pink to spread over her face. Her skin turned hot beneath his fingertips.

Gabriel drew his hand back reluctantly. "I'm not your enemy," he managed to say.

"You're not my fiancé, either."

"Not yet."

"Not *ever.*"

Gabriel wanted to pounce on her. He wanted to haul her into his arms and kiss her senseless. Instead, he said calmly, "Tell me that again in a few days, and I might believe you. In the meantime"—he reached into his coat for another engraved card—"I'm going to give this to Trenear."

Deliberately he gave her a mocking glance, the kind that had never failed to drive his siblings mad . . . and held the card in front of her.

As he'd guessed, Pandora couldn't resist the challenge.

She grabbed for the card. Gabriel made it disappear, seemingly in midair, before she could touch it. As a boy, he'd learned sleight of hand from cardsharps during his visits to Jenner's.

Pandora's expression changed, her eyes widening. "How did you do that?"

Deftly Gabriel made the card reappear. "Learn to ask nicely," he told her, "and I may show you someday."

Her brows lowered. "Never mind. I'm not interested."

But he knew it was a lie. The truth was in her eyes. She *was* interested, no matter how she fought it.

And God help him . . . so was he.

Chapter 3

TWO NIGHTS AFTER THE Chaworth ball, Gabriel practiced at the billiards table in the private apartments above Jenner's. The luxurious rooms, which had once been occupied by his parents in the earliest days of their marriage, were now reserved for the convenience of the Challon family. Raphael, one of his younger brothers, usually lived at the club, but at the moment was on an overseas trip to America. He'd gone to source and purchase a large quantity of dressed pine timber on behalf of a Challon-owned railway construction company. American pine, prized for its toughness and elasticity, was used as transom ties for railways, and it was in high demand now that native British timber was in scarce supply.

The club wasn't the same without Raphael's carefree presence, but spending time alone here was better than the well-ordered quietness of his terrace at Queen's Gate. Gabriel relished the comfortably masculine atmosphere, spiced with scents of expensive liquor, pipe smoke, oiled Morocco leather upholstery, and the acrid pungency of green baize cloth. The fragrance never failed to remind him of the occasions in his youth when he had accompanied his father to the club.

For years, the duke had gone almost weekly to Jenner's to meet with managers and look over the account ledgers. His wife Evie had inherited it from her father, Ivo Jenner, a former professional boxer. The club was an inexhaustible financial engine, its vast profits having enabled the duke to improve his agricultural estates and properties, and accumulate a sprawling empire of investments. Gaming was against the law, of course, but half of Parliament were members of Jenner's, which had made it virtually exempt from prosecution.

Visiting Jenner's with his father had been exciting for a sheltered boy. There had always been new things to see and learn, and the men Gabriel had encountered were very different from the respectable servants and tenants on the estate. The patrons and staff at the club had used coarse language and told bawdy jokes, and taught him card tricks and flourishes. Sometimes Gabriel had perched on a tall stool at a circular hazard table to watch high-stakes play, with his father's arm draped casually across his shoulders. Tucked safely against the duke's side, Gabriel had seen men win or lose entire fortunes in a single night, all on the tumble of the dice.

As Gabriel had grown older, the croupiers had taught him the mathematics of odds and probability. They had also shown him how to detect if someone was using loaded dice or marking cards. Gabriel had become familiar with the signals of collusion—the wink, the nod, the shrug—and all the other subtle techniques used by sharpers. He knew every possible way a man could cheat, having seen cards being marked, concealed, and packed. During those visits to the club, he'd learned a great deal about human nature without even being aware of it.

It hadn't occurred to Gabriel until years later that bringing him to Jenner's had been his father's way of making him a bit more worldly-wise, preparing him for all the future occasions when people would try to take advantage of him. Those lessons had stood him in good stead. When he had finally left the safe environment of his family's home, he'd quickly discovered that, as the Duke of Kingston's heir, he was a mark for everyone.

Lining up five white balls at the head spot, Gabriel positioned the red cue ball for a straight-in shot to the opposite corner. Methodically he dispatched the balls in order, sending each one neatly into the netted pocket. He had always loved billiards, the angles and patterns of it, the way it helped to settle his brain when he needed to think clearly.

As he made the last shot, Gabriel became aware of a presence in the doorway. Still leaning over the table, he glanced up and met his father's light, vibrant gaze. A smile touched his lips. "I wondered how long it would take for you to find out."

Deceptively nonchalant, Sebastian, the Duke of Kingston, entered the room. He always seemed to know everything that occurred in London, even though he lived in Sussex for months at a time. "So far I've heard three different versions of the story."

"Pick the worst, and I'll vouch for that one," Gabriel said dryly, setting aside his cue stick. It was a relief to see his father, who'd always been an unfailing source of reassurance and comfort. They clasped hands in a firm shake, and used their free arms to pull close for a moment. Such demonstrations of affection weren't common among fathers and sons of their rank, but then, they'd never been a conventional family.

After a few hearty thumps on the back, Sebastian drew back and glanced over him with the attentive concern that hearkened to Gabriel's earliest memories. Not missing the traces of weariness on his face, his father lightly tousled his hair the way he had when he was a boy. "You haven't been sleeping."

"I went carousing with friends for most of last night," Gabriel admitted. "It ended when we were all too drunk to see a hole through a ladder."

Sebastian grinned and removed his coat, tossing the exquisitely tailored garment to a nearby chair. "Reveling in the waning days of bachelorhood, are we?"

"It would be more accurate to say I'm thrashing like a drowning rat."

"Same thing." Sebastian unfastened his cuffs and began to roll up his shirtsleeves. An active life at Heron's Point, the family estate in Sussex, had kept him as fit and limber as a man half his age. Frequent exposure to the sunlight had gilded his hair and darkened his complexion, making his pale blue eyes startling in their brightness.

While other men of his generation had become staid and settled, the duke was more vigorous than ever, in part because his youngest son was still only eleven. The duchess, Evie, had conceived unexpectedly long after she had assumed her childbearing years were past. As a result there were eight years between the baby's birth and that of the next oldest sibling, Seraphina. Evie had been more than a little embarrassed to find herself with child at her age, especially in the face of her husband's teasing claims that she was a walking advertisement of his potency. And indeed, there had been a hint of extra swagger in Sebastian's step all through his wife's last pregnancy.

Their fifth child was a handsome boy with hair the deep auburn red of an Irish setter. He'd been christened

Michael Ivo, but somehow the pugnacious middle name suited him more than his given name. Now a lively, cheerful lad, Ivo accompanied his father nearly everywhere.

"You go first," Sebastian said, browsing among the rack of cue sticks and selecting his favorite. "I need the advantage."

"The devil you do," Gabriel replied equably, setting up the game. "The only reason you lost to me the last time was because you let Ivo make so many of your shots."

"Since losing was a foregone conclusion, I decided to use the boy as an excuse."

"Where is Ivo? I can't believe he let you leave him at Heron's Point with the girls."

"He nearly worked himself into a tantrum," Sebastian said regretfully. "But I explained to him that your situation requires my undivided attention. As usual, I'm full of helpful advice."

"Oh, God." Gabriel leaned over the table to make the opening break. Staying down on the shot, he struck the cue ball, which struck the yellow ball and knocked it into the net. Two points. With the next shot, he potted the red ball.

"Well done," his father said. "What a sharper you are."

Gabriel snorted. "You wouldn't say that if you'd seen me two nights ago at the Chaworth ball. You'd have called me a prize idiot—rightly so—for being trapped into marriage by a naïve girl."

"Ah, well, no bull can avoid the yoke forever." Sebastian moved around the table, set up his shot, and executed a perfect in-off. "What is her name?"

"Lady Pandora Ravenel." As they continued to play,

Gabriel explained in disgust, "I didn't want to attend the damned ball in the first place. I was pressed into it by some friends who said that Chaworth had spent a fortune for a crew of self-styled 'fireworks artisans.' There was supposed to be a ripping exhibition at the end of the evening. Since I had no interest in the ball itself, I walked down to the river to watch the workmen set up rockets. As I returned"—he paused to execute a carom, a three-point shot that hit two balls simultaneously—"I happened to hear a girl cursing in the summer house. She had trapped herself arse-upwards on a settee, with her dress caught in the carved scrollwork."

His father's eyes twinkled with enjoyment. "A fiendishly clever lure. What man could resist?"

"Like a clodpate, I went to help. Before I could pull her free, Lord Chaworth and Westcliff happened upon us. Westcliff offered to keep his mouth shut, of course, but Chaworth was determined to bring about my comeuppance." Gabriel sent his father a pointed glance. "Almost as if he had an old score to settle."

Sebastian looked vaguely apologetic. "There may have been a brief dalliance with his wife," he admitted, "a few years before I married your mother."

Gabriel took a heedless shot that sent the cue ball rolling aimlessly around the table. "Now the girl's reputation is ruined, and I have to marry her. The very suggestion of which, I might add, caused her to howl in protest."

"Why?"

"Probably because she doesn't like me. As you can imagine, my behavior was somewhat less than charming, given the circumstances."

"No, I'm asking why you have to marry her."

"Because it's the honorable thing to do." Gabriel paused. "Isn't that what you'd expect?"

"By no means. Your mother is the one who expects you to do the honorable thing. I, however, am perfectly happy for you to do the dishonorable thing if you can get away with it." Leaning down, Sebastian assessed a shot with narrowed eyes, lined it up, and potted the red ball expertly. "Someone has to marry the girl," he said casually, "but it doesn't have to be you." Retrieving the red ball, he returned it to the head spot for another strike. "We'll buy a husband for her. Nowadays most noble families are in debt up to their ears. For the right sum, they'll gladly offer up one of their pedigreed progeny."

Regarding his father with an arrested stare, Gabriel considered the idea. He could foist Pandora onto another man and make her someone else's problem. She wouldn't have to live as an outcast, and he would be free to go on with his life as before.

Except . . .

Except he couldn't seem to stop brooding over Pandora, who was like annoying music he couldn't get out of his head. He'd become so obsessed with her that he hadn't even visited his mistress, knowing that even Nola's extensive repertoire wouldn't serve to distract him.

"Well?" his father prompted.

Preoccupied, Gabriel was slow to reply. "The idea has merit."

Sebastian glanced at him quizzically. "I rather expected something more along the lines of, 'Yes, dear God, I'll do anything to avoid spending a lifetime shackled to a girl I can't abide.'"

"I didn't say I couldn't abide her," Gabriel said testily.

Sebastian regarded him with a faint smile. After a moment, he prodded, "Is she pleasing to the eye?"

Gabriel went to an inset sideboard to pour himself a brandy. "She's bloody ravishing," he muttered.

Looking more and more interested, his father asked, "What is the problem with her, then?"

"She's a perfect little savage. Constitutionally incapable of guarding her tongue. Not to mention peculiar: She goes to balls but never dances, only sits in the corner. Two of the fellows I went drinking with last night said they'd asked her to waltz on previous occasions. She told one of them that a carriage horse had recently stepped on her foot, and she told the other that the butler had accidently slammed her leg in the door." Gabriel took a swallow of brandy before finishing grimly, "No wonder she's a wallflower."

Sebastian, who had begun to laugh, seemed struck by that last comment. "Ahhh," he said softly. "That explains it." He was silent for a moment, lost in some distant, pleasurable memory. "Dangerous creatures, wallflowers. Approach them with the utmost caution. They sit quietly in corners, appearing abandoned and forlorn, when in truth they're sirens who lure men to their downfall. You won't even notice the moment she steals the heart right out of your body—and then it's hers for good. A wallflower never gives your heart back."

"Are you finished amusing yourself?" Gabriel asked, impatient with his father's flight of fancy. "Because I have actual problems to deal with."

Still smiling, Sebastian reached for some chalk and applied it to the tip of his cue stick. "Forgive me. The word makes me a bit sentimental. Go on."

"For all practical purposes, Pandora would be of no use to me other than in bed. She's a novelty. After the newness wore off, I'd be bored within a week. More to the point, she's temperamentally unsuited to be my wife. Anyone's wife." He had to finish his brandy before he could bring himself to admit huskily, "Despite all that . . . I don't want anyone else to have her." Bracing his hands on the edge of the table, he stared blindly at the green baize cloth.

His father's reaction was unexpectedly sanguine. "To play devil's advocate—has it occurred to you that Lady Pandora will mature?"

"I'd be surprised," Gabriel muttered, thinking of those heathen blue eyes.

"But my dear boy, of course you would. A woman will always surprise you with what she's capable of. You can spend a lifetime trying to discover what excites and interests her, but you'll never know it all. There's always more. Every woman is a mystery, not to be understood but enjoyed." Picking up a billiards ball, Sebastian tossed it into the air and caught it deftly. "Your Lady Pandora is young—time will remedy that. She's a virgin—well, there's a problem easily solved. You anticipate marital ennui, which, forgive me, is a pinnacle of arrogance unmatched by anyone except myself when I was your age. The girl sounds anything but boring. Given half a chance, she may please you even more than Mrs. Black."

Gabriel sent him a warning glance.

His father had made no secret of his disapproval of Gabriel's mistress, whose husband was the American ambassador. As the young, beautiful wife of a former Union Army officer whose war injuries prevented him from satisfying her in the bedroom, Mrs. Nola Black took her pleasures where she found them.

For the past two years, Nola had fully indulged Gabriel's every desire, their encounters unhindered by morals or inhibitions. She always knew when to push the limits farther, coming up with new tricks to spark his interest and satisfy his complex desires. Gabriel didn't like it that she was married, he resented her temper and her possessiveness, and lately he had begun to realize that the affair was turning him into the worst possible version of himself.

But he kept going back for more.

"No one pleases me more than Mrs. Black," Gabriel said with difficulty. "That's the problem."

Slowly his father set the cue stick onto the table, his face impassive. "You fancy yourself in love with her?"

"No. God, no. It's just that . . . I . . ." Lowering his head, Gabriel rubbed the back of his neck, which had begun to crawl with discomfort. Although he and his father had always spoken freely on a great variety of subjects, they rarely discussed personal sexual matters. Sebastian, thank God, was not one to meddle in his sons' private lives.

There was no easy way for Gabriel to describe the dark side of his nature, nor was he particularly eager to face it. As the Challon family's oldest son, he had always strived to meet high expectations—his own and other people's. Since a young age, he'd been aware that because of his family name, wealth, and influence, many people actively wanted him to fail. Determined to prove himself, he'd earned high marks at Eton and Oxford. When other boys had wanted to test themselves against him by picking fights or trying to best him in athletics, he'd had to prove himself repeatedly. Whenever he'd identified a weakness in himself, he worked to overcome it. After graduating, he had managed his family's financial affairs competently, and he'd made his own investments in fledgling businesses that had paid off in spades. In most areas of his life, he was self-disciplined and hardworking, a man who took his responsibilities seriously.

But then there was the other side. Sexual, intemperate, and bloody tired of trying to be perfect. The side that made him feel guilty as hell.

Gabriel hadn't yet found a way to reconcile the opposing halves of his nature, the angel and the devil. He doubted he ever would. All he knew for certain was that Nola Black was willing to do anything he wanted, as often as he wanted, and he'd never found that kind of relief with anyone else.

Flushing, Gabriel struggled to explain without making himself sound like a depraved freak of nature. "The problem is that I require particular . . . that is . . . she lets me . . ." He broke off with a guttural curse.

"Every man has his tastes," Sebastian said sensibly. "I doubt yours are all that shocking."

"What your generation considered shocking is probably different from mine."

There was a short, offended silence. When Sebastian replied, his voice was as dry as tinder. "Ancient and decrepit fossil that I am, I believe the ruins of my senile brain can somehow manage to grasp what you're trying to convey. You've indulged in wanton carnal excess for so long that you're disillusioned. The trifles that excite other men leave you indifferent. No virgin's pallid charms could ever hope to compete with the subversive talents of your mistress."

Gabriel glanced up in surprise.

His father looked sardonic. "I assure you, my lad, sexual debauchery was invented long before your generation. The libertines of my grandfather's time committed acts that would make a satyr blush. Men of our lineage are born craving more pleasure than is good for us. Obviously I was no saint before I married, and God knows I never expected to find fulfillment in the arms of one woman for a lifetime. But I have. Which means there's no reason you can't."

"If you say so."

"I do say so." After a contemplative silence, Sebastian spoke again. "Why don't you invite the Ravenels to Heron's Point for a week? Give the girl a sporting chance, and become acquainted with her before you make a decision."

"There's no need to invite her entire family to Sussex for that. It's more convenient for me to visit her here in London."

His father shook his head. "You need to spend a few days away from your mistress," he said frankly. "A man with your developed palate will enjoy the next course far more if you eliminate competing flavors."

Frowning, Gabriel braced his hands on the edge of the table as he considered the suggestion. With each passing day, more people were hounding him about the incipient scandal. Especially Nola, who had already sent a half-dozen notes demanding to know if the rumors were true. The Ravenels must be fending off the same questions, and would probably welcome the opportunity to escape London. The estate at Heron's Point, with its eleven thousand acres of woodland, farmland, and pristine shoreline, offered complete privacy.

His eyes narrowed as he saw his father's bland expression. "Why are you encouraging this? Shouldn't you be a bit more discriminating when it comes to the potential mother of your grandchildren?"

"You're a man of eight-and-twenty who hasn't yet

sired an heir. At this point, I'm not inclined to be overparticular about whom you marry. All I ask is that you produce some grandchildren before your mother and I are too decrepit to pick them up."

Gabriel gave his father a wry glance. "Don't pin your hopes on Lady Pandora. In her opinion, marrying me would be the worst thing ever to happen to her."

Sebastian smiled. "Marriage is usually the worst thing to happen to a woman. Fortunately, that never stops them."

Chapter 4

PANDORA KNEW SHE WAS about to receive bad news when Devon sent for her to come to his study without having requested Cassandra to come down as well. To make matters worse, Kathleen, who usually served as a buffer between Pandora and Devon, wasn't there. She had gone for the afternoon to visit Helen, who was still in childbed after having given birth to a healthy son a week and a half ago. The robust dark-haired infant, named Taron, closely resembled his father—"Except prettier, thank God," Mr. Winterborne had said with a grin. The boy's name had derived from the Welsh word for thunder, and so far he had justified it in full measure every time he was hungry.

During the delivery, Helen had been attended by Dr. Garrett Gibson, a staff physician at Mr. Winterborne's department store. As one of the first few women to have been certified as a physician and surgeon in England, Dr. Gibson was skilled and trained in modern techniques. She had taken excellent care of Helen, who'd had a difficult time during the delivery and had developed a mild case of anemia from loss of blood. The doctor had prescribed iron pills and prolonged bed rest, and Helen was improving every day.

However, Mr. Winterborne, who was overprotective by nature, had so far insisted on hovering over his wife every possible minute, neglecting the mountain of responsibilities accumulating at the store. No matter how Helen reassured him that she was in no danger of falling ill from childbed fever or some other dread condition, he remained at the bedside in a near-constant vigil. Helen spent most of her time reading, nursing the baby, and playing quiet games with Carys, her little half-sister.

This morning Helen had sent a note, begging Kathleen to visit so that Mr. Winterborne would go to his office and attend to some urgent business matters. According to Helen, Winterborne's employees were all going mad without him, and she was going mad *with* him.

The house seemed abnormally quiet as Pandora reached Devon's study. Slants of afternoon light bored through multipaned windows set in deep oak wainscoted recesses.

Devon stood as she entered the room. "I have news." He gestured for her to take the chair beside the desk. "Since it involves Lord St. Vincent, I thought I should tell you before the others."

Her heartbeats stumbled and collided at the sound of the name. Lowering herself to the chair, Pandora balled her hands in her lap. "What is it? Has he withdrawn his offer?"

"Just the opposite." Devon sat and faced her. "St. Vincent has extended an invitation for all of us to visit his family's estate in Sussex. We'll stay for a week. It will allow both families to—"

"*No*," Pandora said, popping up instantly, her nerves clamoring with alarm. "I can't do that."

Devon regarded her with a perplexed frown. "It's an opportunity to become more familiar with them."

That was exactly what Pandora feared. The Duke

and Duchess of Kingston, and their brood of superior offspring, would be sure to look down their elegant noses at her. Only the thinnest veneer of politeness would cover their contempt. Every question they asked her would be a test, and every mistake she made would be noted and stored away for future reference.

Pandora paced around the perimeter of the room in agitation, her skirts whisking the air and sending dust motes swirling upward in tiny glinting constellations. Each time she passed the heavy pedestal desk, stacks of papers fluttered their edges in protest. "By the time they're done with me, I'll be gutted, drawn, and dressed like a trout ready for sautéing."

"Why would they mistreat you after having invited you as their guest?" Devon asked.

"They could be trying to intimidate me into refusing Lord St. Vincent's proposal, so he won't have to withdraw it and look ungentlemanly."

"They only want to become acquainted," Devon said in an extra-patient manner that made her want to explode like an overboiled pudding. "Nothing more, nothing less."

Pandora stopped in her tracks, her heart thrashing in her chest like a wild caged bird. "Does Kathleen know about this?"

"Not yet. But she'll agree that the visit is necessary. The fact is, none of us can go anywhere in London without being badgered with questions about you and St. Vincent. Kathleen and I agreed last night that the family would have to leave town until this situation is resolved."

"I'll go back to Eversby Priory, then. Not Sussex. You'll have to throw me bodily into the carriage, and even then—"

"Pandora. Come here. No, don't be stubborn, I want to talk to you." Devon pointed firmly to the chair. "Now."

It was the first time Devon had ever exerted his authority over her as the head of the family. Pandora wasn't certain how she felt about it. Although she had an innate dislike of authority, Devon had always been fair. He'd never given her reason not to trust him. Slowly she complied, sinking into the chair and gripping the wooden arms with pressure-whitened fingertips. The hated ringing had begun in her left ear. She cupped her palm over it lightly and tapped her forefinger on the back of her skull a few times, which sometimes caused the irritating noise to subside. To her relief, it worked.

Leaning forward in his chair, Devon contemplated Pandora with eyes the same shade of blue-black as her own. "I think I understand what you're afraid of," he said slowly. "At least in part. But I don't think you understand my perspective. In the absence of a father or older brother to protect you, all you have is me. Regardless of what you or anyone else may assume, I'm not going to push you into marrying St. Vincent. In fact, even if you wanted the match, I might not consent to it."

Bewildered, Pandora said, "Lady Berwick told me there's no choice. If I don't marry, the only other option is to hurl myself into the nearest live volcano. Wherever that is."

"Iceland. And the only way you'll marry St. Vincent is if you can convince me that you'd prefer him to the volcano."

"But my reputation . . ."

"Worse things can happen to a woman than a ruined reputation."

Staring at Devon in wonder, Pandora felt herself

begin to relax, her frayed nerves ceasing their frantic shrilling. He was on her side, she realized. Any other man in his position would have forced her into marriage without a second thought.

"You're part of my family," Devon continued evenly. "And I'm damned if I'll hand you over to a stranger without being assured of your well-being. I'll do everything in my power to keep you from making the kind of mistake Kathleen did when she married your brother."

Pandora was silent with surprise. The sensitive subject of Theo was rarely brought up in the Ravenel household.

"Kathleen knew nothing about Theo before their wedding," Devon said. "It was only afterward that she discovered what he was really like. Your brother couldn't hold his liquor, and when he was drunk, he became violent. At times he had to be carried away from his club, or some other public place, by force. It was no secret among his friends, or in the circles he frequented."

"How mortifying," Pandora muttered, her face turning hot.

"Yes. But Theo was careful to conceal his brutish side while he was courting Kathleen. If Lord and Lady Berwick were aware of the rumors about him—and I can't believe they didn't hear some of them—they never discussed it with Kathleen." Devon looked grim. "They bloody well should have."

"Why didn't they?"

"Many people believe marriage will change a man's temperament. Which is absolute rot, of course. One can't love a leopard into changing his spots." Devon paused. "Had Theo lived, he would have made Kathleen's life hell. I won't have you at the mercy of an abusive husband."

"But if I don't marry, the scandal will cause problems for everyone. Especially Cassandra."

"Pandora, sweetheart, do you think any of us could ever be happy if you were mistreated? West or I would end up killing the bastard."

Overwhelmed with gratitude, Pandora felt her eyes sting. How strange it was that her parents and brother were gone, and yet she'd never felt so much like part of a family.

"I don't think Lord St. Vincent would be violent with me," she said. "He seems the kind who would be cold and distant. Which would be a misery in its own way, but I would manage."

"Before we make a decision, we'll try to learn as much as possible about what kind of man Lord St. Vincent is."

"In a week?" she asked doubtfully.

"It's not long enough to delve into complexities," Devon admitted. "But one can discover a great deal about a man by observing him with his family. I'm also going to find out what I can from people who know him. Winterborne is acquainted with him, as a matter of fact. They both sit on the board of a company that manufactures hydraulic equipment."

Pandora couldn't quite imagine the two of them talking together—the son of a Welsh grocer and the son of a duke. "Does Mr. Winterborne like him?" she dared to ask.

"It would seem so. He says St. Vincent is intelligent and practical, and doesn't put on airs. That's high praise, coming from Winterborne."

"Will Mr. Winterborne and Helen come with us to Heron's Point?" Pandora asked hopefully. She would feel better if her entire family were there with her.

"Not so soon after the baby's birth," Devon said gently. "Helen needs to fully regain her health before traveling. Furthermore, I'm going to insist that Lady Berwick *not* accompany us to Heron's Point. I don't want you to be burdened by strict chaperonage. I want you to have an opportunity—or two—to meet with St. Vincent alone."

Pandora's jaw dropped. She would never have expected Devon, who was overprotective to a fault, to say such a thing.

Devon looked slightly uncomfortable as he continued. "I know how a proper courtship is supposed to be conducted. However, Kathleen was never allowed a single moment alone with Theo until they married, and the results were disastrous. I'm damned if I know how else a woman is to evaluate a potential husband other than to have at least a few private conversations with him."

"Well, this is odd," Pandora said after a moment. "No one's ever given me permission to do something improper."

Devon smiled. "Shall we go to Heron's Point for a week, and consider it a fact-finding expedition?"

"I suppose. But what if Lord St. Vincent turns out to be terrible?"

"Then you won't marry him."

"What will happen to the rest of the family?"

"That's for me to worry about," Devon said firmly. "For the time being, all you need to do is become acquainted with St. Vincent. And if you decide you don't wish to marry him, for any reason, you won't have to."

They both stood. Impulsively Pandora stepped forward and dove her face against Devon's chest and hugged him, undoubtedly surprising him as much as herself. She rarely sought out physical contact with anyone. "Thank you," she said in a muffled voice. "It means a great deal that my feelings matter to you."

"Of course they do, sweetheart." Devon gave her a comforting squeeze before drawing back to look down at her. "Do you know the motto on the Ravenel coat of arms?"

"*Loyalté nous lie.*"

"Do you know what it means?"

"'Never make us angry?'" Pandora guessed, and was rewarded by his deep laugh. "Actually, I do know," she said. "It means 'loyalty binds us.'"

"That's right," Devon said. "Whatever happens, we Ravenels will remain loyal to each other. We'll never sacrifice one for the sake of the rest."

Chapter 5

SITTING ON THE FLOOR of the upstairs parlor of Ravenel House, Pandora brushed the pair of black cocker spaniels who had been with the family for ten years. Josephine sat obediently while Pandora drew the soft bristles over her floppy ears. Napoleon lounged nearby with his chin resting on the floor between his paws.

"Are you ready?" Cassandra asked, coming to the threshold. "We can't be late for the train. Oh, don't do that, you'll be covered in dog hair! You have to look presentable for the duke and duchess. And Lord St. Vincent, of course."

"Why bother?" Pandora rose to her feet. "I already know what they're going to think of me." But she stood still as Cassandra moved industriously around her, walloping at her skirts and sending black hairs floating into the air.

"They're going to like you—" *Thwack.* "—if only—" *Thwack. Thwack.* "—you'll be nice to them."

Pandora's traveling dress was made of leaf-green batiste wool with a waistcoat jacket, and a flaring white lace Medici collar that stood up at the back of the neck and tapered down to a point at the top of her basque. It was a smart and stylish ensemble, accessorized with a little feathered emerald velvet hat that matched her sash. Cassandra wore similar garments of pale blue, with a sapphire hat.

"I'll be as nice as nice can be," Pandora said. "But don't you remember what happened at Eversby Priory, when a goose built her nest in the swans' territory? She thought she was enough like them that they wouldn't mind her. Only her neck was too short, and her legs were too long, and she didn't have the right sort of feathers, so the swans kept attacking and chasing the poor thing until finally she was driven off."

"You're not a goose."

Pandora's mouth twisted. "I'm an awfully deficient swan, then."

Cassandra sighed and drew her close. "You mustn't marry Lord St. Vincent for my sake," she said for the hundredth time.

Slowly Pandora laid her head on her twin's shoulder. "I could never live with myself if you had to suffer the consequences of a mistake I made."

"I won't suffer."

"If I become a pariah, no gentleman of rank would ever offer for you."

"I would be happy regardless," Cassandra said stoutly.

"No, you wouldn't. You want to marry someday, and have a home and children of your own." Pandora sighed. "I wish you could be Lord St. Vincent's wife. You would be perfect for each other."

"Lord St. Vincent didn't give me a second glance. All he did was stare at you."

"In sheer horror."

"I think the horror was all on your side," Cassandra said. "He was merely trying to take in the situation." Her light fingers came to smooth Pandora's hair. "They say he's the catch of a century. Last year, Lady Berwick encouraged him to take an interest in Dolly, but he would have none of it."

Cassandra's hand came just a little close to her ear. Flinching reflexively, Pandora drew back. Certain parts of her ear, inside and out, were painfully sensitive. "How do you know that? Dolly never mentioned it to me."

"It was just some ballroom gossip. And Dolly doesn't talk about it because it was a great disappointment."

"Why didn't you tell me before?"

"I didn't think you'd be interested since we'd never even seen Lord St. Vincent, and you said you didn't want to hear anything about eligible bachelors—"

"I do now! Tell me everything you know about him."

After glancing at the empty doorway, Cassandra lowered her voice. "There's a rumor that he keeps a mistress."

Pandora gave her a wide-eyed stare. "Someone told you that in a *ballroom*? During a formal dance?"

"Not openly, it was whispered. What do you think people gossip about during dances?"

"Things like weather."

"It's not gossip when it's about weather, it's only gossip when it's something you know you shouldn't be listening to."

Pandora was indignant at the thought that she'd missed so much interesting information during those hideously dull occasions. "Who is his mistress?"

"No one mentioned her name."

Folding her arms across her chest, Pandora commented sourly, "I'll bet he has the pox."

Cassandra looked bewildered. "What?"

"Heaps of it," Pandora added grimly. "He's a rake, after all. Just like the song."

Cassandra groaned and shook her head, knowing exactly which song Pandora was referring to. They had once overheard one of the stablemen singing a few lines of a ballad called "The Unfortunate Rake," for the amusement of his companions. The bawdy lyrics had told the story of a rake's demise of an unnamed illness after having slept with a woman of ill repute.

Later Pandora and Cassandra had badgered West to explain the mysterious malady, until he had reluctantly told them about the pox. Not smallpox or chicken pox, but a particular strain that infected promiscuous men and women. Eventually it drove one mad and made one's nose fall off. Some called it French pox, some called it English pox. West had told them never to repeat any of it, or Kathleen would have his head.

"I'm sure Lord St. Vincent doesn't have the pox," Cassandra said. "From what I saw the other night, he has a perfectly handsome nose."

"He'll catch the pox someday," Pandora persisted darkly, "if he hasn't already. And then he'll give it to me."

"You're being dramatic. And not all rakes have the pox."

"I'm going to ask him if he does."

"Pandora, you wouldn't! The poor man would be horrified."

"So would I, if I ended up losing my nose."

AS THE RAVENELS rode in the private first-class compartment on the London, Brighton, and South Coast line, Pandora's nerves became more strained with each passing mile. If only the train were headed in another direction, anywhere other than toward Heron's Point.

She couldn't decide whether she was more worried about how she would behave with the Challons, or how they would behave toward her. There was no doubt that Lord St. Vincent resented her for the situation she'd put him in, even though it had been an accident on her part.

God, she was so tired of causing trouble and then having to feel guilty about it. From now on, she would behave like a respectable, proper lady. People would marvel at her restraint and dignity. They might even become a bit concerned—"Is Pandora quite well? She's always so subdued." Lady Berwick would glow with pride, and advise other girls to emulate Pandora's remarkable reserve. She would become known for it.

Sitting by the window, Pandora watched the passing scenery and occasionally glanced at Kathleen, who sat in an opposite seat with little William on her lap. Although they had brought a nursery maid to help with the infant, Kathleen preferred to keep him with her as much as possible. The dark-haired baby played intently with a string of spools, investigating the various sizes and textures, and fitting them against his mouth to gnaw industriously. Entertained by his son's antics, Devon lounged beside them with his arm resting along the back of the bench.

While Cassandra occupied herself with knitting a pair of Berlin wool slippers, Pandora reached into her valise and unearthed her journal, a weighty Coptic-bound volume with a leather cover. Its linen pages were stuffed with clippings, sketches, pressed flowers, tickets, postcards, and all manner of things that had caught her fancy. She had filled at least half of it with ideas and sketches for board games. A silver mechanical pencil dangled from an attached cord that wrapped around the book to keep it closed.

After unwinding the cord, Pandora opened the book to a blank page near the back. She twisted the lower half of the pencil barrel until a nozzle with the lead emerged, and began to write.

JOURNEY TO HERON'S POINT
OR
The Impending Matrimonial Doom
of Lady Pandora Ravenel

Facts and Observations

#1 If people think you're dishonored, it's no different from actually having been dishonored, except you still don't know anything.

#2 When you've been ruined, there are only two options: death or marriage.

#3 Since I am gravely healthy, the first option isn't likely.

#4 On the other hand, ritual self-sacrifice in Iceland cannot be ruled out.

#5 Lady Berwick advises marriage and says Lord St. Vincent is "bred to the bill." Since she once made the same remark about a stud horse she and Lord Berwick bought for their stable, I have to wonder if she's looked in his mouth.

#6 Lord St. Vincent reportedly has a mistress.

#7 The word "mistress" sounds like a cross between mistake and mattress.

"We've crossed into Sussex," Cassandra said. "It's even lovelier than the guidebook led me to expect." She had purchased *The Popular Guide and Visitor's Directory to Heron's Point* at a bookstall in the station, and had insisted on reading parts of it aloud during the first hour of their journey.

Known as the "land of health," Sussex was the sunniest region in England with the purest water, drawn up from deep chalk wells. According to the guidebook, the county possessed fifty miles of coastal shore. Tourists flocked to the town of Heron's Point for its mild, sweet air, and the healing properties of its seawater and hot spring baths.

The guidebook was dedicated to the Duke of Kingston, who had apparently built a seawall to protect erosion of the shore, as well as a hotel, a public esplanade, and a thousand-foot public pier to provide harborage for pleasure steamboats, fishing vessels, and his own private yacht.

#8 The local guidebook doesn't include even one unfavorable detail about Heron's Point. It must be the most perfect town in existence.

#9 Or the author was trying to toady up to the Challons, who own half of Sussex.

#10 Dear God, they're going to be insufferable.

As Pandora looked through the train window, her attention was caught by a flock of starlings that flowed across the sky in synchronized movements, the mass dividing like a water droplet and rejoining before continuing on in a fluid, ribbon-like mass.

The train clicked and clacked its way through a panorama of charming villages, wool-towns with timber-framed houses, picturesque churches, rich green farmland, and smoothly contoured downs carpeted with purple-blooming heath. The sky was vivid and soft, with a few fluffy clouds that appeared to have been freshly laundered and hung up to dry.

#11 Sussex has many picturesque views.

#12 Looking at nature is boring.

As the train neared the station, they passed a waterworks, an alcove of shops, a post office, a row of tidy storage buildings, and a collecting depot where dairy products and market produce were kept chilled until they could be transported.

"There's the Challon estate," Cassandra murmured.

Following her gaze, Pandora saw a white mansion on a distant hill beyond the headland, overlooking the ocean. An imposing marble palace, inhabited by haughty aristocrats.

The train reached the station and came to a halt. The air, so hot that it smelled like ironing, was filled with clanging bells, the voices of signalmen and trackmen, doors opening, and porters wheeling their carts across the platform. As the family disembarked, they were met by a middle-aged man with a pleasant countenance and an efficient manner. After introducing himself as Mr. Cuthbert, the duke's estate manager, he supervised porters and footmen to collect the Ravenels' luggage, including William's handsome wicker pram.

"Mr. Cuthbert," Kathleen asked as the estate manager guided them beneath a vaulted canopy to the other side of the station building, "is it always so warm this time of year?"

Cuthbert blotted a gleam of perspiration from his forehead with a folded white handkerchief. "No, my lady, this is an unseasonably high temperature, even for Heron's Point. A southerly has come in from the continent after a period of dry weather, and it is keeping the cooling sea breezes at bay. Moreover, the promontory"—he gestured to a high cliff that jutted out into the ocean—"helps to create the town's unique climate."

The Ravenels and their retinue of servants proceeded to the vehicle waiting area beside the station's clock tower. The duke had sent a trio of glossy black carriages, their luxurious interiors upholstered in soft ivory Morocco leather and trimmed with rosewood. After climbing into the first carriage, Pandora investigated a fitted tray with a divided compartment, an umbrella that slid cleverly into a socket in the side of the door, and a rectangular leather case tucked beside a folding armrest. The case held a pair of binoculars—not the tiny ones a lady would use at the opera, but a powerful set of field glasses.

Pandora started guiltily as Mr. Cuthbert came to the open carriage door and saw her with the binoculars. "I'm sorry—" she began.

"I was about to bring those to your attention, my lady," the estate manager said, seeming not at all annoyed. "The ocean is visible for most of the drive to the Challon estate. Those aluminum binoculars are the latest design, much lighter than brass. They'll allow you to see clearly at a distance of four miles. You might observe sea birds, or even a shoal of porpoises."

Eagerly Pandora lifted the binoculars to her eyes. Looking at nature might be boring, but it was considerably more entertaining with the aid of technological gadgetry.

"They can be adjusted with the turning mechanism in the center," Mr. Cuthbert advised with a smile. "Lord St. Vincent thought you would enjoy them."

The lenses were briefly filled with the pink blur of his face before Pandora lowered the binoculars hastily. "He put these here for me?"

"Indeed, my lady."

After the estate manager had left, Pandora frowned and handed the binoculars to Cassandra. "Why did Lord St. Vincent assume I would want these? Does he think I need to be distracted by amusements, like little William with his string of spools?"

"It was merely a thoughtful gesture," Cassandra said mildly.

The old Pandora would have loved to use the binoculars during the ride to the house. The new dignified, respectable, proper Pandora, however, would entertain herself with her own thoughts. Ladylike thoughts.

What did ladies think about? Things like starting charities and visiting the tenants, and blancmange recipes—yes, ladies were always bringing blancmange to people. What *was* blancmange, anyway? It had no flavor or color. At best it was only unassertive pudding. Would it still be blancmange if one put some kind of topping on it? Berries or lemon sauce—

Realizing her thoughts had gone off course, Pandora steered them back to the conversation with Cassandra.

"The point is," she told her sister with great dignity, "I have no need of toys to keep me occupied."

Cassandra was looking through the open window with the binoculars. "I can see a butterfly across the road," she marveled, "as clearly as if it were sitting on my finger."

Pandora sat up instantly. "Let me have a look."

Grinning, Cassandra adroitly kept the binoculars out of her grasp. "I thought you didn't want them."

"I do now. Give them back!"

"I'm not finished yet." Maddeningly, Cassandra refused to return the binoculars for at least five minutes, until Pandora threatened to auction her to pirates.

By the time Pandora had reclaimed the binoculars, the carriage had begun the long, gentle ascent up the hill. She managed to obtain glimpses of a seagull in flight, a fishing boat sailing around the headlands, and a hare disappearing beneath a juniper bush. Occasionally a cool breeze from the ocean blew through one of the open hinged windows, bringing momentary relief from the heat. Perspiration gathered and trickled beneath her corset, while the light wool of her traveling dress chafed her prickling skin. Bored and hot, she finally put the binoculars back into the leather case.

"It's like summer," she commented, blotting her forehead on one of her long sleeves. "By the time we arrive, I'll be as red as a boiled ham."

"I already am," Cassandra said, trying to use the guidebook as a fan.

"We're almost there," Kathleen said, resettling William's hot, sleepy form on her shoulder. "As soon as we reach the mansion, we'll be able to change into lighter dresses."

She regarded Pandora with warm concern. "Try not to worry, dear. You're going to have a lovely time."

"You told me the same thing just before I left for the Chaworth ball."

"Did I?" Kathleen smiled. "Well, I suppose I have to be wrong about something every now and then." After a pause, she added gently, "I know you'd rather be safe and snug at home, dear. But I'm glad you agreed to come."

Pandora nodded, squirming uncomfortably as she pulled at the sleeves of her light woolen traveling dress, which was sticking to her skin. "People like me should avoid new experiences," she said. "It never turns out well."

"Don't say that," Cassandra protested.

Devon spoke then, his voice gentle. "Everyone has faults, Pandora. Don't be hard on yourself. You and Cassandra began at a disadvantage after having been raised in seclusion for so long. But you're both learning fast." He smiled down at Kathleen as he added, "As I can personally attest, making mistakes is part of the learning process."

As the carriage proceeded past the main gate, the estate mansion came into view. Contrary to Pandora's expectations, it wasn't at all cold and imposing. It was a gracious, low-slung residence of two stories, inhabiting its surroundings with comfortable ease. Its classic lines were softened by an abundance of glossy green ivy that mantled the cream stucco façade, and arbors of pink roses that arched cheerfully over the courtyard entrance. Two extended wings curved around the front gardens, as if the house had decided to fill its arms with bouquets. Nearby, a slope of dark, dreaming forest rested beneath a blanket of sunlight.

Pandora's interest was caught by the sight of a man making his way to the house. A young child sat on his shoulders, while an older, red-haired boy kept pace at his side. A tenant farmer, perhaps, out walking with his two sons. It was odd that he would stride across the front lawn in such a bold manner.

He wore only trousers, a thin shirt, and an open vest, with no hat or necktie anywhere in sight. He walked with the loose-jointed grace of someone who spent a great deal of time outdoors. It was obvious that he was extraordinarily fit, the simple garments draping lightly over the lean, powerful lines of his body. And he carried the child on his shoulders as if he weighed nothing.

Cassandra leaned closer to stare through Pandora's window. "Is that a worker?" she asked. "A farmer?"

"I would think so. Dressed like that, he couldn't be—" Pandora broke off as the carriage followed the wide arc of the drive, affording her a better view. The man's hair was a distinctive color she'd seen only once before, the dark gold of antique bullion coins. Her insides began to rearrange themselves as if they'd decided to play musical chairs.

The man reached the carriage as it stopped in front of the portico. The driver said something to him, and Pandora heard his relaxed reply, in a cool, deep baritone.

It was Lord St. Vincent.

Chapter 6

AFTER SWINGING THE CHILD easily from his shoulders to the ground, Lord St. Vincent opened the carriage door on Pandora's side. The full blaze of midday gilded his perfect features and struck brilliant lights in his bronze-gold hair.

Fact #13 she wanted to write. *Lord St. Vincent walks around with his own personal halo.*

The man had too much of everything. Looks, wealth, intelligence, breeding, and virile good health.

Fact #14 Some people are living proof of an unjust universe.

"Welcome to Heron's Point," Lord St. Vincent said, his gaze encompassing the entire group. "My apologies—we went to the shore to test my younger brother's new kite design, and it took longer than we expected. I intended to be back in time for your arrival."

"That's quite all right," Kathleen assured him cheerfully.

"The important question is," Devon said, "how did the kite fly?"

The red-headed boy came to the doorway of the carriage. Ruefully he held up a bundle of slender dowels held together by scraps of red fabric and string, so Devon could see it. "Broke apart in mid-flight, sir. I'll have to make modifications to my design."

"This is my brother, Lord Michael," St. Vincent said. "We call him by his middle name, Ivo."

Ivo was a handsome lad of perhaps ten or eleven, with deep auburn hair, sky-blue eyes, and a winning smile. He executed an awkward bow, in the way of someone who'd just had a growth spurt and was trying to manage the new length of his arms and legs.

"What about me?" the barefoot boy on Lord St. Vincent's other side demanded. He was a sturdy, dark-haired, pink-cheeked child, no more than four years old. Like Ivo, he was dressed in a bathing tunic attached at the waist to a pair of short trousers.

Lord St. Vincent's lips twitched as he looked down at the impatient boy. "You're my nephew," he said gravely.

"I know that!" the child said in exasperation. "You're supposed to tell *them*."

Perfectly straight-faced, Lord St. Vincent said to the Ravenels, "Allow me to introduce my nephew Justin, Lord Clare."

A chorus of greetings came from the interior of the carriage. The door on the other side opened, and the Ravenels began to exit the vehicle as a pair of footmen attended them.

Pandora jumped slightly as Lord St. Vincent's inscrutable gaze connected with hers, his eyes as bright and piercing as starlight.

Wordlessly he reached in a hand for her.

Breathless and scattered, Pandora fumbled to find her

gloves, but they seemed to have disappeared along with her valise. A footman was assisting Kathleen and Cassandra as they descended from the carriage on the other side. Turning back to Lord St. Vincent, she reluctantly took his hand and stepped down from the carriage.

He was even taller than she remembered, bigger, his shoulders broader. When she'd seen him before, he'd been constrained in formal black-and-white evening clothes, every inch of him polished and perfect. Now he was in a rather shocking state of undress, coatless and hatless, his shirt open at the throat. His hair was in disarray, the cropped layers sweat-darkened where they tapered at his neck. A pleasant fragrance drifted to her nostrils, the sunny, foresty smell she remembered from before, now infused with a sea-breeze saltiness.

There was a great deal of activity on the drive as servants left the other carriages and footmen unloaded the luggage. Out of the periphery of her vision, Pandora saw her family proceeding into the house. Lord St. Vincent, however, seemed in no hurry to usher her inside.

"Forgive me," he said quietly, looking down at her. "I had intended to be waiting here, appropriately attired, when you arrived. I don't want you to think your visit isn't important to me."

"Oh, but it's not," Pandora said awkwardly. "That is, I didn't expect fanfare when I arrived. You didn't have to be waiting here, or attired at all. I mean, attired well." Nothing that came out of her mouth sounded right. "I expected clothing, of course." Turning crimson, she dropped her head. "*Blast*," she muttered.

She heard his soft laugh, the sound raising gooseflesh on her sweaty arms.

Ivo broke in, looking contrite. "It's my fault we were late. I had to find all the pieces of my kite."

"Why did it break?" Pandora asked.

"The glue didn't hold."

Having learned a great deal about various glue formulations while constructing a prototype for her board game, Pandora was about to ask what kind he had used.

However, Justin interrupted before she could say a word. "It's my fault too. I lost my shoes and we had to look for them."

Charmed, Pandora sank to her haunches to bring her face level with his, heedless of her skirts draping over the dusty graveled drive. "Didn't you find them?" she asked sympathetically, regarding his bare feet.

Justin shook his head and heaved a sigh, a miniature adult plagued by worldly concerns. "Mama won't be happy about this *at all*."

"What do you think happened?"

"I set them on the sand, and they disappeared."

"Perhaps an octopus stole them." Immediately Pandora regretted the remark—it was just the sort of eccentric comment Lady Berwick would have deplored.

But Lord St. Vincent replied with a considering frown, as if the matter were quite serious. "If it's an octopus, he won't stop until he has eight."

Pandora smiled hesitantly up at him.

"I don't have that many shoes," Justin protested. "What can we do to stop him?"

"We could invent some octopus repellent," Pandora suggested.

"How?" The child's eyes sparked with interest.

"Well," Pandora began, "I'm sure we would need some—*oof!*" She was never to finish the thought, as she was startled by a creature that came bounding swiftly around the side of the carriage. A glimpse of floppy ears and jolly brown eyes filled her vision before the enthusiastic canine pounced so eagerly that she toppled backward from her squatting position. She landed on her rump, the impact knocking her hat to the ground. A swath of hair came loose and slid over her face, while a young tan-and-black retriever leapt around her as if he were on springs. She felt a huff of dog breath at her ear and the swipe of a tongue on her cheek.

"Ajax, *no*," she heard Ivo exclaim.

Realizing what a mess she'd become, all in a matter of seconds, Pandora experienced a moment of despair, followed by resignation. *Of course* this would happen. Of course she would have to meet the duke and duchess after tumbling on the drive like a half-witted carnival performer. It was so dreadful that she began to giggle, while the dog nudged his head against hers.

In the next moment, Pandora was lifted to her feet and caught firmly against a hard surface. The momentum threw her off balance, and she clung to St. Vincent dizzily. He kept her anchored securely against him with an arm around her back.

"*Down*, idiot," St. Vincent commanded. The dog subsided, panting happily.

"He must have slipped past the front door," Ivo said.

St. Vincent smoothed Pandora's hair back from her face. "Are you hurt?" His gaze ran over her swiftly.

"No . . . no." Helpless giggles kept bubbling up as her nervous tension released. She tried to smother the giddy sounds against his shoulder. "I was . . . trying so hard to be ladylike . . ."

A brief chuckle escaped him, and his hand moved

over her upper back in a calming circle. "I would imagine it's not easy to be ladylike in the midst of a dog mauling."

"Milord," came the voice of a concerned footman from nearby, "has the young lady been injured?"

Pandora couldn't quite hear Lord St. Vincent's reply over the pounding of her heart. His nearness, the protective arm around her, that gently roaming hand . . . all of it seemed to be awakening parts of her, deep inside, that had never been awake before. A strange new pleasure spread through her and lit every nerve ending like a succession of tiny birthday candles. Her gaze dropped to his shirtfront, the fine layer of handkerchief-weight linen doing little to conceal the hard curves and planes of muscle beneath. Seeing a hint of tawny curling hair where the placket of the shirt fell open, she flushed and recoiled in confusion.

Raising an exploring hand to her hair, she said vaguely, "My hat . . ." She turned to look for it, only to discover that Ajax had found the little velvet hat with its tempting cluster of feathers. Clamping it in his mouth, the dog shook it playfully.

"Ajax, come," Lord St. Vincent said immediately, but the unruly retriever cavorted and jumped, keeping it out of reach.

Ivo approached the dog slowly. "Ajax, let me have it," he said in a coaxing tone. "Come on, boy . . ." The dog turned and took off at a run. "I'll fetch it," Ivo promised, sprinting after the dog.

"Me too!" Justin followed, his short legs a blur. "But it's going to be soggy!" came a dire warning from over his shoulder.

Shaking his head, Lord St. Vincent watched the retriever scamper across the lawn. "I owe you a new hat," he told Pandora. "That one will return in shreds."

"I don't mind. Ajax is still a pup."

"The dog is inbred," he said flatly. "He doesn't retrieve or obey commands, he tries to dig holes in carpets, and as far as I can tell, he's incapable of walking in a straight line."

Pandora grinned. "I rarely walk in a straight line," she confessed. "I'm too distractible to keep to one direction—I keep veering this way and that, to make certain I'm not missing something. So whenever I set out for a new place, I always end up back where I started."

Lord St. Vincent turned to face her fully, the beautiful cool blue of his eyes intent and searching. "Where do you want to go?"

The question caused Pandora to blink in surprise. She'd just been making a few silly comments, the kind no one ever paid attention to. "It doesn't matter," she said prosaically. "Since I walk in circles, I'll never reach my destination."

His gaze lingered on her face. "You could make the circles bigger."

The remark was perceptive and playful at the same time, as if he somehow understood how her mind worked. Or perhaps he was mocking her.

As the empty carriages and wagon were drawn away, Lord St. Vincent guided Pandora toward the entrance of the house. "How was your journey?" he asked.

"You don't have to make small talk with me," she said. "I don't like it, and I'm not very good at it."

They paused in the shade of the portico, beside a sweet-scented bower of roses. Casually Lord St. Vincent leaned a shoulder against a cream-painted column. A lazy smile curved his lips as he looked down at her. "Didn't Lady Berwick teach you?"

"She tried. But I hate trying to make conversation about weather. Who cares what the temperature is? I want to talk about things like . . . like . . ."

"Yes?" he prompted as she hesitated.

"Darwin. Women's suffrage. Workhouses, war, why we're alive, if you believe in séances or spirits, if music has ever made you cry, or what vegetable you hate most . . ." Pandora shrugged and glanced up at him, expecting the familiar frozen expression of a man who was about to run for his life. Instead she found herself caught by his arrested stare, while the silence seemed to wrap around them.

After a moment, Lord St. Vincent said softly, "Carrots."

Bemused, Pandora tried to gather her wits. "That's the vegetable you hate most? Do you mean cooked ones?"

"Any kind of carrots."

"Out of *all* vegetables?" At his nod, she persisted, "What about carrot cake?"

"No."

"But it's *cake*."

A smile flickered across his lips. "Still carrots."

Pandora wanted to argue the superiority of carrots over some truly atrocious vegetable, such as Brussels sprouts, but their conversation was interrupted by a silky masculine voice.

"Ah, here you are. I've been sent out to fetch you."

Pandora shrank back as she saw a tall man approach in a graceful stride. She knew instantly that he must be Lord St. Vincent's father—the resemblance was striking. His complexion was tanned and lightly time-weathered, with laugh-lines at the outer corners of his blue eyes. He had a full head of tawny-golden hair, handsomely silvered at the sides and temples. Having heard of his reputation as a former libertine, Pandora had expected an aging roué with coarse features and a leer . . . not this rather gorgeous specimen who wore his formidable presence like an elegant suit of clothes.

"My son, what can you be thinking, keeping this enchanting creature out in the heat of midday? And why is she disheveled? Has there been an accident?"

"She was assaulted and knocked to the ground," Lord St. Vincent began to explain.

"Surely you don't know her well enough for that yet."

"By the dog," Lord St. Vincent clarified acidly. "Shouldn't you have him trained?"

"Ivo is training him," came his father's prompt reply.

Lord St. Vincent cast a pointed glance toward the distance, where the red-headed boy could be seen chasing after the scampering dog. "It would seem the dog is training Ivo."

The duke grinned and inclined his head to concede the point. His attention returned to Pandora.

Desperately trying to remember her manners, she curtseyed and murmured, "Your Grace."

The smile lines at his eyes deepened subtly. "You appear to be in need of rescue. Why don't you come inside with me, away from this riffraff? The duchess is eager to meet you." As Pandora hesitated, thoroughly intimidated, he assured her, "I'm quite trustworthy. In fact, I'm very nearly an angel. You'll come to love me in no time."

"Take heed," Lord St. Vincent advised Pandora sardonically, fastening the loose sides of his vest. "My father is the pied piper of gullible women."

"That's not true," the duke said. "The non-gullible ones follow me as well."

Pandora couldn't help chuckling. She looked up into silvery-blue eyes lit with sparks of humor and playfulness. There was something reassuring about his presence, the sense of a man who truly liked women.

When she and Cassandra were children, they had fantasized about a handsome father who would lavish them with affection and advice, and spoil them just a little, but not too much. A father who might have let them stand on his feet to dance. This man looked very much like the one Pandora had imagined.

She moved forward and took his arm.

"How was your journey, my dear?" the duke asked as he escorted her into the house.

Before Pandora could reply, Lord St. Vincent spoke from behind them. "Lady Pandora doesn't like small talk, Father. She would prefer to discuss topics such as Darwin, or women's suffrage."

"Naturally an intelligent young woman would wish to skip over mundane chitchat," the duke said, giving Pandora such an approving glance that she fairly glowed. "However," he continued thoughtfully, "most people need to be guided into a feeling of safety before they dare reveal their opinions to someone they've only just met. There's a beginning to everything, after all. Every opera has its prelude, every sonnet its opening quatrain. Small talk is merely a way of helping a stranger to trust you, by first finding something you can both agree on."

"No one's ever explained it that way before," Pandora said with a touch of wonder. "It actually makes sense. But why must it so often be about weather? Isn't there something else we all agree on? Runcible spoons—everyone likes those, don't they? And tea-time, and feeding ducks."

"Blue ink," the duke added. "And a cat's purr. And summer storms—although I suppose that brings us back to weather."

"I wouldn't mind talking about weather with *you*, Your Grace," Pandora said ingenuously.

The duke laughed gently. "What a delightful girl."

They reached the central hall, which was airy and bright, with plasterwork and polished oak flooring. A colonnaded double staircase led to the upper floor, its wide banister rails perfect for sliding. It smelled like beeswax and fresh air, and the perfume of the large white gardenias arranged in vases on pillars.

To Pandora's surprise, the duchess was waiting for them in the hall. She glowed like a flame in the cool white surroundings, with her gold-freckled complexion and a wealth of rose-copper hair that had been pinned up in a braided mass. Her voluptuous but tidy form was covered in a blue muslin dress, with a ribbon belt tied neatly at her trim waist. Everything about her was warm and approachable and soft.

The duke went to his wife, his hand coming to rest at the small of her back. He seemed to luxuriate in her presence like a great cat. "Darling," he murmured, "this is Lady Pandora."

"At last," the duchess said cheerfully, reaching out to take Pandora's hands into her gentle ones. "I w-wondered what they had done with you."

Pandora would have curtseyed, but the duchess was still holding her hands. Was she supposed to curtsey anyway?

"Why did you keep her outside, Gabriel?" the duchess asked, giving Pandora's hands a little squeeze before letting go. Pandora quickly did a belated curtsey, bobbing like a duck in a mud puddle.

Lord St. Vincent described the mishap with Ajax, emphasizing the dog's lack of discipline to great comic effect.

The duchess laughed. "Poor girl. Come, we'll relax and have iced l-lemonade in the summer parlor. It's my favorite room in the house. The breeze comes up from the ocean and blows right thr-through the screened windows." A stammer interrupted the rhythm of her speech, but it was very slight, and she didn't seem at all self-conscious about it.

"Yes, Your Grace," Pandora whispered, determined not to make a mistake. She wanted to be perfect for this woman.

They began to walk through the staircase hall toward the back of the house, while the men followed. "Now, if there is anything that would make your visit more pleasant," the duchess said to Pandora, "you must let me know as soon as you think of it. We put a vase of roses in your room, but if you have a f-favorite flower, you have only to tell us. My youngest daughter Seraphina chose some books for your room, but if there is something more to your taste in the library, we'll switch them out at once."

Pandora nodded dumbly. After some laborious thought, she finally came up with something ladylike to say. "Your house is lovely, ma'am."

The duchess gave her a radiant smile. "If you like, I'll take you on a tour later this afternoon. We have some very good art, and interesting old f-furniture, and some beautiful views from the second floor."

"Oh, that would be—" Pandora began, but to her

annoyance, Lord St. Vincent interrupted from behind them.

"I had already planned to take Lady Pandora on an outing this afternoon."

Pandora glanced over her shoulder with a quick frown. "I would prefer a tour of the house with the duchess."

"I don't trust you around unfamiliar furniture," Lord St. Vincent said. "It could be disastrous. What if I have to pull you out of an armoire, or God forbid, a credenza?"

Embarrassed by the reminder of how they'd met, Pandora said stiffly, "It wouldn't be proper for me to go on an outing without a chaperone."

"You're not worried about being compromised, are you?" he asked. "Because I've already done that."

Forgetting her resolution to be dignified, Pandora stopped and whirled to face the provoking man. "No, you didn't. I was compromised by a settee. You just happened to be there."

Lord St. Vincent seemed to enjoy her indignation. "Regardless," he said, "you have nothing to lose now."

"Gabriel—" the duchess began, but fell silent as he slid her a glance of bright mischief.

The duke regarded his son dubiously. "If you're trying to be charming," he said, "I should tell you that it's not going well."

"There's no need for me to be charming," Lord St. Vincent replied. "Lady Pandora is only pretending disinterest. Beneath the show of indifference, she's infatuated with me."

Pandora was outraged. "That is the most pomposterous thing I've ever heard!" Before she had finished the sentence, however, she saw the dance of mischief in Lord St. Vincent's eyes. He was teasing, she realized. Turning pink with confusion, she lowered her head. Within a few minutes of arriving at Heron's Point, she had tumbled on the drive, lost her hat and her temper, and had used a made-up word. It was a good thing Lady Berwick wasn't there, or she'd have had apoplexy.

As they continued to walk, Lord St. Vincent fell into step beside Pandora while the duchess followed with the duke. "Pomposterous," he murmured, a smile in his voice. "I like that one."

"I wish you wouldn't tease," Pandora muttered. "It's difficult enough for me to be ladylike."

"You don't have to be."

Pandora sighed, her momentary annoyance fading into resignation. "No, I do," she said earnestly. "I'll never be good at it, but the important thing is to keep trying."

IT WAS THE statement of a young woman who was aware of her limitations but was determined not to be defeated by them. Gabriel didn't have to look at his parents to know they were thoroughly charmed by Pandora. As for him . . .

He hardly recognized himself in his reaction to her. She was full of life, burning like sunflowers in the rime of autumn frost. Compared to the languid and diffident girls of London's annual marriage mart, Pandora might have been another species altogether. She was just as beautiful as he'd remembered, and as unpredictable. Laughing after the dog had jumped on her in the front drive, when any other young woman in her place would have been angry or humiliated. As she'd stood there wanting to argue with him about carrots, all Gabriel had been able to think of was how much he wanted to carry her somewhere cool and dark and quiet, and have her all to himself.

But despite Pandora's compelling attractions, there was no doubt she was ill-suited to the only kind of life he could offer. The life he'd been born into. He couldn't renounce his title, nor could he turn his back on the families and employees who depended on him. It was his responsibility to manage the Challons' ancestral lands and preserve their heritage for the next generations. His wife would be saddled with managing multiple households, performing court duties, attending charity organization committee meetings and foundation-layings, and so on.

Pandora would hate it. All of it. Even if she did grow into the role, she would never inhabit it comfortably.

They entered the summer parlor, where the Ravenels chatted amiably with his sisters, Phoebe and Seraphina.

Phoebe, the oldest of the Challon siblings, had inherited their mother's warm and deeply loving nature, and their father's acerbic wit. Five years ago she had married her childhood sweetheart, Henry, Lord Clare, who had suffered from chronic illness for most of his life. The worsening symptoms had gradually reduced him to a shadow of the man he'd once been, and he'd finally succumbed while Phoebe was pregnant with their second child. Although the first year of mourning was over, Phoebe hadn't yet returned to her former self. She went outdoors so seldom that her freckles had vanished, and she looked wan and thin. The ghost of grief still lingered in her gaze.

Their younger sister Seraphina, an effervescent eighteen-year-old with strawberry-blonde hair, was talking to Cassandra. Although Seraphina was old enough to have come out in society by now, the duke and duchess had persuaded her to wait another year. A girl with her sweet nature, her beauty, and her mammoth dowry would be targeted by every eligible man in Europe and beyond. For Seraphina, the London Season would be a gauntlet, and the more prepared she was, the better.

After introductions were made, Pandora accepted a glass of iced lemonade and remained quiet as the conversation flowed around her. When the group discussion turned to the subject of Heron's Point's economy, and its tourism and fishing industries, it was obvious to Gabriel that Pandora's thoughts had drifted in a direction that had nothing to do with the present moment. What was going on in that restless brain?

Moving closer to her, Gabriel asked quietly, "Have you ever gone to a beach? Waded in the ocean and felt the sand beneath your feet?"

Pandora glanced up at him, the vacant expression leaving her face. "No, I—there's a sand beach here? I thought it would be all pebbles and shingle."

"The estate has a private sandy cove. We walk to it along a holloway."

"What's a holloway?"

"It's what they call a sunken lane, here in the southern counties." Gabriel loved the way she shaped the word silently with her lips . . . *holloway* . . . seeming to savor it as if it were a bonbon. Glancing at Seraphina, who was standing nearby, he said, "I'm going to take Lady Pandora to the cove this afternoon. I expect Ivo will come too. Would you like to join us?"

Pandora frowned. "I didn't say—"

"That would be lovely," Seraphina exclaimed, and

turned to Cassandra. "You must come with us. It's refreshing to splash about in the ocean on a day like this."

"Actually," Cassandra said apologetically, "I would rather take a nap."

"How could you possibly want a nap?" Pandora demanded, incredulous. "We've done nothing but sit all day."

Cassandra was instantly defensive. "Doing nothing is exhausting. I need to rest in case we do nothing again later."

Looking nettled, Pandora turned back to Gabriel. "I can't go, either. I have no bathing costume."

"You can wear one of mine," Seraphina volunteered.

"Thank you, but without a chaperone, I couldn't—"

"Phoebe has agreed to chaperone us," Gabriel interrupted.

His older sister, who had been listening to the exchange, raised her brows. "I did?" she asked coolly.

Gabriel gave her a meaningful glance. "We discussed it this morning, remember?"

Phoebe's gray eyes narrowed. "Actually, I don't."

"You said you'd spent too much time inside lately," he told her. "You said you needed a walk and some fresh air."

"Goodness, how talkative I was," Phoebe said in a caustic tone, her gaze promising retribution. But she didn't argue.

Gabriel grinned as he saw Pandora's mutinous expression. "Don't be stubborn," he coaxed in an undertone. "I promise you'll enjoy yourself. And if you don't . . . you'll have the satisfaction of proving me wrong."

Chapter 7

After being shown to a pretty bedroom with delicate pink walls, and wide windows opening to a view of the ocean, Pandora changed into a bathing costume that had been brought by Seraphina's maid. The ensemble consisted of a dress with short puffed sleeves and a shockingly brief skirt, and a pair of Turkish trousers to wear underneath. Sewn of light blue flannel trimmed with white braid, the bathing costume was wonderfully light and loose.

"If only women could dress like this all the time," Pandora enthused, twirling experimentally. Losing her balance, she fell dramatically backward onto the bed with her white-stockinged legs in the air like an upended tea table. "I feel so free without a creaky old corset."

Her lady's maid, a stout fair-haired girl named Ida, regarded her doubtfully. "Ladies need corsets to support their weak backs."

"I don't have a weak back."

"You should pretend to. Gentlemen prefer a delicate lady." Ida, who had pored over hundreds of ladies' fashion periodicals, continued with authority. "Take my advice and find a reason to swoon when you're at the beach, so Lord St. Vincent can catch you."

"Swoon from what?"

"Say a crab frightened you."

Still lying on the bed, Pandora began to laugh. "It's after me!" she exclaimed theatrically, opening and closing her hands like pincers.

"Don't snort, if you please," Ida said sourly. "You sound like a trumpet-major."

Raising up on her elbows, Pandora regarded her with a crooked grin. Ida had been hired at the beginning of the Season, when it had been decided the twins each needed her own lady's maid. Both Ida and the other maid, Meg, had vied eagerly for the position of attending Cassandra, who had lovely golden hair and a far more compliant disposition than Pandora.

Cassandra had chosen Meg, however, which had forced Ida to settle for becoming Pandora's maid. Ida had made no secret of her disappointment. To Pandora's amusement, Ida had dispensed with most of the usual courtesies and pleasantries, and had remained surly ever since. In fact, when the two of them were in private, her remarks bordered on insulting. However, Ida was efficient and hardworking, and determined to make a success of her charge. She went to great lengths to keep Pandora's clothing in perfect condition, and was proficient at arranging her heavy, slippery hair so that it stayed firmly in its pins.

"Your tone lacks deference, Ida," Pandora said.

"I'll treat you with all the deference in the world, milady, if you can manage to bring Lord St. Vincent up to scratch. Word among his servants is, the Challons will arrange for someone else to marry you, if you don't suit Lord St. Vincent."

Instantly annoyed, Pandora climbed off the bed and tugged the bathing costume back into place. "As if this were a game of pass-the-parcel? With me as the parcel?"

"It wasn't Lord St. Vincent who said so," Ida interrupted. She held up a hooded robe, which had also been brought by Seraphina's lady's maid. "It was his servants, and they were only speculating."

"How do you know what his servants are saying?" Fuming, Pandora turned and thrust her arms into the robe. "We've only been here for an hour."

"It's all everyone is talking about belowstairs." Ida fastened the robe at the waist. It matched the rest of the bathing costume and gave the ensemble the appearance of a proper dress. "There, you're presentable." She knelt and guided Pandora's feet into little canvas slippers. "Mind you don't become loud and wild during your outing. His lordship's sisters will notice everything, and tell the duke and duchess."

"Bother," Pandora grumbled. "I wish I weren't going at all now." Scowling, she jammed a low-brimmed straw hat over her coiffure and left the room.

THE GROUP HEADING to the beach consisted of Lord St. Vincent, Seraphina, Ivo, Phoebe and her son Justin, Pandora, and Ajax, who bounded ahead and barked as if urging them to hurry. The boys were in high spirits, carrying an assortment of tin pails, spades, and kites.

The holloway was only wide enough to accommodate a single cart or wagon, and so deeply sunken in some places that its banks were taller than Pandora. Tussocks of gray-green Marram grass grew in places along its walls, interspersed with long-stalked flowers and spiny shrubs of sea buckthorn laden with brilliant orange berries. White-and-gray herring gulls spiraled on ocean-flung breezes, their stiffly spread wings carving through the soft sky.

Still brooding over the idea that she was on trial—that Lord St. Vincent was assessing her and would most likely decide to foist her off on someone else—Pandora spoke as little as possible. To her discomfiture, the rest of the group seemed inclined to draw away from the two of them. Phoebe made no effort to watch over them, instead walking far in front, hand-in-hand with Justin.

Obliged to keep pace with Lord St. Vincent's more relaxed stride, Pandora saw the distance between them and their companions increase. "We should try to catch up to the others," she said.

His lazy pace didn't alter. "They know we'll reach them eventually."

Pandora frowned. "Does Lady Clare know nothing about chaperoning? She's paying no attention to us."

"She knows the last thing we need is close supervision, since we're trying to become familiar with each other."

"That's rather a waste of time, isn't it?" Pandora couldn't resist asking. "In light of your plans."

Lord St. Vincent glanced at her alertly. "What plans?"

"To pawn me off on some other man," she said, "so you don't have to marry me."

Lord St. Vincent stopped in the middle of the holloway, obliging her to halt as well. "Where did you hear that?"

"It's household gossip. And if it's true—"

"It's not."

"—I don't need you to dredge up an unwilling bridegroom from somewhere and bully him into marrying me just so you don't have to. Cousin Devon says I won't be made to marry anyone if I don't wish it. And I don't. Furthermore, I don't want to spend my visit trying to win your approval, so I hope—"

She broke off, startled as Lord St. Vincent moved toward her in two fluid strides. Instinctively she backed away until her shoulders encountered the side bank of the holloway.

Looming over her, Lord St. Vincent braced one hand against an exposed tree root that ran up the wall. "I'm not planning to give you to another man," he said evenly, "if only because for the life of me, I can't think of a single acquaintance who would begin to know how to handle you."

Her eyes narrowed. "But you can?"

Lord St. Vincent didn't reply, but his mouth twisted in a way that seemed to imply the answer to the question was obvious. As he saw the fist she had clenched in the folds of her robe, something in his face softened. "You're not here to win my approval. I invited you to find out more about who you are."

"Well, that won't take long," Pandora muttered. In response to his quizzical glance, she continued, "I've never been anywhere, or done any of the things I've dreamed about. I haven't finished becoming myself. And if I marry you, I'll never be anything except Lord St. Vincent's peculiar wife who talks too fast and never knows the order of precedence for the dinner guests." Hanging her head, Pandora swallowed against the sharp constriction of her throat.

After a speculative silence, his long, graceful fingers came to her jaw, tipping it upward. "What do you say to lowering our guards?" he asked gently. "A temporary disarmament."

Fidgeting, Pandora looked away from him and happened to see a nearby vine bearing an enormous cup-shaped pink blossom with a white star at its center. "What kind of flower is that?"

"Sea bindweed." Lord St. Vincent guided her face back to his. "Are you trying to distract me, or did that question just pop into your head?"

"Both?" she offered sheepishly.

Amusement flicked one corner of his mouth upward. "What would it take to keep your attention fixed on me?"

Pandora stiffened as his fingertips traced the edge of her jaw, leaving behind a ticklish trail of warmth. Her throat felt thick, as if she'd just swallowed a spoonful of honey. "I am paying attention to you."

"Not fully."

"I am, I'm looking at you, and—" A shaky breath escaped her as she recalled that Lord Chaworth had called this man a notorious rake. "Oh, no. I hope this isn't—you're not going to try to kiss me, are you?"

One of his brows arched. "Do you want me to?"

"No," she said hastily. "No, thank you, no."

Lord St. Vincent laughed gently. "One refusal is enough, darling." The backs of his fingers stroked the frantic pulse in her throat. "The fact is, we have a decision to make by the end of the week."

"I don't need a week. I can tell you right now."

"No, not until you find out more about what you might be turning down. Which means we're going to have to condense six months of courtship into six days." He let out a breath of rueful amusement as he read her expression. "You look like a patient who's just been informed she needs surgery."

"I'd rather not be courted."

"Could you help me understand why?" he asked, relaxed and patient.

"I just know it would turn out badly, because . . ." Pandora hesitated, considering how to explain the side of herself she'd never liked but couldn't seem to change. The side that perceived intimacy as a threat, and feared being controlled. Manipulated. Damaged. "I don't want you to find out more about who I am, when so many things about me are wrong. I've never been able to think or behave the way other girls do. I'm even different from my own twin. People have always called us hellions, but the truth is, *I'm* the hellion. I should be put on a leash. My sister is only guilty by association. Poor Cassandra." Her throat cinched around an ache of misery. "I've caused a scandal, and now she'll be ruined, and she'll end up a spinster. And my family will suffer. It's all my fault. I wish none of this had happened. I wish—"

"Easy, child. Good Lord, there's no need for all this self-flagellation. Come here." Before Pandora quite knew what was happening, she was in his arms, clasped against the warm, breathing strength of him. As he brought her head to his shoulder, her hat was dislodged and fell to the ground. Shocked and bewildered, she felt his masculine form pressed all along hers, and clarions of alarm sang through her blood. What was he doing? Why was she allowing it?

But he was speaking to her, his voice low and soothing, and it was so comforting that her startled tension dissolved like a sliver of ice in the sun. "Your family isn't as fragile as all that. Trenear is more than capable of seeing to their welfare. Your sister is an attractive girl with good blood and a dowry, and even in the shadow of family scandal, she won't go unmarried." His hand moved over her back with easy, hypnotic strokes until Pandora began to feel like a cat whose fur was being smoothed just the right way. Slowly her cheek came to rest upon the smooth linen weave of his vest, her eyes half-closing as she inhaled the hint of laundry soap, and the crisp, resinous dryness of cologne on hot male skin.

"Of course you don't fit in with London society," he was saying. "Most of them have no more imagination or originality than the average sheep. Appearances are all they understand, and therefore—however maddening you find it—you're going to have to heed some of the rules and rituals that make them comfortable. The unfortunate fact is, the only thing worse than being a part of society is living outside of it. Which is why you may have to let me help you out of this situation, just as I pulled you out of that settee."

"If by 'help' you mean marriage, my lord," Pandora said, her voice muffled against his shoulder, "I would rather not. I have reasons you don't know about."

Lord St. Vincent studied her half-hidden face. "I'll be interested to hear them." Lightly he fingered a tendril of hair at her temple, and smoothed it into place with his fingertips. "Let's use first names from now on," he suggested. "We have a great deal to talk about in a short amount of time. The more honest and direct we are with each other, the better. No secrets, no evasions. Will you agree to that?"

Reluctantly lifting her head, Pandora gave him a doubtful glance. "I don't want this to be a one-sided arrangement," she said, "in which I tell all my secrets while you withhold yours."

A smile edged his lips. "I promise full disclosure."

"And everything we say will be confidential?"

"God, I hope so," he said. "My secrets are far more shocking than yours."

Pandora didn't doubt it. He was a seasoned, self-assured man, well acquainted with the world and all its vices. There was an almost preternatural maturity about him, a sense of authority that couldn't have been more unlike her father and brother, with their hair-trigger tempers.

This was the first time she'd truly been able to relax after days of anguish and guilt. He was so large and substantial that she felt like a small wild creature who'd just found refuge. She let out a quivering sigh of relief, a regrettably childish sound, and he began to stroke her again. "Poor mite," he murmured. "You've had a time of it, haven't you? Relax. There's nothing for you to worry about."

Pandora didn't believe that, of course, but it felt so lovely to be treated like this, soothed and coddled into a good humor. She tried to absorb every sensation, every detail, so she could remember it later.

His skin was smooth everywhere except for the texture of beard-grain where he'd shaved. There was an intriguing triangular hollow at the base of his throat, near his collarbone. His bare neck was very strong-looking except for that one shadowed place, vulnerable amid the tough construction of muscle and bone.

An absurd thought occurred to her. What would it be like to kiss him there?

It would feel like satin against her lips. His skin would taste as nice as he smelled.

The insides of her cheeks watered.

The temptation grew with every passing second, impossible to ignore. It was the feeling that sometimes came over her when an impulse was so overpowering that she had to obey it or die. That lightly shadowed hollow had its own gravity. It was pulling her closer. Blinking, Pandora felt her body camber forward.

Oh no. The urge was too much to resist. Helplessly she leaned forward and closed her eyes and just did it, kissed him right there, and it was even more satisfying than she'd thought it would be, her mouth finding tender warmth, a vibrant pulse.

Gabriel's breath caught hard, and his body jolted. His fingers sank into her coiffure and he eased her head back, his wide, wondering eyes staring down into hers. His lips parted as he struggled for words.

Pandora's face was scorched with shame. "I'm so sorry."

"No, I . . ." He sounded nearly as breathless as she was. "I don't mind. I was just . . . surprised."

"I can't control my impulses," she said hastily. "I'm not responsible for what just happened. I have a nervous condition."

"A nervous condition," Gabriel repeated, his white teeth catching at his lower lip in the prelude to a grin. For a moment, he looked heart-stoppingly boyish. "Was that an official diagnosis?"

"No, but according to a book I once read, *Phenomena Produced By Diseases Of The Nervous System,* it's very likely that I have hyperesthesia or periodic mania, or both." Pandora paused with a frown. "Why are you smiling? It's not nice to laugh at other people's diseases."

"I was remembering the night we met, when you told me about your unwholesome reading material." One of his palms came to rest low on her spine. His other hand slid around the back of her neck, closing tenderly around the small muscles. "Have you ever been kissed, love?"

Pandora's stomach suddenly went very light, as if she were falling. She stared up at him mutely. Her entire vocabulary had collapsed. Her head was nothing but a box of loose moveable type.

Gabriel smiled slightly at her dumbstruck silence. "I'll assume that means no." His lashes lowered as his gaze fell to her mouth. "Take a breath, or you might faint from lack of oxygen and miss the whole thing."

Pandora obeyed jerkily.

Fact #15 she would write in her book later. *Today I found out why chaperones were invented.*

Hearing the wheeze of her anxious breath, Gabriel gently massaged her neck muscles. "Don't be afraid. I won't kiss you now, if you don't want it."

Pandora managed to find her voice. "No, I . . . if it's going to happen, I would rather you went ahead and did it now. Then we'll have it out of the way and I won't dread it." Realizing how that sounded, she said apologetically, "Not that I should dread it, because I'm sure your kissing is well above average, and many ladies would be delighted by the prospect."

She felt a tremor of laughter run through him. "My kisses are above average," he conceded, "but I wouldn't say *well* above average. That might be overstating my abilities, and I wouldn't want you to be disappointed."

Pandora looked up at him suspiciously, wondering if he were teasing her again. His expression was perfectly bland. "I'm sure I won't be," she said, and steadied herself. "I'm ready," she said bravely. "You can do it now."

Perversely, Gabriel made no move to kiss her right away. "You're interested in Charles Darwin, as I recall. Have you read his latest book?"

"No." Why was he talking about books? She was shaky with nerves, and rather annoyed that he was drawing the whole thing out like this.

"*The Expression of Emotion In Man and Animals*," Gabriel continued. "Darwin writes that the custom of kissing can't be considered an innate human behavior, as it doesn't extend to every culture. New Zealanders, for example, rub noses in lieu of kissing. He also references an account of tribal societies in which they greet each other by blowing air softly against the face." He gave her an innocent glance. "We could start that way, if you like."

Pandora had no idea how to respond. "Are you mocking me?" she demanded.

Laughter danced in his eyes. "Pandora," he chided, "don't you know when someone is flirting with you?"

"No. All I know is that you're looking at me as if I'm excessively amusing, like a trained monkey playing a tambourine."

With his hand still supporting her nape, Gabriel brought his lips to her forehead and smoothed out the furrow of her frown. "Flirting is like playing. It's a promise you may or may not keep. It could be a provocative glance . . . a smile . . . the touch of a fingertip . . . or a whisper." His face was right over hers, so close that she could see the gold tips on his feathery dark lashes. "Should we rub noses now?" he whispered.

Pandora shook her head. She had the sudden urge to tease him, catch him off guard. Pursing her lips, she blew a soft, cool stream of air against his chin.

To her satisfaction, Gabriel reacted with a quick double-blink of surprise. A flush of color made his eyes fever-bright, the irises spangled with glints of wondering amusement. "You win at flirting," he told her, and his hand cradled her jaw, his thumb stroking a circle over her cheek.

Pandora tensed as his mouth came to hers, as light as a brush of silk or a zephyr breeze. He was almost tentative at first, making no demands, only feeling the contours of her mouth with his. Softly, softly . . . his lips moved over hers in sensuous touches that quieted the usual chaos of her brain. Mesmerized, she answered with hesitant pressure, and he shaped her response, played with her, until she began to dissolve in the slow, endless teasing. There was no interference of thought or time, no past or future. There was only this moment, the two of them standing together in a sun-drenched path of flowering vines and sweet dry grass.

He caught gently at her lower lip, and then the upper, the tender nibbling sending vibrant shocks down to the quick of her body. Pressing deeper, he coaxed her lips to part until an unfamiliar flavor whispered across her senses, something clean and soft and stirring. She felt the tip of his tongue, an intrusion of pure heat into the private space that had always belonged only to her. Bewildered, trembling in surprise, she opened to him.

His fingers spread over the back of her head, cupping the curve of her skull, and he broke the kiss to work his way down the side of her throat. She began to breathe in gasps at the feel of his lips moving slowly over the most deliriously sensitive places, the most delicate skin. The wet velvet friction caused gooseflesh to rise all over. She lost the feel of her bones, sinking against him while pleasure pooled at the pit of her stomach like melted sun.

Reaching the joint where her neck connected with her shoulder, Gabriel lingered there, touching it with his tongue. The edges of his teeth clamped down in a soft bite, and a helpless shiver wracked her. He worked his way back up with supple, searching kisses. By the time he reached her mouth again she couldn't hold back a mortifying whimper of eagerness. Her lips felt swollen, and the firm, savoring pressure was an exquisite relief. Clutching her arms around his neck, she pulled his head down, urging him to kiss her harder, longer. She dared to explore his mouth the way he had hers, and that drew a low pleasured sound from his throat. He was so delicious and silky that she couldn't stop herself from putting her hands on the sides of his face and claiming him aggressively. She kissed him harder, deeper, feasting on the luscious interior of his mouth with uncontrollable greed.

With a smothered laugh, Gabriel pulled his head back and gripped a hand in her hair. Like her, he was panting for breath. "Pandora, love," he said, his eyes brilliant with mingled heat and amusement, "you kiss like a pirate."

She didn't care. She needed more of him. She was throbbing in every limb, feeling too much at once, shaking with a hunger she didn't know how to satisfy. Clutching his shoulders, she sought his mouth again and arched against the hard masculine contours of his body. Not enough . . . she wanted him to crush her, take her to the ground, and hold her there with his full weight.

Gabriel kept the kiss light, trying to gentle her. "Easy, my wild girl," he whispered. When she refused to calm down, still shaking, he relented and gave her what she wanted, fastening his mouth over hers, siphoning pleasure from her with sweet erotic pulls.

"Oh, for God's sake." A woman's exasperated voice came from several yards away, startling Pandora as if someone had just tossed a bucket of cold water on them.

It was Phoebe, who had come back along the holloway to find them. She had discarded her robe and stood there in her bathing costume, hands braced on slender hips. "Are you coming to the beach," she asked her brother irritably, "or are you going to seduce the poor girl in the middle of the holloway?"

Disoriented, Pandora became aware of a flurry of jubilant movement near her legs. Ajax had run back along the holloway to bounce and prance around them, and paw at the skirt of her robe.

Feeling the way she was trembling, Gabriel kept holding her, his palm resting on her back between her shoulder blades. His chest moved with the ragged rhythm of his breathing, but he sounded calm and collected as he replied. "Phoebe, the fact that I asked you to be a chaperone should have made it obvious that I didn't want a chaperone at all."

"I have no desire to be one," Phoebe retorted. "However, the children are asking why you're taking so long, and I can't very well explain to them that you're a libidinous goat."

"No," Gabriel replied, "because then you would sound like a parsimonious prig."

Pandora was perplexed by the quick, fond grins the siblings exchanged after the sharp words.

Rolling her eyes, Phoebe turned and strode away. Ajax bolted after her—with Pandora's hat clamped in his mouth.

"That dog will cost me a fortune in hats," Gabriel said dryly. His hands stroked her back and neck, while the rough pounding of her heart eased slowly.

It took at least a half-minute before Pandora could speak. "Your sister—she saw us—"

"Don't worry, she won't say a word to anyone. She and I like to bait each other, that's all. Come." Nudging her chin upward, he stole a last swift kiss, and pulled her along the path with him.

Chapter 8

THEY EMERGED FROM THE holloway into a landscape unlike anything Pandora had seen except in photographs or engravings . . . a wide belt of pale sand extending toward a white-frothed ocean, and more blue sky than she'd ever seen at one time. The foreshore was backed by dunes anchored in place with bushy grasses and spiky flowering plants. Toward the west, the sand graded to pebble and shingle before the ground ascended to chalk cliffs that bordered the promontory. The air was filled with the rhythmic collapse of waves and soft rushes of water flattening across the sand. A trio of herring gulls pecked over a bit of food, squabbling with thin, sharp cries.

It didn't look like Hampshire or London. It didn't seem like England at all.

Phoebe and the two boys stood farther along the shore, engaged in unwinding the string of a kite. Seraphina, who had been wading in ankle-deep water, noticed Pandora and Gabriel, and scampered toward them. She had removed her shoes and stockings, and the trousers of her bathing costume were sodden from the knees down. Her strawberry-blonde hair hung in a loose braid over one shoulder.

"Do you like our cove?" Seraphina asked, with an expansive gesture at their surroundings.

Pandora nodded, her awed gaze traveling across the scenery.

"I'll show you where to put your robe." Seraphina led her to a bathing-machine that had been left near a dune. It was a small enclosed room set on high wheels, with a set of steps leading up to a door. A removable hook ladder had been affixed to one of the outside walls.

"I've seen one of these in pictures," Pandora said regarding the contraption dubiously, "but I've never been inside one."

"We never use it, unless we have a guest who insists. Then we have to hitch up a horse to pull it out to waist-deep water, and the lady steps into the ocean on the other side, so no one can see. It's a lot of bother, and rather silly, since a bathing costume covers just as much as an ordinary dress." Seraphina opened the door of the bathing-machine. "You can take off your things in there."

Pandora went into the bathing-machine, which had been supplied with shelves and a row of hooks, and removed her robe, stockings, and canvas slippers. As she emerged into the sunshine dressed in the bathing costume with its short skirt and trousers, and her feet and ankles bare, she turned as red as if she were naked. To her relief, Gabriel had gone to help with the kite, and was standing at a distance with the two boys.

Seraphina smiled, brandishing a small tin pail. "Let's go look for shells."

As they headed toward the ocean, Pandora was amazed by the feeling of sun-warmed sand conforming to her soles and slipping up between her toes. Closer to the water, the sand became firm and moist. She stopped to glance back at the trail of footprints behind her. Experimentally she hopped forward on one foot for a few yards, and turned to view her tracks.

Soon Justin ran to them with something clasped in his cupped hands, while Ajax trotted at his heels. "Pandora, put out your hand!"

"What is it?"

"A hermit crab."

Cautiously she extended her hand, and the boy deposited a round object into her palm, a shell no bigger than the tip of her thumb. Slowly a set of miniature claws emerged, followed by thread-like antennae and black pinhead eyes.

Pandora inspected the tiny creature closely before handing it back to Justin. "Are there many of them in the water?" she asked. Although one hermit crab by itself was rather adorable, she wouldn't care to go wading with a consortium of them.

A shadow crossed over her, and a pair of bare masculine feet came into her vision. "No," came Gabriel's reassuring reply, "they live under rocks and shingle on the far side of the cove."

"Mama says I have to put him back later," Justin said. "But first I'm going to build a sandcastle for him."

"I'll help," Seraphina exclaimed, kneeling to fill the tin pail with wet sand. "Go fetch the other pails and spades by the bathing-machine. Pandora, will you join us?"

"Yes, but . . ." Pandora glanced at the waves surging and breaking on the shore in tumbles of foam. "First I'd like to go exploring a little, if I may."

"Of course." Seraphina was using both hands to load sand into the pail. "You certainly don't need to ask for *my* consent."

Pandora was both amused and chagrined. "After a year of Lady Berwick's instructions, I feel as if I should have permission from someone." She glanced at Phoebe, who was at least a dozen yards away, looking out at the ocean. Obviously the woman couldn't have cared less about what Pandora was doing.

Gabriel followed her gaze. "You have Phoebe's permission," he said dryly. "Let me walk with you."

Still feeling shy from their earlier encounter, Pandora accompanied him across the cool, compacted sand. Her senses were overwhelmed by a deluge of sight, sound, and sensation. Every breath filled her lungs with vibrant, living air and left the taste of salt spindrift on her lips. Farther out, the ocean rolled in wind-harried billows, trimmed with ruffles of white foam. Pausing to stare out at the vast blue infinity, she tried to imagine what might be concealed in its mysterious depths, shipwrecks and whales and exotic creatures, and a pleasant shiver went through her. She bent to pick up a tiny cup-shaped shell that had been partially embedded in the sand, and rubbed her thumb across its rough gray-striped surface. "What is this?" she asked, showing it to Gabriel.

"A limpet."

She found another shell, round and ridged. "And this? Is it a scallop?"

"A cockleshell. You can tell the difference by looking at the hinge-line. A scallop has a triangle on each side."

As Pandora collected more shells—whelks, a winkle, mussels—she gave them to Gabriel, who carried them for her in one of his trouser pockets. She noticed he had rolled the hems of his trousers to the middle of his calves, which were lightly dusted with glinting tawny fleece.

"Do you have a bathing-suit?" she dared to ask shyly.

"Yes, but it's not for mixed company." At her questioning glance, Gabriel explained, "A man's bathing-suit isn't like the ones Ivo and Justin are wearing. It consists of flannel trunks that tie at the waist with a string. Once they're wet, they leave so little to the imagination that a man may as well wear nothing at all. Most of us at the estate don't bother with them when we go for a swim."

"You swim naked?" Pandora asked, so flustered that a shell dropped from her lax fingers.

Gabriel bent to retrieve it. "Not with ladies present, of course." He smiled at her pink face. "I usually go in the mornings."

"The water must be like ice."

"It is. But there are benefits to a cold ocean swim. Among other things, it stimulates the circulation."

The idea of him swimming without a stitch on had certainly affected *her* circulation. She wandered to the water's edge where the sand was glossy. It was too wet to leave a footprint: As soon as she took another step, silt flowed into the depression. A wave rolled in and thinned until it reached her toes. She started at the biting cold of it but took a few steps forward. The next surge flooded over her ankles and almost up to her knees in a rush of chilling, bubbling lightness. She gave a little squeal and a surprised laugh at the feel of it. The wave slackened, its forward momentum halting.

As the water retreated in a long pull, towing sand back with it, Pandora had the sensation of sliding backward even though she was standing still. At the same time, sand eroded from beneath her feet, as if someone were yanking away a rug she happened to be standing on.

The ground tilted sharply and she staggered, her equilibrium lost.

A pair of strong hands caught her from behind. Blinking, Pandora found herself pulled back against

Gabriel's hard, warm chest, with his thighs braced on either side of hers. She heard the baritone of his voice, but he spoke near her bad ear, and the sound of the surf muffled his words.

"Wh-what?" she asked, turning her head to the side.

"I said I have you," Gabriel murmured at her other ear. The brush of his lips at the delicate outer rim sent an electric feeling through her. "I should have warned you. As the waves ebb, it can make you feel as if you're moving even when you're standing still."

Another wave approached. Pandora tensed and backed up against him more tightly, and she was vaguely annoyed to feel him chuckle.

"I won't let you fall." His arms slid securely around her front. "Just relax."

He steadied her as the wave broke and surged around her legs, its eddies raking up sand and shells. As the water retreated, Pandora considered fleeing to higher ground. But it felt so pleasant to lean back against Gabriel's sturdy form that she hesitated, and then another surge was coming. She gripped his arm hard, and it tightened reassuringly across her middle. Shoaling water rose and broke with the sounds of shattering crystal, followed by swooshes as if something were being mopped. Over and over, in hypnotic rhythm. Gradually her breathing turned deep and regular.

The experience began to feel rather dreamlike. The world had become nothing but coldness, heat, sun, sand, the scent of brine and minerals. Gabriel's torso was a wall of muscle at her back, flexing subtly as he adjusted for balance, keeping her braced and supported and safe. Random thoughts drifted through her mind, the way they did in early morning, in the margin between sleep and wakefulness. A breeze carried the sounds of the children laughing, the dog barking, Phoebe's and Seraphina's voices, but they all seemed removed from what was happening to her.

Forgetting herself entirely, Pandora let her head loll back against Gabriel's shoulder. "What kind of glue does Ivo use?" she asked languidly.

"Glue?" he echoed after a moment, his mouth close to her temple, grazing softly.

"For his kites."

"Ah." He paused while a wave retreated. "Joiner's glue, I believe."

"That's not strong enough," Pandora said, relaxed and pensive. "He should use chrome glue."

"Where would he find that?" One of his hands caressed her side gently.

"A druggist can make it. One part acid chromate of lime to five parts gelatin."

Amusement filtered through his voice. "Does your mind ever slow down, sweetheart?"

"Not even for sleeping," she said.

Gabriel steadied her against another wave. "How do you know so much about glue?"

The agreeable trance began to fade as Pandora considered how to answer him.

After her long hesitation, Gabriel tilted his head and gave her a questioning sideways glance. "The subject of glue is complicated, I gather."

I'm going to have to tell him at some point, Pandora thought. *It might as well be now.*

After taking a deep breath, she blurted out, "I design and construct board games. I've researched every possible kind of glue required for manufacturing them. Not just for the construction of the boxes, but the best kind to adhere lithographs to the boards and lids. I've registered a patent for the first game, and soon I intend to apply for two more."

Gabriel absorbed the information in remarkably short order. "Have you considered selling the patents to a publisher?"

"No, I want to make the games at my own factory. I have a production schedule. The first one will be out by Christmas. My brother-in-law, Mr. Winterborne, helped me to write a business plan. The market in board games is quite new, and he thinks my company will be successful."

"I'm sure it will be. But a young woman in your position has no need of a livelihood."

"I do if I want to be self-supporting."

"Surely the safety of marriage is preferable to the burdens of being a business proprietor."

Pandora turned to face him fully. "Not if 'safety' means being owned. As things stand now, I have the freedom to work and keep my earnings. But if I marry you, everything I have, including my company, would immediately become yours. You would have complete authority over me. Every shilling I made would go directly to you—it wouldn't even pass through my hands. I'd never be able to sign a contract, or hire employees, or buy property. In the eyes of the law, a husband and wife are one person, and that person is the husband. I can't bear the thought of it. It's why I never want to marry."

THE LITTLE SPEECH was astounding. It was the most transgressive talk Gabriel had ever heard from a woman. In a way, it was more shocking than any of his mistress's most salacious words and acts.

What in God's name had Pandora's family been thinking, encouraging such ambitions? Granted, it was hardly unheard-of for someone like a middle-class widow to run a business inherited from her late husband, or for a milliner or seamstress to have her own little shop. But it was well nigh unimaginable for a peer's daughter.

A high-waxing wave rushed at Pandora from behind, impelling her against him. Gabriel steadied her, his hands clamping at her waist. When the water had retreated, he put a hand at the small of her back and guided her back toward the shore, where his sisters were sitting.

"A wife trades her independence in return for a husband's protection and support," he said, his mind bristling with questions and arguments. "That's the marriage bargain."

"I think it would be foolish—no, stupid—of me to agree to bargain in which I would be worse off after I agreed to it."

"How could you be worse off? There's precious little freedom in long work hours and endless worry over profits and expenses. As my wife, you'll live in security and comfort. I'll settle a fortune on you, to spend any way you wish. You'll have your own carriage and driver, and a house full of servants to do your bidding. You'll have a position in society that any woman would envy. Don't lose sight of all that by focusing on technicalities."

"If it were your legal rights at stake," Pandora said, "you wouldn't dismiss them as technicalities."

"But you're a woman."

"And therefore inferior?"

"No," Gabriel said swiftly. He had been raised to respect the intelligence of women, in a household where his mother's authority was heeded no less than his father's. "Any man who chooses to believe women's minds are inferior is underestimating them at his own peril. However, nature imposes certain domestic roles by making the wife the bearer of children. That being said, no man has the right to run his marriage as a dictatorship."

"But he does. According to the law, a husband can behave any way he likes."

"Any decent man treats his wife as a partner, as is the case with my own parents."

"I don't doubt that," Pandora said. "But that's the *spirit* of their marriage, not the legal reality. If your father decided to treat your mother unfairly, no one could stop him."

He felt a tiny muscle in his jaw twitch irritably. "I would stop him, damn it."

"But why must her welfare be left to his or your mercy? Why can't she have the right to decide how she should be treated?"

Gabriel wanted to argue with Pandora's position, and point out the rigidity and impracticality of her argument. It was also on the tip of his tongue to ask her why millions of other women had willingly agreed to the marital union she found so offensive.

But he couldn't. As much as he hated to admit it . . . her logic was sound.

"You're . . . not entirely wrong," he forced himself to say, nearly choking on the words. "Regardless of the law, however, it all comes down to a matter of trust."

"But you're saying I should trust a man with the lifelong power to make all my decisions the way I would wish them to be made, when I would rather make them for myself." With a touch of honest bewilderment, Pandora asked, "Why would I do that?"

"Because marriage is more than a legal arrangement. It's about companionship, security, desire, love. Are none of those things important to you?"

"They are," Pandora said, her gaze falling to the ground before them. "Which is why I could never feel them for a man if I were his property."

Well, hell.

Her objections to marriage went far deeper than Gabriel could have imagined. He'd assumed she was a nonconformist. She was a bloody insurrectionist.

They had almost reached his sisters, who were sitting together while Ivo and Justin had gone to fill their pails with more wet sand.

"What are you talking about?" Seraphina asked Gabriel.

"Something private," he said curtly.

Phoebe leaned toward Seraphina and said *sotto voce*, "I think our brother may be having a moment of enlightenment."

"Is he?" Seraphina regarded Gabriel as if he were a particularly thrilling form of wildlife trying to peck out of its shell.

Gabriel gave them both a sardonic glance before returning his attention to Pandora's mutinous face. He touched her elbow lightly and drew her aside for a last word. "I'll find out what the legal options are," he muttered. "There may be some loophole that would allow a married woman to own a business without having it held in trust or controlled by her husband."

To his annoyance, Pandora didn't appear impressed in the least, nor did she seem to recognize the enormity of the concession. "There isn't," she said flatly. "But even if there were, I'd still be worse off than if I'd never married at all."

For the next hour, the subject of Pandora's board game business was discarded as the group worked on the sandcastle. They paused at intervals to drink thirstily from jugs of cold water and lemonade that had been sent down from the house. Pandora threw herself into the project with enthusiasm, consulting with Justin, who had decided the castle must have a moat, square corner towers, a front gatehouse with a drawbridge, and battlement walls from which the occupants could drop scalding water or molten tar onto the advancing enemy.

Gabriel, who'd been instructed to dig the moat, stole frequent glances at Pandora, who had enough energy for ten people. Her face glowed beneath her battered straw hat, which she had managed to pry away from Ajax. She was sweaty and covered with sand, a few escaped locks of hair trailing over her neck and back. She played with the unselfconscious ease of a child, this woman of radical thoughts and ambitions. She was beautiful. Complex. Frustrating. He'd never met a woman who was so wholly and resolutely herself.

What the devil was he going to do about her?

"I want to decorate the castle with shells and seaweed," Seraphina said.

"You'll make it look like a girl's castle," Justin protested.

"Your hermit crab might be a girl," Seraphina pointed out.

Justin was clearly appalled by the suggestion. "He's *not!* He's not a girl!"

Seeing his little cousin's gathering outrage, Ivo intervened quickly. "That crab is definitely male, sis."

"How do you know?" Seraphina asked.

"Because . . . well, he . . ." Ivo paused, fumbling for an explanation.

"Because," Pandora intervened, lowering her voice confidentially, "as we were planning the layout of the castle, the hermit crab discreetly asked me if we would include a smoking room. I was a bit shocked, as I thought he was rather young for such a vice, but it certainly leaves no doubt as to his masculinity."

Justin stared at her raptly. "What else did he say?" he demanded. "What is his name? Does he like his castle? And the moat?"

Pandora launched into a detailed account of her conversation with the hermit crab, reporting that his name was Shelley, after the poet, whose works he admired. He was a well-traveled crustacean, having flown to distant lands while clinging to the pink leg of a herring gull who had no taste for shellfish, preferring hazelnuts and bread crumbs. One day, the herring gull, who possessed the transmigrated soul of an Elizabethan stage actor, had taken Shelley to see *Hamlet* at the Drury Lane theater. During the performance, they had alighted on the scenery and played the part of a castle gargoyle for the entire second act. Shelley had enjoyed the experience but had no wish to pursue a theatrical career, as the hot stage lights had nearly fricasseed him.

Gabriel stopped digging and listened, transported by the wonder and whimsy of Pandora's imagination. Out of thin air, she created a fantasy world in which animals could talk and anything was possible. He was charmed out of all reason as he watched her, this sandy, disheveled, storytelling mermaid, who seemed already to belong to him and yet wanted nothing to do with him. His heart worked in strange rhythms, as if it were struggling to adjust to a brand new metronome.

What was happening to him?

The rules of logic by which he'd always lived had

somehow been subverted so that marrying Lady Pandora Ravenel was now the only acceptable outcome. He was unprepared for this girl, this feeling, this infuriating uncertainty that he might not end up with the one person he *absolutely must* be with.

But how the devil could he make the prospect of marriage acceptable to her? He had no desire to bully her into it, and he doubted that was possible anyway. Nor did he want to take away her choices. He wanted to *be* her choice.

Bloody hell, there wasn't enough time. If they weren't engaged when she returned to London, the scandal would erupt full-force, and the Ravenels would have to act decisively. Pandora would most likely leave England and take up residence in a place where she could produce her games. Gabriel had no desire to find himself chasing after her across the continent, or possibly all the way to America. No, he had to persuade her to marry him now.

But what the devil could he offer that would mean more to her than her freedom?

By the time Pandora had finished the story, the castle was completed. Justin regarded the tiny crab with awe. He demanded to hear more about Shelley's adventures with the herring gull, and Pandora laughed.

"I'll tell you another story," she said, "while we carry him back to the rocks where you found him. I'm sure he misses his family by now." They clambered to their feet, and Justin carefully lifted the crab from his perch on a castle turret. As they headed toward the water, Ajax left the shade beneath the bathing-machine and trotted after them.

When they were out of earshot, Ivo announced, "I like her."

Seraphina grinned at her younger brother. "Last week you said you were finished with girls."

"Pandora's a different kind of girl. Not like the ones who are afraid to touch frogs and are always talking about their hair."

Gabriel barely listened to the exchange, his gaze fastened on Pandora's retreating form. She went to the verge of the high water mark where the sand was glossy, and stopped to pick up an interesting shell. Glimpsing another one behind her, she retrieved that as well, and another. She would have continued if Justin hadn't seized her hand and tugged her back on course.

Good God, she really did walk in circles. A pang of tenderness centered in Gabriel's chest like an ache.

He wanted all her circles to lead back to him.

"We should leave soon," Phoebe said, "if we're to have time to wash and dress for dinner."

Seraphina stood, grimacing at her sand-encrusted hands and arms. "I'm all sandy and sticky. I'm going to rinse off what I can in the water."

"I'll collect the kites and pails," Ivo said.

Phoebe waited until their younger siblings had gone before speaking. "I overheard part of your conversation with Pandora," she said. "Your voices carried across the sand."

Brooding, Gabriel reached over to adjust the front brim of her hat. "What do you think, redbird?" It was a pet name that only he and their father used for her.

Frowning thoughtfully, Phoebe used the flat of her palm to smooth one of the castle walls. "I think if you wanted a peaceful marriage and orderly household, you should have proposed to any one of the well-bred simpletons who've been dangled in front of you for years. Ivo's right: Pandora is a different kind of girl. Strange and marvelous. I wouldn't dare predict—" She broke off as she saw him staring at Pandora's distant form. "Lunkhead, you're not even listening. You've already decided to marry her, and damn the consequences."

"It wasn't even a decision," Gabriel said, baffled and surly. "I can't think of one good reason to justify why I want her so bloody badly."

Phoebe smiled, gazing toward the water. "Have I ever told you what Henry said when he proposed, even knowing how little time we would have together? 'Marriage is far too important a matter to be decided with reason.' He was right, of course."

Gabriel took up a handful of warm, dry sand and let it sift through his fingers. "The Ravenels will sooner weather a scandal than force her to marry. And as you probably overheard, she objects not only to me, but the institution of marriage itself."

"How could anyone resist you?" Phoebe asked, half-mocking, half-sincere.

He gave her a dark glance. "Apparently she has no problem. The title, the fortune, the estate, the social position . . . to her, they're all detractions. Somehow I have to convince her to marry me despite those things." With raw honesty, he added, "And I'm damned if I even know who I am outside of them."

"Oh, my dear . . ." Phoebe said tenderly. "You're the brother who taught Raphael to sail a skiff, and showed Justin how to tie his shoes. You're the man who carried Henry down to the trout stream, when he wanted to go fishing one last time." She swallowed audibly, and sighed. Digging her heels into the sand, she pushed them forward, creating a pair of trenches. "Shall I tell you what your problem is?"

"Is that a question?"

"Your problem," his sister continued, "is that you're too good at maintaining that façade of godlike perfection. You've always hated for anyone to see that you're a mere mortal. But you won't win this girl that way." She began to dust the sand from her hands. "Show her a few of your redeeming vices, dear. She'll like you all the better for it."

Chapter 9

ALL THROUGH THE NEXT DAY, and the day after that, Lord St. Vincent—Gabriel—made no further attempts to kiss Pandora. He was a perfect gentleman, respectful and attentive, making certain they were chaperoned or in full view of others at all times.

Pandora was very glad about that.

Mostly glad.

More or less glad.

Fact #34 Kissing is like one of those electrical experiments in which one makes a fascinating new discovery but is fried like a mutton-chop in the process.

Still, she couldn't help wondering why Gabriel hadn't tried again since that first day.

Admittedly, she shouldn't have allowed it to begin with. Lady Berwick had once told her that a gentleman might sometimes test a lady by making an improper advance and judging her severely if she didn't resist. Although it seemed very unsporting for Gabriel to do something like that, Pandora didn't know enough about men to rule out the possibility.

But the most likely reason Gabriel hadn't tried to kiss her again was that she was bad at it. She'd had no idea how to kiss, what to do with her lips or tongue. But the sensations had been so extraordinary that her excitable nature had taken over, and she'd virtually attacked him. And then he'd made that pirate remark, which she had puzzled over incessantly. Had he meant it in a disparaging way? It hadn't sounded like a complaint, exactly, but could one reasonably take it as a compliment?

Fact #35 No list of ideal feminine qualities has ever included the phrase "you kiss like a pirate."

Although Pandora felt mortified and defensive every time she thought about her kisstastrophe, Gabriel had been so charming for the past two days that she couldn't help enjoying his company anyway. They had spent a great deal of time together, talking, walking, riding, playing lawn tennis, croquet, and other outdoor games, always in the company of family members.

In some ways, Gabriel reminded her of Devon, with whom he seemed to have struck up a fast friendship. Both were quick-witted and irreverent men, tending to view the world with a mixture of irony and clear-eyed pragmatism. But whereas Devon's nature was spontaneous and occasionally volatile, Gabriel was more careful and considered, his character tempered with a maturity that was rare for a man of relatively young age.

As the duke's firstborn son, Gabriel was the future of the Challons, the one to whom the estate, title, and family holdings would fall. He was well educated, with a complex understanding of finance and commerce, and a comprehensive knowledge of estate management. In these days of industrial and technological development, the peerage could no longer afford to depend only on the yields from their ancestral land holdings. One heard more and more often of impoverished noblemen who had been unable to adapt their old-fashioned ways of thinking, and were now being forced to abandon their estates and sell their property.

There was no doubt in Pandora's mind that Gabriel would rise to the challenges of a fast-changing world. He was astute, intelligent, cool-headed, a natural leader. Still, she thought, it must be difficult for any man to live under the burden of such expectations and responsibilities. Did he ever worry about making mistakes, looking foolish, or failing at something?

On the third day of Pandora's visit, they spent the afternoon at the estate's archery grounds with Cassandra, Ivo, and Seraphina. Realizing it was time to go inside and change for dinner, the group went to collect their arrows from the row of targets backed by grass-covered mounds.

"Don't forget," Seraphina cautioned, "we're to dress a bit more formally than usual for dinner tonight. We've invited two local families to join us."

"How formal?" Cassandra asked, instantly worried. "What are you going to wear?"

"Well," Ivo said thoughtfully, as if the question had been meant for him, "I thought I would wear my black velveteen trousers, and my waistcoat with the fancy buttons—"

"Ivo," Seraphina exclaimed with mock solemnity, "this is no time for teasing. Fashion is a serious matter."

"I don't know why girls keep changing their fashions every few months and making such a fuss about it," Ivo said. "We men had a meeting a long time ago, and we all decided, 'It's trousers.' And that's what we've worn ever since."

"What about the Scots?" Seraphina asked slyly.

"They couldn't give up their kilts," Ivo said reasonably, "because they'd become so accustomed to having the air swirling around their—"

"Knees," Gabriel interrupted with a grin, tousling Ivo's gleaming red hair. "I'll see to your arrows, brat. Go to the house and find your way into a pair of velveteen trousers."

Ivo grinned up at his older brother and trotted off.

"Hurry inside with me," Seraphina told Cassandra, "and we'll have just enough time for me to show you my dress."

Cassandra cast a worried glance at her target, which was still bristling with uncollected arrows.

"I'll take care of it," Pandora told her. "I never need more than a few minutes to change for dinner."

Cassandra smiled and blew her a kiss, and ran toward the house with Seraphina.

Grinning at her sister's haste, Pandora cupped her hands around her mouth and shouted after them in her best imitation of Lady Berwick, "Ladies do not gallop like chaise horses!"

Cassandra's reply floated back from a distance, "Ladies do not screech like vultures!"

Laughing, Pandora turned and found Gabriel's intent gaze on her. He seemed fascinated by . . . something . . . although she couldn't imagine what he would find so interesting about her. Self-consciously she brushed at her cheeks with her fingers, wondering if there were a smudge on her face.

Gabriel smiled absently and gave a slight shake of his head. "Am I staring? Forgive me. It's only that I adore the way you laugh."

Pandora blushed up to her hairline. She went to the

nearest target and began to jerk out arrows. "Please don't compliment me."

Gabriel went to the next target. "You don't like compliments?"

"No, they make me feel awkward. They never seem true."

"Perhaps they don't seem true to you, but that doesn't mean they're not." After sliding his arrows into a leather quiver, Gabriel came to help collect hers.

"In this case," Pandora said, "it's definitely not true. My laugh sounds like a serenading tree frog swinging on a rusty gate."

Gabriel smiled. "Like silver wind chimes in a summer breeze."

"That's not *at all* how it sounds," Pandora scoffed.

"But that's how it makes me feel." The intimate note in his voice seemed to vibrate along the network of fine, taut nerves strung all through her.

Refusing to look at him, Pandora fumbled a little with the cluster of arrows in the canvas target. The shots had landed so deep and close that some of the shafts had wedged against each other in the stuffing of flax tows and shavings. This target had been Gabriel's, of course. He'd released the arrows with almost nonchalant ease, hitting the gold center every time.

Pandora twisted the arrows carefully as she pulled them free, to keep the poplar shafts from breaking. After extricating the last arrow and handing it to Gabriel, she began to remove her glove, which consisted of leather finger-sheaths attached to flat straps, all leading to a band that buckled around her wrist.

"You're an excellent marksman," she said, prying at the stiff little buckle.

"Years of practice." Gabriel reached for the buckle and unfastened it for her.

"And natural ability," Pandora said, refusing to let him be modest. "In fact, you seem to do everything perfectly." She held still as he reached for her other arm and began on the fastenings of her Morocco leather arm-guard. More hesitantly, she said, "I suppose people expect it of you."

"Not my family. But the outside world—" Gabriel hesitated. "People tend to notice my mistakes, and remember them."

"You're held to a higher standard?" Pandora ventured. "Because of your position and name?"

Gabriel gave her a noncommittal glance, and she knew he was reluctant to say anything that might sound like complaining. "I've found it's better to be careful about revealing weaknesses."

"You have weaknesses?" Pandora asked in pretend surprise, only half-joking.

"Many," Gabriel said with rueful emphasis. Carefully he drew the arm-guard away from her and dropped it into a side pouch of the quiver.

They were standing so close that Pandora saw the tiny silver threads that striated the translucent blue depths of his eyes. "Tell me the worst thing about yourself," she said impulsively.

A peculiar expression flashed across his face, uncomfortable and almost . . . ashamed? "I will," he said quietly. "But I'd rather discuss it later, in private."

A sick weight of dread settled at the bottom of her stomach. Would her worst suspicion about him turn out to be true?

"Does it have something to do with . . . women?"

Pandora brought herself to ask, her pulse beating a rapid tattoo of alarm in her throat and wrists.

He gave her an oblique glance. "Yes."

Oh God, no, *no*. Too upset to guard her tongue, she burst out, "I knew it. You have the pox."

Gabriel shot her a startled look. The quiver of arrows dropped to the ground with a clatter. *"What?"*

"I knew you'd probably caught it by now," Pandora said distractedly, as he pulled her around the nearest target and behind one of the earthworks mounds, where they were obscured from the view of the house. "Heaven knows how many kinds. English pox, French pox, Bavarian pox, Turkish—"

"Pandora, wait." He gave her a slight shake to capture her attention, but the words kept tumbling out.

"—Spanish pox, German pox, Australian pox—"

"I've never had the pox," he interrupted.

"Which one?"

"All of them."

Her eyes turned huge. "You've had *all* of them?"

"No, damn it—" Gabriel broke off and turned partially away. He began to cough roughly, his shoulders trembling. One of his hands lifted to cover his eyes, and with a pang of horror, she thought he was weeping. But in the next moment, she realized he was laughing. Every time he glanced at her indignant face, it started a new round of irrepressible choking. She was forced to wait, annoyed at finding herself the object of hilarity while he struggled to control himself.

Finally Gabriel managed to gasp, "I've had *none* of them. And there's only one kind."

A tide of relief swept away Pandora's annoyance. "Why are there so many different names, then?"

His chuckles subsided with a last ragged breath, and he wiped at the wet inner corners of his eyes. "The English began calling it French pox when we were at war, and naturally they returned the favor by calling it English pox. I doubt anyone has ever called it Bavarian or German pox, but if someone did, it would have been the Austrians. The point is, I don't have it, because I've always used protection."

"What does that mean?"

"Prophylactics. Viscera of *ovis aries*." His tone had turned lightly caustic. "French letters, English hats, *baudruches*. Take your pick."

Pandora puzzled over the French word, which sounded somewhat familiar. "Isn't baudruche the fabric made from, er . . . sheep's innards . . . that they use for making hot air balloons? What does a sheep balloon have to do with warding off the pox?"

"It's not a sheep balloon," he said. "I'll explain if you think you're ready for that level of anatomical detail."

"Never mind," she replied quickly, having no desire to be embarrassed further.

With a slow shake of his head, Gabriel asked, "How the devil did you come by the idea that I had the pox?"

"Because you're a notorious rake."

"No, I'm not."

"Lord Chaworth said you were."

"My *father* was the notorious rake," Gabriel replied with poorly contained exasperation, "in the days before he married my mother. I've been tarred by the same brush because I happen to look like him. And because I inherited his old title. But even if I wanted to acquire legions of amorous conquests, which I don't, I wouldn't have the damned time."

"But you've 'known' many women, haven't you? In the Biblical sense."

Gabriel's eyes narrowed. "How are we defining *many*?"

"I don't have a particular quantity in mind," Pandora protested. "I wouldn't even know—"

"Give me a number."

Pandora rolled her eyes and sighed shortly to convey that she was humoring him. "Twenty-three."

"I've known fewer than twenty-three women in the Biblical sense," Gabriel said promptly, seeming to think that would end the discussion. "Now, I think we've spent enough time indulging in filthy conversation on the archery grounds. Let's go back to the house."

"Have you been with twenty-two women?" Pandora asked, refusing to move.

A rapid succession of emotions crossed his face—annoyance, amusement, desire, warning. "No."

"Twenty-one?"

There was a moment of absolute stillness before something in him seemed to snap. He pounced on her with a sort of tigerish delight, and clamped his mouth over hers. She squeaked in surprise, wriggling in his hold, but his arms clamped around her easily, his muscles as solid as oak. He kissed her possessively, almost roughly at first, gentling by voluptuous degrees. Her body surrendered without giving her brain a chance to object, applying itself eagerly to every available inch of him. The luxurious male heat and hardness of him satisfied a wrenching hunger she hadn't been aware of until now. It also gave her the close-but-not-close-enough feeling she remembered from before. Oh, how confusing this was, this maddening need to crawl inside his clothes, practically inside his skin.

She let her fingertips wander over his cheeks and jaw, the neat shape of his ears, the taut smoothness of his neck. When he offered no objection, she sank her fingers into his thick, vibrant hair and sighed in satisfaction. He searched for her tongue, teased and stroked intimately until her heart pounded in a tumult of longing, and a sweet, empty ache spread all through her. Dimly aware that she was going to lose control, that she was on the verge of swooning, or assaulting him again, she managed to break the kiss and turn her face away with a gasp.

"Don't," she said weakly.

His lips grazed along her jawline, his breath rushing unsteadily against her skin. "Why? Are you still worried about Australian pox?"

Slowly it registered that they were no longer standing. Gabriel was sitting on the ground with his back against the grass-covered mound, and—heaven help her—she was in his lap. She glanced around them in bewilderment. How had this happened?

"No," she said, bewildered and perturbed, "but I just remembered that you said I kissed like a pirate."

Gabriel looked blank for a moment. "Oh, that. That was a compliment."

Pandora scowled. "It would only be a compliment if I had a beard and a peg leg."

Setting his mouth sternly against a faint quiver, Gabriel smoothed her hair tenderly. "Forgive my poor choice of words. What I meant to convey was that I found your enthusiasm charming."

"Did you?" Pandora turned crimson. Dropping her head to his shoulder, she said in a muffled voice, "Because I've worried for the past three days that I did it wrong."

"No, never, darling." Gabriel sat up a little and cradled her more closely against him. Nuzzling her cheek, he whispered, "Isn't it obvious that everything about you gives me pleasure?"

"Even when I plunder and pillage like a Viking?" she asked darkly.

"Pirate. Yes, especially then." His lips moved softly along the rim of her right ear. "My sweet, there are altogether too many respectable ladies in the world. The supply has far exceeded the demand. But there's an appalling shortage of attractive pirates, and you do seem to have a gift for plundering and ravishing. I think we've found your true calling."

"You're mocking me," Pandora said in resignation, and jumped a little as she felt his teeth gently nip her earlobe.

Smiling, Gabriel took her head between his hands and looked into her eyes. "Your kiss thrilled me beyond imagining," he whispered. "Every night for the rest of my life, I'll dream of the afternoon in the holloway, when I was waylaid by a dark-haired beauty who devastated me with the heat of a thousand troubled stars, and left my soul in cinders. Even when I'm an old man, and my brain has fallen to wrack and ruin, I'll remember the sweet fire of your lips under mine, and I'll say to myself, 'Now, that was a kiss.'"

Silver-tongued devil, Pandora thought, unable to hold back a crooked grin. Only yesterday, she'd heard Gabriel affectionately mock his father, who was fond of expressing himself with elaborate, almost labyrinthine turns of phrase. Clearly the gift had been passed down to his son.

Feeling the need to put some distance between them, she crawled out of his lap.

"I'm glad you don't have the pox," she said, standing and tugging at the wild disorder of her skirts. "And your future wife—whoever she is—will certainly be glad as well."

The pointed comment didn't escape him. He gave her an acerbic glance and rose to his feet in an easy movement. "Yes," he said dryly, brushing at his own trousers, and raking a hand through the brilliant layers of his hair. "Thank God for sheep balloons."

Chapter 10

THE LOCAL FAMILIES THAT came to dinner were quite sizeable, each with an array of children of varying ages. It was a merry gathering, with lively conversation flowing across the long table where the adults were seated. The youngest children were eating upstairs in the nursery, while the older children occupied their own table in a room adjoining the main dining room. The atmosphere was embellished with the soft music of a harp and a flute, played by local musicians.

The Challons' cook and kitchen staff had outdone themselves with a variety of dishes featuring spring vegetables and local fish and game. Although the cook back home at Eversby Priory was excellent, the food at Heron's Point was a cut above. There were colorful vegetables cut into tiny julienne strips, tender artichoke hearts roasted with butter, steaming crayfish in a sauce of white burgundy and truffles, and delicate filets of sole coated with crisp breadcrumbs. Pheasant covered with strips of bacon and roasted to juicy, smoky perfection was served with a side of boiled potatoes that had been whipped with cream and butter into savory melting fluff. Beef roasts with peppery crackled hides were brought out on massive platters, along with golden-crusted miniature game pies, and macaroni baked with Gruyère cheese in clever little tart dishes.

Pandora was quiet, not only out of fear of saying something awkward or gauche, but also because she was determined to eat as much of the delicious food as possible. Unfortunately, a corset was a misery for anyone fond of eating. Swallowing one mouthful beyond the point of comfortable fullness would cause sharp pains behind the ribs, and make it difficult to breathe. She wore her best dinner dress, made of silk dyed in a fashionable shade called *bois de rose*, a deep earthy pink that flattered her fair complexion. It was a severely simple style, with a low square-cut bodice and skirts pulled back tightly to reveal the shape of her waist and hips.

To her disgruntlement, Gabriel wasn't seated by her as he had been the past few nights. Instead, he was at the duke's end of the table, with a matron and her daughter on either side. The women laughed and chatted easily, delighted to have the attention of two such dazzling men.

Gabriel was slim and handsome in formal black evening clothes, a white silk waistcoat, and a crisp white necktie. He was flawless, ice-cool, utterly self-possessed. The candlelight played gently over him, striking golden sparks from his hair, flickering over the high cheekbones and the firm, full curves of his mouth.

Fact #63 I couldn't marry Lord St. Vincent if for no other reason than the way he looks. People would think I was shallow.

Remembering the erotic pressure of his lips against hers only two hours earlier, Pandora squirmed a little in her chair and tore her gaze from him.

She had been seated close to the duchess's end of the table, between a young man who seemed not much older than herself, and an older gentleman who was obviously smitten with the duchess and was doing his best to monopolize her attention. There was little hope of any conversation from Phoebe, who sat across from Pandora looking distant and detached, consuming her food in tiny bites.

Risking a glance at the dignified young man beside her—what was his name?—Mr. Arthurson, Arterton?—Pandora decided to try her hand at some small talk.

"It was very fine weather today, wasn't it?" she said.

He set down his flatware and dabbed at both corners of his mouth with his napkin before replying. "Yes, quite fine."

Encouraged, Pandora asked, "What kind of clouds do you like better—cumulus or stratocumulus?"

He regarded her with a slight frown. After a long pause, he asked, "What is the difference?"

"Well, cumulus are the fluffier, rounder clouds, like this heap of potatoes on my plate." Using her fork, Pandora spread, swirled, and dabbed the potatoes. "Stratocumulus are flatter and can form lines or waves—like this—and can either form a large mass or break into smaller pieces."

He was expressionless as he watched her. "I prefer flat clouds that look like a blanket."

"Altostratus?" Pandora asked in surprise, setting down her fork. "But those are the boring clouds. Why do you like them?"

"They usually mean it's going to rain. I like rain."

This showed promise of actually turning into a conversation. "I like to walk in the rain too," Pandora exclaimed.

"No, I don't like to walk in it. I like to stay in the

house." After casting a disapproving glance at her plate, the man returned his attention to eating.

Chastened, Pandora let out a noiseless sigh. Picking up her fork, she tried to inconspicuously push her potatoes into a proper heap again.

Fact #64 Never sculpt your food to illustrate a point during small talk. Men don't like it.

As Pandora looked up, she discovered Phoebe's gaze on her. She braced inwardly for a sarcastic remark.

But Phoebe's voice was gentle as she spoke. "Henry and I once saw a cloud over the English Channel that was shaped in a perfect cylinder. It went on as far as the eye could see. Like someone had rolled up a great white carpet and set it in the sky."

It was the first time Pandora had ever heard Phoebe mention her late husband's name. Tentatively she asked, "Did you and he ever try to find shapes in the clouds?"

"Oh, all the time. Henry was very clever—he could find dolphins, ships, elephants, and roosters. I could never see a shape until he pointed it out. But then it would appear as if by magic." Phoebe's gray eyes turned crystalline with infinite variations of tenderness and wistfulness.

Although Pandora had experienced grief before, having lost both parents and a brother, she understood that this was a different kind of loss, a heavier weight of pain. Filled with compassion and sympathy, she dared to say, "He . . . he sounds like a lovely man."

Phoebe smiled faintly, their gazes meeting in a moment of warm connection. "He was," she said. "Someday I'll tell you about him."

And finally Pandora understood where a little small talk about the weather might lead.

AFTER DINNER, INSTEAD of the customary separation of the sexes, the assemblage retired together to the second floor family room, a spacious area arranged with clusters of seating and tables. Like the downstairs summer parlor, it faced the ocean with a row of screened windows to catch the breeze. A tea tray, plates of sweets, port, and brandy were brought up, and a box of cigars was set out on the shaded balcony for gentlemen who wished to indulge. Now that the formal dinner was concluded, the atmosphere was wonderfully relaxed. From time to time, someone would go to the upright piano and plunk out a tune.

Pandora went to sit in a group with Cassandra and the other young women, but she was obliged to stop as a set of warm masculine fingers closed around her wrist.

Gabriel's voice fell gently against her ear. "What were you discussing with the prim Mr. Arterson while stirring your potatoes so industriously?"

Pandora turned and looked up at him, wishing she didn't feel such a leap of gladness at the fact that he'd sought her out. "How did you notice what I was doing all the way from the other end of the table?"

"I nearly did myself injury, straining to see and hear you all through dinner."

As she stared up into his smiling eyes, she felt as if her heart were opening all its windows. "I was demonstrating cloud formations with my potatoes," she said. "I don't think Mr. Arterson appreciated my stratocumulus."

"I'm afraid we're all a bit too frivolous for him."

"No, one can't blame him. I knew better than to play with my food, and I've resolved never to do it again."

Mischief flickered in his eyes. "What a pity. I was about to show you the one thing carrots are good for."

"What is it?" she asked, her interest piqued.

"Come with me."

Pandora followed him to the other side of the room. Their progress was briefly interrupted as a half-dozen children crossed in front of them to pilfer sweets from the sideboard.

"Don't take the carrot," Gabriel told them, as a multitude of small hands snatched almond and currant cakes, sticky squares of quince paste, crisp snow-white meringues, and tiny chocolate biscuits.

Ivo turned and replied with a chocolate biscuit making a bulge in his cheek. "No one is even thinking of taking the carrot," he told his older brother. "It's the safest carrot in the world."

"Not for long," Gabriel said, reaching over the herd of feasting children to retrieve a single raw carrot from the side of a dessert tray.

"Oh, you're going to do *that*," Ivo said. "May we stay and watch?"

"Be my guest."

"What is he going to do?" Pandora asked Ivo, wildly curious, but Ivo was prevented from answering as a matron approached to shoo the marauders away from the plates of sweets.

"Off with you, now!" the vexed mother exclaimed. "Begone! Those sweets are too rich for you, which is why you were all given plain sponge cake at the end of your dinner."

"But sponge cake is just *air*," one of the children grumbled, while pocketing an almond cake.

Suppressing a smile, Gabriel addressed his younger brother in a quiet undertone. "Ivo, weren't you put in charge of managing this lot? It's time to demonstrate some leadership."

"This is leadership," Ivo informed him. "I'm the one who led them in here."

Pandora exchanged a laughing glance with Gabriel. "No one likes dry sponge cake," she said in Ivo's defense. "One may as well eat a sponge."

"I'll take them out in a minute," Ivo promised. "But first I want to fetch Lord Trenear—he'll want to see the carrot trick." He dashed off before anyone could reply. The boy had taken a liking to Devon, whose straightforward masculine character and ready sense of humor appealed to him.

After settling the matron's ruffled feathers, and cautioning the children not to take *all* the sweets, Gabriel led Pandora toward a narrow pier table in the corner of the room.

"Now, what is that for?" she asked, watching as he took out a pocket knife and pared the end of the carrot.

"It's part of a card trick." Casually Gabriel set the carrot into a silver candleholder on the pier table. "In the absence of an honest talent such as singing or playing piano, I've had to develop what few skills I possess. Especially since for the greater part of my youth"—he had raised his voice just enough that his father, who sat at a nearby table playing whist with the other gentlemen, could hear—"I was abandoned to the unwholesome companionship of the sharpers and criminals who frequented my father's club."

The duke glanced over his shoulder with an arched brow. "I thought it would benefit you to learn about worldly vice firsthand, so you would know what to avoid in the future."

Gabriel turned back to Pandora with a glint of self-mocking amusement in his eyes. "Now I'll never know if I could have earned a misspent youth on my own, instead of having it handed to me on a silver platter."

"What are you going to do to the carrot?" she demanded.

"Patience," he cautioned, retrieving a fresh deck of cards from a stack on a nearby tray table. He opened the box and set it aside. Not above showing off, he shuffled the cards in midair, executing a riffle and bridge cascade.

Pandora's eyes widened. "How do you do that without a table?" she asked.

"It's all in how you hold the deck." With one hand, he divided the deck in half and flipped both halves onto the back of his hand. With breathtaking dexterity, he tossed the two packets of cards into the air so that they spun around completely and landed in perfect reverse order in his palm. He continued with a rapid succession of flourishes, making the cards fly from one hand to the other in a fluid stream, then blossom into a pair of circular fans that snapped shut. All of it was magically graceful and quick.

Devon, who had come with Ivo to watch the proceedings, gave a low whistle of admiration. "Remind me never to play cards with him," he told Ivo. "I would lose my entire estate within minutes."

"I'm a mediocre player at best," Gabriel said, spinning a single card on his fingertip as if it were a pinwheel. "My talent with cards is limited to pointless entertainment."

Leaning close to Pandora, Devon counseled as if imparting a great secret, "Every card sharp begins by lulling you into a false sense of superiority."

Pandora was so mesmerized by Gabriel's card manipulations that she barely heard the advice.

"I may not be able to do this straight off," Gabriel warned. "Usually I need some practice first." He retreated to a distance of approximately fifteen feet from the table, and the nearby whist game paused temporarily as the gentlemen watched the proceedings.

Holding the corner of a single card between his index and middle fingers, Gabriel drew his arm back as if for an overhand throw. He focused on the carrot with narrowed eyes. His arm moved in a fast forward pitch, finishing with a flick of his wrist, and the card shot through the air. An inch-long section of the carrot was instantly severed. Lightning-fast, Gabriel threw a second card, and the rest of the carrot was divided in half.

Laughter and a smattering of applause came from around the room, and the children at the sideboard exclaimed in delight.

"Impressive," Devon said to Gabriel with a grin. "If I could do that in a tavern, I'd never have to pay for a drink. How much practice did it take?"

"Regrettably, bushels of innocent carrots were sacrificed over a period of years."

"Well worth it, I'd say." Devon glanced at Pandora, his eyes twinkling. "With your permission, I'll rejoin the whist game before they boot me out of it."

"Of course," she said.

Ivo observed the group of children still at the sideboard, and heaved a sigh. "They're out of control," he said. "I suppose I'll have to do something about it." He executed a precise bow in Pandora's direction. "You look very pretty tonight, Lady Pandora."

"Thank you, Ivo," she said demurely, and grinned as Ivo hurried away to herd his charges from the room. "What a little rogue," she said.

"I think our grandfather—his namesake—would have doted on him," Gabriel replied. "There's more Jenner than Challon in Ivo, which is to say more fire than ice."

"The Ravenels are rather too fiery," Pandora said ruefully.

"So I've heard." Gabriel looked amused. "Does that include you?"

"Yes, but I'm not angry all that often, it's more that I'm . . . excitable."

"I enjoy a woman with a lively nature."

"That's a very nice way to put it, but I'm not just lively."

"Yes, you're also beautiful."

"No"—Pandora swallowed back an uncomfortable laugh—"no compliments, remember. I didn't say 'I'm not just lively' to imply that I have other qualities, I meant that I'm extremely, inconveniently lively in a way that makes me terribly difficult to live with."

"Not for me."

She glanced at him uncertainly. Something in his voice caused a flutter in her stomach, like flower tendrils delicately searching for places to adhere.

"Would you like to play a game of whist?" he asked.

"Just the two of us?"

"At the small table near the window." As she hesitated, he pointed out, "We're in the company of at least two dozen people."

There could be no harm in that. "Yes, but you should be warned: My cousin West taught me whist, and I'm very good at it."

He smiled. "I'll expect a fleecing, then."

After Gabriel had obtained a sealed deck of cards, they went to the screened windows. He seated Pandora at a small marquetry table inlaid with precious woods that depicted a Japanese bonsai tree and a pagoda hung with tiny mother-of-pearl lanterns.

Gabriel opened the cards, shuffled them expertly and dealt thirteen apiece. He set the rest of the deck facedown on the table and turned the top card faceup. Whist was a trick-taking game with two stages: In the first stage, players tried to collect the best cards for themselves, and in the second, they competed to win the most tricks.

To Pandora's satisfaction, she had acquired an exceptionally good hand with numerous trumps and high cards. She enjoyed herself immensely, taking risks whereas Gabriel was, predictably, more careful and conservative. As they talked, he entertained her with stories about his family's gaming club. Pandora was especially amused by one about a card cheat, who had always ordered a plate of sandwiches during the game. It turned out that he had been slipping unwanted cards into his sandwiches. The scheme had been discovered when another player tried to eat a ham and potted cheese on rye, and ended up with a two of spades caught between his teeth.

Pandora had to cover her mouth to keep from laughing too loudly. "Gaming is illegal, isn't it? Are there ever raids on your club?"

"Usually the respectable West End clubs are left alone. Especially Jenner's, since half the legislators in

England are members. However, we've taken precautions in the event that a raid occurs."

"Such as?"

"Such as installing metal-plated doors that can be bolted shut until the evidence is disposed of. And there are escape tunnels for club members who can't afford to be seen. Also, I regularly grease a few palms in the police force to ensure that we have adequate warning before a raid."

"You bribe the police?" Pandora whispered in surprise, mindful of being overheard.

"It's a common practice."

The information wasn't at all appropriate for a young lady's ears, which of course made it all the more fascinating. It was a glimpse of a side of life that was utterly foreign to her.

"Thank you for being so frank with me," she said spontaneously. "It's nice to be treated like an adult." With a quick, awkward laugh, she added, "Even if I don't always behave like one."

"Being imaginative and playful doesn't make you any less of an adult," Gabriel said gently. "It only makes you a more interesting one."

No one had ever said anything like that to her before, praising her faults as if they were virtues. Did he mean it? Blushing and perplexed, Pandora lowered her gaze to her cards.

Gabriel paused. "While we're on the subject of Jenner's," he said slowly, "there's something I want to tell you. It's nothing of import, but I feel I should mention it." Faced with her quizzical silence, he explained, "I met your brother a few years ago."

Thunderstruck by the revelation, Pandora could only stare at him. She tried to imagine Theo in the company of this man. They had been similar in the most obvious ways, both tall, wellborn, handsome, but they couldn't have been more different beneath the surface.

"He visited the club with a friend," Gabriel continued, "and decided to apply for membership. The manager referred him to me." He paused, his expression unreadable. "I'm afraid we had to refuse him."

"Because of his credit?" Pandora faltered. "Or was it his temperament?" At his long hesitation before replying, she said anxiously, "Both. Oh, dear. Theo didn't take it well, did he? Was there an argument?"

"Something like that."

Which meant that her volatile brother must have behaved very badly indeed.

Her face heated with shame. "I'm sorry," she said. "Theo was always crossing swords with people he couldn't intimidate. And you're the kind of man he was always pretending to be."

"I didn't tell you to make you uncomfortable." Gabriel used the pretext of reaching for a card to inconspicuously stroke the back of her hand. "God knows his behavior was no reflection on you."

"I think he felt like a fraud inside," she said pensively, "and that made him angry. He was an earl, but the estate was a shambles and in terrible debt, and he knew practically nothing about how to manage it."

"Did he ever discuss it with you?"

Pandora smiled without humor. "No, Theo never discussed anything with me, or with Cassandra and Helen. My family wasn't like yours at all. We were like . . ." She hesitated thoughtfully. "Well, there was something I once read . . ."

"Tell me," Gabriel said softly.

"It was an astronomy book that said in most of the

constellations, the stars don't actually belong together. They only appear to. They look to us as if they're close to each other, but some of them exist in another part of the galaxy altogether. That's how my family was. We seemed to belong to the same group, but we were all very far apart. Except for me and Cassandra, of course."

"What about Lady Helen?"

"She's always been very loving and kind, but she lived in her own world. We're much closer now, actually." Pandora paused, staring at him fixedly and thinking she could try for hours to describe her family, and she still wouldn't be able to convey the truth of it. The way her parents' love for each other had been conducted like warfare. The glittering beauty of her untouchable mother, who would disappear to London for long stretches of time. Her father, with his unpredictable mixture of violence and indifference. Helen, who had appeared only rarely, like a visiting wraith, and Theo, with his occasional moments of careless kindness.

"Your life at Eversby Priory was very secluded," Gabriel commented.

Pandora nodded absently. "I used to fantasize about being out in society. Having hundreds of friends, going everywhere, and seeing everything. But if you live in isolation long enough, it becomes part of you. And then when you try to change, it's like looking into the sun. You can't bear it for too long."

"It's only a matter of practice," he said gently.

They continued the first hand of cards, which Pandora ended up winning, and played another, which she lost to Gabriel. After congratulating him good-naturedly, she asked, "Shall we stop now, and leave it a draw?"

His brows lifted. "With no victor?"

"I'm a better player than you," she told him kindly. "I'm trying to spare you the inevitable defeat."

Gabriel grinned. "Now I insist on a third hand." He slid the deck of cards toward her. "Your turn to deal." As Pandora shuffled the cards, he leaned back in his chair and regarded her speculatively. "Shall we make the game more interesting by having the loser pay a forfeit?"

"What kind of forfeit?"

"The winner decides."

Pandora chewed her lower lip, mulling over possibilities. She sent him a mischievous grin. "Are you truly bad at singing, as you said before?"

"My singing is an insult to the very air."

"Then if I win, your forfeit is to sing 'God Save The Queen' in the middle of the entrance hall."

"Where it will echo unmercifully?" Gabriel sent her a glance of mock-alarm. "Good God. I had no idea you were so ruthless."

"Pirate," Pandora reminded him regretfully, and dealt.

Gabriel gathered up his cards. "I was going to suggest a fairly easy forfeit for you, but now I see I'll have to come up with something more severe."

"Do your worst," Pandora said cheerfully. "I'm already accustomed to looking foolish. Nothing you propose will bother me."

But as she should have expected, that turned out not to be true.

Gabriel's gaze lifted slowly from his cards, eyes bright in a way that caused the back of her neck to prickle. "If I win," he said, his voice low, "you'll meet me back here at half past midnight. Alone."

Unnerved, Pandora asked, "For what?"

"A midnight rendezvous."

She looked at him without comprehension.

"I thought you might like to experience one for yourself," he added.

Her stunned mind recalled the first night they'd met, when they'd argued over Dolly's rendezvous with Mr. Hayhurst. Hot blood rose to her cheeks. He had been so nice—she'd been feeling so comfortable with him—and now he'd made a proposition that any decent woman would find insulting.

"You're supposed to be a gentleman," she whispered sharply.

Gabriel tried—and failed—to look apologetic. "I have lapses."

"You can't possibly think I would agree to that."

To her annoyance, he regarded her as if she had all the worldly experience of a new-laid egg. "I understand."

Her eyes narrowed. "You understand what?"

"You're afraid."

"I am not!" With as much dignity as she could summon, she added, "But I would like a different forfeit."

"No."

Pandora's incredulous gaze flew to his, while the Ravenel temper blazed up like freshly stirred coals. "I've been trying very hard not to like you," she said darkly. "Finally, it's working."

"You can call off the rest of the game, if you wish," Gabriel said in a matter-of-fact tone. "But if you decide to play—and you lose—that's the forfeit." He sat back in his chair and watched as she struggled to recover her composure.

Why had he challenged her like this? And why was she hesitating?

Some lunatic impulse kept her from backing down.

It made no sense. She didn't understand herself. A confusion of recoil and attraction filled her. Glancing at Gabriel, she saw that although he appeared relaxed, his gaze was keen, taking in every detail of her reaction. Somehow he'd known that she would have trouble refusing him.

The room was filled with an ambient mix of conversation, piano music, laughter, the rattling of teacups and saucers, the clinking of crystal decanters and glasses, the riffling of cards from the nearby whist game, the tactful murmuring of servants, gentlemen coming in after having cigars on the balcony. She found it nearly impossible to believe that she and Gabriel were discussing something so outrageous in the midst of a respectable family gathering.

Yes. She was afraid. They were playing a very adult game, with real risks and consequences.

Looking through the screened window, Pandora saw that the balcony was empty and shadowy, with night closing around the nearby headland. "May we step outside for a moment?" she asked quietly.

Gabriel stood and helped her from her chair.

They went out on the covered balcony, which extended the entire length of the house's main section, the sides framed with latticework and climbing roses. By tacit agreement, they went as far away as possible from the family parlor windows. A westering breeze carried the sounds of the surf and the cry of an errant seabird, and whisked away the last pungent wisps of tobacco smoke.

Leaning back against one of the white-painted support columns, Pandora folded her arms tightly across her chest.

Gabriel stood beside her, facing the opposite direction, his hands braced on the balcony railing as he looked out to sea. "A storm is coming," he commented.

"How can you tell?"

"Clouds on the horizon, moving in on a crosswind. The heat will break tonight."

Pandora looked at his profile, silhouetted against the red tarnish of sunset. He was a fantasy figure—the kind who existed in other girls' dreams. Not hers. Before she came to Heron's Point, she had known exactly what she wanted, and what she didn't want, but now everything was muddled. She thought Gabriel might be trying to convince himself that he liked her well enough to marry her. However, she had come to understand enough about his commitment to his family and responsibilities to be certain that he would never voluntarily choose someone like her as his wife. Not unless it was a point of honor, to save her ruined reputation. Even if she didn't want to be saved.

Squaring her shoulders, she turned to face him fully. "Are you going to try to seduce me?"

Gabriel had the gall to smile at her bluntness. "I might try to tempt you. But the choice would be yours." He paused. "Are you worried that you might not want me to stop?"

Pandora snorted. "After what my sister Helen told me about the conjugal embrace, I can't fathom why any woman would willingly consent to it. But I suppose if any man could make it slightly less revolting than it sounds, it would be you."

"Thank you," Gabriel said, sounding bemused. "I think."

"But no matter how non-repulsive you might be able to make it," Pandora continued, "I still have no desire to try it."

"Even with a husband?" he asked softly.

Pandora hoped the shadows helped to conceal her reddening face. "If I were married, I would have no choice but to fulfill my legal spousal obligation. But I still wouldn't *want* to."

"Don't be so sure. I have persuasive skills you don't know about yet." His lips twitched at her expression. "Shall we go inside and finish the game?"

"Not when you've demanded a forfeit that goes against every principle."

"You're not worried about principles." Gabriel leaned closer, crowding her gently back against the column. His taunting whisper curled in her right ear like a wisp of smoke. "You're worried that you might do something naughty with me and enjoy it."

Pandora was silent, trembling with mortified surprise at the slow burn of excitement that had awakened in all the intimate places of her body.

"Let fate decide," Gabriel said. "What's the worst that could happen?"

Her reply was honest and a bit wobbly. "I could end up having no choices left."

"I'll leave you a virgin. Only a little less innocent." His fingertips found the inside of her wrist, his fingertips stroking a tiny pulse. "Pandora, you're not living up to your reputation as the misbehaving twin. Take a risk. Have a little adventure with me."

Pandora had never imagined being vulnerable to this kind of temptation, never guessed at how difficult it would be to resist. Meeting him in secret, at night, would be the most genuinely disgraceful thing she'd ever done, and she wasn't entirely certain that he would keep his promise. But conscience was putting up the flimsiest, most feeble possible defense against a desire that seemed shameful in its blind power. Weak with nerves and hunger and anger, she made her decision too quickly, the way she made most of her decisions.

"I'll finish the game," she said crisply. "And before the night ends, the entrance hall will be echoing with your stirring rendition of the national anthem. All six verses."

His eyes gleamed with satisfaction. "I only know the first verse, so you'll have to settle for hearing that one six times."

In retrospect, Pandora shouldn't have been surprised that the last hand of whist proceeded in an entirely different manner than the first two hands. Gabriel's playing style altered drastically, no longer cautious but aggressive and swift. He won trick after trick with miraculous ease.

It wasn't a fleecing. It was a massacre.

"Are these cards marked?" Pandora asked irritably, trying to inspect the backs of them without revealing her hand.

Gabriel looked affronted. "No, it was a sealed deck. You saw me open it. Would you like me to fetch a new one?"

"Don't bother." Doggedly she played out the rest of the hand, knowing already how it would end.

There was no need to tally up the points. He'd won by such a large margin that it would have been a pointless exercise.

"Cousin Devon was right to warn me," Pandora muttered in disgust. "I've been flamboozled. You're not a mediocre player at all, are you?"

"Sweetheart," he said softly, "I learned how to play

cards from the best sharpers in London while I was still in short trousers."

"Swear to me these cards weren't marked," she demanded, "and that you weren't hiding any up your sleeve."

He gave her a level glance. "I swear it."

In a turmoil of anxiety, anger, and self-blame, Pandora pushed back from the table and stood before he could move to help her. "I've had enough of games for now. I'm going to sit with my sister and the other girls."

"Don't be cross," Gabriel coaxed, rising to his feet. "You can back out if you wish."

Although she knew the offer was meant to be conciliatory, Pandora was highly insulted nonetheless. "I take games seriously, my lord. Paying a debt is a matter of honor—or do you assume that because I'm a woman, my word means less than yours?"

"No," he said hastily.

She gave him a cold glance. "I will meet you later." Turning on her heel, she walked away, trying to keep her stride relaxed and her face expressionless. But her insides had frozen with abject fear as she thought of what she would soon face.

A rendezvous . . . alone with Gabriel . . . at night . . . in the dark.

Oh God, what have I done?

Chapter 11

GRIPPING A BRASS CANDLEHOLDER by its finger ring and thumb hold, Pandora made her way slowly along the upstairs hallway. Black shadows appeared to slide across the floor, and she ignored the illusion of movement, grimly determined to keep her balance.

One flickering candle flame was all that stood between her and disaster. The lights had been extinguished, including the hanging lamp in the central hall. Aside from the occasional flash of distant lightning, the only source of illumination was a faint glow coming from the threshold of the family room.

As Gabriel had predicted, a storm had rolled in from the ocean. Its first rise was rough and furious, as it wrestled with trees and flung stray twigs and branches in every direction. The house, built low and sturdy to accommodate coastal weather, endured the gale stoically, shrugging off sheets of rain from its oak-timbered roof. Still, the sound of thunder made Pandora shiver.

She was dressed in a muslin nightgown and a plain flannel wrap, its sides folded around the front and tied with a plaited belt. Although she'd wanted to wear a day dress, there had been no way to avoid the nightly ritual of bathing and taking her hair down without making Ida suspicious.

Her feet were tucked into the Berlin wool slippers

Cassandra had made, which, owing to an accidental misreading of the pattern, had resulted in two different sizes. The slipper for the right foot was perfect, but the left one was loose and floppy. Cassandra had been so apologetic that Pandora had made a special point of wearing them, insisting they were the most comfortable slippers ever made.

She stayed close to the wall, occasionally reaching out to graze it with her fingertips. The darker her surroundings, the worse her equilibrium, the signals in her head refusing to match up with what her body told her. At certain moments, the floor, walls, and ceiling might all abruptly switch places for no reason, leaving her flailing. She had always relied on Cassandra to help her if they had to go somewhere at night, but she couldn't very well ask her twin to escort her to an illicit meeting with a man.

Breathing with effort, Pandora stared fixedly at the hushed amber glow down the hallway. The carpeting stretched like a black ocean between her and the family parlor. Holding the wavering lit candle far out in front of her, she took one step after another, straining to see through the shadows. A window had been left open somewhere. Moist, rain-scented air kept whisking against her face and across her bare ankles, as if the house were breathing around her.

A midnight rendezvous was supposed to be romantic and daring, something done by girls who were not wallflowers. But this was an exercise in misery. She was exhausted and worried, fighting to keep her balance in the darkness. All she wanted was to be safe in bed.

As she stepped forward, the loose slipper on her left foot flopped just enough to make her trip and stumble, nearly falling to her knees. Somehow she managed to catch her balance, but the candleholder flew out of her hand. The wick was instantly extinguished as it hit the floor.

Gasping, disoriented, Pandora stood engulfed in darkness. She didn't dare move, only kept her arms suspended in midair, fingers spread like cat's whiskers. Shadow-currents flowed around her, gently pushing her off balance, and she stiffened against their intangible momentum.

"Oh, damn," she whispered. Icy sweat broke out on her forehead as she worked to think past the first rush of panic.

The wall was on her left side. She had to reach it. She needed stability. But the first cautious step made the floor drop from beneath her feet, and the world lurched in a diagonal tilt. She staggered and landed on the floor with a heavy thud . . . or was it the wall? Was she leaning upright or lying down? Leaning, she decided. She was missing her left slipper, and her bare toes were flat against a hard surface. Yes, that was the floor. Pressing her damp cheek to the wall, she willed her surroundings to sort themselves out, while a high-pitched tone rang in her left ear.

There were too many heartbeats in her chest. She couldn't breathe around them. Her pained intakes of air sounded like sobs. A large, dark form approached so swiftly that she shrank against the wall.

"Pandora." A pair of hard arms closed around her. She quivered as she heard Gabriel's low voice, and felt herself wrapped in the reassurance of his body. "What happened? My God, you're shaking. Are you afraid of the dark? The storm?" He kissed her damp forehead and pressed soothing murmurs into her hair. "Easy. Softly, now. You're safe in my arms. Nothing's going to harm you, my sweet girl." He had discarded his black formal coat, and the turndown collar of his shirt had been unfastened. She could smell the spice of shaving soap on his skin, the acrid tang of starched linen and the hint of cigar smoke absorbed by his silk waistcoat. The fragrance was masculine and comforting, making her shiver in relief.

"I . . . I dropped my candle," she wheezed.

"Don't worry about that." One of his hands curved around the back of her neck, fondling gently. "Everything's all right now."

Her heart began to measure out beats more evenly, no longer casting them out in careless handfuls. The waking-nightmare feeling began to dissipate. But as her alarm faded, a hideous tide of embarrassment overwhelmed her. Only she could have botched a midnight rendezvous so terribly.

"Feeling better?" he asked, one of his hands sliding down to enfold hers in a reassuring grasp. "Come with me to the family parlor."

Pandora wanted to die. She didn't move, only let out a defeated breath. "I can't," she blurted out.

"What is it?" came the gentle question.

"I can't move at all. I lose my balance in the dark."

His lips went to her forehead again, and he kept them there for a long moment. "Put your arms around my neck," he eventually said. After she obeyed, he lifted her easily, clasping her high against his chest.

Pandora kept her eyes closed as he carried her along the hallway. He was strong and superbly coordinated, sure-footed as a cat, and she felt a pang of envy. She couldn't remember what it was like to move so confidently through the night, fearing nothing.

The family parlor was lit only by a fire in the hearth.

Gabriel went to a low, deeply upholstered empire sofa with a curved back and arms, and settled with her in his lap. Her pride objected feebly to the way he was holding her, as if she were a frightened child. But his hard chest was comforting, and his hands slowly chased the nervous tremors that ran through her limbs, and it was the nicest, warmest feeling she'd ever known. She needed this. Just for a few minutes.

Reaching over to a mahogany sofa table, Gabriel picked up an engraved dram glass half-filled with inky liquid. Without a word, he pressed the glass to her lips as if she couldn't be trusted to hold it on her own without spilling it.

Pandora sipped cautiously. The drink was delicious, with rich flavors of toffee and plum leaving mellow heat on her tongue. She took another, deeper taste, her hands creeping up to take the glass from him. "What is this?"

"Port. Have the rest." He curled his arm loosely around her bent knees.

Pandora drank it slowly, relaxing as the port sent warmth all the way down to her toes. The storm whistled impatiently, rattling the windows, calling back and forth with the sea as it leapt in roaring liquid hills. But she was warm and dry, resting in Gabriel's arms while the snapping light of the hearth played over them.

He reached into the pocket of his waistcoat for a soft folded handkerchief, and blotted the last traces of perspiration from her face and throat. After setting the cloth aside, he stroked back a lock of dark hair and tucked it carefully behind her left ear. "I've noticed you don't hear as well on this side," he said quietly. "Is that part of the problem?"

Pandora blinked in amazement. In a mere handful of days, he had detected something that even her family, the people who actually lived with her, hadn't perceived. They had all learned to accept, as a matter of course, that she was careless and inattentive.

She nodded. "I hear only about half as well in this ear as I do in the other. At night . . . in the dark . . . everything goes topsy-turvy, and I can't tell what's up or down. If I turn too quickly, I drop to the floor. I can't control it; it's like being pushed by invisible hands."

Gabriel cradled her cheek in his palm, regarding her with a steady tenderness that sent her pulse into confusion. "That's why you don't dance."

"I can manage a few of the dances at a slow pace. But waltzing is impossible. All that whirling and pivoting." Self-consciously she looked away and drained the last few drops of port.

He took the empty glass from her and set it aside. "You should have told me. I would never have asked you to meet me at night if I'd known."

"It wasn't far. I thought a candle would be enough." Pandora fidgeted with the belt of her flannel robe. "I didn't count on tripping over my own slippers." She extended her bare left foot from beneath her nightgown and frowned at it. "I've lost one of them."

"I'll find it later." Taking one of her hands in his, Gabriel lifted it to his lips. He wove a pattern of gentle kisses over her cold fingers. "Pandora . . . what happened to your ear?"

Her soul revolted at the prospect of discussing it.

Turning her hand over, Gabriel kissed her palm and shaped her fingers against his cheek. His shaven skin was smooth in one direction and softly abrasive in the other, like a cat's tongue. The firelight had turned him golden everywhere except for those eyes, the clear blue of an arctic star. He waited, damnably patient, while Pandora summoned the nerve to reply.

"I . . . can't talk about it if I'm touching you." Drawing her hand from his cheek, she crawled out of his lap. There was a persistent high-pitched ringing in her ear. Covering it lightly with her palm, she tapped her fingers on the back of her skull a few times. To her relief, the trick worked.

"Tinnitus," Gabriel said, watching closely. "One of our older family solicitors has it. Does it trouble you often?"

"Only now and then, when I'm distressed."

"There's no need to be distressed now."

Pandora cast him a brief, distracted smile, and knotted her fingers into a tight ball. "I brought this on myself. Do you remember when I told you that I eavesdrop? I don't do it as much as I used to, actually. But when I was little, it was the only way to find out anything that was happening in our household. Cassandra and I took all our meals in the nursery and played by ourselves. Sometimes weeks would go by before we saw anyone other than Helen and the servants. Mama would leave for London, or Father would go on a hunting trip, or Theo would be off to boarding school, without even saying goodbye. When my parents were at home, the only way to attract their notice was to misbehave. I was the worst, of course. I dragged Cassandra into my plots and schemes, but everyone knew she was the nice twin. Poor Helen spent most of her time reading books in the corner and trying to be invisible. I preferred causing trouble to being ignored."

Gabriel picked up the length of her braid and played with it as he listened.

"I was twelve when it happened," she continued. "Or maybe eleven. My parents were arguing in the master bedroom with the door closed. Whenever they fought, it was dreadful. They would scream and smash things. Naturally, I poked my nose where it didn't belong, and went to eavesdrop. They were fighting about a man my mother was . . . involved with. My father was shouting. Every word sounded like a piece of something broken. Cassandra started trying to pull me away from the door. Then it swung open and my father stood there, in a rage. He must have seen movement in the crack at the bottom of the casing. He reached for me, and fast as lightning, he boxed my ears. All I remember is the world exploding. Cassandra says she helped me back to our room, and there was blood coming from my left ear. My right ear mended in a day or two, but I could only hear a little out of the left one, and there was a beating pain deep down. Soon I took ill with fever. Mama said that had nothing to do with the ear, but I think it did."

Pandora paused, unwilling to relate any of the distasteful details of her ear suppurating and draining. She glanced cautiously at Gabriel, whose face was averted. He was no longer playing with her braid. His hand had clenched around it until the muscles of his forearms and wrist stood out.

"Even after I recovered from the fever," Pandora said, "the hearing didn't come back all the way. But the worst part was that I kept losing my balance, especially at night. It made me afraid of the dark. Ever since then—" She stopped as Gabriel lifted his head.

His face was hard and murderous, the hellfrost in his eyes frightening her more than her father's fury ever had.

"That bloody son of a bitch," he said softly. "If he were still alive, I'd beat him with a thresher's flail."

Pandora reached out with a fluttering motion, patting the air near him. "No," she said breathlessly, "no, I wouldn't want that. I hated him for a long time, but now I feel sorry for him."

Gabriel caught her hand in midair, swift but gentle, as if it were a bird he wanted to hold without injuring. His eyes had dilated until she could see reflections of herself in the dark centers. "Why?" he whispered after a long moment.

"Because hurting me was the only way to hide his own pain."

Chapter 12

GABRIEL WAS STUNNED BY Pandora's compassion for a man who had caused her such harm. He shook his head in wonder as he stared into her eyes, as dark as cloud-shadow on a field of blue gentian. "That doesn't excuse him," he said thickly.

"No, but it helped me to forgive him."

Gabriel would never forgive the bastard. He wanted vengeance. He wanted to strip the flesh from the bastard's corpse and hang up his skeleton to scare crows. His fingers contained a subtle tremor as he reached out to trace the fine edges of her face, the sweet, high plane of her cheekbone. "What did the doctor say about your ear? What treatment did he give?"

"It wasn't necessary to send for a doctor."

A fresh flood of rage seared his veins as the words sunk in. "Your eardrum was ruptured. What in God's name do you mean a doctor wasn't necessary?" Although he had managed to keep from shouting, his tone was far from civilized.

Pandora quivered uneasily and began to inch backward.

He realized the last thing she needed from him was a display of temper. Battening down his rampaging emotions, he used one arm to bring her back against his side. "No, don't pull away. Tell me what happened."

"The fever had passed," she said after a long hesitation, "and . . . well, you have to understand my family. If something unpleasant happened, they ignored it, and it was never spoken of again. Especially if it was something my father had done when he'd lost his temper. After a while, no one remembered what had really happened. Our family history was erased and rewritten a thousand times.

"But ignoring the problem with my ear didn't make it disappear. Whenever I couldn't hear something, or when I stumbled or fell, it made my mother very angry. She said I'd been clumsy because I was hasty or careless. She wouldn't admit there was anything wrong with my hearing. She refused even to discuss it." Pandora stopped, chewing thoughtfully on her lower lip. "I'm making her sound terrible, and she wasn't. There were times when she was affectionate and kind. No one's all one way or the other." She flicked a glance of dread in his direction. "Oh God, you're not going to pity me, are you?"

"No." Gabriel was anguished for her sake, and outraged. It was all he could do to keep his voice calm. "Is that why you keep it a secret? You're afraid of being pitied?"

"That, and . . . it's a shame I'd rather keep private."

"Not your shame. Your father's."

"It feels like mine. Had I not been eavesdropping, my father wouldn't have disciplined me."

"You were a child," he said brusquely. "What he did wasn't bloody discipline, it was brutality."

To his surprise, a touch of unrepentant amusement curved Pandora's lips, and she looked distinctly pleased with herself. "It didn't even stop my eavesdropping. I just learned to be more clever about it."

She was so endearing, so indomitable, that Gabriel was wrenched with a feeling he'd never known before, as if all the extremes of joy and despair had been compressed into some new emotion that threatened to crack the walls of his heart.

Pandora would never bend to anyone else's will, she would never surrender . . . she would only break. He'd seen what the world did to spirited and ambitious women. She had to let him protect her. She had to take him as a husband, and he didn't know how to convince her. The usual rules didn't apply to someone who lived by her own logic.

Reaching for her, he gathered her close against his thumping heart. A thrill went through him as she relaxed automatically.

"Gabriel?"

"Yes?"

"How did you win that last hand of whist?"

"I counted cards," he admitted.

"Is that cheating?"

"No, but it still wasn't fair." He stroked back the wayward strands of hair that crossed her forehead. "My only excuse is that I've wanted to be alone with you for days. I couldn't leave it to chance."

"Because you want to do the honorable thing," Pandora said seriously.

His brows lifted as he looked askance at her.

"You want to save me and my family from scandal," she explained. "Seducing me is the obvious shortcut."

Gabriel's mouth quirked with a sardonic smile. "You and I both know this doesn't have a damned thing to do with honor." At her perplexed look, he added, "Don't pretend you don't know when a man wants you. Even you're not that naïve."

She continued to stare at him, a twitch of worry appearing between her brows as she realized there was something she was supposed to know, something she should have understood. Christ. She *was* that naïve. There had been no flirtations or romantic interests that would have taught her how to interpret the signs of a man's sexual interest.

He certainly would have no problem demonstrating it. Bending his head to kiss her, he let his mouth drift back and forth until her lips trembled and parted. Their tongues met in a slide of tender wet silk. As he deepened the kiss, it became more and more delicious, her mouth lush and clinging and innocently erotic.

Carefully he lowered her to the velvet brocade cushions, keeping a supportive arm beneath her neck. His body was sweltering beneath the layers of his clothes, so uncomfortably aroused that he had to reach down and adjust himself. "Sweetheart . . . being around you makes me as hot as a buck in running-time. I thought that was obvious."

Turning crimson, Pandora ducked her face against his shoulder. "Nothing about men is obvious to me," came her muffled voice.

He smiled slightly. "How fortunate for you, then, that I'm here to enlighten you on every particular." Aware of her fidgeting, he glanced down to see her trying to pull down the hem of her robe where it had ridden up to her knee. Once that was accomplished, she lay there unmoving, contained fire seething beneath the calm surface.

Bringing his lips closer to her exposed ear, Gabriel spoke very softly. "You dazzle me, Pandora. Every beautiful, fascinating, kinetic molecule of you. The night we met, I felt you like an electric shock. Something about you calls to the devil in me. I want to take you to bed for days at a time. I want to worship every inch of you while the minutes smolder like moths that dance too close to the flame. I want to feel your hands on me, to—what is it, sweet?" He paused as he heard her indistinguishable muttering.

Pandora flipped onto her back, looking disgruntled. "I said you're talking into my bad ear. I can't hear what you're saying."

Gabriel regarded her blankly, then dropped his head with a smothered laugh. "I'm sorry. I should have noticed." He took a steadying breath. "Perhaps it's just as well. I've thought of another way to make my point." He levered himself up from the sofa cushions and brought Pandora with him. Sliding his arms beneath her slim body, he lifted her easily.

"What are you doing?" she asked, floundering.

For answer, he settled her deliberately onto his lap.

Pandora frowned and squirmed uncomfortably. "I don't see why you—"

Suddenly her eyes widened, and she went very still. A rapid sequence of expressions crossed her face: astonishment, curiosity, mortification . . . and the awareness of a robust male erection beneath her.

"And you said men weren't obvious," Gabriel mocked gently. As she wriggled to adjust her position, it sent exquisite pulses of feeling through his groin and belly. He steeled himself to endure the sensation, breathlessly aware that it wouldn't take much more than this to send him rocketing to climax. "Darling, would you mind . . . not moving . . . quite so much?"

Pandora gave him an indignant glance. "Have you ever tried sitting on a cricket bat?"

Biting back a grin, Gabriel moved most of her weight

to one of his thighs. "Here, lean against my chest, and put your . . . yes, like that." When he'd settled her more comfortably, he loosened the belt of her robe. "You look overheated," he said. "Let me help you off with this."

Pandora was undeceived by his solicitous tone. "If I'm overheated," she told him, pulling her arms from the sleeves, "it's because you've embarrassed me." With a severe glance, she added, "On purpose."

"I was only trying to make it clear how much I desire you."

"It's clear now." She was pink and flustered.

Gabriel tugged the robe out from beneath her and tossed it aside, leaving her clad only in the muslin nightdress. He tried to remember the last time one of his sexual partners had been shy. He couldn't recall what it was like to feel embarrassed during intimacy, and he was charmed out of his wits by Pandora's modesty. It made something familiar seem entirely new.

"Didn't your sister explain what happens to a man's body when he's aroused?" he asked.

"Yes, but she didn't tell me it could happen in the parlor, of all places."

His lips curved. "I'm afraid it can happen anywhere. The parlor, the drawing room, a carriage . . . or a summer house."

Looking scandalized, Pandora asked, "Then you think *this* is what Dolly and Mr. Hayhurst were doing in the summer house?"

"There's no doubt." He began to unfasten the top buttons of her nightgown, and kissed the newly revealed skin of her throat.

Pandora, however, hadn't yet finished with the subject of the summer house rendezvous. "But Mr. Hayhurst wouldn't have returned to the ballroom with a . . . a protrusion like that. How do you deflate it?"

"I usually distract myself by thinking about the latest analysis of foreign securities on the stock exchange. That usually takes care of the problem right away. If that fails, I picture the Queen."

"Really? I wonder what Prince Albert used to think about? It couldn't have been the Queen—they had nine children together." As Pandora continued to chatter, Gabriel spread the sides of the nightgown open and kissed the tender valley between her breasts. Her fingers fidgeted at the back of his neck. "Do you suppose it was something like educational reform? Or Parliamentary procedure, or—"

"Shhh." He found the tracery of a blue vein in the alabaster glow of her skin, and touched it with his tongue. "I want to talk about how beautiful you are. About how you smell like white flowers and open windows and spring rain. About how soft and sweet you are . . . so sweet . . ." His mouth wandered over the gentle curve of her breast, and Pandora jerked, her breath stopping. A rush of excitement flooded him as he sensed her awakening pleasure. His lips traversed her chest in a pattern of lightly grazing touches. Reaching the pink bud of a nipple, he parted his lips and drew it into the hot interior of his mouth. He circled and teased with the tip of his tongue until the peak was textured and velvety.

His mind was swimming with thoughts of the endless ways he wanted to take her, the desires he longed to satisfy. It took all his self-control to caress her slowly, deliberately, when he wanted to devour her. But everything was new to her, every intimacy unnerving, and he would be patient if it killed him. As he licked and tugged gently, he heard a frayed whimper in her throat. She touched his shoulders and chest hesitantly, as if she didn't know where to put her hands.

Lifting his head, he found her lips and possessed them hungrily. "Pandora," he said when the kiss broke, "you can touch me any way you'd like. You can do anything that pleases you."

She gave him a long, wondering gaze. Her fingers went tentatively to the white necktie that hung loosely on either side of his open collar. At his lack of objection, she pulled it free and reached down to the fastenings of his low-cut silk waistcoat. He moved to help her, removing the garment and dropping it to the floor. Next she unbuttoned the placket of his shirt to where it ended mid-chest. Staring at the triangular notch at the base of his throat as if riveted, she leaned forward to kiss him there.

"Why do you like that place?" Gabriel asked, his heart slamming against his ribs as he felt the delicate lap of her tongue.

"I don't know." Her smile curled against his skin. "It seems made for my—" She paused. "For kissing."

Closing his hand in her hair, he guided her to meet his gaze. "For your kisses," he said gruffly, ceding ownership of the spot whether she wanted it or not.

Her inquisitive hands explored the contours of his torso and chest. Carefully her fingers slipped beneath the straps of the braces that went over his shoulders and eased them down. It was the most erotic torture Gabriel had ever experienced, disciplining himself to stay still while Pandora took inventory of this new masculine territory. She kissed the side of his neck and played with the hair on his chest. Finding the flat circle of a male nipple, she rubbed the pad of her thumb over it, raising a tiny aroused point. Growing bolder, she maneuvered over him in a tangle of coltish limbs, trying to press closer, until one of her knees jabbed perilously close to his groin. Hastily he reached down to grasp her hips. "Careful, love. You don't want me to spend the rest of the evening in a sobbing heap on the sofa."

"Did I hurt you?" Pandora asked anxiously, subsiding on his lap.

"No, but for men, that place is . . ." Gabriel broke off with a primal grunt as he felt her straddling him. The feel of it was so scorching, so exquisitely incendiary, that he found himself only a few heartbeats away from release. His hands tightened on her hips to keep her still, while he closed his eyes with a quiet curse. Any movement at all on her part, if only to lift away from him, would cause him to erupt like a stripling lad with his first woman.

"Oh," he heard Pandora exclaim softly. Her thighs tensed on either side of his. "I didn't mean to—"

"Hold still," he rasped. "Sweet merciful God, don't move. Please."

To his vast relief, she stayed in place. He could hardly think past the insane desire, his body struggling in every muscle. He could feel how hot she was even through the fabric of his trousers. *Mine,* his blood screamed. He needed to have her. Mate her. Taking deep, calming breaths, he shivered and gulped, and painstakingly brought himself under control.

"Are you thinking about the Queen?" he heard Pandora ask eventually, while the engorged length of his shaft throbbed vehemently between them. "Because if you are, it's not working."

Gabriel's lips twitched at the helpful observation. He replied with his eyes still closed. "With you sitting on me in that sweet little nightdress, it wouldn't matter if the Queen were standing in this room with a contingent of guards in full uniform."

"What if she were scolding you? What if she were pouring cold water on your feet?"

Entertained, he regarded her with a one-eyed squint. "Pandora, I have the feeling you're trying to deflate my protrusion."

"What if all the guards had drawn their swords and were pointing them at you?" she persisted.

"I would reassure them that the Queen was in absolutely no danger from me."

"Am I in danger?" Pandora asked hesitantly, which certainly wasn't an inappropriate question for a virgin sitting on a half-naked man to be asking.

"Of course not," Gabriel said, although he wasn't certain either of them found that entirely convincing. "The safest place in the world for you is in my arms." Sliding his arms around her, he eased her closer. As she leaned forward, the swollen ridge of his erection aligned with her soft cleft, and she caught her breath. He patted her hip reassuringly. "Does it make you nervous to feel how much I want you? The only purpose of *this*"—he nudged upward gently—"is to give you pleasure."

Pandora glanced down between them dubiously. "Helen said it does more than that."

A quiet laugh broke from him. He'd never known it was possible to be this amused and aroused at the same time. "Not tonight," he managed to say. "I promised I wouldn't take away your choices. And I'll always keep my promises to you."

Contemplating him with those wondrous blue eyes, Pandora rested more heavily on him, her lashes flickering in a double-blink as she felt the thick, involuntary twitch of his hard flesh nestled against her. "What are we going to do now?" she whispered.

"What do you want to do?" he whispered back, watching her in fascination.

They studied each other, both of them unmoving and pleasurably tense, invisible fuses burning. Very carefully, as if she were experimenting with some violently unstable substance, Pandora brought her mouth to his, trying different angles, searching and tasting with increasing fervor.

No woman had ever kissed Gabriel the way she did, wringing out sensation and soft fire as if she were sucking raw honey from the comb. The longer it went on, however, the wilder she became. One of them had to stay in control, and it clearly wasn't going to be her, and she was making it hard. He groaned as she writhed on his lap. *So* damned hard.

Framing her face in his hands, he pulled back and tried to gentle her. "Easy, love. Relax. I'll give you everything you—"

Before he could even finish the sentence, Pandora dove back in and captured his mouth with take-no-prisoners enthusiasm. Panting, she tried to feel more of his chest, fumbling at the bottom of the shirt placket, but there were no more buttons left to unfasten. She grasped the sides of the placket and tugged roughly, trying to tear the garment open. It might have worked with an ordinary shirt, but the front of an evening shirt was sewn with an extra thickness of cloth and pressed with a double portion of starch to keep it smooth.

Despite Gabriel's acute arousal, he felt an irresistible laugh swell in his chest as he looked down at her, his small and determined pirate, who was having a moment of unexpected difficulty with bodice-ripping. But there was no way in hell he would risk hurting her feelings at such a moment. After brutally quelling the laughter, he sat up straight to tug the hem of his shirt upward and over his head, baring his chest completely.

As soon as the garment was stripped away, Pandora attached herself to him with a wrenching sigh, her hands wandering over his chest and sides with unbridled greed. Gabriel eased back in his seated position. Later he would teach her about pacing and control, about the slow build of desire, but for now, he would allow her free rein. Her braid had come unraveled, the long trailing locks as shiny as moonlight on ripples of dark water. It caressed and tickled his body as she moved on him, her hips grinding in urgent and unmeasured patterns.

Gabriel's entire body was as taut as a man on a medieval dungeon rack. His hands clenched into the sofa cushion until his fingers threatened to punch holes through the brocade. He fought to keep his mind focused, restraining his own desire as Pandora continued to kiss him, rising and subsiding in his lap.

Tearing her mouth from his with a frazzled, wordless exclamation, Pandora dropped her head to his shoulder. She breathed in gasps, clearly not knowing what she wanted, only that the pleasure was woven with frustration, and everything she did to satisfy it only made it worse.

It was time to take control. With a sympathetic murmur, Gabriel stroked her heaving back, and gathered her loose hair into a single stream. "I want to do something for you, little love. Will you trust me for a few minutes?"

Chapter 13

PANDORA CONSIDERED THE QUESTION without moving. She felt hot and unsatisfied, her nerves tight-strung with something like hunger, only much worse. Something gnawing and sharp and shaky. "What are you going to do?" she asked.

Gabriel's hands moved over her with tantalizing lightness. "You know I would never hurt you."

It didn't escape her that he hadn't answered the question directly. She pushed herself up on his chest then, looking down at him. He was inhumanly beautiful as he lay there beneath her, all whipcord muscle and golden sleekness, his face like something from a dream. A flush of color burnished his cheekbones and the bridge of his nose, as if he'd been out in the sun too long. His light blue eyes glinted with mischief and secrets, shadowed by a tangle of long lashes. *A living, breathing Adonis,* she thought, a wave of gloom breaking over her.

"I think we should stop now," she said reluctantly.

Gabriel shook his head, squinting slightly as if mystified by the statement. "We've barely started."

"This can't lead to anything. Prince Charming doesn't belong with a girl who sits in corners, he belongs with a girl who can waltz."

"What the devil does waltzing have to do with this?"

"It's a metaphor."

"For what?" Gabriel moved her off his lap, sat up, and raked his hands through his hair. Despite his attempts to restore order, the golden-bronze locks fell back into disheveled layers, some sliding over his forehead, and it looked wonderful. He laid an arm across the back of the sofa, his gaze locked on her.

Pandora was so distracted by his tautly muscled torso and arms, and the tantalizing fleece of hair on his chest, she could barely recall the answer. "For all the things I can't do. Your wife will have to act as hostess for all kinds of events, and attend balls and soirées with you, and what woman with two perfectly good legs can't dance with her husband? People would ask. What excuse could I give them?"

"We'll say I'm a jealous husband. That I never want you to be in any man's arms but mine."

Pandora frowned, pulling the front of her nightdress together. She felt aggrieved and even a bit self-pitying—and there was nothing she despised more than self-pity. "As if anyone would believe that," she muttered.

Gabriel took her upper arms in a firm grip. His eyes were as bright as lit matches as he stared at her. "I never want you to be in any man's arms but mine."

The world stopped on its axis. Pandora was stricken and frightened to think there might be even a grain of truth in his words. No, he didn't mean it. He was manipulating her.

She pushed at his chest. It was as hard as a stone wall. "Don't say that."

"You belong with me."

"No."

"You feel it," he insisted, "every time we're together. You want—"

She tried to hush him with her mouth, which in retrospect was not the wisest tactic. Gabriel responded immediately, his kiss deep and demanding.

In the next moment she was on her back, stretched out beneath him. He braced enough of his weight on his elbows and knees to keep from crushing her, but she was still anchored securely, pressed into the sofa cushions while he kissed her with slow, consuming ardor. He seemed determined to prove something, as if she didn't already want him, as if she weren't already weak with hunger. Her mouth opened to his, absorbing the intoxicating taste of him, the smooth male heat, the erotic exploration of his tongue. She couldn't stop her hands from sliding over the heavy muscles of his back, the skin luxurious to the touch, thicker and more satiny than her own.

His parted lips dragged slowly over her neck and down to her breasts. She arched as he captured a taut nipple with his mouth, flicking it with his tongue, catching at it lightly with his teeth. His hand covered her other breast, shaping the malleable flesh, before sliding along the side of her body, charting the curves of waist and hip. The hem of her nightdress had ridden up on her thighs, making it easy for him to tug it up to her waist. Shocked, she clamped her thighs together.

Her toes bunched at the sound of his soft laugh. Devilish, sensuous, knowing. Easing to his side, Gabriel trailed his fingertips across her stomach to her navel, caressing around it with lazy circles. At the same time, he kissed and sucked at the tip of her breast until it was wet and unbearably sensitive.

His fingertips tickled their way down to the thatch of silky-coarse curls between her thighs, stroking idly. Pandora writhed, her gaze unfocused. Oh God, was she really letting him do this? Yes, she was. Moaning with shame and worry, she felt him playing softly with her, the tip of his middle finger sliding into the top of the delicate furrow of her sex. A brief, ticklish swirl left her gasping. Her legs pressed together more tightly.

His mouth released her breast. "Open to me," he whispered.

She bit her lip as he stroked through the curls, the darting touches of his fingers making her weak. Her body was nothing but heat driven by heartbeats. Nothing was clear anymore. Nothing mattered except what he was doing to her. Her legs shook, and she whimpered at the effort it took to keep them together.

"Pandora . . ." His voice was soft and seductive. "Open to me." His fingertip insinuated between the sensitive folds of her sex and wriggled gently. The sensation rippled through her like flickers of white flame. "So stubborn," he whispered. "Oh, Pandora, don't tempt me. You're going to make me do something wicked." His forefinger slid along the seam of her closed thighs. "Just part them one inch. For me." A hot breath of laughter fanned against her skin. "Not even an inch?"

"It's embarrassing," she protested. "You're bothering my nervous condition."

"This is a well-known treatment for female nerves."

"It's not helping. You're . . . *ahh!* . . . making it worse . . ."

Gabriel was moving lower, tasting her skin, biting softly, using his teeth . . . lips . . . tongue . . . She tried to roll out from beneath him, but he caught her hips and held her in place. There was a wet swirl around her navel, painting it with liquid fire before trailing downward. Her heart thudded painfully as she felt him breathe against the most intimate place of her body. He nuzzled into the wispy curls, separating them with his tongue. A peculiar slide of heat, a slithery tickle.

Astonished, she shrank away from him, but he stayed with her, licking into wet-rose tenderness, teasing it open. Her thighs fell apart in helpless surrender. His tongue found moist silken flesh, the soft-secreted bud, and circled lightly, delicately, while his hands moved slowly up and down her thighs.

Pleasure was spreading everywhere, beneath her skin and in the spaces between her heartbeats. All her senses focused on the spell he was working, an enchantment of fire wrapped in darkness. He rested the flat of his tongue against her, and to her everlasting embarrassment, her hips pushed against him. After a few fluttering strokes, his tongue went flat and still again. She couldn't stop herself from writhing, and she felt the heat of his chuckle against her. He was playing with her, making her do shameful things. As her hands fumbled to push his head away, he caught her shaking wrists and pinned them to the sofa. He found a rhythm of light, steady flicks that made her insides clench rhythmically, like a heartbeat. He knew what he was doing, relentlessly stoking the feeling higher, higher, until it turned molten and began to flood every part of her. She tried to hold it back, but that only made it worse, setting off long, bone-deep shudders that wracked her entire frame. She felt her eyes roll back in her head, her limbs drawing up with the primitive urge to close around something.

As the last tremors smoothed into peacefulness, Gabriel rose over her and pulled her into his arms. She stretched and nestled against his side, hitching a thigh over one of his. Her limbs felt pleasantly heavy, as if she were waking from a long sleep, and for once her mind was utterly focused, without the distraction of too many thoughts. She felt the shapes of words brushing her ear as he whispered something, the same few words over and over, until Pandora stirred and mumbled, "That's my bad ear."

His smile curved against her cheek, and he lifted his head. "I know."

What had he been whispering? Bemused, Pandora let her hand drift over his chest, playing with the light, glinting fur, feeling the armor of ribs and hard muscle beneath. The flesh of his stomach and sides was so different from hers, tough and sinewy, the skin gleaming like polished marble.

Fascinated, she let the backs of her fingers inch timidly to the front of his trousers, where the heavy ridge of his aroused flesh strained against the black broadcloth. Turning over her hand, she dared to curve her palm against the shaft, and followed it all the way down to the base and up again. It was scary and exciting and unbelievable to be touching him like this. His breath quickened, and an involuntary quiver chased across his stomach as she gripped over the stiffness.

Beneath her fingers, the hard flesh seemed to possess its own pulses and responsive twitches. She wanted to see this mysterious part of him. She wanted to find out what it felt like. The front of his trousers had been styled in the classic formal design, a fall attached with two side rows of buttons. Timidly her hand slid to the nearest row of buttons.

His hand came to hers, arresting her wandering touch, and his lips grazed her temple. "Better not, sweet."

Pandora frowned. "But it's not fair for you to treat my nervous condition, and me to do nothing for yours."

His gentle laugh filtered through her hair. "We'll take care of mine later." Leaning over her, he took her lips with a brief, ardent kiss. "Let me carry you to bed now," he whispered, "and tuck you in like a good little girl."

"Not yet," she protested. "I want to stay here with you." The storm rolled over the house, rain falling with the force of bronze pennies. She snuggled more tightly into the warm crook of Gabriel's arm. "Besides . . . you still haven't answered the question I asked you at the archery grounds."

"What question?"

"You were going to tell me the worst thing about yourself."

"God. Do we have to discuss that now?"

"You said you wanted to talk about it in private. I don't know when we'll have another chance."

Gabriel frowned and remained silent, occupied with thoughts that seemed far from pleasant. Perhaps he wasn't certain how to begin.

"Does it have something to do with your mistress?" she asked helpfully.

Gabriel gave her a narrowed glance, as if the question had taken him aback. "So you've heard about that."

She nodded.

He let out a controlled sigh. "The devil knows I'm not proud of it. However, I thought it better than resorting to harlotry or seducing innocents, and I'm not exactly suited for celibacy."

"I don't think badly of you for it," Pandora hastened to assure him. "Lady Berwick says it's often done by gentlemen, and ladies must pretend not to know about it."

"All very civilized," Gabriel muttered. His expression was dark as he continued. "There's nothing wrong with the arrangement unless one or both of the parties involved are married. I've always considered marriage vows to be sacred. To lie with another man's wife is . . . unforgivable."

His tone remained even and calm, except for the self-loathing that colored the last word.

For a moment Pandora was too surprised to speak. It seemed impossible that this man, with his golden good looks and sophistication—a man so perfect in every way—would feel ashamed about anything. Then the surprise melted into a tender feeling as she reflected that he was not some godlike being, but a man with very human flaws. It wasn't an unwelcome discovery.

"Your mistress is married," she said without asking.

"She's the wife of the American ambassador."

"Then how do you and she . . ."

"I bought a house where we meet whenever possible."

Pandora felt something clutch at her chest, like a set of claws digging into her heart. "No one lives there?" she asked. "The house is only for rendezvous-ing?"

Gabriel gave her a sardonic glance. "I thought it preferable to rutting behind the potted palms at the latest soirée."

"Yes, but to buy an *entire house* . . ." Pandora knew she was belaboring the point. But it rankled, the idea that he had bought a private, special place for himself and his mistress. *Their* house. It was probably smart and fashionable, one of those detached villas with bow windows, or perhaps a cottage *orné* with its own little kitchen garden.

"What is Mrs. Black like?" she asked.

"Vivacious. Confident. Worldly."

"Beautiful too, I suppose."

"Very."

The invisible claws sank deeper. What a nasty feeling this was. It almost felt like . . . jealousy? No. *Yes.* It was jealousy. Oh, this was awful.

"If the idea of taking a married woman as a mistress bothers you," she asked, trying not to sound snide, "why didn't you look for someone else?"

"It's not as if one can advertise for a mistress in the papers," Gabriel said dryly. "And attraction doesn't always happen with convenient people. It bothered me a great deal that Nola was married. But that wasn't enough to stop me from pursuing her, once I realized—" He broke off and rubbed the back of his neck, his mouth clamping in a sullen line.

"Realized what?" Pandora asked with a touch of dread. "That you loved her?"

"No. I'm fond of her, but nothing more." Gabriel's color heightened as he forced himself to continue. "I realized that she and I were very well-matched in the bedroom. I've rarely ever found a woman who can satisfy me the way she does. So I overlooked the fact that she was married." His lips twisted. "When it comes to matters of character, it seems I'll toss out every scruple in favor of sexual gratification."

Pandora was baffled. "Why is it so difficult for women to please you?" she demanded. "What exactly do you ask them to do?"

The audacious question seemed to jar Gabriel out of his bleak mood. He returned his gaze to her, the corners of his mouth deepening. "I only ask that a woman be available, willing . . . and uninhibited." Turning his attention to the buttons of Pandora's nightdress, he began to fasten them with undue concentration. "Unfortunately, most women are taught never to enjoy the sexual act unless it's for procreation."

"But you think they should?"

"I think there are few enough pleasures for a woman in this world. I think only a selfish idiot would deny his partner the same satisfaction she gives him, especially when her pleasure enhances his own. Yes, I believe women should enjoy it, radical as that might sound. Nola's lack of inhibition makes her unique, and very desirable."

"I don't have inhibitions," Pandora blurted out, feeling competitive. She regretted the comment as soon as she saw the sparkle of amusement in Gabriel's eyes.

"I'm glad," he said gently. "You see, there are things a gentleman isn't supposed to ask of his wife. But if we were to marry, I would have to ask them of you."

"If we were to marry, I suppose I wouldn't mind. But we're not—" She was forced to pause as an irresistible yawn took over, and she covered her mouth with her hand.

Gabriel smiled and pulled her close, as if he were trying to absorb the feel of her. Pandora let herself rest quietly against the deep warmth of his flesh and the satiny golden skin. She was surrounded by the vibrant scent of him, fresh with hints of evergreen and dark spice. How familiar his smell had become in a handful of days. She would miss it. She would miss being held like this.

For a moment of biting envy, she imagined Gabriel going back to London, to the intimate little house he'd bought for himself and his mistress. Mrs. Black would be there waiting for him, perfumed and dressed in a beautiful negligée. He would take her to bed, and do wicked things to her, and even though Pandora had little idea of what those things were, she couldn't help wondering what it would be like to spend hours in bed with him. Butterflies swirled in her stomach.

"Gabriel," she said uncertainly, "I didn't quite tell you the truth."

His hand played in her hair. "About what, love?"

"I shouldn't have said I have no inhibitions. The truth is that I *mostly* don't have inhibitions, but I think there are a few. I just don't know exactly what they are yet."

A dark, soft whisper nearly singed her ear. "I can help you with those."

Her heartbeats came even faster than falling rain. It felt disloyal to want him like this . . . disloyal to herself . . . but she couldn't seem to stop.

Gabriel loosened the embrace and reached for her discarded robe, intending to dress her again. "I have to carry you to bed now, Pandora," he said ruefully. "Or our rendezvous is going to turn into outright debauchery."

Chapter 14

"ARE YOU ILL, MILADY?" Ida asked the next morning, standing at Pandora's bedside.

Feeling her consciousness dragged upward, kicking and screaming, from the depths of comfortable oblivion, Pandora squinted up at her lady's maid.

"I'm lying in bed in a dark room," she said grumpily, "with my head on a pillow and my eyes closed. People tend to do this when they're sleeping."

"By this time every morning, you're usually jumping about and chirping like a cricket in a hen yard."

Pandora rolled to face away from her. "I didn't sleep well last night."

"The rest of the household is awake. You're going to miss breakfast unless I can manage to make you presentable in the next half hour."

"I don't care. Tell whoever wants to know that I'm resting."

"What about the housemaids? They'll want to come in and clean."

"The room is already tidy."

"It most certainly is not. The carpet must be swept, and . . . why is your wrapper draped at the foot of the bed instead of hanging in the wardrobe?"

Pandora burrowed more deeply beneath the covers, turning pink all over. She remembered Gabriel carrying her to her room last night and laying her on the bed. It had been so dark that she could hardly make out anything, but Gabriel had exceptional night vision.

"Arms in or out?" he'd asked, straightening the covers efficiently.

"Out." Pandora had been nonplussed and amused. "I didn't know one of your bedroom skills was tucking people in."

"Only very small people until now. Justin routinely gives me low marks for leaving the covers too loose." Gabriel's weight had depressed the mattress as he'd braced a hand and bent over her. As his lips had touched her forehead, Pandora had circled her arms around his neck and sought his mouth. He'd resisted briefly, his soft laugh rushing against her cheek. "You've had enough kissing for one night."

"One more," she had insisted.

He had obliged her, and she had no idea how long he'd stayed there with his lips playing against hers, while she'd responded with deep-dreaming intensity. Eventually he'd left her, vanishing into the darkness like a cat.

Pandora was wrenched away from the pleasurable memory as she heard the clang of the tin slipper-box lid.

"There's only one slipper," she heard Ida say suspiciously. "Where's the other?"

"I don't know."

"Why were you out of bed?"

"I was looking for a book, since I couldn't sleep," Pandora replied irritably, filled with worry. What if Gabriel hadn't remembered to retrieve the other slipper from the hallway? And what about the fallen candle? If one of the servants had found the items . . .

"It must be here somewhere," Ida fretted, crouching to look under the bed. "How do you lose things so easily? Gloves, handkerchiefs, pins—"

"Your talking is waking up my brain," Pandora said. "I would have thought you'd be pleased for me to stay unconscious longer than usual."

"I would," Ida retorted, "but I have other things to do besides wait on you all morning, Lady Slugabed." Standing with a huff, she left the room, and closed the door behind her.

Fluffing up her pillow, Pandora dove her head into it. "I'm going to hire a *nice* lady's maid someday," she grumbled. "One who doesn't call me names and lecture me at dawn." She turned to her back and then to her other side, trying to find a comfortable position. It was no use. She was awake, and that was that.

Would it be worth the effort to ring for Ida and try to dress in time for breakfast? No, she didn't feel at all like hurrying. In fact, she didn't know what she felt like. A strange mixture of emotions whisked around inside her . . . nervousness, excitement, melancholy, yearning, fear. Tomorrow was her last full day at Heron's Point. She dreaded having to leave. She especially dreaded the things that would have to be said.

Someone tapped quietly on the door. Pandora's heart lurched as she wondered if it might be Gabriel trying to return the missing slipper. "Yes?" she called out in a hushed voice.

Kathleen came into the room, her red hair glowing even in the dimness. "I'm sorry to disturb you, dear," she said gently, coming to the bedside, "but I wanted to ask how you were feeling. Are you ill?"

"No, but my brain is tired." Pandora inched closer to the edge of the mattress as she felt Kathleen's cool, small hand smoothing back her hair and resting briefly on her forehead. From the moment Kathleen had come to the estate, she had been the closest thing to a mother Pandora had ever known, despite the fact that she was still a young woman herself.

"You have a great deal to think about," Kathleen murmured, her face soft with sympathy.

"Whatever I decide is going to feel like a mistake." Pandora's throat cinched tight. "I wish Lord St. Vincent were a warty old windbag. Then everything would be easy. Instead, he's odiously attractive and charming. It's like he's deliberately trying to make my life as difficult as possible. *This* is why I've never understood why people think the devil is a hideous beast with horns and claws and a forked tail. No one would be tempted by that."

"You're saying Lord St. Vincent is the devil in disguise?" Kathleen asked, sounding vaguely amused.

"He may as well be," Pandora said morosely. "He's made everything confusing. I'm like a goldfinch, thinking 'Oh, that little cage looks so awfully nice with its gold bars and cozy velvet perch and that dish of milletseed—it might be worth having my wings clipped for that.' And then when the door latches shut, it will be too late."

Kathleen patted her back comfortingly. "No one's wings have to be clipped. I'll support whatever you decide to do."

Oddly, Pandora felt frightened rather than comforted by the reassurance. "If I don't marry him, will our family be ruined? And Cassandra?"

"No. We'll be grist for the gossip mill for a little while, but time will eventually soften everyone's memory, and then any lingering stain on our reputation will only serve to make us very interesting dinner companions. And I promise we'll find a perfectly nice husband for Cassandra." Kathleen hesitated. "However, should you wish to marry in the future, this scandal might pose a problem for some men. Not all, but a few."

"I won't marry until women have the right to vote and make the laws fair. Which means never." Pandora buried her face in the pillow. "Even the Queen opposes suffrage," she added in a smothered voice.

She felt Kathleen's gentle hand on her head. "It takes time and patience to change people's way of thinking. Don't forget that many men are speaking up for women's equality, including Mr. Disraeli."

Pandora flopped over to look up at her. "I wish he would speak up a bit more loudly, then."

"One has to speak to people in a way they can hear." Kathleen regarded her thoughtfully. "In any case, the law won't change in the next two days, and you have a decision to make. Are you absolutely certain that Lord St. Vincent wouldn't be supportive of your board game company?"

"Oh, he would support it, in the way a man supports his wife's hobby. But it would always have to come second to everything else. It wouldn't be convenient to have a wife who's visiting her factory instead of planning out the dinner party. I'm afraid if I marry him, I'll end up making one compromise after another, and all my dreams will die slowly while I'm busy looking the other way."

"I understand."

"Do you?" Pandora asked earnestly. "But you wouldn't make the same choice, would you?"

"You and I have different fears, and different needs."

"Kathleen . . . Why did you marry Cousin Devon after Theo treated you so badly? Weren't you afraid?"

"Yes, I was very afraid."

"Why did you do it, then?"

"I loved him too much to be without him. And I realized I couldn't let fear make the decision for me."

Pandora looked away, while melancholy fell over her like a shadow.

Kathleen smoothed out a wrinkle on the counterpane. "The duchess and I are taking the girls for an outing to the seashore promenade in town. We're planning to visit some shops and have fruit ices. Would you like to come? We'll wait until you're ready."

Sighing shortly, Pandora pulled the soft linen sheet over her head. "No, I don't want to pretend to be cheerful when I'm feeling so floppulous."

Kathleen folded down the sheet and smiled at her. "Then do whatever you like. Everyone has scattered in different directions, and the house is quiet. Devon has gone to the pier with the duke and Ivo to find out if the storm did any damage to the family yacht. Lady Clare is out on a walk with her children."

"What about Lord St. Vincent? Do you know where he is?"

"I believe he's taking care of business correspondence in the study." Kathleen bent to kiss Pandora's forehead, the movement diffusing a whiff of roses and mint. "Darling, let me leave you with a thought: There's very little in life that doesn't require a compromise of one kind or another. No matter what you choose, it won't be perfect."

"So much for happy-ever-after," Pandora said sourly.

Kathleen smiled. "But wouldn't it be dull if ever-after was always happy, with no difficulties or problems to solve? Ever-after is far more interesting than that."

LATER IN THE MORNING, Pandora ventured downstairs in a lavender dress of delicately ribbed grosgrain silk, with layered white underskirts that had been pulled back into a cascade of flounces. Ida, despite her earlier cantankerous attitude, had brought up tea and toast for Pandora, and had taken special pains to arrange her hair. After curling the long dark locks with hot tongs, Ida had carefully pinned it up at the crown of her head into a mass of ringlets and clusters. Whenever a lock of Pandora's obstinately straight hair had refused to hold a curl, Ida had misted it with quince seed tonic, resulting in a coil as sturdy as a steel spring. As a finishing touch, the lady's maid had accented the style with a few randomly placed pearls affixed to silver pins.

"Thank you, Ida," Pandora had said, viewing the results in the looking glass with the aid of a hand mirror. "You're the only person my hair has ever obeyed." After a pause, she had added humbly, "I'm sorry I lose things. I'm sure it would drive anyone mad to have to look after me."

"Keeps me in a job," Ida had said philosophically. "But don't apologize, milady—you should never tell a servant you're sorry. It upsets the order of things."

"But what if I feel so sorry that I must say it or burst?"

"You can't."

"Yes, I can. I'll look at you and tap my forehead with three fingertips—like this. There—that's our signal for 'I'm sorry.'" Enthused by the idea, Pandora had continued, "I could come up with other signals—we'll have our own language!"

"Milady," Ida had begged, "*please* don't be so odd."

The house was bright with slants of sunlight, now that the storm had cleared. Although no one was in sight, Pandora heard the bustling of servants in various rooms as she walked along the hallway. There was the rattle of a coal scuttle, the swishing of carpet brooms, the scrape of scouring paper on fire irons. All the industry taking place around her made Pandora long to return home and resume work on her board game business. It was time to visit potential locations for a small factory space, and meet with her printer, and begin to interview prospective employees.

The door of the study had been left open. As Pandora approached the threshold, her pulse escalated until she could feel it beating at her throat, wrists, and knees. She hardly knew how to face Gabriel, after the things they'd done last night. Stopping at the side of the doorway, she peeked around the edge of the jamb.

Gabriel was sitting at a heavy walnut desk, his profile edged in sunlight. He was reading a document with a slight frown of concentration, pausing to write on a scrap of notepaper. Dressed in a morning suit, with his hair neatly brushed and his face clean-shaven, he looked as fresh as a new-minted sovereign.

Although Pandora made no movement or sound, Gabriel's gaze flickered to her. His slow smile made her lightheaded. "Come in," he said, pushing back from the desk.

Feeling acutely self-conscious, Pandora approached him with flaming cheeks. "I was on my way to—well, I'm just wandering, but—I wanted to ask you about my slipper. Did you find it? Do you have it?"

He stood and looked down at her, his eyes like hot starlight, and for a moment all she could think of was the lick of firelight on shadowed skin. "I have the slipper," he said.

"Oh, thank goodness. Because my lady's maid is on the brink of reporting it to Scotland Yard."

"That's too bad. I've already decided to keep it."

"No, you can only do that if it's a dainty glass slipper. If it's a big floppy slipper made out of fuzzy wool, you have to give it back."

"I'll consider it." After glancing at the doorway to make certain they were unobserved, Gabriel bent to steal a swift kiss. "Will you talk with me for a few minutes? Or let me wander with you. There's something important I want to discuss."

Pandora's stomach did a somersault. "You're not going to propose, are you?"

His lips twitched. "Not right now."

"Then yes, you can walk with me."

"Outside? Through the gardens?"

She nodded.

As they exited from the side of the house and set out on a finely graveled walk, Gabriel seemed relaxed, his expression carefully neutral, but there was no hiding the faint pull of tension between his brows.

"What do you want to discuss?" Pandora asked.

"A letter I received this morning. It's from Mr. Chester Litchfield, a solicitor in Brighton. He represented Phoebe in a dispute with her in-laws over some provisions in her late husband's will. Litchfield is well versed in the property law, so I wrote to him immediately after I learned about your board game business. I asked him to find a way for you to legally maintain control over your company as a married woman."

Surprised and uneasy, Pandora veered to the side of the path. She affected interest in a six-foot-tall shrub that bore massive white flowers the size of camellias. "What was Mr. Litchfield's response?"

Gabriel approached her from behind. "He didn't give the answers I wanted."

Pandora's shoulders drooped slightly, but she remained silent as he continued.

"As Litchfield put it," Gabriel continued, "once a woman marries, she becomes more or less 'civilly dead.' She can't legally enter into a contract with anyone, which means that even if she owns land, she can't rent it out or build upon it. Even if property has been secured to her as a separate estate, her husband receives all the interest and profits. In the view of the government, a woman who tries to own anything separately from her husband is, in essence, stealing from him."

"I already knew that." Pandora wandered to the other side of the path to stare blindly at a bed of yellow primroses. What was the meaning of primroses? Chastity? No, that was orange blossoms . . . Was it constancy? . . .

Gabriel was still speaking. "Litchfield believes property law will continue to be reformed in the future. But as things stand now, the moment after the marriage vows are spoken, you'll lose your legal independence and control of your business. However—" He paused. "Don't start drifting. This next part is important."

"I wasn't drifting. I was only trying to remember what primroses mean. Would it be innocence, or is that for daisies? I think it's for—"

"I can't live without you."

Pandora turned to face him sharply, her eyes wide.

"The meaning of primroses," Gabriel said in a matter-of-fact tone.

"How do you know that?"

He looked wry. "My sisters often discuss drivel like flower symbolism. No matter how I try to ignore it, some of it seeps through. Now, back to Litchfield—he said that according to a recent amendment of the Married Women's Property Act, if you earn a salary, you'll be able to keep it."

Pandora blinked and focused on him alertly. "*Any* amount of earnings?"

"As long as you're seen to perform work that would justify it."

"What does that mean?"

"In your case, you would have to take an active interest in the management of the company. You could also keep an annual bonus payment. I'll ask Litchfield about sales commissions and a pension—you may be able to retain those as well. Here's how we would structure it: Upon our marriage, when your business automatically transfers to me, I'll put it in trust for you and hire you as the company president."

"But . . . what about legal contracts? If I can't sign anything, how could I enter into agreements with suppliers and stores, and how could I hire people—"

"We could hire a manager to assist you, on condition that he always comply with your wishes."

"What about the company's profits? They would go to you, wouldn't they?"

"Not if you folded them back into the business."

Pandora stared at him fixedly, her mind working over the idea, trying to comprehend what such a future would look and feel like.

The arrangement would give her more independence and authority than the law had ever intended a married woman to have. But she still wouldn't be able to employ or fire anyone, or sign checks, or make decisions on her own. She would have to ask a male manager to sign contracts and agree to business deals on her behalf, as if she were a toddler. It would be difficult to negotiate for goods and services, because everyone would know that the ultimate authority lay not with her, but her husband.

It wouldn't be ownership, but it would have the appearance of it. Rather like wearing a tiara and asking everyone to pretend she was royalty, when they all knew it was a sham.

Tearing her gaze from him, Pandora quivered with frustration. "Why can't I own my business the way a man would, so no one could take it away from me?"

"I won't let anyone take it from you."

"That's not the same. It's all convoluted. It's compromised."

"It's not perfect," Gabriel agreed quietly.

Pandora paced in a small, tight circle. "Do you want to know why I love board games? The rules make sense, and they're the same for everyone. The players are equal."

"Life isn't like that."

"It certainly isn't for women," she said acidly.

"Pandora . . . we'll set our own rules. I'll never treat you as anything less than my equal."

"I believe you. But to the rest of the world, I would be legally nonexistent."

Gabriel reached out and caught lightly at her upper arm, interrupting her pacing. There was a ragged edge to his calmness now, like a hem that was coming unstitched. "You'll be able to do the work you love. You'll be a wealthy woman. You'll be treated with respect and affection. You'll—damn it, I'm not going to plead like a street beggar holding out his cap. There's a way for you to have most of what you want—isn't that enough?"

"What if our situations were reversed?" she shot back. "Would you give up all your legal rights and surrender everything you own to me? You'd never be able to touch a penny of your money, except by my leave. Think of it, Gabriel—the last contract you'd ever sign would be our marriage contract. Would marrying me be worth that?"

"That's not a sane comparison," he said with a scowl.

"Only because in one case, a woman gives up everything, and in the other, a man does."

His eyes flashed dangerously. "Is there nothing to be gained, then? Does the prospect of living as my wife have no appeal at all?" He took her in both hands, bringing her closer. "Say you don't want me. Say you don't want more of what we did last night."

Pandora turned scarlet, her pulse running riot. She wanted to sink against him right then, and tug his head to hers and let him kiss her into obliviousness. But some stubborn, rebellious part of her brain wouldn't be subdued.

"Would I have to obey you?" she heard herself ask.

His lashes lowered, and one of his hands came to the back of her head. "Only in bed," he growled softly. "Outside of that . . . no."

She took an unsteady breath, aware of strange pangs and zings of heat all through her body. "Then you'll promise never to stop me from making my own decisions, even if you think it's a mistake? And if you decide someday that my work isn't good for me, that it poses a risk to my health or wellbeing or even my safety, you'll guarantee that you'd never forbid me from doing it?"

Gabriel let go of her abruptly. "Damn it, Pandora, I can't promise not to protect you."

"Protecting can turn into controlling."

"No one has absolute freedom. Not even me."

"But you have so much of it. When someone has only a little of something, they have to fight to keep from losing any of it." Realizing she was on the verge of crying, Pandora lowered her head. "You want to argue, and I know if we did, you'd score points and make it seem as if I were being unreasonable. But we could never be happy together. Some problems can never be solved. Some things about me can never be fixed. Marrying me would be just as impossible a compromise for you as it would be for me."

"Pandora—"

She strode away without listening, nearly breaking into a run.

AS SOON AS Pandora reached her room, she went back to bed, fully dressed, and lay unmoving for hours.

She felt nothing, which should have been a relief. But somehow it was even worse than feeling awful.

Thinking about things that usually made her happy had no effect. It didn't help to envision her future of independence and freedom, and what it would look like to see stacks of her board games displayed on store tables. There was nothing to look forward to. Nothing would ever give her pleasure again.

Maybe she needed some kind of medicine—she was so terribly cold—could she have a fever?

Kathleen and the others had probably returned from their outing by now. But Pandora couldn't turn to anyone for comfort. Not even her own twin. Cassandra would try to offer solutions or say something loving and encouraging, and Pandora would end up having to pretend to feel better to keep from worrying her.

Her chest and throat wouldn't stop hurting. Maybe if she let herself cry, it would make her feel better.

But the tears wouldn't come. They stayed locked inside the frozen vault of her chest.

This had never happened before. She started to become seriously worried. How long would this go on? She felt like she was turning into a stone statue, starting from the inside out. She would end up on a marble pedestal with birds perched on her head—

Tap, tap, tap. The bedroom door opened slightly. "Milady?"

Ida's voice.

The lady's maid came into the dim room, holding a little round tray. "I brought you some tea."

"Is it morning again?" Pandora asked, in a daze.

"No, it's three in the afternoon." Ida came to the bedside.

"I don't want tea."

"It's from his lordship."

"Lord St. Vincent?"

"He sent for me and asked me to fetch you, and when I said you were resting, he said, 'Give her some tea, then. Pour it down her throat if necessary.' Then he handed me a note for you."

How annoying. How incredibly highhanded. A flicker of actual feeling seared through the numbness. Groggily Pandora struggled to sit up.

After giving her the cup of tea, Ida went to draw back the curtains. The glare of daylight made Pandora flinch.

The tea was hot, but it had no flavor. She forced herself to drink it, and rubbed her dry, burning eyes with her knuckles.

"Here, milady." Ida gave her a small sealed envelope, and took the empty cup and saucer.

Pandora looked dully at the red wax seal on the envelope, stamped with an elaborate family crest. If Gabriel had written something nice to her, she didn't want to read it. If he'd written something not nice, she didn't want to read that either.

"By the holy poker," Ida exclaimed, "just open it!"

Reluctantly Pandora complied. As she pulled a small folded note from the envelope, a tiny, fuzzy object fell out. Reflexively she yelped, thinking it was an insect. But at second glance, she realized it was a bit of fabric. Picking it up gingerly, she saw that it was one of the decorative felt leaves from her missing Berlin wool slipper. It had been carefully snipped off.

My lady,

Your slipper is being held for ransom. If you ever want to see it again, come alone to the formal drawing room. For every hour you delay, an additional embellishment will be removed.

—St. Vincent

Now Pandora was exasperated. Why was he doing this? Was he trying to draw her into another argument?

"What does it say?" Ida asked.

"I have to go downstairs for a hostage negotiation," Pandora said shortly. "Would you help put me to rights?"

"Yes, milady."

The lavender silk dress had been crushed and crumpled into a mass of wrinkles, which obliged Pandora to change into a fresh day gown of plain-woven yellow faille. This frock wasn't as fine as the first one, but it was lighter and more comfortable, without so many underskirts. Fortunately her elaborate hairstyle had been so well anchored and pinned that it needed minimal repair.

"Will you take out the pearl pins?" Pandora asked. "They're too nice for this dress."

"But they look pretty," Ida protested.

"I don't want to look pretty."

"What if his lordship proposes?"

"He won't. I've already made it clear that if he did, I wouldn't accept."

Ida looked aghast. "You . . . but . . . *why?*"

It was over the line, of course, for a lady's maid to ask such a thing, but Pandora answered nonetheless. "Because then I'd have to be someone's wife instead of having my own board game company."

A hairbrush dropped from Ida's lax fingers. Her eyes were like saucers as she met Pandora's gaze in the vanity mirror. "You're refusing to marry the heir to the Duke of Kingston because you'd rather *work*?"

"I like work," Pandora said curtly.

"Only because you don't have to do it all the time!" A thunderous expression contorted Ida's round face. "Of all the ninny-pated things I've heard you say, that is the *worst thing ever.* You've gone off your nob. To refuse a man such as that—*what can you be thinking*? A man almost too beautiful to live . . . a young, strapping man in the full vigor of his years, mind you . . . and on top of that, he's rich as the Royal Mint. Only a donkey-headed halfwit would turn him away!"

"I'm not listening to you," Pandora said.

"Of course you're not, because I'm making sense!" Heaving a tremulous sigh, Ida bit her lip. "Blest me if I'll ever understand you, milady."

The outburst from her overbearing lady's maid did little to improve Pandora's mood. She went downstairs, feeling like she had a brick in her stomach. If only she'd never met Gabriel, she wouldn't have to face this right now. If only she hadn't agreed to help Dolly, and managed to trap herself in a settee. If only Dolly hadn't lost her earring in the first place. If only she'd never gone to the ball. If only, if only . . .

As Pandora reached the formal drawing room, she heard piano music through the closed doors. Was it Gabriel? Did he play the piano? Perplexed, she opened one of the doors and went inside.

The drawing room was handsome and spacious, with intricate parquetry wood floors, wainscoted walls painted a creamy shade of white, and abundant windows draped with soft folds of pale, semi-transparent silk. The carpets had been rolled back to the side of the room.

Gabriel stood at a mahogany grand piano in the corner, riffling through sheet music, while his sister Phoebe sat on a bench in front of the keyboard. "Try this one," he said, handing her a piece of paper. He turned at the sound of the door closing, his gaze meeting with Pandora's.

"What are you doing?" Pandora asked. She approached him in cautious steps, tense as a horse ready to bolt. "Why did you send for me? And why is Lady Clare here?"

"I asked Phoebe to help us," Gabriel said pleasantly, "and she kindly agreed."

"I was coerced," Phoebe corrected.

Pandora shook her head in confusion. "Help us to do what?"

Gabriel came to her, his shoulders blocking them from his sister's view. His voice lowered. "I want you to waltz with me."

Pandora felt her face go bleach-white with hurt, then red with shame, then white again, like the alternating stripes on a barber's pole. She would never have imagined him capable of such vicious mockery. "You know I can't waltz," she managed to say. "Why would you say something like that?"

"Just try it with me," he coaxed. "I've been thinking about it, and I believe there are ways I can make waltzing easier for you."

"No, there aren't," Pandora retorted in a scalding whisper. "Did you tell your sister about my problem?"

"Only that you have difficulty dancing. I didn't tell her why."

"Oh, *thank you,* now she thinks I'm clumsy."

"We're in a large, basically empty room," Phoebe said from the piano. "There's no point in whispering, I can hear everything."

Pandora turned to flee, but Gabriel moved to block her.

"You're going to try this with me," he told her.

"What is the matter with you?" Pandora demanded. "If you deliberately tried to come up with the most unpleasant, embarrassing, *frustrating* activity for me to attempt in my currently unstable emotional condition, *it would be waltzing.*" Fuming, she looked at Phoebe and spread her palms upward, as if to ask what could be done with such an impossible human being.

Phoebe gave her a commiserating glance. "We have

two perfectly nice parents," she said. "I have no idea how he turned out this way."

"I want to teach you how my parents learned to waltz," Gabriel told Pandora. "It's slower and more graceful than the current fashion. There are fewer turns, and the steps are gliding rather than springing."

"It doesn't matter how many turns there are. I can't even do one turn."

Gabriel's expression was unyielding. Clearly he didn't intend to let her leave the drawing room until she humored him.

Fact #99 Men are like chocolate bonbons. The ones with the most attractive outsides have the worst fillings.

"I won't push you too hard," he said gently.

"You're pushing me too hard right now!" Pandora found herself trembling with outrage. "What do you want?" she asked through gritted teeth.

Her pulse was pounding in her ears, nearly obscuring his quiet murmur. "I want you to trust me."

To Pandora's horror, the tears that wouldn't come earlier now threatened to burst out. She swallowed repeatedly and willed them back, and stiffened against the caress of his hand at her waist. "Why don't you trust *me*?" she asked bitterly. "I've already told you this is impossible, but apparently I have to prove it. Very well. I'm not afraid of ritual humiliation: I've survived three months of the London Season. I'll stumble through a waltz for your amusement, if that's what it takes to be rid of you."

She dragged her gaze to Phoebe. "I might as well

tell you: my father boxed my ears when I was younger, and now one ear is mostly deaf and I have no balance."

To her relief, Phoebe didn't look pitying, only concerned. "That's appalling."

"I just wanted you to know there's a reason my dancing resembles the flailing of a demented octopus."

Phoebe gave her a slight, reassuring smile. "I like you, Pandora. Nothing will change that."

Some of Pandora's anguished shame faded, and she took a deep breath. "Thank you."

Reluctantly she turned back to Gabriel, who didn't look one bit sorry for what he was doing to her. The corners of his mouth tipped in an encouraging curve as he reached for her.

"Don't smile at me," Pandora said. "I'm angry at you."

"I know," he said gently. "I'm sorry."

"You're going to be even sorrier when I heave-ho all over your shirtfront."

"It's worth the risk." Gabriel slid his right hand over her left shoulder blade, the tips of his long fingers reaching her spine. Reluctantly Pandora assumed the waltz position she'd been taught, resting her left hand on his upper arm.

"No, put it directly on my shoulder," he said. At her hesitation, he added, "It will give you more support."

Pandora let him arrange her in a closed hold position, with her right hand clasped in his left. As they faced each other, she couldn't help remembering those moments of being lost in the darkness, when his arms had closed around her and he'd whispered, *Nothing's going to harm you, my sweet girl.* How could that man have changed into this heartless fiend?

"Shouldn't we stand farther apart?" she asked, staring miserably at his chest.

"Not for this style of waltzing. Now, on the first count, as I start the turn, step forward with your right, so your foot is between mine."

"But I'll trip you."

"Not if you follow my lead." He nodded to Phoebe to begin playing, and slowly he guided Pandora through the first rotation. "Instead of an even one-two-three count, the third step will be a long glide, like this."

Stiffly Pandora tried to move with him. She stumbled, stepped on his foot and made an exasperated sound. "Now I've maimed you."

"Let's try again."

Gabriel led her through the pattern of the waltz, which was indeed different from the usual repetitive circles. In the first measure, they completed only three-quarters of a turn, followed by a closed change in the next measure, and then three-quarters of a turn in the other direction. It was a beautiful gliding pattern, and no doubt it was very graceful when executed correctly. But as soon as they went into a turn, Pandora lost all sense of up and down, and the room spun. She clutched at him in panic.

Gabriel stopped and held her steady.

"You see?" Pandora asked breathlessly. "Everything tilts, and I start to fall."

"You weren't falling. You only felt like you were." He reached over to press her palm more firmly against his shoulder. "Feel how sturdy that is? Feel my hand on your back, and my arms around you? Forget your sense of balance and use mine. I'm rock-solid. I won't let you fall."

"It's impossible to ignore what my own senses are telling me, even when they're wrong."

Gabriel led her through another few measures. He was the only steady thing in a world that swayed and careened. Even though this variation of the waltz was much smoother and more controlled than the one she'd been taught, her inner gyroscope couldn't manage even three-quarter turns. Soon she felt herself break out in a cold sweat, a queasy feeling coming over her.

"I'm going to be sick," she panted.

Gabriel halted immediately and pulled her against him. He was blessedly solid and still, holding her, while she struggled to bring the nausea under control. Slowly the sickness retreated.

"To put it in terms you would understand," Pandora finally said, blotting her damp forehead against his shoulder, "waltzing is my carrots."

"If you'll bear with this a little longer," Gabriel said, "I'll eat an entire carrot in front of you."

She slitted a glance up at him. "Would I be able to choose the carrot?"

His chest vibrated with his low laugh. "Yes."

"This might be worth it, for that." Easing apart from him, she put her hand back on his shoulder and doggedly resumed the waltz position.

"If you choose a fixed point somewhere in the room," Gabriel said, "and stare at it as long as possible during the turn—"

"No, I've tried that. It doesn't work for me."

"Then look straight at me and let the surroundings rush by you without trying to focus on them. I'll be your fixed point."

As he guided her into the pattern once more, Pandora had to admit grudgingly that when she stopped trying to orient herself to her surroundings, and focused only on Gabriel's face, she didn't feel quite so sick. He was relentlessly patient, leading her through turns, glides, and change steps, paying attention to every detail of what she said and did. "Don't lift so high on the balls of your feet," he advised at one point. And when she wobbled dangerously at the end of a turn, he said, "When that happens, let me adjust your balance."

The problem was fighting her instincts, which screamed at her to lean in precisely the wrong direction whenever her balance was off, which was most of the time. At the end of the next turn, she tensed and tried to stabilize herself when it felt like she was pitching forward. She ended up tripping over Gabriel's foot. Just as the floor began to rush up toward her, he caught her easily and held her close.

"It's all right," he murmured. "I have you."

"Bollocks," she said in frustration.

"You didn't trust me."

"But it felt like I was going to—"

"You have to let me do it." One of his hands moved up and down her back. "I can read your body. I can feel just before your balance falters, and I can tell how to compensate." His face lowered over hers, and his free hand came up to caress her cheek. "Move with me," he said softly. "Feel the signals I'm giving you. It's a matter of letting our bodies communicate. Will you try to relax and do that for me?"

His touch on her skin . . . that low, velvety voice . . . it seemed to ease every tight place inside her. The knots of fear and resentment melted into fluid warmth. As they took up the position again, it started to feel like they were working together, striving for a common goal.

It felt like a partnership.

Through one waltz after another, they negotiated through various difficulties. Was a turn easier this way or that? Was it better if they made the steps longer or more compact? Perhaps it was Pandora's imagination, but the turns weren't making her quite as dizzy and disoriented as they had at first. It seemed as if the more she did them, the more her body became accustomed.

It was annoying whenever Gabriel praised her . . . *good girl . . . yes, that's perfect* . . . and it was even more annoying that the words made her flush with gratification. She felt herself surrendering by gradual degrees, focusing on the subtle pressures of his hands and arms. There were a few remarkably satisfying moments when their steps matched exactly. There were also moments of near-disaster, when she lost the measure and Gabriel fixed the break in their rhythm. He was a superb dancer, of course, skilled at managing his partner and timing their steps. "Relax," he would murmur every now and then. "Relax."

Gradually Pandora's brain quieted and she stopped straining to oppose the rushing, wheeling scenery and the constant deceptive sensation of falling. She let herself trust him. It wasn't that she was enjoying the experience, exactly . . . but it was an interesting feeling to be so completely out of control and yet realize at the same time that she was safe.

Gabriel's steps slowed before he brought them both to a full stop, lowering their clasped hands. The music had ceased.

Pandora looked up into Gabriel's smiling eyes. "Why are we stopping?"

"The dance is over. We just completed a three-minute waltz with no problems." He pulled her close.

"You'll have to find another excuse for sitting in corners now," he said near her good ear. "Because you can waltz." A pause. "But I'm still not giving your slipper back."

Pandora was very still, unable to take it in. No words would come, not even a syllable. It was as if some huge smothering curtain had been drawn back to reveal another side of the world, a view of places she'd never known existed.

Clearly puzzled by her silence, Gabriel loosened his arms and looked down at her with those eyes like a clear winter morning, while a tawny lock of hair slid over his forehead.

In that moment, Pandora realized it would kill her not to have him. She might actually expire of heartbreak. She was becoming someone new, with him—they were becoming something together—and nothing was going to turn out the way she'd expected. Kathleen had been right—whatever she chose, it wouldn't be perfect. She would have to lose something.

But no matter what else she gave up, this man was the thing she couldn't lose.

She burst into tears. Not dainty, feminine tears, but a messy, red-faced explosion of sobs. The most terrible, beautiful, stunning feeling she'd ever known had come crashing over her in a huge wave, and she was drowning in it.

Gabriel stared at her with alarm, fumbling in his coat pocket for a handkerchief. "No, no . . . you weren't supposed to . . . my God, Pandora, don't do that. What is it?" He mopped at her face until she took the handkerchief from him and blew her nose, her shoulders shaking. As he continued to hover and ask worried questions, Phoebe left the piano and came to them.

Keeping Pandora folded deeply in his embrace, Gabriel cast a distracted glance at his sister. "I don't know what's wrong," he muttered.

Phoebe shook her head and reached up to ruffle his hair fondly. "Nothing's wrong, lunkhead. You came into her life like a lightning strike. Anyone would feel a bit scorched."

Pandora was only dimly aware of Phoebe leaving the drawing room. When the storm of tears had ebbed enough that she could bring herself to look up at Gabriel, she was caught in his transfixed stare.

"You're crying because you want to marry me," he said. "Is that it?"

"No." A hiccupping sob escaped her. "I'm crying because I don't want to *not* marry you."

Gabriel drew in a sharp breath. His mouth came down over hers in a kiss so rough that it almost hurt. As he searched her hungrily, his entire body vibrated with thrills.

Breaking the kiss, Pandora put her hands on his cheeks, and stared at him woefully. "Wh-what rational woman would ever want a husband who looks like you?"

He took her mouth again, fierce and demanding. She closed her eyes, surrendering in a dark half-swoon of pleasure.

Eventually Gabriel's head lifted and he asked huskily, "What's wrong with my looks?"

"Isn't it obvious? You're too handsome. Other women will flirt and try to attract your attention, and chase after you *forever.*"

"They've always done that," he said, kissing her cheeks, chin, throat. "I won't even notice."

She squirmed to evade his marauding lips. "But I

will, and I'll hate it. And it will be so monotonous, looking at a perfectly beautiful person day after day. You could at least try to grow fat, or sprout some hair out of your ears, or lose a front tooth—No, even then you'd still be too handsome."

"I could develop a receding hairline," he offered.

Pandora considered that, reaching up to push back the heavy gold-shot locks that had fallen over his forehead. "Are there bald people in your family? On either side?"

"Not that I know of," he admitted.

She scowled. "Don't give me false hope, then. Just admit it: You're always going to be handsome, and somehow I'll have to find a way to live with it."

Gabriel tightened his arms as she tried to pull away. "Pandora," he whispered, holding her firmly. "Pandora."

If only she could stop the terrible-wonderful feelings that flooded her. Hot. Cold. Happy. Afraid. She couldn't make sense of what was happening to her. Gabriel was murmuring, pouring delicious words into her ear. "You're so beautiful . . . so precious to me. I'm not asking for a surrender, I'm offering you one. I'll do anything. It has to be you, Pandora . . . only you . . . for the rest of my life. Marry me . . . say you'll marry me . . ."

His mouth was on hers, stroking deeply, his hands moving over her, his fingers spreading as if he couldn't feel enough of her. The heavy muscles of his body tensed and relaxed as he altered his hold, trying to fit her closer against him. Then he went still with his lips against her throat, as if he'd realized the futility of words. He was silent, except for his unsteady breathing. The side of her face was pressed against his hair, the gleaming locks smelling like sun and ocean salt. His scent filled her. His warmth was all around her. He waited with merciless, devastating patience.

"All right," she croaked.

His breath stopped, and his head jerked up. "You'll marry me?" He spoke with great care, as if he wanted to make certain there was no misunderstanding.

"Yes." She could barely speak.

A flush of color rose through his tan, and a slow grin emerged, so brilliant that it nearly blinded her. "Lady Pandora Ravenel . . . I'm going to make you so happy that you won't even care about losing your money, freedom, and your entire legal existence."

Pandora groaned. "Don't even joke about it. I have conditions. Thousands of them."

"Yes to all of them."

"Starting with . . . I want my own bedroom."

"Except for that one."

"I'm used to privacy. A lot of it. I need a room in the house that's only mine."

"You can have several rooms for privacy. We'll buy a big house. But we're going to share a bed."

Pandora decided to argue about the bed later. "The important thing is that I won't promise to obey you. I *literally* can't. The word has to be removed from the wedding vows."

"Agreed," he said readily.

Pandora's eyes widened in surprise. "Really?"

"You'll have to replace it with some other word." Gabriel bent over her, the tip of his nose touching hers. "A good one."

It was hard to think with his mouth so close.

"Fondle?" she suggested breathlessly.

He made a sound of amusement. "If you like." As he tried to kiss her again, she strained her head back.

"Wait, there's another condition. About your mistress." Pandora felt him go still, his gaze encompassing her. "I wouldn't like—that is, I can't—" She broke off, impatient with herself, and forced the words out. "I won't share you."

The glow in his eyes was like the innermost heart of a flame. "I said, 'only you,'" he reminded her. "I meant it." His lashes lowered, and his lips came to hers.

And for a long time after that, there was no more discussion.

THE REST OF that day was a colorful blur in Pandora's memory. Only a few moments stood out in the dreamlike haze. First they went to share the news with her family, who seemed delighted to the point of elation. As Kathleen and Cassandra embraced Gabriel by turns and inundated him with questions, Devon took Pandora aside.

"This is what you want?" he asked softly, staring down at her with those black-rimmed blue eyes so much like her own.

"Yes," she said on a faint note of amazement. "It is."

"St. Vincent came to talk with me this afternoon about the solicitor's letter. He said that if he could persuade you to marry him, he would do everything possible to encourage you in your business, and refrain from interfering. He understands what it means to you." Devon paused to glance at Gabriel, who was still talking with Kathleen and Cassandra, before continuing in a low tone. "The Challons come from a tradition in which a gentleman's word is ironclad. They still honor tenant agreements that were made a century ago over a simple handshake."

"Then you think we can rely on his promise."

"Yes. But I also told him that if he doesn't keep it, I'll break both his legs."

Pandora smiled and leaned her head against his chest.

". . . we'll want it to occur soon," she heard Gabriel saying to Kathleen.

"Yes, but there's so much to plan—the trousseau, the ceremony and reception, the wedding breakfast and honeymoon, and of course things like flowers and bridesmaids' dresses—"

"I'll help," Cassandra exclaimed.

"I can't do all of that," Pandora burst out anxiously, whirling around to face them. "In fact, I can't do any of it. I have to submit two more patent applications, and meet with my printer, and look for factory space to lease, and . . . no, I can't let the wedding stand in the way of all the important things I need to take care of."

Gabriel's lips twitched at the comparative importance of the wedding to her board game company.

"I'd rather elope, so I can go right to work," Pandora continued. "A honeymoon would be a waste of time and expense."

She was well aware, of course, that a honeymoon had become traditional for upper- and middle-class newlyweds. But she was terrified of being swallowed up in a new life while all her plans and dreams fell by the wayside. She wouldn't enjoy going away somewhere, thinking about all that awaited her at home.

"Pandora, dear—" Kathleen began.

"We'll discuss it later," Gabriel said in a relaxed manner, and sent Pandora a reassuring smile.

Turning back to Devon, Pandora muttered, "Did you see that? He's managing me already. And he's good at it."

"I know the feeling well," Devon assured her, his sparkling gaze flickering to Kathleen.

In the evening, the Challons and Ravenels gathered in the family parlor before going down to dinner. Champagne was brought out, and toasts were made to congratulate the betrothed couple and celebrate the union of their two families. Gabriel's entire family received the news with a warmth and ready acceptance that almost overwhelmed Pandora.

Taking Pandora lightly by the shoulders, the duke smiled and bent to press a warm kiss to her forehead. "What a welcome addition you are to the family, Pandora. Be forewarned—from now on, the duchess and I will consider you as one of our own children, and spoil you accordingly."

"I'm not spoiled," Ivo, who was standing nearby, protested. "Mother thinks I'm a jewel."

"Mother thinks everyone is a jewel," Phoebe said dryly, as she and Seraphina came to join them.

"We'll have to wire Raphael right away," Seraphina exclaimed, "so he can come back from America in time for the wedding. I wouldn't want him to miss it."

"I wouldn't worry about that," Phoebe said. "A wedding this large will take months to plan."

Pandora lapsed into uneasy silence while they continued to chatter. None of this seemed quite real. In a mere week her life had changed entirely. Her head was full of commotion, and she needed to go somewhere quiet and sort out her thoughts. She tensed as she felt a gentle arm curve behind her shoulders.

It was the duchess, her blue eyes radiant with kindness and a hint of concern, as if she understood how frightening it was to have made the most important decision of her life based on a few days' acquaintance. But there was no way this woman would understand what it was like to face the prospect of marrying a virtual stranger.

Wordlessly the duchess drew Pandora away with her through one of the doors that led to the outside balcony. Although they had spent time together in the company of others, they hadn't yet found an opportunity to talk alone. There were more or less constant demands on the duchess's time: everyone from her infant grandson to the duke himself desired her attention. In her quiet way, the duchess was the hub around which the entire estate revolved.

It was cold and dark out on the balcony, the breeze causing Pandora to shiver. She hoped the duchess hadn't brought her out here to say something disapproving. Something like, *You certainly have a lot to learn*, or *You're not what I would have chosen for Gabriel, but it seems we'll have to make do.*

As they stood side by side at the railing, facing the dark ocean, the duchess took the shawl from her shoulders, unfolded it, and draped it over them both. Pandora was still with astonishment. The cashmere was light and warm, fragrant with lilac water and a hint of talcum. Tongue-tied, Pandora stood next to her while they listened to the soothing *chirr* of a nightjar, and the musical trills of nightingales.

"When Gabriel was about Ivo's age," the duchess remarked almost dreamily, staring out at the plum-colored sky, "he found a pair of orphaned fox cubs in the woods, at a country manor we'd leased in Hampshire. Has he told you about that?"

Pandora shook her head, her eyes wide.

A reminiscent smile curved the duchess's full lips. "It was a pair of females, with big ears, and eyes like shiny black buttons. They made chirping sounds, like small birds. Their mother had been killed in a poacher's trap, so Gabriel wrapped the poor th-things in his coat and brought them home. They were too young to survive on their own. Naturally, he begged to be allowed to keep them. His father agreed to let him raise them under the gamekeeper's supervision, until they were old enough to return to the f-forest. Gabriel spent weeks spoon-feeding them with a mixture of meat paste and milk. Later on, he taught them to stalk and catch prey in an outside pen."

"How?" Pandora asked, fascinated.

The older woman glanced at her with an unexpectedly mischievous grin. "He dragged dead mice through their pen on a string."

"That's horrid," Pandora exclaimed, laughing.

"It was," the duchess agreed with a chuckle. "Gabriel pretended not to mind, of course, but it was qu-quite disgusting. Still, the cubs had to learn." The duchess paused before continuing more thoughtfully. "I think for Gabriel, the most difficult part of raising them was having to keep his distance, no matter how he loved them. No p-petting or cuddling, or even giving them names. They couldn't lose their fear of humans, or they wouldn't survive. As the gamekeeper told him, he might as well murder them if he made them tame. It tortured Gabriel, he wanted to hold them so badly."

"Poor boy."

"Yes. But when Gabriel finally let them go, they scampered away and were able to live freely and hunt for themselves. It was a good lesson for him to learn."

"What was the lesson?" Pandora asked soberly. "Not to love something he knew he would lose?"

The duchess shook her head, her gaze warm and encouraging. "No, Pandora. He learned how to love them without changing them. To let them be what they were meant to be."

Chapter 15

"I SHOULD HAVE STOOD MY ground about the honeymoon," Pandora groaned, hanging her head over the railing of the paddle steamer.

Gabriel removed his gloves, tucked them into a coat pocket, and gently massaged the back of her neck. "Breathe in through your nose and out through your mouth."

They had wed that morning, only a fortnight after he'd proposed. Now they were crossing the Solent, the narrow channel between England and the Isle of Wight. The voyage of three miles took no more than twenty-five minutes from Portsmouth to the harbor town of Ryde. Unfortunately Pandora was prone to seasickness.

"We're almost there," Gabriel murmured. "If you lift your head, you can see the pier."

Pandora risked a glance at the approaching view of Ryde, with its long line of white houses and delicate spires bristling from wooded shores and inlets. Dropping her head again, she said, "We should have stayed at Eversby Priory."

"And spent our wedding night in your childhood bed?" Gabriel asked dubiously. "With the house full of our assembled relations?"

"You said you liked my room."

"I found it charming, love. But it's not the appropriate setting for the activities I have in mind." Gabriel smiled slightly at the recollection of her bedroom, with its quaint framed needlework samplers, the much-loved wax doll with a tangled wig and one missing glass eye, and the bookcase of well-worn novels. "Besides, the bed is too small for me. My feet would hang over the edge."

"I suppose you have a large bed at your terrace?"

He toyed softly with the dark wisps of hair at her nape. "We, madam," he murmured, "have a very large bed at our terrace."

Pandora hadn't yet seen his house at Queen's Gate, in the Royal Borough of Kensington. Not only would such a visit have gone against all propriety, even in the presence of chaperones, but there hadn't been time in the mad flurry of wedding arrangements.

It had taken Gabriel nearly the entire two weeks to find a way for the word "obey" to be struck from the wedding vows. He had been informed by the Lord Bishop of London that if a bride didn't vow obedience to her husband during the ceremony, a marriage would be ruled unlawful by the ecclesiastical court. Gabriel had then gone to the Archbishop of Canterbury, who had reluctantly agreed to give him a special and highly unusual dispensation, as long as certain conditions were met. One of them being an enormous "private fee" that amounted to bribery.

"The dispensation will render our marriage lawful and valid," Gabriel explained to Pandora, "as long as we allow the priest to 'set before you' the necessity of wifely obedience."

Pandora had frowned. "What does that mean?"

"It means you have to stand there and pretend to listen while the priest explains why you should obey your husband. As long as you don't object, it will be implied that you agree with him."

"But I won't have to promise to obey? I won't have to say the word?"

"No."

She had smiled, looking both pleased and contrite. "Thank you. I'm sorry you've had to go to so much trouble on my account."

Sliding his arms around her, Gabriel had viewed her with a mocking grin. "What would I do with a meek and submissive Pandora? There would be no sport in that."

Obviously theirs had been no ordinary courtship, and the need for an expedient wedding was obvious. But as tempting as the idea of an elopement had been, Gabriel had rejected the idea. With all the newness and uncertainty Pandora faced, she had needed the comfort of her loved ones and familiar surroundings on her wedding day. When Devon and Kathleen had offered the use of the chapel at their estate, Gabriel had agreed immediately.

It had made sense to have the wedding ceremony in Hampshire, and spend their honeymoon at the Isle of Wight, just off the southern coast. Often referred to as "the garden of England," the small island was flourishing with gardens, woodlands, tidy coastal villages, and an assortment of inns and luxurious hotels.

But as they approached the island, its charms appeared to be lost on his impatient bride.

"I don't need a honeymoon," Pandora said, glowering at the picturesque town rising steeply from the water. "My board game has to be stocked in stores in time for the Christmas holiday."

"Anyone else in our circumstances would honeymoon for at least a month," Gabriel pointed out. "I've only asked for a week."

"But there won't be anything to do."

"I'll try to keep you entertained," Gabriel said dryly. He moved to stand at her back, his hands gripping the rail on either side of hers. "Spending a few days together will help us ease into our new life. Marriage will be a considerable change, especially for you." He lowered his mouth close to her ear. "You'll be living in an unfamiliar house, with an unfamiliar man—who'll be doing *very* unfamiliar things to your body."

"Where will you be?" Pandora asked, and barely restrained a yelp as he nipped at her earlobe.

"If you change your mind midway through the honeymoon," he told her, "we can go back to London. We'll board a steamer bound for Portsmouth Harbour Station, ride a direct train line to Waterloo station, and reach our front doorstep in no more than three hours."

The statement seemed to mollify her. As the steamer continued the crossing, Pandora tugged off her left glove to admire her wedding ring, as she'd already done a dozen times that day. Gabriel had chosen a loose sapphire from the collection of Challon family jewels, and had it set in a gold and diamond ring mounting. The Ceylon sapphire, cut and polished into a smooth dome, was a rare stone that gleamed with a twelve-ray star instead of six. To his satisfaction, Pandora seemed inordinately pleased by the ring, and was fascinated by the way the star seemed to move across the surface of the sapphire. The effect, called *asterism*, was especially noticeable in sunlight.

"What causes the star?" Pandora asked, as she tilted her hand this way and that.

Gabriel tucked a kiss behind the soft lobe of her ear.

"A few tiny imperfections," he murmured, "that make it all the more beautiful."

She turned and nestled against his chest.

Their wedding had been a three-day affair, attended by the Challons, Ravenels, and a limited number of close friends, including Lord and Lady Berwick. To Gabriel's regret, there had been no time for his younger brother Raphael to return from his business trip to America in time for the ceremony. Raphael had sent a telegram, however, and promised to celebrate with them when he returned home later in the spring.

As Pandora had taken Gabriel on a private tour around her family's estate, Gabriel had begun to comprehend exactly how secluded she and her sisters had been for most of their lives. Eversby Priory was a world unto itself. The rambling Jacobean manor, set among ancient forests and remote green hills, had been largely unchanged for two centuries. Devon had begun making much-needed improvements to the estate ever since inheriting the earldom, but it would take time to fully renovate the house. They had installed modern plumbing only two years ago. Before then, they had used chamber pots and outdoor privies, leading Pandora to tell Gabriel with mock gravity, "I'm barely housebroken."

The festivities had provided an opportunity for Gabriel to meet the two Ravenels he hadn't yet encountered: Devon's younger brother West, and Pandora's older sister, Lady Helen. Gabriel had taken an instant liking to West, a charming rogue with a sharp wit and an irreverent manner. As the manager of Eversby Priory's farms and tenants, West seemed to have a thorough grasp of all their issues and concerns.

Lady Helen, who had been accompanied by her husband, Mr. Rhys Winterborne, was far more reserved than the twins. Instead of Pandora's raw and radiant energy, or Cassandra's effervescent charm, she possessed a quality of sweet, patient gravity. With her silver-blonde hair and willowy slenderness, Helen seemed as ethereal as a figure from a painting by Bougereau.

Few people would have envisioned a match between such a delicate creature and a man like Rhys Winterborne, a big, black-haired Welshman whose father had been a grocer. Now the owner of the largest department store in England, Winterborne was a man of considerable financial power, known for his forceful and decisive nature. Since his marriage, however, Winterborne seemed to have become far more relaxed and content, smiling with an ease Gabriel hadn't seen in him before.

Gabriel had met Winterborne several times over the past four years, at the biannual board meetings of a hydraulic equipment manufacturing company. Winterborne had shown himself to be a pragmatic and decent man, with remarkable intuition and shrewdness in business matters. Gabriel liked the Welshman, for all that he lacked polish, but they moved in very different social circles and had never encountered each other outside of business meetings.

Now it seemed that Gabriel and Winterborne would be seeing a great deal of each other. Not only had they both married into an extraordinarily close-knit family, but Winterborne was a mentor to Pandora. For the past year, he had encouraged and advised Pandora about her board game company, and had made a firm commitment to stock her game in his department store. Pandora made no secret of her gratitude and affection for the man. In fact, she hung on to his every word, and glowed at his attention.

As Gabriel had seen how comfortable they were with each other, he'd struggled with an unexpected pang of jealousy. The realization appalled him. He'd never been jealous or possessive of anyone in his life, having considered himself above such petty emotions. But when it came to Pandora, he was no better than a primitive brute. He wanted her all to himself, every word and glance, every touch of her hand, every glint of light on her hair and breath from her lips. He was jealous of the air that touched her skin.

It didn't help that Pandora was so determined to remain independent from him, like a small sovereign nation afraid of being conquered and absorbed by a powerful neighbor. Every day she added more conditions to her list of marital boundaries, as if she needed to protect herself from him.

When Gabriel had discussed it privately with Phoebe, his sister had given him an incredulous glance and said, "There are items in the meat larder that are older than your relationship with Pandora. You can't expect eternal love and devotion from a woman after a mere two weeks' acquaintance." She had laughed affectionately at his disgruntled expression. "Oh, I forgot. You're Gabriel, Lord St. Vincent—of course you would expect that."

His thoughts were drawn back to the present as Pandora lifted her face to the cooling breeze.

Wondering what was going on in her restless brain, Gabriel stroked back a lock of loose hair that clung to her cheek. "What are you thinking about?" he asked. "The wedding? Your family?"

"A rhombus," Pandora said absently.

His brows lifted. "You're referring to the parallelogram with opposite equal obtuse angles?"

"Yes, Cousin West told me the Isle of Wight is shaped like a rhombus. I was just thinking that if 'rhombus' were an adjective . . ." Raising a gloved hand to her chin, Pandora tapped her fingertips against her lips. "It would be rhombuseous."

Gabriel toyed with a tiny silk flower on her hat. "Rhombusphobia," he said, entering into the game. "Fear of rhombus."

That earned him a spontaneous grin. Her deep blue eyes became places to frolic and revel in. "Rhombusolotry. Worship of rhombus."

Stroking the exquisite line of her cheek, Gabriel murmured, "I'd like to worship you."

Pandora barely seemed to have heard him, her mind still occupied with the word game. Smiling, Gabriel kept an arm around her as the steamer approached the dock.

After disembarking, they went to a horse-drawn tram which would convey them to the fashionable promenade a mile away. In the meantime, Gabriel's valet, Oakes, directed porters and managed the transfer of luggage from the steamer. The valet would then travel separately to the hotel along with the lady's maid.

Once they reached the promenade, it was only a five-minute carriage ride to the Empire, an opulent seafront hotel situated on a sand beach. The magnificent lodging was equipped with every possible modern convenience, such as hydraulic lifts for conveying packages to all floors, and suites with private bathrooms.

Having never stayed in a hotel before, Pandora was mesmerized by the lush surroundings. She turned in circles to take in every detail of the blue, gold, and white interior, lavishly appointed with marble pillars, hand-painted wallpaper and Italian plasterwork. The maître d'hôtel, who could hardly fail to notice Pandora's interest, offered to give the newlywed couple a personal tour around the public rooms.

"Thank you, but—" Gabriel began.

"We would *love* that," Pandora exclaimed, bouncing slightly on her heels before she recalled herself and went still in a belated attempt at dignity. Gabriel bit back a smile.

Gratified by her enthusiasm, the maître d'hôtel gave her his arm and escorted her through the hotel, while Gabriel followed behind. They went first to the picture gallery, where their guide proudly pointed out the fine portraits of the hotel owner's family, as well as a landscape by Turner and a painting of children and dogs by the Dutch master Jan Steen.

Next they visited the hotel's French restaurant, where Pandora was shocked and delighted to observe that mixed dining was allowed in the main room, instead of relegating ladies to small private rooms. The maître d'hôtel assured Pandora that men and women dining together in fine hotel restaurants was already the done thing in Paris. In a manner of highest confidentiality, he discreetly pointed out a table occupied by an Indian prince and his wife, and another where a renowned American financier dined with his wife and daughters.

The tour continued along a wide gallery surrounding an indoor garden with a soaring roof of iron and glass. As the maître d'hôtel expounded on the amenities of the hotel . . . a water supply drawn from its own artesian well . . . sea-breeze gardens where afternoon tea was served daily . . . a full ballroom paneled with red Verona marble and lit with Louis XIV crystal chandeliers . . . Gabriel's patience rapidly wore thin.

"Thank you for the tour," Gabriel finally interrupted as they neared the grand staircase with its balustrade of wrought bronze imported from Brussels, decorated with scenes of the twelve feats of Hercules. There was no doubt the maître d'hôtel would describe each feat in excruciating detail. "We are much obliged. However, I'm afraid Lady St. Vincent and I have already taken up too much of your time. We'll retire to our suite now."

"But my lord . . . I have not yet related the story of Hercules defeating the Lernean Hydra," the maître d'hôtel said, gesturing to a scene on the balustrade. At Gabriel's glance of refusal, he persisted hopefully, "Hercules and the Horses of Diodemes . . . ?"

Ignoring Pandora's longing glance at the staircase, Gabriel thanked the man once more and tugged her up the steps with him.

"But he was about to tell us a dozen stories," Pandora protested in a whisper.

"I know." Gabriel didn't stop until they had reached their private suite, where their valet and lady's maid had just finished unpacking their luggage. Although Ida was ready to help Pandora change from her traveling clothes, Gabriel decided to dismiss her. "I'll take care of Lady St. Vincent. You and Oakes won't be needed for a while."

Although the statement was hardly salacious, either in content or delivery, the fair-haired, round-faced lady's maid blushed a deep shade of pink and bobbed a curtsey. She paused only for a brief, tersely muttered exchange with Pandora before departing the suite with the valet.

"What did she say to you just now?" Gabriel asked Pandora, following as she investigated the suite, which including sitting rooms, service rooms, bedrooms, bathrooms, and a private veranda with a view of the ocean.

"She told me to drape my dress across a chair rather than throw it on the floor. Also she complained because I set my hat on a chair and soon someone's going to sit on it."

Gabriel frowned. "Her manner with you is too familiar. I've half a mind to dismiss her."

"Ida is the Genghis Khan of lady's maids," Pandora conceded, "but she's very good at reminding me about things I tend to forget, and finding things I've lost." Her voice echoed slightly as she went into the marble-tiled bathroom. "Also, she told me I was a donkey-headed halfwit if I didn't marry you."

"We'll keep her," he said decisively. Entering the bathroom, he found Pandora bending over the large porcelain bathtub, fiddling with two sets of spigots and faucets, one silver-plated, the other polished brass.

"Why are there so many of these fixtures?" she asked.

"One set is for freshwater bathing, the other for seawater."

"Truly? I could take a seawater bath right here?"

"Indeed." Gabriel grinned at her expression. "Are we a bit less surly about our honeymoon now?"

Pandora gave him a sheepish smile. "Perhaps a little," she admitted. In the next moment she threw herself at him impulsively, her arms circled around his neck.

Feeling the fine tremors that ran continuously through her slender body, Gabriel held her more firmly, his amusement fading. "Why are you trembling, love?"

Pandora kept her face against his chest. "I'm dreading tonight."

Of course. She was a bride on her wedding night, facing the prospect of climbing into bed with a man she scarcely knew, with the certainty that there would be pain and embarrassment. A wave of tenderness came over him, but at the same time, disappointment settled like a stack of bricks on his chest. There would likely be no consummation tonight. He would have to be patient. He would resign himself to whatever preliminaries she would allow, and then perhaps in a day or two, she might be willing to—

"I'd rather do it right now," she said, "so I can stop worrying."

The statement derailed Gabriel so completely that he couldn't speak.

"I'm as nervous as a Christmas Eve goose," Pandora continued. "I won't be able to eat dinner, or read, or do anything until it's over with. Even if it turns out to be pure agony, I'd prefer that to waiting."

His heart leapt in relief and desire, and he let out a controlled breath. "Darling love, it won't be agony. I promise you'll enjoy it." He paused before adding wryly, "Most of it." Ducking his head, he found a soft place on her throat with his lips, and felt the tight ripple of her swallow. "You liked our midnight rendezvous, didn't you?" he asked softly. Another swallow, and she nodded. He could feel the effort she was making to relax, to trust him.

He sought her lips, urging them to part with the lightest touches of his tongue. Her response was soft at first, the innocently carnal mouth following his teasing caresses. She relaxed and leaned against him, and he could feel her attention centering on him, all her vitality pouring into him. The hairs at the back of his neck bristled in excitement, while heat danced and rioted in every part of his body. With difficulty, he ended the kiss, cradling her face in his hands, watching her long inky lashes sweep upward to reveal drowsy blue-black eyes.

"Why don't I send for some champagne?" he suggested. "It will help you to relax." He stroked her cheeks with his thumbs. "And then I want to give you a present."

Pandora's dark winged brows drew together. "A literal present?"

Gabriel responded with a puzzled smile. "Yes. How could it be otherwise?"

"I thought 'give you a present' might be a metaphor." Her gaze flicked in the direction of the bedroom. "For *that*."

He began to laugh. "I wouldn't presume to flatter myself quite so extravagantly. You'll have to inform me later if my lovemaking is a gift or not." Still chuckling, he bent to press his lips to hers.

He adored her. There was no one like her, and she belonged to him completely . . . although he knew better than to say that out loud.

ANY OF THE awkwardness Pandora might have felt while being undressed by a man was eclipsed by Gabriel's continuing amusement. He kept breaking out into chuckles until she demanded, "Are you still laughing over your metaphor?"

That set him off again. "It wasn't a metaphor."

Although Pandora wanted to point out that most brides would not appreciate their husbands laughing like hyenas while removing their clothing, she was fairly certain that anything she said would only prolong his amusement. She waited until her corset was unhooked, leaving her only in her chemise and drawers, and then she dashed to the bed and plunged beneath the covers. "Gabriel?" she asked, pulling the bedclothes up to her neck. "Instead of champagne . . . may I have a glass of port? Or is that only for gentlemen?"

Her husband came to the bedside and bent to kiss her. "If you like port, my love, that's what you shall have."

While he left to ring for a servant, Pandora removed her undergarments beneath the covers. She dropped them over the edge of the mattress and propped an extra pillow behind her.

In a few minutes, Gabriel returned and sat on the edge of the bed. Taking one of her hands, he placed a rectangular leather case on her palm.

"Jewelry?" Pandora asked, suddenly feeling shy. "There was no need for that."

"It's customary for the groom to give the bride a gift on the wedding day."

After unlatching the tiny gold clasp, Pandora opened the case and beheld a double-stranded pearl necklace on a bed of red velvet. Her eyes widened, and she lifted one of the strands, gently rolling the lustrous ivory pearls between her fingers. "I never imagined having something so fine. Thank you."

"Do they please you, sweet?"

"Oh, so very much—" Pandora began, and stopped as she saw the gold clasp, glittering with diamonds. It was fashioned with two interlocking parts of swirling, deeply cut leaves. "Acanthus scrolls," she said with a crooked grin. "Like the ones in the settee at the Chaworth ball."

"I have a fondness for those acanthus scrolls." His gaze caressed her as she put on the necklace. The double strands were so long that there was no need to unfasten the clasp. "They kept you in place just long enough for me to catch you."

Pandora grinned, enjoying the cool, sensuous weight of the pearls as they slid against her neck and chest. "I think you were the one who was caught, my lord."

Gabriel reached out to touch the curve of her bare shoulder with his fingertips, and followed the pearl strands over her breast. "Your captive for life, my lady."

Pandora leaned forward to kiss him. His mouth was warm and firm, shaping hers deliciously. Her eyes closed and her lips parted, and she was conscious of nothing in the world except the tantalizing stroke of his mouth, and the silky touches of his tongue. She was lightheaded from the penetrating sweetness of his kiss, her lungs dilating as if she were inhaling hot mist. She didn't realize the sheets and blankets had fallen to her waist until she felt his hand at her breast. His thumb lightly rolled a strand of pearls across the sensitive peak, back and forth. A quiver ran through her, and the pounding of her heart strengthened until she could feel it in her cheeks, throat, breasts, and wrists.

He kissed her slowly, his tongue sinking deeper, deeper, until she moaned at the pleasure of it. She tried to squirm free of the covers, forgetting everything but the need to be closer to him. In the next moment he had her stretched out on the mattress, his fully clothed body covering her naked one. The masculine weight of him was satisfying and exciting, his aroused flesh jutting against her stomach and between her thighs. As she writhed upward into the stimulating pressure, she felt as if butterflies were dancing and fluttering inside.

Gabriel breathed as if he were in torment, claiming her mouth with long, fevered kisses, murmuring darkly as his hands roamed over her. "Your body is so exquisite . . . so strong and soft . . . the way it curves here . . . and here . . . God, I want you so much . . . I need more hands to feel you with."

If she'd had the breath, she would have told him that he was quite dangerous enough with two.

Wanting to feel his skin, she tugged at his clothes. He moved to help her, although the process was complicated by his reluctance to stop kissing her for more than a few seconds at a time. One garment after another was flung over the side of the bed, until his naked body was revealed, flushed and golden, his torso smooth except for his hair-roughened chest and groin.

After risking a glance at the startling sight of his erection, Pandora's stomach clenched with nerves, and she pressed her face against his shoulder. Once, on one of their rambles around the estate, she and Cassandra had glimpsed a pair of small boys splashing in a shallow creek, while their mother, a tenant farmer's wife, watched over them. The boys had been naked and hairless, and their private parts had been so innocently small as to be hardly noticeable.

This, however, would have been noticeable at a hundred yards.

Gabriel's hand came to her jaw and nudged her to meet his gaze. "Don't be afraid," he said thickly.

"I'm not," she said quickly. Perhaps a little too quickly. "I was only surprised because . . . well . . . it's not like a little boy's."

Gabriel blinked, and amusement deepened the creases at the outer corners of his eyes. "It is not," he agreed. "Thank God."

Taking a deep breath, Pandora tried to think past the attack of nerves. He was her husband, and a beautifully made man, and she was determined that every part of him would be dear to her. Even this rather intimidating part. No doubt his former mistress would have known exactly what to do with it. The thought awakened Pandora's competitive instincts. Now that she'd asked him to discard his mistress, she could hardly prove herself a poor replacement.

Taking the initiative, she pushed at his shoulder, trying to urge him onto his back. He didn't budge, only gave her a quizzical glance.

"I want to look at you," she said, pushing again.

This time he rolled easily, lying down with one muscular arm curled behind his neck. He looked like a lion sunning itself. Propping herself up on an elbow, Pandora set a tentative hand on his midriff, the flesh lean and tightly knit with muscle. She leaned over him to nuzzle the coarsely silky fleece on his chest. His breathing changed as she used the tip of her tongue on a flat male nipple, raising a tiny, diamond-hard point. When he offered no objections, she continued to explore him, trailing the backs of her knuckles to the sleek line of his hip, and down toward his groin, where the sun-colored skin became silkier and warmer. As she reached the verge of softly springy curls, she hesitated and glanced up at his face. The trace of a smile had vanished. His color had heightened, and his lips had parted as if he wanted to speak but couldn't.

For such an articulate man, Pandora thought wryly, her husband had certainly chosen the wrong time to keep his mouth shut. A few instructions, a suggestion here or there, would not have gone amiss. But Gabriel only stared down at her hand as if spellbound, and breathed like a broken steam boiler. He seemed positively helpless with anticipation.

Some mischievous corner of Pandora's heart relished the discovery that this large, virile creature wanted her touch so badly. She scratched her fingertips lightly through the coarse, silky hair, and the heavy shaft twitched against the taut surface of his stomach. A faint groan came from over her head, while the powerful muscles of his thighs contracted visibly. Feeling braver, she scooted down on the bed and delicately grasped the rigid length of him. It was as hot as a fire-iron, and very nearly as hard. The skin was satiny and fever-colored, and judging from the way he shivered, intensely sensitive. Fascinated, she dared to fondle up and down the shaft, and molded her fingers over the tight-mounded weights below.

His breathing roughened. The scent of him here was clean like white soap, but tempered with a hint of salty pungency. Pandora drew closer, drawing in more of the beguiling scent. On impulse, she pursed her lips and blew a long, cool stream of air all along the length of him.

Gabriel reached down to her head with an incoherent sound. Leaning closer, she touched him with her tongue, and licked upward as if it were a stick of sugar-candy. The texture of him was silken and plush, like nothing she'd ever felt before.

Catching her beneath her arms, Gabriel pulled her upward until she straddled his hips, with his hard-swollen erection pressed between them. "You drive me mad," he muttered before crushing his lips against hers. He cupped the back of her head in one hand, carelessly dislodging a few hairpins from the upswept curls, while the other hand slid over her naked bottom.

As Pandora squirmed over him, he guided her floundering movements into a lazy rhythm, his hardness spreading the folds of her sex with silky friction.

The crisp fur on his chest teased the tips of her breasts and sent darts of fire down to the quick of her body. The strokes against her sex became even smoother and silkier, a strange and lascivious feeling, glides of heat and moisture . . .

Her head jerked up, and she froze, her face turning scarlet.

"I . . . it's wet . . ." she whispered, mortified.

"Yes." Gabriel's eyes were heavy-lidded, lashes shadowing drowsy depths of starlight blue. Before she could say another word, he had pulled her high enough to fasten his mouth to her breast. She moaned as he resumed the rhythm beneath her, making her ride the slick, searing hardness, his hands kneading her bottom. He was slow and relentless, teasing until she was brimming with sensation, desperate for the tension to spill into relief.

Rolling carefully, Gabriel pressed her onto her back and began to browse over her body with hot, feathery kisses. His hands wandered over her skillfully, causing downy hairs to prickle and lift everywhere. His fingertips traced sinuous patterns inside her leg, venturing higher and higher, finally reaching the smoldering softness between her thighs. How gently he touched her. She felt the subtle, centering pressure of a fingertip, and stiffened as it slid forward. The intrusion burned as her inner muscles tightened to keep him out. He murmured against her stomach, and although she couldn't make out the words, the low resonance of his voice soothed her.

The finger worked deeper, finding sensitive places that made her gasp. His mouth descended to the triangle of curls, searching among the soft folds. He kept her balanced on the edge of intense pleasure, kissing and suckling at the little crest of her sex, while his finger played inside her. She couldn't help grinding her hips in tightly curtailed movements, begging wordlessly for relief. His touch withdrew briefly, only to return with more pressure, and she realized he had added another finger. She began to protest, but then his mouth did something so amazing that she gasped and spread her shaking thighs.

Patiently, tenderly, he coaxed and caressed her, his tongue flicking at a steady pace, bringing up the pleasure in a powerful surge. She moaned and strained against him, her pelvis tilting upward. A moment of stillness came over her right before the blinding release began, rushing all through her. She twisted, cried out, panted, sobbed, lost to shame in her husband's arms. After the last faint quivers had faded, she was too dazed to move. His fingers slid from her, leaving her with a strange, empty feeling, the entrance to her body dilated and throbbing.

Moving over her, Gabriel settled between her thighs and slid an arm beneath her neck. "Stay relaxed, sweet," he whispered. "Just like that."

Pandora didn't have a choice—her body was as limp as an empty glove.

He reached down, and she felt a glassy-smooth hardness stroking over her vulnerable opening, circling slowly. Searing-hot, heavy, the blunt tip nudged into the soft cove. He filled her gradually, the pressure enormous and inescapable, and the pain took her breath away as she felt herself being stretched wider than she would have thought possible. Her flesh throbbed sharply around scalding tightness.

Gabriel held still and stared down at her with concern, waiting for her to adjust to him. Smoothing wisps of hair back from her face, he kissed her forehead.

"You don't have to wait," Pandora said, closing her eyes against a sudden smart of tears.

She felt the brush of his lips against her eyelids. "I want to," he whispered. "I want to stay inside you as long as possible. The pleasure you give me . . . it's like discovering lovemaking for the first time." He brought her mouth to his in a softly erotic blaze that sent the butterflies whirling in her stomach again. Her muscles clamped convulsively on the hardness inside her, and she felt him push deeper each time. Somehow her body made room for him, yielding to the insistent penetration. It wasn't quite as painful now, subtle ripples of pleasure rising through the discomfort. He moved with great care, the heat of him pressing astonishingly deep within her, sliding in like silk.

Pandora lifted her arms around his neck, and tilted her head back as he kissed her throat. "What should I do?" she asked breathlessly.

Gabriel let out a quiet groan, his forehead drawn as if he were in pain. "Just hold me," he said hoarsely. "Keep all the pieces of me together. My God—I've never—" He broke off and thrust deep, and shuddered until she felt his rough tremors at her core, and she wrapped her arms and legs around him, holding him with every part of herself.

After a long time, he stopped shivering and collapsed in weary satisfaction, moving partially to the side to keep from crushing her.

Pandora played with the damp locks of his hair at the back of his neck, and traced the neat shape of his ear. "Your lovemaking," she informed him, "is a gift."

And she felt the curve of his smile against her shoulder.

Chapter 16

"I'VE NEVER SPENT SO much time in bed," Pandora said four days later, as late-morning light stole in through a crack in the draperies. "Not even when I was sick." Other than a handful of outings, such as a walking excursion to view ancient Saxon statues, and taking afternoon tea in the hotel's outside gardens—they had stayed in the privacy of their suite. "I need to do something productive."

A lazy masculine arm curved around her front, pulling her back against a hard, furry chest. Gabriel's voice was like dark velvet against her ear. "I, for one, have been exceptionally productive."

"I meant something useful."

"You have been useful." His palm smoothed over her naked hip.

"Doing what?"

"Satisfying my needs."

"Not very well, it seems, or I wouldn't have to keep doing it." Pandora began to crawl across the mattress as if to escape the bed, and giggled as he pounced on her.

"You do it too well. It makes me want you all the more." Gabriel settled over her, pinning her in place. His mouth lowered to her shoulder for a brief, soft bite. "You obsess me, with your sweet mouth and clever little hands . . . your beautiful back . . . and legs . . ."

"You need a hobby," Pandora said severely as she felt his erection against her bottom. "Have you ever tried writing poetry? Building a ship in a bottle?"

"You're my hobby." He pressed his lips to the back of her neck, having discovered it was a particularly sensitive place.

Gabriel was a tender and passionate lover, exploring every inch of her with ruthless patience. He taught her about the slow build of anticipation, about the infinite ways to heighten desire. For languid hours he would guide her from one erotic sensation to the next, until she was overcome with shuddering waves of pleasure. At other times, he played rough-and-tumble, teasing her into a state of wildness and satisfying her with deep, powerful thrusts. She was always a little disoriented afterward, euphoric and shaky, but he would hold and caress her until she relaxed into a dreamless sleep. She'd never slept like this in her life, all through the night and late into the morning.

When evening approached, they would order dinner up to their suite. A pair of hotel stewards, both wearing noiseless slippers, would come to the sitting room to cover the round table with spotless white linen, and arrange place settings of china, silver, and crystal. They would set out little bowls of water, each topped with a perfect sprig of lemon verbena, for rinsing one's fingers between courses. After bringing trays of steaming silver-covered dishes, the stewards would leave to allow them to serve themselves in privacy.

During dinner, Gabriel was an entertaining companion, amusing her with an endless supply of stories. He was willing to discuss any subject, and encouraged her to speak frankly and ask as many questions as she liked. Whenever she jumped from one topic to another seemingly unrelated one, it didn't appear to bother him. It seemed that no matter what her faults were, he was willing to accept her for who she was, and who she was not.

At the end of the meal, the house stewards would return to remove the dishes, and bring tiny cups of Turkish coffee, a plate of French cheese, and a tray of bottled liqueurs. Pandora loved the jewel-colored liqueurs, which were served in miniature crystal glasses shaped like thimbles with flared rims. However, they were deceptively strong, as she discovered one evening when she made the mistake of trying three different kinds. As she tried to rise from her chair, her legs wobbled dangerously, and Gabriel quickly reached out to pull her into his lap.

"My balance is off," she said in befuddlement.

Gabriel smiled. "I suspect it was that extra glass of *Crème de Noyaux*."

Pandora twisted to cast a perplexed glance at the half-filled glass of almond cream liqueur. "But I didn't even finish it." With effort, she leaned over to grasp it, downed the rest in a gulp, and set the empty glass on the table. "There, that's better," she said in satisfaction. Spying Gabriel's liqueur, which he had barely sipped from, she began to reach for that one as well, but he hauled her back with a smothered laugh.

"No, sweet, you don't want a headache in the morning."

Pandora looped her arms around his neck and stared at him with owlish concern. "Have I had too many? Is that why I feel so swignorant?" As Gabriel began to reply, she interrupted him with her mouth and wrapped herself around him passionately.

In the morning, she awoke with a hazy memory of having done remarkably indecent things with him on the chair . . . clothes had been discarded or pulled to the side . . . and at some point she vaguely remembered squirming and bouncing on his lap while savaging him with kisses . . . oh, she wanted to die of embarrassment.

Also, she had a headache.

Mercifully, upon seeing her discomfort, Gabriel didn't tease, although his mouth worked briefly as if to hold back a smile. He had a glass of peppermint water and a headache powder waiting for her, the moment she awakened. After she downed the medicine, he put her in a warm scented bath.

"My head feels like a threshing machine," Pandora grumbled.

Gabriel bathed her with a soapy sponge while she rested her head back against the rim of the tub. "The Germans call it *katzenjammer*," he said. "The way one feels the morning after an evening of drinking. Translated, it means 'the wailing of cats.'"

Pandora smiled slightly, keeping her eyes closed. "I would be wailing, if I thought it would make me feel any better."

"I should have stopped you after the second glass. But I overestimated your tolerance."

"Lady Berwick says a lady always takes wine or spirits within a sober limit. She would be disappointed that I behaved badly."

She felt Gabriel lean over her, his lips brushing her water-speckled cheek. "Let's not tell her, then," he whispered. "Because you're so delightful when you behave badly."

After her bath, he wrapped her in a thick flannel towel and carried her into the bedroom. Sitting on the bed with her, he carefully pulled out the tortoiseshell combs that anchored her hair. Pandora turned onto her front and rested her head on his chest as he began to massage her scalp with gentle fingertips. The slow kneading sent a delicious tingly sensation down the back of her neck. But she couldn't let herself enjoy it fully.

"What's worrying you?" Gabriel asked, his fingertips especially gentle around her bad ear.

"Part of me doesn't want to go back to London," she admitted.

The soothing massage didn't cease. "Why not, darling?"

"As soon as we return, we'll have to send out wedding cards to let people know they can call on us, and pay calls in return, and I'll have to learn the servants' names and the domestic expenses, and make certain the larder inventory matches the butcher's bill. And someday I'll have to give a *dinner party*."

"Is that bad?" he asked sympathetically.

"I'd rather be guillotined."

Gabriel eased her up higher on his chest and began to smooth her hair. "We'll postpone sending out wedding cards until you feel more settled. People can wait to call until you're ready. As for the servants—they won't expect you to know everything straight off. Moreover, the housekeeper has managed the household efficiently for years, and if you don't wish to involve yourself in the details, she'll proceed as usual unless you tell her to change something." His fingertips traced a light pattern over her bare upper back, eliciting a pleasant shiver. "You'll feel better when you make some progress with your board game company. When we return, you'll have your own carriage, driver, and personal footman, to allow you to go wherever you like."

"Thank you," Pandora said, pleased. "Although

there's no need to hire an extra footman. I'll have the second footman accompany me when necessary, the way Kathleen does."

"I'd prefer to hire a special footman, for your convenience and my peace of mind. There's a particular fellow I'm considering—he's vigilant, capable, and trustworthy, and in need of a new position."

Pandora frowned. "I think I should have a say in choosing him, if he's to accompany me everywhere."

Gabriel smiled, stroking the shape of her cheek. "What qualities do you have in mind?"

"I would like my footman to have a cheerful disposition and twinkling eyes, like Father Christmas. And he must be kind and have a good sense of humor. Also patience, and excellent reflexes, because if I'm out walking and thinking too hard, I may not notice if I'm about to be mown down by a speeding carriage."

Gabriel actually paled a shade or two, and gripped her closer.

"There's no need to be alarmed," Pandora said with a grin. "I have yet to be flattened under a carriage wheel."

Looking no less anxious, Gabriel continued to hold her a little too tightly. "The man I have in mind has all those qualities and more. I'm sure you'll be pleased with him."

"I probably will," Pandora allowed. "After all, look at what I tolerate from my lady's maid. A footman would have to be absolutely impossible for me to dislike him."

Chapter 17

"MY FOOTMAN IS IMPOSSIBLE," Pandora exclaimed a week after their return to London. "I have to find another one right away." She had just come back from her first outing in her new carriage, and it didn't appear to have gone well. Closing the bedroom door behind her, she advanced on Gabriel with a scowl while he unbuttoned his waistcoat.

"There's a problem?" Gabriel asked in concern. He tossed aside his waistcoat and began to unknot his necktie.

"*A* problem? No. Many problems. A plethora of problems. I went to visit Helen and the new baby, and then I stopped at Winterborne's, and—Good God, what is that smell?" Pandora stopped in front of him, sniffing close to his chest and throat. "It's all over you. A sort of metal-polish smell, and a bit like something's gone bad in the larder."

"I've just come from the swimming club," Gabriel said, smiling at her expression. "They added chlorine and other chemicals to the swimming bath to keep the water from turning foul."

Pandora wrinkled her nose. "In this case, the solution may be worse than the problem." She retreated to the bed and hoisted herself onto the mattress, watching him undress.

"You were saying about the footman," Gabriel prompted, unbuttoning his cuffs.

He'd been prepared for a few objections about Drago, a former employee from Jenner's, who was admittedly an unconventional choice for a footman. Drago had started working at the club at the age of twelve, and had risen through the ranks from messenger boy to night porter, and eventually to main hall steward. He had no family to speak of, having been abandoned at an orphanage with a note bearing his name.

Gabriel had known him for years. There was no man in London he would trust more to watch over his wife during her excursions about town, which was why he'd ended up paying a small fortune to hire him as a lady's footman.

The role wasn't as improbable a fit as one might have assumed. One of the requirements of a footman was to be well acquainted with the terrain of London, and Drago knew every nook and cranny of the city. He was a physically imposing man, large and muscular, with an air of quiet menace that would intimidate anyone who even thought about approaching Pandora. His disposition was steady, if humorless, and he was not easily provoked. It was second nature for him to notice details of people's dress, postures, and expressions, and identify risks and problems before they occurred.

Although Drago had reluctantly accepted the position, his lack of enthusiasm had been obvious.

"Lady St. Vincent doesn't pay attention to time," Gabriel had told him, "so you'll have to mind her schedule. She tends to lose things easily. Keep an eye out for dropped gloves, handkerchiefs, books, anything she might accidentally leave behind. She's sweet-natured and impulsive, so for God's sake keep swindlers, street-sellers, pickpockets, and beggars away from her. Also, she's often distracted, so don't let her trip on the pavement or veer into the street." Gabriel had hesitated before adding, "She's hard of hearing in her right ear, and it sometimes causes vertigo, especially in poor lighting when she can't orient herself. She'd have my head if she knew I'd told you. Now, do you have any questions?"

"Yes. Am I supposed to be a footman or a bloody nanny?"

Gabriel had leveled a steady gaze at him. "I understand this may seem like a step down from working at the club. But to me, there is nothing more important than her safety. Lady St. Vincent is a young, curious, very active woman who doesn't think in conventional ways. She has much to learn about the world—and the world has much to learn about her. Protect my wife, Drago. It won't be as easy as you think."

Drago had given him a short nod, the hint of annoyance fading.

Gabriel's thoughts returned to the present as Pandora aired her grievances.

"I wanted a footman with twinkly eyes like Father Christmas, not the eyes of a Viking mercenary. Footmen are supposed to be clean-shaven and pleasant-looking, and have nice names like Peter or George. But mine is scowly and growly, and his name is Drago and he has a black beard. You should have seen when I stopped by the toy department at Winterborne's. He stood by the door, glowering with his arms folded, and all the children grew nervous and started looking for their mothers." She gave Gabriel a suspicious glance. "Does he know anything about being a footman?"

"Not much," he admitted. "Drago has worked at the

club in various positions. But the butler is training him, and he learns quickly."

"Why can't I have an ordinary footman like the other ladies have?"

"Because you won't always be going to the places other ladies go." Gabriel sat on a chair to remove his shoes and stockings. "You'll be looking for factory space, and meeting with suppliers, retailers, and wholesale traders, and so forth. If you take Drago with you, it will ease my mind about your safety." As he saw the mulish set of Pandora's jaw, Gabriel decided to take another tack. "Of course, we'll replace him if you wish," he said with a casual shrug. He began to unfasten the buttons of his braces. "But it would be a pity. Drago grew up in an orphanage and has no family. He's always lived in a small room at the club. He was looking forward to living in a real household for the first time in his life, and seeing what family life was like." That last sentence was pure conjecture, but it did the trick.

Pandora sent him a long-suffering glance and heaved a sigh. "Oh, all right. I suppose I'll have to keep him. And train him not to scare people." Dramatically she fell backward on the bed, arms and legs akimbo. Her small, glum voice floated up to the ceiling. "My very own footmonster."

Gabriel regarded the small, splayed figure on the bed, feeling a rush of mingled amusement and lust that made his breath catch. Before another second had passed, he'd climbed over her, crushing her mouth with his.

"What are you doing?" Pandora asked with a spluttering laugh, twisting beneath him.

"Accepting your invitation."

"What invitation?"

"The one you gave me by reclining on the bed in that seductive pose."

"I flopped backward like a dying trout," she protested, squirming as he began to hike up her skirts.

"You knew I wouldn't be able to resist."

"Take a bath first," she implored. "You're not fit for the house. I should take you out to the stables and scrub you like one of the horses, with carbolic soap and a birch brush."

"Oh, you naughty girl . . . yes, let's do that." His hand wandered lecherously under her skirts.

Pandora yelped with laughter and wrestled him. "Stop, you're contaminated! Come to the bathroom and I'll wash you."

He pinned her down. "You'll be my bath handmaiden?" he asked provocatively.

"You'd like that, wouldn't you?"

"I would," he whispered, touching his tongue to the center of her lower lip.

Her dark blue eyes were bright with mischief. "I'll bathe you, my lord," she offered, "but only if you agree to keep your hands to yourself, and remain as still and stiff as a statue."

"I'm already as stiff as a statue." He nudged her to demonstrate.

Pandora rolled out from under him with a grin and headed toward the bathroom, while he followed readily.

It amazed Gabriel to reflect that just a short time ago, he'd believed that no woman would ever please him as Nola Black had, with her "subversive talents," as his father had dryly put it. But even in their most passionate moments, his encounters with Nola had always left him hungering for something nameless and elusive. An intimacy that went beyond the joining of physical parts. Whenever he and Nola had tried to let down their guards with each other, even briefly, her sharp edges—and his—had left mutual scars. Neither of them had been able to take the risk of sharing the flaws and weaknesses they each guarded so fiercely.

But everything was different with Pandora. She was a force of nature, unable to be anything other than entirely herself, and somehow that made it impossible for him to maintain any pretenses around her. Whenever he admitted to having flaws or making mistakes, she seemed to like him all the better for them. She had unlocked his heart with terrifying ease, and thrown away the key.

He loved her more than was good for either of them. She filled him with a wellspring of joy he'd never connected to the sexual act before. No wonder he lusted after her constantly. No wonder he felt so possessive, and worried every moment she was out of his sight. Pandora had no idea how fortunate she was that he didn't insist on sending her out with a bodyguard of assorted marksmen, cavalry, Scottish archers, and a few Japanese samurai thrown in for good measure.

It was insane to let a creature so perfectly beautiful and artlessly spirited and vulnerable as his wife venture out into a world that could crush her with casual unconcern, and he had no choice but to allow it. But he had no illusions about ever being comfortable with it. For the rest of his life, he would feel a stab of dread every time she walked out the door, leaving him there with his heart wide open.

BEFORE GABRIEL DEPARTED the next morning for a business meeting with an architect and builder—something about granting a speculative building lease on property he owned in Kensington—he set a stack of letters in front of Pandora.

She looked up from the parlor writing desk, where she was laboriously composing a letter to Lady Berwick. "What are those?" she asked with a slight frown.

"Invitations." Gabriel smiled slightly at her expression. "The Season isn't over. I assume you'll wish to decline them, but there may be one or two of interest."

Pandora regarded the stack of envelopes as if they were a coiled snake. "I suppose I can't be unsociable forever," she said.

"That's the spirit." Gabriel grinned at her lackluster tone. "There's an upcoming reception at the Guildhall for the Prince of Wales, now that he's returned from his tour of India."

"I might consider something like that," she said. "It would be better than attending some small, stuffy dinner, where I would feel as conspicuous as the bearded lady at a country fair. Speaking of beards—is there a reason Drago hasn't removed his? He really should remove it, now that he's a footman."

"I'm afraid it wasn't open for negotiation," Gabriel said ruefully. "He's always had it. In fact, whenever he makes an ironclad vow, he swears by his beard."

"Well, that's silly. No one can swear by a beard. What if it catches fire?"

Gabriel smiled and leaned over her. "Take the matter up with Drago, if you wish. But be forewarned: he's very attached to it."

"Well, of course he's attached to it, it's his beard."

His lips caressed hers with lingering pressure, until her mouth opened to take in more of the sultry heat and sweetness. Tenderly his fingertips stroked her throat, teasing a flush to the surface of her skin. He licked into the kiss, the velvety stroke awakening an erotic pang low in her stomach. Her head swam, and she reached out to steady herself by gripping his forearms. He was slow to finish the kiss, taking a last deep taste before reluctantly easing his mouth from hers. "Be a good girl today," he murmured.

Pandora smiled, her cheeks aflame, and she tried to gather her wits as he left. Picking up a glass paperweight with little glass flowers embedded within, she rolled it absently between her palms and listened to the sounds of the household around her. Shutters being opened and dusted, things being scoured, polished, and brushed, rooms being aired out and tidied.

Although Pandora agreed with Gabriel's assertion that they would need to find a bigger house soon, she liked the terrace house, which wasn't nearly as spare and bachelor-ish as she'd anticipated. It was a corner house in a row of terraces, with wide bay windows, high vaulted ceilings, and balconies with wrought-iron balustrades. The house had every possible modern convenience, including a tiled entrance hall that was heated with hot water coils and fitted with a dinner lift from the basement. While Pandora had been away on the honeymoon, Kathleen and Cassandra had brought a few items from Ravenel House to make her new surroundings feel familiar and cozy. Among them were a flowered needlepoint pillow, a soft lap blanket with tasseled corners, some favorite books, and a collection of tiny colored glass candle cups. From Helen and Winterborne, there had been a beautiful new cabinet desk, with a multitude of drawers and compartments, and a gold clock built into the top panel.

The terrace was well maintained by an amiable group of servants, who were in general quite a bit younger than the staff at Eversby Priory, and Heron's Point too, for that matter. They all worked hard to please the housekeeper, Mrs. Bristow, who directed their daily tasks with crisp efficiency. She treated Pandora with a mixture of friendliness and deference, although she was understandably perplexed by the new countess's utter lack of interest in domestic affairs.

Actually, there were a few small things that Pandora was tempted to mention. Afternoon tea, for example. Teatime had always been a cherished ritual for the Ravenels, even in the days when they hadn't been able to afford it. Every afternoon they indulged in an ample selection of tarts and cream cakes, plates of biscuits and finger rolls, scones, and miniature sweet puddings, while steaming pots of freshly brewed tea were brought out at regular intervals.

Tea in this household, however, consisted of either a plain toasted muffin or a lone currant bun, served with butter and a pot of jam. Perfectly nice fare, to be certain, but when Pandora thought of the long, lavish Ravenel teas, this was quite boring and crumb-drum by comparison. The problem was that even minor involvement in household management might lead to more involvement and responsibility. Therefore, it was wiser to stay silent and eat her muffin. Besides, now that she had her own carriage, she could visit Kathleen for tea whenever she wished.

The thought of the carriage reminded her of the footman.

Picking up a brass bell on the desk, Pandora rang it tentatively, wondering if Drago would answer. Within a minute, he was at the threshold.

"Milady."

"Come in, Drago."

He was a large, muscular man with the broad-shouldered build that was ideal for a footman's livery, but for some reason the long-skirted coat, knee breeches and silk stockings didn't suit him. He seemed ill at ease, as if the dark blue velvet and gold braiding were an affront to his dignity. As he watched her with those alert black eyes, she noticed a small crescent-shaped scar that went from the end of his left brow almost to the outer corner of his eye, a permanent reminder of some dangerous event from long ago. His black beard, short and neatly trimmed, looked as impenetrable as otter fur.

Pandora regarded him thoughtfully. Here was a person who was trying to do his best in a situation that was uncomfortable for him. She understood that feeling. And that beard . . . it was symbolic, whether or not he realized it. A sign that he would only go so far in compromising who he was. She understood that, too.

"How do you like your name to be pronounced?" she asked. "Lord St. Vincent says it with an *ah* sound, but I heard the butler pronounce it with a long *a*."

"Neither's right."

As she had learned from their brief, awkward outing yesterday, he preferred to speak with a minimum of words.

She gave him a perplexed glance. "Why haven't you said anything?"

"No one asked."

"Well, I'm asking."

"It's like dragon, without an n."

"Oh." A smile spread across Pandora's face. "I like that much better. I'll call you Dragon."

His brows lowered. "It's Drago."

"Yes, but if we add that one extra letter, people

would always know how to pronounce it, and more importantly, *everyone* likes dragons."

"I don't want to be liked."

With that coal-black hair and his dark eyes—and the way he looked just now, as if he were actually capable of breathing fire—the nickname was so perfect as to be sublime. "Won't you at least consider—" Pandora began.

"No."

She stared at him speculatively. "If you shaved off your beard, would you turn out to be improbably handsome?"

The quick change of subject seemed to throw him slightly off balance. "No."

"Well, in any case, footmen can't have beards. I think it's the law."

"It's not the law."

"It's tradition, however," she said wisely, "and going against tradition is almost like breaking the law."

"Coachman has a beard," Drago pointed out.

"Yes, coachmen can have them, but footmen can't. I'm afraid you'll have to get rid of it. Unless . . ."

His eyes narrowed as he realized she was going in for the *coup de grâce*. "Unless?"

"I would be willing to overlook your inappropriate facial foliage," Pandora offered, "if you let me call you Dragon. If you don't, the beard goes."

"The beard stays," he snapped.

"Very well." Pandora gave him a satisfied smile. "I'll need the carriage ready at two o'clock, Dragon. That will be all for now."

He gave her a surly nod and began to leave, but he stopped at the threshold as Pandora spoke again. "There's one more thing I want to ask. Do you like wearing livery?" Dragon turned to face her. At his long hesitation, Pandora said, "I have a reason for asking."

"No, I don't like it. Too much cloth flying about—" He flipped the skirted hem of the livery coat contemptuously. "And up top, it's cut too tight to let a man move his arms properly." Glancing down at himself, he said in disgust, "Bright colors. Gold braid. I look like a great peacock."

Pandora gave him a sympathetic glance. "The fact is," she said earnestly, "you're not really a footman, you're a bodyguard who sometimes performs the duties of a footman. Inside the house, while you're assisting the butler with dinner and all that, I'm sure they'll insist on livery. But whenever you accompany me outside the house, I think it would be best if you wore your own clothes, as befitting a private bodyguard." She paused before adding frankly, "I've seen the way street urchins and ruffians taunt liveried servants, especially in the more common parts of town. There's no need to subject you to such annoyances."

His shoulders relaxed slightly. "Yes, milady." Before he turned away, she could have sworn that a faint smile had stirred within the depths of his beard.

THE MAN WHO accompanied Pandora out to her carriage was a far different version of Dragon than the awkward footman bound up in livery. He moved with easy confidence in a suit consisting of a well-cut black coat and trousers, and a dark gray waistcoat. The beard that had looked so out of place on a footman now seemed appropriate. One might have even said he looked dashing, were he not so charmless. But then, dragons weren't supposed to be charming.

"Where do you wish to go, milady?" Dragon asked, after he let down the step of the carriage.

"O'Cairre Print Works, on Farringdon Street."

He gave her a sharp glance. "In Clerkenwell?"

"Yes. It's in the Farringdon Works building, behind the—"

"There are three prisons in Clerkenwell."

"There are also flower-sellers, candle-makers, and other respectable businesses. The area is being reclaimed."

"By thieves and Irishmen," Dragon said darkly as Pandora ascended into the carriage. He handed in the leather valise stuffed with papers, sketches, and game prototypes, and she set it on the seat beside her. After closing the carriage door, he went to sit up top with the driver.

Pandora had pored over a list of printers before narrowing down her choices to the final three. O'Cairre Print Works was of special interest because the proprietor happened to be a widow who had run the business since her husband's death. Pandora liked the idea of supporting other women in business.

Clerkenwell was hardly the most dangerous place in London, although its reputation had been tarnished by a prison bombing nine years ago. The Fenians, a secret society fighting for the cause of Irish self-government, had unsuccessfully tried to free one of their members by blowing a hole in a prison wall, resulting in the deaths of twelve people and injuries to scores of others. It had resulted in a public backlash and resentment against the Irish that had been slow to fade. Which was a shame, in Pandora's opinion, since the hundred thousand peaceful Irish-born residents of London shouldn't be punished for the actions of a few.

Once a respectable middle-class area that had fallen to hard times, Clerkenwell bristled with tall, densely crowded buildings sandwiched between tumbledown properties. New road construction would someday ease the warren of congested alleys, but for now the ongoing work had created a series of detours that made parts of Farringdon Street difficult to access. Fleet Ditch, a river that had devolved into a sewer, had been covered by the roadway, but its ominous slushing could occasionally be heard—and unfortunately smelled—through grids in the pavement. The rumbles and whistling of trains cut through the air as they approached the temporary terminus of the Farringdon Street station and a large goods depot that had been built by the railway company.

The carriage stopped in front of a utilitarian red-and-yellow brick warehouse building. Pandora's heart skipped with excitement as she saw the double-fronted shop faced with segmented windows and a carved pediment over the entrance. *O'Cairre Print Works* had been painted on the pediment in elaborate gold lettering.

Dragon was quick to open the carriage door and reach in for Pandora's valise before pulling down the step. He was careful not to let Pandora's skirt touch the wheel as she emerged from the carriage. Efficiently he opened the shop door, and closed it after she entered. However, instead of waiting outside the shop as a footman would, he went inside and stood beside the door.

"You don't need to wait in the shop with me, Dragon," Pandora murmured as he gave her the valise. "My appointment will last at least an hour. You can go somewhere and drink some ale, or something."

He ignored the suggestion and remained exactly where he was.

"I'm visiting a printer," Pandora couldn't resist

pointing out. "The worst thing that could happen to me is a paper cut."

No response.

Sighing, Pandora turned and went to the first in a row of counters that extended across the large interior and divided it into several departments. The print works was the most wonderfully cluttery, colorful place she had ever been in, except perhaps Winterborne's department store, which was an Aladdin's cave of sparkling glass and jewels and luxury items. But this was a fascinating new world. The walls were liberally papered with caricature prints, cards, playbills, engravings, penny-sheets, and toy theater backdrops. The air was perfumed with an intoxicating mixture of fresh paper, ink, glue, and chemicals, a smell that made Pandora want to snatch up a pen and frantically start drawing something. At the back of the shop, machinery clacked and clattered with a start-run-stop rhythm as apprentices operated hand presses.

Overhead, prints had been hung up to dry on hundreds of lines strung across the room. There were towers of mill-board and card stock everywhere, and high columns of paper in greater quantities and varieties than Pandora had ever seen in one place. The counters were piled with trays of printing blocks carved with letters, animals, birds, people, stars, moons, Christmas symbols, vehicles, flowers, and thousands of other delightful images.

She *loved* this place.

A young matron approached. She was tidy and slender and bosomy, with curly brown hair and long-lashed hazel eyes. "Lady St. Vincent?" she asked, and curtseyed deeply. "Mrs. O'Cairre."

"A pleasure," Pandora said, beaming.

"I've never been so intrigued as I was by your letter," Mrs. O'Cairre said. "Your board game sounds very clever, milady." She was a well-spoken woman with the musical hint of a brogue. There was a lively air about her that Pandora liked exceedingly. "Would you like to sit with me and discuss your plans for it?"

They went to sit at a table in a sheltered spot at the side of the room. For the next hour, they talked about Pandora's game and what components it would require, while she unearthed sketches, notes, and prototypes from her valise. It was a shopping-themed game, with pieces that moved around a track that wove through the departments of a whimsically detailed store. It would include merchandise cards, play money, and chance cards that would either help or hinder the players' progress.

Mrs. O'Cairre was enthusiastic about the project, making suggestions about various materials to use for the game components.

"The most important issue is the folding game board. We can do lithograph printing directly onto the board with a flat-bed press. If you want a multi-colored game board, we could create a metal plate for each color—five to ten would be sufficient—and apply ink to the board in layers until the image is complete." Mrs. O'Cairre viewed Pandora's hand-painted game board thoughtfully. "It would be much cheaper if we only applied the image in black and white, and you hired women to hand-color the image. But of course, that would be much slower. If your board game is in high demand, which it will be, I'm sure, you'll make greater profits by producing the game entirely by machine."

"I would prefer the hand-colored option," Pandora said. "I want to provide good jobs for women who are trying to support themselves and their families. There's more than profits to consider."

Mrs. O'Cairre stared at her for a long moment, her eyes warm. "I admire that, milady. Very much. Most ladies of your rank, if they think of the poor at all, do little more than knit stockings and caps for charity groups. Your business would help the poor far more than knit-work."

"I hope so," Pandora said. "Believe me, my knitting wouldn't help anyone."

The woman laughed. "I do like you, milady." She stood and rubbed her hands together briskly. "Come to the back rooms, if you please, and I'll give you a pile of samples to take home and view at your leisure."

Scooping up her papers and game materials, Pandora dumped them into her valise. She glanced over her shoulder at Dragon, who was watching her from beside the door. He stepped forward as he saw that she was heading to the back of the shop, but she shook her head and gestured for him to stay there. Frowning slightly, he folded his arms and remained in place.

Pandora followed Mrs. O'Cairre past a waist-high counter where a pair of boys were busy collating pages. To the left, an apprentice worked a treadle-operated letter press with huge gears and levers, while another man operated a machine with large copper rollers that pressed images continuously on long rolls of paper.

Mrs. O'Cairre led her to a sample room brimming with materials. Moving along a wall of shelves and drawers, Mrs. O'Cairre began to collect pieces of paper, card stocks, boards, binding canvas and muslins, and a variety of type-specimen lettering sheets. Pandora followed closely behind her, receiving handfuls of pages and dropping them into her valise.

They both paused at a discreet knock.

"It's likely the warehouse boy," Mrs. O'Cairre said, heading to the other side of the room. While Pandora continued to browse among the shelves, the printer opened the door just enough to reveal a boy in his teens, with a cap pulled low over his forehead. After a brief, muttered exchange, Mrs. O'Cairre closed the door. "Milady," she said, "I beg your pardon, but I have to give instructions to a deliveryman. Will it trouble you if I leave you here for one minute?"

"Certainly not," Pandora said. "I'm as happy as a clam at high water." She paused to look more closely at the woman, who was still smiling . . . but distress had exerted subtle tension over her features like a drawstring bag being cinched. "Is something wrong?" Pandora asked in concern.

The woman's face cleared instantly. "No, milady, it's only that I don't like to be interrupted when I'm with a customer."

"Don't worry on my account."

Mrs. O'Cairre went to a set of drawers and pulled out an open-ended envelope. "I'll be back sooner than you can take a hop, skip, and a jump."

As the printer exited through the warehouse door, closing it firmly behind her, something fluttered to the floor in her wake. A slip of paper.

Frowning, Pandora set down her valise and went to retrieve the small piece of paper. It was blank on one side and printed on the other with what appeared to be different samples of typographic lettering, but it wasn't organized like the type-specimen sheets. Had it fallen from the envelope that Mrs. O'Cairre had just pulled from the drawer? Was it important?

"Bother," she muttered. Opening the door, she went

after the printer, calling her name. When there was no reply, Pandora proceeded cautiously through a dimly lit gallery that opened to a warehouse working space. A row of segmented windows near the roof let in a wash of greasy light that fell over lithographic stones and metal plates, rollers, machinery parts, and stacks of filter troughs and vats. The heavy smell of oil and metal was cut with the welcome pungency of wood shavings.

As Pandora emerged from the gallery, she saw Mrs. O'Cairre standing with a man, next to the massive bulk of a nearby steam-powered printing machine. He was tall and solid-looking, with a square face and a broad, bunchy chin, as if more than one chin had gone into the making of it. Fair-haired and moon-pale, he possessed brows and lashes so light as to appear nonexistent. Although he was dressed in inconspicuous dark clothes, his stylish chimney pot hat would only have been worn by a gentleman of means. Whatever else he might be, this was no deliveryman.

"Forgive me," Pandora said, approaching them, "I wanted to ask—" She halted in her tracks as Mrs. O'Cairre whirled to face her. The flash of undisguised horror in the woman's eyes was so startling that Pandora's mind went blank. Her gaze darted back to the stranger, whose lash-less cobra eyes regarded her in a way that made her flesh creep.

"Hello," Pandora said faintly.

He took a step toward her. Something about the movement sparked the same instinctive response she felt upon seeing a spider's articulated skitter, or a snake's undulation.

"Milady," Mrs. O'Cairre burst out, quickly moving into his path and taking Pandora's arm, "the warehouse is no place for you . . . your fine dress . . . there's grime and oil everywhere. Let me take you back inside."

"I'm sorry," Pandora said in confusion, letting the woman bustle her quickly to the gallery and into the shop offices. "I didn't mean to interrupt your meeting, but—"

"You didn't." The woman forced a light laugh. "The deliveryman was just telling me about a problem with an order. I'm afraid I must see to it right away. I hope I've given you enough information and samples."

"Yes. Have I caused a problem? I'm sorry—"

"No, but it would be best if you left now. There is much to do here." She ushered Pandora through the office, snatching up the valise by its handles without stopping. "Here is your bag, milady."

Confused and chagrinned, Pandora went through the shop with her, toward the front where Dragon was waiting.

"I'm afraid I don't know how much time it will take," Mrs. O'Cairre said. "The problem with the order, that is. If it turns out that we'll be too busy to print your game, there's a printer I can recommend. Pickersgill's, in Marylebone. They're very good."

"Thank you," Pandora said, staring at her in concern. "Again, I'm sorry if I did something wrong."

The printer smiled slightly, although her air of urgency remained. "Bless you, milady. I wish you very well." Her gaze flickered to Dragon's unreadable face. "You'd best go quickly—the construction and street traffic worsens toward the evening."

Dragon responded with a short nod. He took the bag from Pandora, opened the door, and whisked her outside unceremoniously. They proceeded along the wooden plank walk toward the waiting carriage.

"What happened?" Dragon asked brusquely, reaching out to steer her around a rotting hole in the planks.

"Oh, Dragon, it was so very odd." Pandora described the situation rapidly, some of her words tumbling over each other, but he seemed to follow without difficulty. "I shouldn't have gone out to the warehouse," she finished contritely. "But I—"

"No, you shouldn't." It wasn't a reprimand, only a quiet confirmation.

"I think it was bad that I saw that man. Perhaps there's a romantic involvement between him and Mrs. O'Cairre, and they don't want to be found out. But it didn't look that way."

"Did you see anything else? Anything in the warehouse that didn't seem to belong?"

Pandora shook her head as they reached the carriage. "I can't think of anything."

Dragon opened the door and pulled the step down for her. "I want you and the driver to wait here for five minutes. I have to do something."

"What is it?" Pandora asked, climbing into the carriage. She sat and took the valise from him.

"Call of nature."

"Footmen don't really have calls of nature. Or at least they're not supposed to mention it."

"Keep the shades down," he told her. "Lock the door, and don't open it for anyone."

"What if it's you?"

"Don't open it for anyone," Dragon repeated patiently.

"We should come up with a secret signal. A special knock—"

He closed the door firmly before she could finish.

Disgruntled, Pandora settled back into the seat. If there was anything worse than feeling bored or anxious, it was feeling both things at the same time. She cupped her hand over her ear and tapped the back of her skull, trying to settle an annoying high-pitched tone. It took a few minutes of dedicated tapping. Finally she heard Dragon's voice outside the carriage, and felt the faint jostle of the vehicle as he climbed up beside the driver. The carriage pulled away and proceeded along Farringdon, heading out of Clerkenwell.

By the time they returned to the Queen's Gate terrace, Pandora was nearly beside herself with impatient curiosity. It took all her self-restraint to keep from exploding out of the carriage when Dragon opened the door and pulled down the step.

"Did you go back into the printer's shop?" she demanded, remaining seated. It would be improper to stand outside and talk with him on the street, but there would be no privacy once they entered the house. "Did you talk to Mrs. O'Cairre? Did you see the man I told you about?"

"I pushed my way in to have a look around," Dragon admitted. "She was none too pleased, but no one there could stop me. I didn't see the man."

He stood back, waiting for Pandora to leave the carriage, but she didn't move. She was certain there was something he hadn't told her. If so, he would talk to Gabriel about it, and then she would have to find out about it secondhand.

When he moved back into the doorway and gave her a questioning glance, Pandora said earnestly, "If I'm to trust you, Dragon, you can't hide things from me, or I'll never be sure of you. Besides, withholding important information isn't protecting me. Just the opposite. The more I know, the less likely I am to do something foolish."

Dragon considered that and relented. "I walked through the office rooms, and went out to the warehouse. I saw . . . things, here and there. Glass and rubber tubes, metal cylinders, traces of powdered chemical compounds."

"But those things are common at a printer's works, aren't they?"

A notch appeared between his black brows, and he nodded.

"Then why are you concerned?" she asked.

"They're also used for making bombs."

Chapter 18

As soon as Gabriel arrived home after a long day of meetings, he was greeted by the sight of Drago awaiting him in the entrance hall.

"Milord." Drago moved forward to assist him, but was pointedly shouldered aside by the first footman, who collected Gabriel's hat and gloves. Gabriel sternly suppressed a smile, knowing that Drago hadn't yet learned the order of precedence concerning the small rituals of the household. Certain tasks defined a servant's status and would not be relinquished easily.

After shooting a quick, scathing glance at the first footman's back, Drago returned his attention to Gabriel. "A word with you, milord?"

"Of course." Gabriel led the way to the nearby morning room, where they both went to stand at one of the front bay windows.

As Drago gave him a succinct account of the visit to the Clerkenwell printer's shop, including their abrupt exit, and the suspicious items in the offices and warehouse, Gabriel listened with a growing frown. "What was the chemical compound? Could you hazard a guess?"

For answer, Drago pulled a small, cork-stoppered glass tube from his coat pocket and handed it to him.

Gabriel held it up and rotated it slowly, watching a few salt-like grains roll inside.

"Chloride of potash," Drago said.

It was a common and easily recognizable chemical, used in soap, detergents, friction matches, fireworks, and ink. Gabriel handed the tube back to him. "Most people wouldn't see cause for concern upon finding this at a printer's works."

"No, milord."

"But something about it seemed dodgy to you."

"It was the look of things. The way Mrs. O'Cairre behaved. The man Lady St. Vincent saw. Something's not right about the place."

Bracing one hand on the niche framing of the bay window, Gabriel regarded the quiet street outside, and drummed his fingers on the wood paneling. "I trust your instincts," he finally said. "You've seen enough trouble to know when it's brewing. But the police will dismiss this out of hand for lack of compelling evidence. And I don't know of a detective in the entire department who isn't corrupt or an idiot."

"I know who to talk to."

"Who?"

"Doesn't like his name to be mentioned. He says most London detectives are too well known by their appearance and habits to be of any use. Soon they'll make a clean sweep of the department and create a special branch. That's a secret, by the way."

Gabriel's brows lifted. "How do you know all this when I don't?"

"You've gone missing of late," Drago said. "Something about a wedding."

A smile tugged at Gabriel's lips. "Talk to your contact as soon as possible."

"I'll go tonight."

"One more thing." Gabriel hesitated, almost dreading the answer to what he was about to ask. "Did you have any difficulties with Lady St. Vincent? She didn't argue or try to evade you?"

"No, milord," Drago replied in a matter-of-fact manner. "She's a brick."

"Oh," Gabriel said, bemused. "Good." He headed upstairs to find his wife, puzzling over the statement. In London street cant, calling someone a *brick* was the highest possible praise, used only for a man who was exceptionally loyal and good-hearted. Gabriel had never heard Drago pay such a compliment to anyone. In fact, he'd never heard of a woman being called a brick until now.

Pandora's voice drifted from the direction of her bedroom, where she changed her clothes and had her hair arranged. At his insistence, she slept in his bed each night. She'd offered a few half-hearted objections at first, pointing out that she was a restless sleeper, which was true. However, whenever she awakened him with her tossing and turning, he solved her problem—and his—by making love to her until she fell into an exhausted slumber.

Drawing closer to the room, Gabriel paused with a smile as he heard Ida delivering a lecture about ladylike delicacy, which appeared to have been inspired by an article in a recent periodical.

". . . ladies aren't supposed to rush from room to room trying to help people," the lady's maid was saying. "The article said you should recline on a chaise, all fragile and wan, and make people help *you*."

"And be an inconvenience to everyone?" Pandora asked heatedly.

"Everyone admires delicate ladies," the lady's maid informed her. "The article quoted Lord Byron: 'There's a sweetness to woman's decay.'"

"I've read plenty of Byron," Pandora said indignantly, "and I'm sure he never wrote such twaddle. Decay, my foot. What periodical was that? It's appalling enough to advise healthy women to act like invalids, but to misquote a fine poet in the bargain—"

Gabriel knocked at the door, and the voices fell silent. Making his face impassive, he pushed his way in, and was greeted with the charming sight of his wife dressed in nothing but her corset, chemise, and drawers.

Staring at him with wide eyes, Pandora blushed from head to toe. She cleared her throat and said breathlessly, "Good evening, my lord. I'm . . . changing for dinner."

"So I see." His gaze traveled slowly over her, lingering at the gentle weight of her breasts pushed upward and outward by the corset.

Ida snatched up the circle of a discarded dress on the floor, and said to Pandora, "Milady, I'll fetch a robe—"

"No need," Gabriel said. "I'll take care of my wife."

Looking flustered, Ida bobbed a curtsey and fled, closing the door behind her.

Pandora stood still, radiating nervous energy as Gabriel came farther into the room. "I . . . I suppose Dragon talked to you."

He arched a brow at the nickname but didn't comment. His gaze took in the worried pucker of her forehead, the twitching fingers and fidgeting toes, those eyes as round as a punished child's, and a feeling of overwhelming tenderness poured through him. "Why are you uneasy with me, love?" he asked softly.

"I thought you might be angry, because I went alone into the warehouse."

"I'm not angry. Just slightly tormented by the thought of anything happening to you." Taking one of her hands, Gabriel drew her to a nearby chair and sat with her slight weight on his knee. She relaxed in relief, her arms linking around his neck. She was wearing perfume, a light touch of something flowery and crisp, but he preferred the silky, salty fragrance of her unadorned skin, more potent than any aphrodisiac. "Pandora, you can't take risks by going into unfamiliar places without protection. You're too important to me. Besides, if you deprive Drago of the chance to intimidate and oppress people, you'll demoralize him."

"I'll remember next time."

"Promise me."

"I promise." She laid her head on his shoulder. "What's going to happen now? Is Dragon going to tell the police about what he saw?"

"Yes, and until we find out whether or not it's worth investigating, I'd rather you not venture far from home."

"Gabriel . . . Mrs. O'Cairre is a nice woman. She was very kind and encouraging about my board game company, and I'm sure she would never hurt anyone knowingly. If she's caught up in something dangerous, it can't possibly be her fault."

"Let me caution you, love: Sometimes people you want to believe in will disappoint you. The more you learn about the world, the fewer illusions you'll have."

"I don't want to become cynical."

Gabriel smiled against her hair. "Being just a little cynical will make you a much safer optimist." He kissed the side of her neck. "Now, let's decide how I should punish you."

"Punish me?"

"Mmm." His hands wandered over her slender bare

legs. "You can't learn your lesson properly if I don't reinforce it."

"What are my choices?"

"They all begin with removing your drawers."

A smile deepened the curve of her cheek as he sought her lips. "There's not enough time before dinner," she said, squirming as he reached for the drawstring just below her waist.

"You might be surprised at what I can accomplish in five minutes."

"Based on recent experience, I wouldn't be surprised at all."

Gabriel laughed against her mouth, relishing her impudence. "A challenge. Well, you can forget all about dinner now."

Pandora struggled and squeaked as he divested her of her drawers and pulled her fully onto his lap, with her naked legs dangling on either side of his waist. The corset, with its stiffened fabric and stays, forced her back to remain straight. He tugged down the shoulders of her chemise and lifted her breasts from the supportive half-cups of the corset. He kissed the pale curves, leisurely catching the soft pink nipples with his lips, flicking them with his tongue. Her breathing grew labored within the confining grip of the corset, and she reached down to the front hooks.

Gabriel stopped her, gently grasping her wrists and drawing them back around his neck. "Leave it on," he murmured, forestalling arguments by taking her mouth with his. It was a decoy she couldn't resist, heat instantly taking hold like flame racing through kindling.

Adjusting her weight, he let her bottom settle between his spread knees, leaving her open and exposed. He kept one arm behind her back, while he slid his hand between her thighs. His fingers tickled and stirred through petals and silkiness and tender wet heat, until Pandora quivered in his lap. He knew what was happening to her, the way the corset redirected sensation below her waist in unfamiliar ways. Pressing a fingertip just above the hidden peak of her clitoris, he agitated it softly. Pandora's moans grew louder. He circled the emerging bud and slid his finger to the little cove below, and sank it inside her. He felt her thighs and hips flexing, muscles struggling to bring their bodies closer, to close around the teasing stimulation.

Withdrawing the gentle invasion, he continued to play with her idly, making her wait, making her arch and squirm in rising frustration. He caressed her with skillful, circuitous strokes, avoiding the place she most wanted him to touch. Her eyes were heavy-lidded and unfocused, her face exquisitely flushed. He kept her hovering at the edge of release, gentling his touch every time the erotic torment seemed about to spill over into pleasure.

Cupping his free hand behind her head, he brought her lips to his, and she kissed him almost violently, trying to draw his tongue into her mouth. He gave it to her, and covered her sex with his entire hand, savoring the fiery damp softness of her.

Breaking the kiss with a sigh, Pandora let herself fall forward stiffly and dropped her head to his shoulder.

Relenting, he picked her up and carried her to the bed. He set her feet on the floor and bent her over the mattress. She braced for him, shaking visibly, while he unfastened his trousers. His flesh was hard and almost obscenely swollen, his groin filled with a savage ache at the sight of his wife laying there waiting for him, so trusting and still. So innocent. He thought of what he'd once told her, that there were certain things gentlemen didn't ask of their wives. She'd said something about being willing, but it had been obvious she didn't understand a damned thing about what he'd meant.

His hand moved over her narrow corseted back, hesitating at the bow-knot of laces. Erotic thoughts floated through his head, and he didn't want to hide them from her. He wasn't sure whether revealing more about his private desires would change the way she felt about him. But if there was ever a woman who could be both wife and mistress, who might be able to accept the whole of him, including the complexity of secret cravings and foolish fantasies, it would be her.

Before he let himself think twice about it, he untied the knot of the corset laces. Wordlessly he reached for Pandora's arms, guiding them downward and behind her back. She tensed but didn't resist. The position drew her shoulders taut and arched her bottom upward. His heart drummed as he deftly tied her wrists to the corset, taking care not to make the cords too tight.

The sight of her lightly trussed on the bed sent a wave of overwhelming heat through him. Breathing unsteadily, he kneaded and stroked her bottom. He sensed her bewilderment and curiosity, and saw her wrists flex tentatively against the cord restraints. She was half-naked and he was the one who was fully clothed, but he'd never felt more exposed. He waited for her reaction, ready to free her instantly if she objected. But she was silent, unmoving except for the quick rise and fall of her lungs.

Slowly his hand wandered down between her legs, coaxing them wider. He grasped the aching stiffness of his erection and stroked the head across her melting flesh, back and forth. The arch of her back deepened, and her fingers began to curl and straighten like delicate anemone fronds. She made a low, vibrant sound, and pushed backward against him, signaling not only permission but pleasure. Clearly she would allow this, and other intimacies in the future, as long as she trusted him.

Suffused with relief and excitement, he leaned over her and groaned out a few words, some of them tender, some crude, but he was beyond controlling anything. The second he entered her, she cried out and began to spasm, her inner muscles tightening while his hips rolled in continuous nudges that almost lifted her feet from the floor. Driving deep into the wet pulsations, he rode out her climax to the last helpless shudder, and when at last she lay still and gasping, he tugged at the laces to free her wrists.

He crawled onto the bed with her and unhooked her corset with savage tugs. After spreading the garment open, he tore the thin layer of her chemise down the front. He bent to lick upward from her navel to her breasts. She wriggled as if to escape, and laughed breathlessly as he growled and pinned her hips to the mattress. But he was too far gone for amusement, too maddened by need. He mounted her, his shaft roughly probing until he found the right angle. As he slid inside, her intimate muscles gripped him fluidly, pulling him in to the hilt.

Pandora's face changed, and she turned docile in the way of a wild creature accepting her mate, her hips canting upward to cradle and welcome him. He took her mouth with his, and thrust into the depths of her, building sensation until she began to gasp. He circled his hips, grinding sinuously, sending her into another climax. She nipped at his shoulder, dug in her nails, the little stings of pain inflaming him beyond sanity. Plunging deep, he took his own pleasure, letting it explode and shatter and dissolve him until he was lost in her, surrendering completely, wanting no other woman, no other fate.

Chapter 19

THE FOLLOWING DAY, Dragon reported that his contact in the detective department had agreed to visit the print works in Clerkenwell and question Mrs. O'Cairre. In the meantime, Pandora could go about her usual activities, as the detective saw no reason for undue alarm.

The news was welcome, since Pandora and Gabriel had already agreed to attend a play that evening with Helen and Mr. Winterborne, and have a late dinner afterward. The comedy, a revival of *The Heir-At-Law*, was playing at the Haymarket Royal Theatre, the most fashionable playhouse in London.

"I'd rather not take you to a public place until the investigation is concluded," Gabriel said with a frown, pulling on a shirt in his bedroom. "The area around the Haymarket is notoriously dangerous."

"But I'll be with you," Pandora pointed out, "and Mr. Winterborne will be there as well. Furthermore, Dragon has insisted on going even though it's supposed to be his night off. What could possibly happen to me?" She glanced in the mirror on top of the mahogany dresser and adjusted the drape of her double-stranded pearls over the lace bodice of her lavender-and-ivory evening gown.

Gabriel made a noncommittal sound, folding back

the cuffs of his shirt. "Would you hand me the cuff-links on the dresser?"

She brought them to him. "Why aren't you allowing Oakes to help you? Especially when you're dressing for a formal evening. He must be distraught."

"Probably. But I'd rather not have to explain where the marks came from."

"What marks?"

For an answer, he pulled aside the open placket of his shirt, revealing the little red places on his shoulder where her teeth had nipped him.

Contritely Pandora stood on her toes to examine the marks, her color rising. "I'm so sorry. Do you think he would gossip about it?"

"Good God, no. As Oakes likes to say, 'Discretion is the better part of valets.' However"—his golden-bronze head lowered over hers—"there are some things I'd rather keep private."

"Poor man. You look as though you'd been attacked by a wild beast."

A husky laugh escaped him. "Just a small vixen," he said, "who grew a bit fierce in her play."

"You should bite her back," Pandora said against his chest. "That would teach her to be gentler with you."

Curving his hand along the side of her face, Gabriel tilted her head upward. After nibbling gently at her lower lip, he whispered, "I want her just the way she is."

THE INTERIOR OF the Haymarket was luxurious and opulent, with cushioned seats and tiers of boxes decorated with gold moldings of antique lyres and oak wreaths. The domed rose-colored ceiling was covered in gilded ornamentation and hand-painted depictions of Apollo, while cut-glass chandeliers shed rich light on the fashionably dressed crowd below.

Before the performance began, Pandora and Helen sat in the theater box and talked, while their husbands hobnobbed with a group of men in the nearby box-lobby. Helen was in glowing good health and full of news, and seemed determined to persuade Pandora to join a ladies' fencing class with her.

"You must learn to fence as well," Helen urged. "It's very good for posture and breathing, and my friend Garrett—that is, Dr. Gibson—says it's an exhilarating sport."

Pandora had no doubt that was all true, but she was fairly certain that putting a woman with balance problems in the proximity of pointy objects would have no good outcome. "I wish I could," she said, "but I'm too clumsy. You know I don't dance well."

"But the fencing-master would teach you how to . . ." Helen's voice faded as she looked in the direction of the upper dress circle seats, which were on the same level as their box. "My goodness. Why is that woman staring at you so fiercely?"

"Where?"

"On the left side of the dress circle seats. The brunette in the first row. Do you know her?"

Pandora followed her gaze to a dark-haired woman who was affecting interest in her theater program. She was slim and elegant, with classic features, deep-set eyes with extravagant lashes, and a pencil-slim nose angled perfectly over full red lips. "I haven't a clue who she is," Pandora said. "She's quite beautiful, isn't she?"

"I suppose. All I can see is that dagger-like stare."

Pandora grinned. "It seems my skill at annoying people has now extended to ones I don't even know."

The striking woman was seated next to a stocky older gentleman with prodigious whiskers and a curiously two-toned beard, dark gray on the cheeks and jaw and white on the chin. His posture was military-straight, as if his back had been tied to a cart axle. The woman touched his arm and murmured to him, but he seemed not to notice, his attention fixed on the theater stage as if he were watching some invisible play.

Pandora felt an unpleasant shock as the brunette woman's gaze met hers directly. No one had ever stared at her with such cold hatred before. She couldn't think of anyone who would have a reason to look at her that way, except . . .

"I think I might know who she is," she whispered.

Before Helen could respond, Gabriel came to occupy the empty seat next to Pandora. He turned so that his shoulder partially blocked her from the woman's lethal stare. "That is Mrs. Black and her husband, the American ambassador," he said quietly, his features hard. "I had no idea they would be here."

Comprehending that it was a private matter, Helen hastily turned away to talk with her husband.

"Of course you didn't," Pandora murmured, surprised as she saw a tiny muscle jumping in Gabriel's clenched jaw. Her husband, always so calm and sure of himself, was on the verge of losing his temper right there in the Royal Theatre.

"Would you like to leave?" he asked grimly.

"Not at all, I want to see the play." Pandora would have rather died before giving his former mistress the satisfaction of making her leave the theater. She peeked around Gabriel's shoulder and saw that Mrs. Black was still glaring at her as if she'd been wronged. For heaven's sake, the woman's husband was sitting beside her. Why didn't he tell her to stop making a public display? The minor drama had now started to attract the attention of others who were seated in the dress circle, as well as some in the mezzanine boxes.

It must have seemed like a nightmare to Gabriel, whose every accomplishment and mistake had been scrutinized for his entire life. He had always been careful to protect his privacy and maintain an invulnerable façade. But apparently Mrs. Black was determined to make it clear to most of London society . . . and his wife . . . that they had been lovers. Knowing what a source of shame it was for Gabriel to have slept with another man's wife . . . and to have it made public in this fashion . . . Pandora's heart ached for him.

"She can't hurt us," she said softly. "She can glare until her eyeballs fall out, and it won't bother me in the least."

"This won't happen again, by God. I'll go to her tomorrow, and tell her—"

"No, you mustn't. I'm sure Mrs. Black would love nothing better than for you to visit her. But I forbid it."

There was a dangerous cold flicker in Gabriel's eyes. "You forbid?"

It was quite possible no one had ever said such a thing to him before. He certainly didn't seem to like it.

Pandora touched his face with her gloved hand, gently stroking his cheek. She knew that demonstrations of affection in public, even between husband and wife, were highly inappropriate, but at the moment, all that mattered was comforting him. "Yes. Because you're mine now." She smiled faintly, holding his gaze. "All mine, and I won't share you. She's not allowed to have even five minutes of your time."

To her relief, Gabriel took a slow breath and seemed to relax. "You're my wife," he said quietly, catching her hand as she began to lower it. "No other woman has claim on me." He held it in midair and deliberately unfastened the three pearl buttons at the wrist of her elbow-length kid glove. Pandora gave him a questioning glance. Staring steadily into her eyes, Gabriel tugged at the fingertips of the glove, one by one. Her breath caught as she felt the glove loosen.

"What are you doing?" she whispered.

Gabriel didn't reply, only pulled the glove slowly until it slid away from her arm. Hectic color spread over every inch of Pandora's skin. The sensuous way he'd removed it, in front of so many curious gazes, sent a wash of hectic color over every inch of her skin.

Lifting her bare hand, Gabriel turned it over and pressed his mouth against her sensitive inner wrist, before nuzzling a kiss into the vulnerable cup of her palm. A few happily scandalized gasps and murmurs came from the crowd. It was a gesture of ownership, of intimacy, intended not only to demonstrate his passion for his new bride, but also to rebuke his former mistress. By tomorrow, every fashionable parlor in London would be buzzing with the gossip that Lord St. Vincent had been seen openly fondling his wife at the Haymarket, in view of his former mistress.

Pandora didn't want to be used to hurt anyone, not even Mrs. Black. However, as Gabriel gave her a warning glance, daring her to protest, she kept her mouth shut and decided to take issue with him later.

Mercifully the lights were soon lowered, and the

play began. It was a testament to the quality of the production and the skill of the actors that Pandora was able to relax and laugh at the quicksilver dialogue. However, she was aware that Gabriel was enduring the comedy rather than enjoying it.

At intermission, while Gabriel and Winterborne met with acquaintances in the hallway just outside the box, Pandora and Helen talked privately.

"Dear," Helen murmured, covering Pandora's gloved hand with hers, "I can say from personal experience that it's not pleasant to learn about the women a husband may have known in his past. But very few men lead a chaste life before marrying. I hope you won't—"

"Oh, I don't blame Gabriel for having had a mistress," Pandora whispered. "I don't *like* it, of course, but I can hardly complain about anyone else's faults when I have so many of my own. Gabriel told me about Mrs. Black before we married, and promised to end the relationship, and obviously he has. She doesn't seem to have taken it well, however." She paused. "I don't think he broke the news to her the right way."

Helen's lips quirked. "I don't think there's any way to end an affair happily, no matter how well-chosen the words are."

"The question is, why would her husband tolerate her behavior? She was trying to make a scene right in front of him, and he did nothing about it."

Helen glanced at their surroundings to make certain the box was quite empty, and held up her program on the pretext of reading about the next act. "Rhys told me just before intermission," she said in an undertone, "that Ambassador Black was a Lieutenant General in the Union Army, during the American Civil War. It's rumored that he sustained injuries in battle that make it difficult for him to . . ." Blushing, Helen gave a little shrug.

"To do what?"

"Perform his husbandly duties," Helen whispered, turning even redder. "Mrs. Black is his second wife—he was a widower when they met—and obviously she's still a young woman. That's why he chooses to look the other way when she strays."

Pandora sighed shortly. "Now I almost feel sorry for her." With a wry grin, she added, "But she still can't have my husband."

AT THE CONCLUSION of the performance, Pandora and Gabriel made their way slowly past the swarming hallways, foyers, and box-lobbies to the colonnaded entrance hall. Helen and Winterborne were a few yards ahead of them, but they were difficult to see amid the close-packed crowd. The play had been heavily attended, and the press of bodies was so close that Pandora began to feel anxious.

"We're almost through it," Gabriel murmured, keeping a protective arm around her.

As they emerged from the theater, the crowding was even worse. People jostled and milled in the portico area, clustering among the six Corinthian columns that extended to the edge of the pavement. A long row of private carriages and hansom cabs had massed along the thoroughfare, trapping some vehicles in place. Making matters worse, the gathering of theatergoers had attracted pickpockets, confidence tricksters, muggers, and beggars from nearby alleys and streets. A lone uniformed policeman could be seen trying to bring order to the scene, with little apparent success.

"Both your driver and mine are hemmed in," Winterborne came to tell Gabriel, having pushed his way through the gathering. He gestured toward the southern end of Haymarket. "They've stopped over there. They'll have to wait for some of the street traffic to depart before there's room to move."

"We can walk to the carriages," Gabriel said.

Winterborne gave him a glance of wry amusement. "I wouldn't advise it. A flock of cyprians has just crossed over from Pall Mall, and we'd have to go through the lot of them."

"Do you mean prostitutes, Mr. Winterborne?" Pandora asked, forgetting to modulate her voice.

A few people in the crowd turned to look at her with raised brows.

Gabriel grinned for the first time all evening, and pulled Pandora's head against his chest. "Yes, he means prostitutes," he murmured, and kissed her ear gently.

"Why are they called cyprians?" Pandora asked. "Cypress is an island in Greece, and I'm sure they don't all come from there."

"I'll explain later."

"Pandora," Helen exclaimed, "I want to introduce you to some of my friends from the Ladies' Book Club, including Mrs. Thomas, its founder. They're in the group standing near the last column."

Pandora looked up at Gabriel. "Do you mind if I go with Helen for a moment?"

"I'd rather you stayed with me."

"It's just over there," she protested. "We're going to have to wait for the carriage regardless."

Reluctantly Gabriel let go of her. "Stay where I can keep an eye on you."

"I will." Pandora gave him a warning glance. "Don't talk to Grecian women."

He smiled and watched as she made her way through the crowd with Helen.

"Mrs. Thomas is working to establish reading rooms around London for the poor," Helen told Pandora. "She's incredibly generous, and fascinating. You'll adore each other."

"Can anyone join the book club?"

"Anyone who's not a man."

"Perfect, I qualify," Pandora exclaimed.

They stopped at the edge of a small group of women, and Helen waited for an opportune moment to break into the conversation.

Standing behind her, Pandora pulled her soft white gauze wrap farther over her shoulders and fingered the double strand of pearls around her neck.

Without warning, a smooth voice spoke next to her ear—a woman's voice with an American accent. "You're nothing but a skinny, awkward child, just as he described. He's visited me since the wedding, you know. He and I have laughed together over your juvenile infatuation with him. You bore him senseless."

Pandora turned and found herself confronted by Mrs. Nola Black. The woman was breathtaking, her features creamy-skinned and flawless, her eyes deep and dark under brows so perfectly groomed and delineated, they looked like thin strips of velvet. Although Mrs. Black was approximately the same height as Pandora, her figure was a remarkable hourglass shape, with a waist so small one could have buckled a cat's collar around it.

"That's nothing but bitchful thinking," Pandora said calmly. "He hasn't visited you, or he would have told me."

Mrs. Black was clearly "picking for a fight," as Winterborne would have put it. "He'll never be faithful to you. Everyone knows you're a peculiar girl who tricked him into marriage. He appreciates novelty, to be sure, but it will wear off, and then he'll send you packing to some remote country house."

Pandora was filled with a confusing mixture of feelings. Jealousy, because this woman had known Gabriel intimately, and had meant something to him . . . and antagonism, but also a stirring of pity, because there was something wounded in the biting darkness of her eyes. Behind the stunning façade, she was a savagely unhappy woman.

"I'm sure you think that's what I should fear," Pandora said, "but I actually don't worry about that at all. I didn't trick him, by the way." She paused before adding, "I'll admit to being peculiar. But he seems to like that."

She saw a twitch of perplexity between those perfect brows, and realized the other woman had expected a different reaction, perhaps tears or rage. Mrs. Black wanted to do battle, because in her view Pandora had stolen away a man she cared about. How painful it must be every time she realized she would never have Gabriel in her arms again. "I'm sorry," Pandora said softly. "These past few weeks must have been dreadful for you."

Mrs. Black's gaze turned poisonous. *"Don't you dare condescend to me."*

Becoming aware that Pandora was talking to someone, Helen turned around and blanched as she saw the American woman. She extended a protective arm around Pandora.

"It's all right," Pandora told her sister. "There's nothing to worry about."

Unfortunately, that wasn't quite accurate. In the next moment Gabriel had reached them, his eyes light and murderous. He hardly seemed to notice Pandora or

Helen, all his attention riveted on Mrs. Black. "Have you gone mad?" he asked the American woman in a quiet voice that curdled Pandora's blood. "Approaching my wife—"

"I'm perfectly fine," Pandora broke in hastily.

By this time, the group of Ladies' Book Club members had swiveled en masse to watch the growing scene.

Closing his hand around one of Mrs. Black's gloved wrists, Gabriel muttered, "I'm going to talk to you."

"What about me?" Pandora protested.

"Go to the carriage," he told her brusquely. "It's in front of the portico now."

Pandora glanced at the row of vehicles. Their carriage had indeed drawn up to the curbstone, and she caught a glimpse of Dragon dressed in his livery. However, something in her rebelled at the idea of going to the carriage like a dog that had just been commanded to slink off to its kennel. Even worse, Mrs. Black was sending her a triumphant glance behind Gabriel's back, having succeeded in gaining the attention she'd craved.

"Now see here—" Pandora began, "I don't think—"

Another man joined the conversation. *"Take your hand off my wife."* The saw-toothed voice belonged to the American ambassador. He regarded Gabriel with a sort of resigned hostility, as if they were a pair of reluctant roosters who'd just been thrown into a cockpit.

The situation was worsening rapidly. Pandora looked at Helen in alarm. *"Help,"* she whispered.

Helen, bless her, swept into action, moving between the two men. "Ambassador Black, I am Lady Helen Winterborne. Do forgive my forwardness, but I thought perhaps we might have met at Mr. Disraeli's dinner last month?"

The older man blinked, caught off guard by the sudden appearance of a luminous young woman with silver-blonde hair and the eyes of an angel. He didn't dare treat her discourteously. "I don't recall having had the honor."

To Pandora's satisfaction, she saw Gabriel release Mrs. Black's arm.

"And here is Mr. Winterborne," Helen said, barely concealing her relief as her husband arrived to help defuse the situation.

Winterborne exchanged a swift glance with Gabriel, silent messages flying through the air like invisible arrows. Looking composed and capable, Winterborne began to make conversation with the ambassador, who replied stiffly. It would have been difficult to imagine a more awkward scene, with Helen and Winterborne behaving as if nothing were amiss, while Gabriel stood there in a silent fury. And Mrs. Black was reveling silently in the turmoil she'd created, having proved—at least, in her mind—that she was still a significant part of Gabriel's life. She fairly glowed with excitement.

Any flicker of sympathy Pandora had felt for the woman had vanished. She was rather annoyed with Gabriel for falling right in with Mrs. Black's plan, by reacting angrily when he should have simply ignored her. It had been atrociously easy for Gabriel's former mistress to drag his male instincts down to the level of the farmyard.

Sighing shortly, Pandora reflected that she probably should go to the carriage. Her presence wasn't helping at all, and she was feeling more exasperated by the minute. Even Dragon's limited reserves of conversation would be better than this. Stepping back from the group, she looked for the clearest path to the curbstone.

"Milady," someone said hesitantly. "Lady St. Vincent?"

Pandora's gaze fell upon the lone figure of a woman standing beside a Corinthian column at the end of the portico. She was wearing a plain bonnet, a dark dress, and a blue shawl. As the woman smiled, Pandora recognized her.

"Mrs. O'Cairre," she exclaimed in concern, going to her at once. "What are you doing here? How are you?"

"I'm well enough, milady. And you?"

"I'm well enough too," Pandora said. "I'm sorry about the way my manservant barged into your shop yesterday. He's very protective. There was no way I could stop him, other than crowning him with a heavy object. Which I considered doing, incidentally."

"No harm done." Mrs. O'Cairre's smile dampened slightly, and her clear hazel eyes clouded with worry. "But a man came to the shop today, asking questions. He wouldn't give his name, or say what business he was about. I beg your pardon for asking, milady, but have you talked to the police?"

"No." Pandora regarded her with increasing concern, noticing a film of sweat on the woman's face, and the dilated blackness of her pupils. "Mrs. O'Cairre, are you in some kind of trouble? Are you ill? Tell me how I can help you."

The woman tilted her head, regarding Pandora with an almost affectionate regret. "You're a sweet soul, milady. Forgive me."

A hoarse male shout distracted Pandora's attention. She glanced toward the crowd, startled to see Dragon violently pushing and shoving his way toward her. He looked absolutely berserk. What was the matter with him?

He was upon them before Pandora could take a breath. She was stunned to feel him slam his wrist and forearm hard against her collarbone as if he were trying to break it. A frightened breath escaped her at the impact, and she reeled backward. He caught her and pulled her against his massive chest.

Bewildered, she spoke against the soft velvet of his livery coat. "Dragon, why did you hit me?"

He made a brief reply, but she couldn't hear him above high-pitched screams that had begun to erupt around them. As he eased her away from his chest, she saw that his sleeve had been cut open, as if with a pair of scissors, and the fabric was dark and wet. *Blood.* She shook her head in confusion. What was happening? His blood was all over her. There was so much of it. The coppery smell rose thickly to her nostrils. She closed her eyes and turned her face away.

In the next second, she became aware of Gabriel's arms around her. He seemed to be shouting orders at people.

Thoroughly baffled, Pandora stirred and looked around. What was this? She was on the ground, half-propped in Gabriel's lap. And Helen was kneeling beside them. People were crowding all around them, offering coats, calling out advice, while a policeman worked to hold them back. It was strange and frightening to wake up in such a situation.

"Where are we?" she asked.

Helen answered, her face very white but calm. "We're still at the Haymarket, dearest. You fainted."

"I did?" Pandora tried to gather her wits. It wasn't easy to think, with the way her husband was gripping her shoulder like a vise. "My lord, you're holding my shoulder too tightly. You're hurting me. Please—"

"Darling love," he said in a muffled voice, "hold still. I'm applying pressure to the wound."

"What wound? I have a wound?"

"You were stabbed. By your Mrs. O'Cairre."

Pandora looked up at him in amazement, her brain slow to absorb the revelation. "Not *my* Mrs. O'Cairre," she said after a moment, her teeth chattering. "If she's going around stabbing people, I'm disowning her." Her shoulder was beginning to hurt more and more, the dull throbbing sharpening into pain that pierced down to her marrow. Her entire skeleton rattled constantly, as if she were being shaken by invisible hands. "What about Dragon? Where is he?"

"He went after her."

"But his arm . . . he was hurt . . ."

"He said the cut wasn't deep. He'll be fine."

Her shoulder felt like it had been burned with scalding grease. The ground was hard and cold beneath her, and her entire bodice was strangely soggy. She looked down, but Gabriel had covered her front with his coat. Tentatively she maneuvered her arm to lift the garment.

Helen stopped her, pressing a light hand to her chest. "Dear, try not to move. You must stay covered."

"My dress is clammy," Pandora said fitfully. "The pavement is hard. I don't like this. I want to go home."

Winterborne pushed through the crowd and crouched beside them. "Has the bleeding slowed enough to move her?"

"I think so," Gabriel replied.

"We'll take my carriage. I've already sent word to my staff physicians—they'll meet us at Cork Street. There's a new surgery and clinic in the building next to my store."

"I'd rather take her to my family doctor."

"St. Vincent, she needs to be seen by someone quickly. Cork Street is only a half-mile away."

She heard Gabriel curse quietly. "Let's go, then."

Chapter 20

NOTHING GABRIEL HAD EVER been through had felt like this, real and yet not real. A waking nightmare. Nothing had ever made him afraid like this. Staring down at his wife, he wanted to howl with anguish and rage.

Pandora's face was strained and white, her lips blue-tinged. Blood loss had weakened her severely. She was propped in his lap with her legs extended across the carriage seat. Although she was weighted with coats and lap blankets, she shivered continuously.

Tucking the coats around her more snugly, he checked the bandage he'd fashioned with a pad of clean handkerchiefs. He'd bound it with neckties that went around her arm, crossed over the joint of her neck and shoulder and wrapped beneath her opposite arm. His mind kept returning to the moment when she'd collapsed in his arms, blood welling from the incised wound.

It had happened within seconds. He'd looked up to make certain Pandora had crossed the short distance to the carriage. Instead, he'd seen Dragon fighting his way through the crowd and running full-bore toward the corner of the building, where Pandora was standing with an unfamiliar woman. The woman had been pulling something from her sleeve, and he'd seen the telltale shake of her arm as she flipped open a folding knife. The short blade had flashed in the reflected theater lights as she'd raised it.

Gabriel had reached Pandora just a second after Dragon, but by that point the knife blade had already driven downward.

"Wouldn't it be strange if I died from this?" Pandora chattered, trembling against his chest. "Our grandchildren wouldn't be at all impressed. I'd rather have been stabbed while doing something heroic. Rescuing someone. Maybe you could tell them . . . oh, but . . . I s'pose we wouldn't have grandchildren if I died, would we?"

"You're not going to die," Gabriel said shortly.

"I still haven't found a printer," Pandora fretted.

"What?" he asked, thinking she was delirious.

"This might delay my production schedule. My board game. Christmas."

Winterborne, who was sitting with Helen in the opposite seat, interrupted gently. "There's still time for that, *bychan*. Don't worry about your game."

Pandora relaxed and subsided, her fist closing in a fold of Gabriel's shirt like a baby's.

Winterborne glanced at Gabriel, seeming to want to ask something.

On the pretext of smoothing Pandora's hair, Gabriel settled his palm gently over her good ear, and gave the other man a questioning glance.

"Was the blood spurting?" Winterborne asked softly. "As if in time to a heartbeat?"

Gabriel shook his head.

Winterborne relaxed only marginally, rubbing the lower half of his jaw.

Removing the hand from Pandora's ear, Gabriel continued to stroke her hair, and saw that her eyes had closed. He propped her up slightly higher. "Darling, don't go to sleep."

"I'm cold," she said plaintively. "And my shoulder hurts, and Helen's carriage is lumpy." She made a pained sound as the vehicle turned a corner and jolted.

"We've just turned onto Cork Street," he said, kissing her cool, damp forehead. "I'm going to carry you inside, and they'll give you some morphine."

The carriage stopped. As Gabriel lifted Pandora with care and brought her into the building, she felt terrifyingly light in his arms, as if her bones were hollow like a bird's. Her head rested on his shoulder, rolling slightly as he walked. He wanted to pour his own strength into her, fill her veins with his blood. He wanted to beg, bribe, threaten, hurt someone.

The interior of the building had recently been renovated, with a well-ventilated and brightly lit entrance. They went through a set of self-closing doors to a large block of rooms identified with neatly lettered signs, including an infirmary, a dispensary, administrative offices, consulting and examination rooms, and an operating room at the end of a long corridor.

Gabriel had already been aware that Winterborne employed two full-time physicians for the benefit of the hundreds of men and women who worked for him. However, the best doctors usually attended upper-class patients, whereas the middle and working class had to make do with practitioners of lesser talent. Gabriel had vaguely envisioned a set of shabby offices and a mediocre surgery, occupied by a pair of indifferent physicians. He should have known that Winterborne would have spared no expense in building an advanced medical facility.

They were met in the surgery lobby by a middle-aged physician with a shock of white hair, a broad brow, penetrating eyes, and a handsomely craggy face. He looked exactly how a surgeon should look, capable and dignified, with decades' worth of knowledge earned by vast experience.

"St. Vincent," Winterborne said, "this is Doctor Havelock."

A slender brown-haired nurse strode briskly into the lobby area, waving away Winterborne's attempt at introductions. She was dressed in a divided skirt and wore the same kind of white linen surgeon's gown and cap as Havelock. Her face was young and clean-scrubbed, her green eyes sharp and assessing.

"My lord," she said to Gabriel without preamble, "please bring Lady St. Vincent this way."

He followed her into an examination room, which was brilliantly lit with surgical lamps and reflectors. It was also immaculately clean, the walls lined with glass plates, the floor paved with glazed tiles and scored with gutters to divert liquid. Chemicals scented the air: carbolic acid, distilled alcohol, and a hint of benzene. Gabriel's gaze swept across an assortment of metal vessels and apparatus for steam sterilizing, tables bearing washbasins and trays of instruments, and a stoneware sink.

"My wife is in pain," he said curtly, glancing over his shoulder and wondering why the doctor hadn't accompanied them.

"I've already prepared a hypodermic of morphine," the nurse replied. "Has she eaten during the past four hours?"

"No."

"Excellent. Lay her gently on the table, please."

Her voice was clear and decisive. It grated a bit, her authoritative manner, the surgeon's cap, the way she seemed to be posturing as a doctor.

Although Pandora had compressed her lips tightly, a whimper broke from her as Gabriel settled her onto the leather table. It had been constructed with moveable framework, and was positioned to elevate the upper body slightly. The nurse whisked away the coat draped over Pandora's blood-soaked white lace bodice and covered her with a flannel blanket.

"Oh, hello," Pandora said faintly, drawing in quick, reedy breaths and looking up at the woman with dull, pain-hazed eyes.

Smiling briefly, the nurse took up Pandora's wrist and checked her pulse. "When I invited you to tour the new surgery," she murmured, "I didn't necessarily mean as a patient."

Pandora's dry lips quirked as the woman noted the dilation of her eyes. "You'll have to patch me up," she said.

"I certainly will."

"You know each other?" Gabriel asked, puzzled.

"Indeed, my lord. I'm a friend of the family." The nurse picked up a contraption with an earplate, a flexible silk-covered tube, and a trumpet-shaped wooden piece. Lifting one end to her ear, she applied the other end to various places on Pandora's chest and listened intently.

Increasingly perturbed, Gabriel glanced at the door, wondering where Dr. Havelock was.

The nurse reached for a swab of cotton, dampened it with solution from a small bottle, and cleaned a patch of skin on Pandora's left arm. Turning to a tray of instruments, she picked up a glass syringe fitted with a hollow needle. She tilted the needle upward and depressed the piston to drive the air out of the chamber.

"Have you had an injection before?" she asked Pandora gently.

"No." Pandora's free hand crept toward Gabriel, and he engulfed her cold fingers in his.

"You'll feel a sting," the nurse said, "but it will be brief. Then you'll feel a wave of warmth, and all the pain will vanish."

As she searched for a vein in Pandora's arm, Gabriel asked abruptly, "Shouldn't the doctor be doing that?"

The nurse delayed answering, having already inserted the needle. She depressed the plunger slowly, while Pandora's fingers tightened on Gabriel's. He watched her face helplessly, and he fought to keep himself calm and steady, when everything inside was imploding. Everything that mattered was encompassed in this frail body on the leather table. He saw the morphine take effect, her limbs relaxing, the strain easing from around her eyes and mouth. *Thank God.*

Setting aside the empty hypodermic, the young woman said, "I'm Dr. Garrett Gibson. I'm a fully licensed physician, trained by Sir Joseph Lister in his antiseptic method. In fact, I assisted him in surgeries at the Sorbonne."

Caught thoroughly off guard, Gabriel asked, "A female physician?"

She looked wry. "The only certified one in England so far. The British medical association has done its best to ensure that no other woman will follow in my footsteps."

Gabriel didn't want her assisting Havelock. There was no way of knowing what to expect of a female physician in the operating room, and he didn't want anything unusual or outlandish connected with his wife's surgery. He wanted steady, experienced male doctors. He wanted everything to be conventional and safe and normal.

"I want to talk to Havelock before the surgery proceeds," he said.

Dr. Gibson didn't seem at all surprised. "Of course," she replied evenly. "But I would ask that you delay the conversation until after we've assessed Lady St. Vincent's condition."

Dr. Havelock entered the room and approached the examination table. "The nurse arrived and is washing up," he murmured to Dr. Gibson, and turned to Gabriel. "My lord, there is a seating area beside the operating room. While you wait there with the Winterbornes, we'll have a look at this young lady's shoulder."

After pressing a kiss to Pandora's chilled fingers and giving her a reassuring smile, Gabriel left the examination room.

Finding the waiting area, he strode to where Winterborne was seated. Lady Helen was nowhere in sight.

"A female physician?" Gabriel demanded with a scowl.

Winterborne looked faintly apologetic. "I didn't think to warn you about that. But I can vouch for her—she oversaw Helen's childbirth and lying-in."

"That's a far different matter than surgery," Gabriel said curtly.

"There have been female physicians in America for over twenty years," Winterborne pointed out.

"I don't give a damn what they do in America. I want Pandora to have the best possible medical treatment."

"Lister has said publicly that Dr. Gibson is one of the best surgeons he's ever trained."

Gabriel shook his head. "If I'm to put Pandora's life into strangers' hands, it has to be someone with experience. Not a woman who barely looks old enough to be out of the schoolroom. I don't want her assisting in the surgery."

Winterborne parted his lips to argue, then appeared to think better of it. "I would probably have similar thoughts, were I in your place," he admitted. "The idea of a female physician takes some getting used to."

Gabriel sat heavily in a nearby chair. He became aware of a fine vibration running through his limbs, a constant hum of nervous tension.

Lady Helen entered the waiting room with a small, folded white towel. The cloth was damp and steaming. Wordlessly she approached Gabriel and wiped his cheek and lower jaw. When the cloth came away he saw that it was smudged with blood. Lifting his hands by turn, she began to clean the bloodstains from the creases of his knuckles and between his fingers. He hadn't even noticed that. He began to take the cloth from her to do it himself, but her grip tightened on it.

"Please," Helen said quietly. "I need to do something for someone."

He relaxed and let her continue. By the time she'd finished, Dr. Havelock had entered the waiting area. Gabriel stood, his heart pounding with anxiety.

The physician looked grave. "My lord, upon examining Lady St. Vincent with a stethoscope, we detected a rushing noise at the site of the injury, which indicates the forcible ejection of arterial blood. The subclavian artery has been nicked or partially severed. If we try to repair the laceration, there's a risk of life-threatening complications. Therefore, the safest solution is to tie it off with a double ligature. I will assist Dr. Gibson in the process, which could possibly take as long as two hours. In the meantime—"

"Wait," Gabriel said warily. "You mean Dr. Gibson will assist you."

"No, my lord. Dr. Gibson will be performing the surgery. She is versed in the newest and most advanced techniques."

"I want you to do it."

"My lord, there are very few surgeons in England who would attempt this operation. I am not one of them. Lady St. Vincent's damaged artery is deeply placed and partially covered by the clavicle bone. The entire area of operation is perhaps an inch and a half wide. Saving your wife will be a matter of millimeters. Dr. Gibson is a meticulous surgeon. Cool-headed. Her hands are steady, thin, and sensitive—perfect for delicate procedures such as this. Furthermore, she has been trained in modern antiseptic surgery, which makes the ligature of major arteries far less dangerous than in the past."

"I want a second opinion."

The physician nodded calmly, but his gaze was piercing. "We'll make the facilities available to anyone you choose, and assist in any way we can. But you had better fetch him quickly. I know of only a half-dozen cases in the past thirty years with an injury similar to Lady St. Vincent's that have ever made it to the operating table. She's minutes away from heart failure."

Every muscle coiled. Gabriel's throat closed on a cry of anguish. He couldn't accept what was happening.

But there was no choice. In a life that had been filled with infinite opportunities, possibilities, and alternatives than most human beings had ever been blessed with . . . there was no choice, now when it mattered most.

"Of the cases that made it to the operating table," he asked hoarsely, "how many survived?"

Havelock averted his gaze as he replied. "The prognosis for such an injury is unfavorable. But Dr. Gibson will give your wife the best chance of pulling through."

Which meant none.

Gabriel's legs weren't quite steady beneath him. For a moment he thought he might drop to his knees.

"Tell her to go ahead," he managed to say.

"You consent to have Dr. Gibson perform the surgery?"

"Yes."

Chapter 21

For the next two hours, Gabriel occupied a corner of the waiting area with his coat draped across his knees. He was silent and withdrawn, only distantly aware that Devon, Kathleen, and Cassandra had come to wait with him and the Winterbornes. Thankfully they seemed to understand that he didn't want to be approached. The sound of their quiet voices was an irritant, as was Cassandra's sniffling. He didn't want emotion around him or he would crumble. Finding Pandora's necklace in one of his coat pockets, he held the rust-smeared pearls in his hands, rolling them in his fingers. She'd lost so much blood. How long did it take for the human body to produce more?

He stared down at the tiled flooring, the same kind that had been in the examination room, except they'd installed gutters in there. The operating room must have them too. His mind kept returning helplessly to the thought of his wife unconscious on the operating table. A knife had pierced that smooth ivory flesh, and now more knives were being used to repair the damage.

He thought of those moments leading up to the stabbing, the unholy fury he'd felt upon seeing Nola with Pandora. He knew Nola well enough to be certain she'd said something poisonous to his wife. Was that going to be the last memory Pandora had of him? His hand tightened on the necklace until one of the strands broke, sending pearls scattering.

Gabriel sat unmoving while Kathleen and Helen bent to retrieve the pearls, and Cassandra went around the waiting area to pick up the strays.

"My lord," he heard her say. She was standing in front of him, reaching out her cupped hands. "If you give them to me, I'll make certain they're cleaned and restrung."

Reluctantly he let them slide into her hands. He made the mistake of glancing at her face, and started at the sight of her wet eyes, blue rimmed with black. Dear God, if Pandora died, he was never going to be able to see these people again. He wouldn't be able to bear looking into those damned Ravenel eyes.

Standing, he left the waiting area and went to the hallway, setting his back against the wall.

In a few minutes, Devon came around the corner and approached him. Gabriel kept his head lowered. This man had entrusted him with Pandora's safety, and he'd failed utterly. The guilt and shame was overpowering.

A silver flask was thrust into his field of vision. "My butler, in his infinite wisdom, handed this to me as I left the house."

Gabriel took the flask, uncapped it, and took a swallow of brandy. Its smooth fire seared its way down and thawed his frozen insides a degree or two. "It's my fault," he eventually said. "I didn't watch over her well enough."

"Don't be an idiot," Devon said. "No one could watch over Pandora every minute. You can't keep her under lock and key."

"If she lives through this, I'll bloody well have to." Gabriel broke off, his throat knotting, and he had to take another swallow of brandy before he could speak again. "We haven't even been married for one blasted month, and she's on an operating table."

"St. Vincent . . ." Devon's voice was edged with rueful amusement. "When I inherited the title, I wasn't at all prepared to take responsibility for three innocent girls and an ill-tempered widow. They were always heading in different directions, acting on impulse, and landing themselves in trouble. I thought I'd never be able to control them. But then one day I realized something."

"What was it?"

"That I'll never be able to control them. They are who they are. All I can do is love them, and try my damnedest to keep them safe, even knowing it won't always be possible." Devon sounded wry. "Having a family has made me a happy man. It's also robbed me of all peace of mind, probably forever. But on the whole . . . not a bad bargain."

Gabriel recapped the flask and silently extended it to him.

"Keep it for now," Devon said, "I'll go back to wait with the others."

Just before the end of the third hour, a hush fell over the waiting area, followed by a few quiet murmurs.

"Where is Lord St. Vincent?" he heard Dr. Gibson ask.

Gabriel's head jerked up. He waited like a damned soul, watching the woman's slim form appear from around the corner.

Dr. Gibson had removed the cap and surgeon's gown. Her chestnut hair was confined in neat braids that went along the sides of her head and joined in a coil at the back, a tidy style vaguely reminiscent of a schoolgirl. Her green eyes were weary but alert. As she faced him, a faint smile broke through the layers of formidable self-possession.

"We've passed the first hurdle," she said. "Your wife came through the operation in good condition."

"Jesus," he whispered. Covering his eyes with one hand, he cleared his throat and hardened his jaw against a rough tremor of emotion.

"I was able to reach the damaged portion of the artery without having to resection the clavicle," Dr. Gibson continued. At his lack of response, she continued speaking, as if trying to allow him time to recover himself. "Rather than tie it off with silk or horsehair, I used specially treated catgut ligatures that are eventually absorbed into the tissues. They're still in the late developmental stage, but I prefer to use them in special cases like this. No sutures will need to be removed later, which minimizes the risk of infection and hemorrhage."

Finally controlling the surge of excess emotion, Gabriel looked at her through a hot blur. "What's next?" he asked gruffly.

"The main concern is keeping her completely still and relaxed, to minimize the risk of having a ligature give way and causing hemorrhage. If there's a problem, it will occur within the first forty-eight hours."

"Is that why none of them survived? Hemorrhage?"

She gave him an inquiring glance.

"Havelock told me about the previous cases like Pandora's," he said.

Dr. Gibson's gaze softened. "He shouldn't have. At least not without putting it in proper perspective. Those cases were unsuccessful for two reasons: the doctors relied on old-fashioned surgical techniques, and the operations took place in contaminated environments. Pandora's situation is quite different. All of our instruments were sterilized, every square inch of the operating room was disinfected, and I sprayed carbolic solution on every living thing in sight, including myself. We've cleaned the wound thoroughly and covered it with an antiseptic dressing. I'm quite optimistic about Pandora's recovery."

Gabriel let out a shaken sigh. "I want to believe you."

"My lord, I never try to make people feel better by shading the truth one way or the other. I merely relate the facts. How you react to them is your responsibility, not mine."

The resolutely unsentimental words almost made him smile. "Thank you," he said sincerely.

"You're quite welcome, my lord."

"May I see her now?"

"Soon. She's still recovering from the anesthesia. With your permission, I will keep her here in a private room for at least two or three days. I'll stay around the clock, of course. In the event that a hemorrhage occurs, I'll be able to operate right away. Now, I must assist Dr. Havelock with some postoperative . . ." The doctor's voice faded as she noticed two men entering the front door and walking through the lobby. "Who are they?"

"One of them is my footman," Gabriel said, recognizing Dragon's towering form. The other man was a stranger.

As they approached, Dragon's gaze fastened on Gabriel with dark intensity, trying to read his expression.

"The operation was successful," Gabriel told him.

A look of relief came over the footman's face, and his shoulders relaxed.

"Did you find Mrs. O'Cairre?" Gabriel asked.

"Yes, milord. She's being held at Scotland Yard."

Realizing he hadn't yet made introductions, Gabriel murmured, "Dr. Gibson, this is my footman, Dragon. That is . . . Drago."

"It's Dragon now," the footman told him in a matter-of-fact tone. "As her ladyship prefers." He gestured to the man beside him. "Here is the acquaintance I told you about, milord. Mr. Ethan Ransom, of Scotland Yard."

Ransom was improbably young for a man of his profession. Usually by the time a man was promoted to detective, he had served on the force for a number of years, and had been worn down by the physical hardships of the police beat. He was lean and big-boned, well over the height of five feet and eight inches required by the Metropolitan force. His coloring was Black Irish, with dark hair and dark eyes, and fair skin warmed with a hint of ruddiness.

Gabriel stared at the detective closely, thinking there was something familiar about him.

"Have we met before?" Dr. Gibson demanded of the detective, evidently thinking the same thing.

"We have, doctor," Ransom replied. "A year and a half ago, Mr. Winterborne asked me to watch over you and Lady Helen, as you went on an errand in a dangerous part of town."

"Oh, yes." Dr. Gibson's eyes narrowed. "You're the man who stalked after us and skulked in the shadows, and interfered needlessly as we went to hire a hansom cab."

"You were being attacked by a pair of dockyard navvies," Ransom pointed out gently.

"I had the situation well in hand," came her brisk reply. "I had already dispatched one man, and was about to put away the other, when you jumped into the fray without even asking."

"I beg your pardon," Ransom said gravely. "I thought you might need assistance. Obviously my assumption was incorrect."

Mollified, Dr. Gibson said in a grudging tone, "I suppose you could hardly be expected to stand by and let a woman do all the fighting. The masculine sense of pride is fragile, after all."

A smile flashed in Ransom's eyes, but disappeared quickly. "Doctor, could you briefly describe Lady St. Vincent's wound for me?"

After receiving a nod of consent from Gabriel, Dr. Gibson replied. "It was a single acute puncture just to the right of the neck, entering an inch above the clavicle and extending three inches deep. It pierced the anterior scalene muscle and lacerated the subclavian artery. Had the artery been severed completely, it would have caused unconsciousness in ten seconds and death in approximately two minutes."

Gabriel's stomach dropped at the thought. "The only reason that didn't happen," he said, "is because Dragon blocked the forward tug of the knife with his arm." He glanced at the footman quizzically. "How did you know what she was going to do?"

Dragon spoke while tucking in the loose edge of the makeshift bandage over his arm. "As soon as I saw Mrs. O'Cairre aim for the top of the shoulder, I thought she would jerk the knife down like a pump handle. I once saw a man killed that way in an alley near the club, when I was a boy. Never forgot it. An odd way to stab someone. It made him drop to the ground, and there was no blood."

"The blood would have drained into the chest cavity and collapsed the lung," Dr. Gibson said. "Quite an efficient way to murder someone."

"It's not the method of a street thug," Ransom commented. "It's . . . professional. The technique requires some knowledge of physiology." He sighed shortly. "I'd like to find out who instructed Mrs. O'Cairre how to do it."

"Can you not question her?" Dr. Gibson asked.

"Unfortunately the detectives with the seniority are managing the interrogation, and they're fouling it up so badly, it almost seems deliberate. The only real information we'll end up with is what Mrs. O'Cairre told Dragon when he caught her."

"Which is?" Gabriel asked.

"Mrs. O'Cairre and her late husband were part of a group of Irish anarchists who aspire to overthrow the government. *Caipíní an Bháis,* they call themselves. A splinter group of the Fenians."

"The man Lady St. Vincent saw in the warehouse is a collaborator," Dragon added. "Mrs. O'Cairre said he's a man of position. When he feared his anonymity had been compromised, he told Mrs. O'Cairre to take a knife to Lady St. Vincent. Mrs. O'Cairre says she's sorry it had to be done, but she couldn't refuse."

In the silence that followed, Dr. Gibson glanced at Dragon's bandaged arm and said, "Has that cut been seen to?" She continued without waiting for an answer. "Come with me and I'll take a look at it."

"Thank you, but I don't need—"

"I'll disinfect and bandage it properly. You may require stitches."

Dragon followed her reluctantly.

Ransom's gaze lingered on the doctor for a few extra

seconds as she strode away, the divided skirt swishing around her hips and legs. He returned his attention to Gabriel. "My lord, I hesitate to ask at such a time. But at your earliest convenience, I'd like to see the materials that Lady St. Vincent brought back from the print works."

"Of course. Dragon will help you with anything you need." Gabriel gave him a hard glance. "I want someone to pay for what was done to my wife."

Chapter 22

"SHE'S STILL DISORIENTED FROM the anesthesia," Dr. Gibson cautioned as she brought Gabriel to Pandora's private room. "I've given her another dose of morphine, not only for the pain but also to ease the nausea from the chloroform. Therefore, don't be alarmed by anything she says. She probably won't pay close attention to you, and she may jump to a different topic in the middle of a sentence, or say something confusing."

"So far you've described an average conversation with Pandora."

The doctor smiled. "There's a bowl of ice chips beside the bed—try to coax her to take some. You've washed your hands with the carbolic soap? Good. We want to keep her environment as aseptic as possible."

Gabriel walked into the small underfurnished room. The gas lighting had been turned off, leaving only the quiet glow of a glass spirit lamp on a table beside the bed.

Pandora looked very small on the bed. Her motionless body was arranged with her limbs perfectly straight, arms by her sides. She never slept that way. At night she was always curled up, or sprawling, or hugging the pillow, or kicking the blankets off one leg while keeping the other covered. Her complexion was unnaturally pale, like a porcelain bisque cameo.

Gabriel sat on the bedside chair and carefully took her hand. Her fingers were light and loose, as if he were holding a little bundle of wood spills.

"I'll leave you to spend a few minutes alone with her," Dr. Gibson said from the doorway. "Then, if you wouldn't mind, I'll let the family members see her briefly, so we can send them all home. If you wish, you can sleep tonight in a spare bedroom at the Winterbornes' residence—"

"No, I'll stay here."

"We'll bring in a moveable cot, then."

Curling Pandora's fingers around his, Gabriel pressed the backs of them to his cheek and held them there. Her familiar scent had been obliterated by a blank, sterile too-clean smell. The surface of her lips was rough and chapped. But her skin had lost the frightening chill, and her breathing was steady, and he was steeped in the relief of being able to sit there and touch her. He settled his free hand lightly on her head, his thumb stroking the silky verge of her hairline.

The crescents of her lashes fluttered, and she stirred. Slowly her face turned toward him. He looked into the midnight blue of her eyes, and was pierced with a tenderness so acute that it made him want to weep.

"There's my girl," he whispered. He reached for a chip of ice from the bowl and fed it to her. Pandora held it in her mouth, letting the liquid absorb into the dry inner tissues of her cheeks. "You'll be all better soon," he said. "Are you in pain, love?"

Pandora shook her head slightly, her gaze locking on his. A furrow of puzzled concern gathered on her forehead. "Mrs. Black . . ." she croaked.

His heart twisted in his chest like a scullery rag

being wrung out. "Whatever she told you, Pandora, it wasn't true."

"I know." She parted her lips, and he fished in the bowl for another ice chip. Sucking on the bit of ice, she waited until it had dissolved. "She said I bore you."

Gabriel looked at her blankly. Of all the lunatic notions Nola could have come up with. . . . Burying his head in his arm, he gasped with amusement, his shoulders shaking. "I have not been bored," he eventually managed to say, looking at her. "Not for one second since I first met you. In truth, love, after this I wouldn't mind a few days of boredom."

Pandora smiled slightly.

Unable to resist the temptation, Gabriel leaned forward and pressed a fleeting, dry kiss against her mouth. He glanced at the empty doorway first, of course, suspecting that if Dr. Gibson had seen him, she would have had his lips sterilized.

For the next two days, Pandora slept heavily, waking only for brief intervals and exhibiting little interest in her surroundings. Even though Dr. Gibson assured Gabriel the symptoms were common for a patient after undergoing anesthesia, it was unnerving to see his energetic young wife reduced to this condition.

Pandora showed glimmers of her usual liveliness only twice. The first time was when her cousin West came to sit by her bedside, having traveled by train from Hampshire. She had been delighted to see him and spent ten minutes trying to convince him that the lyrics to the song "Row, Row, Row Your Boat" included the phrases "gently down the string" and "life's a butter dream."

The second time was when Dragon had come to the doorway to look in on her, his usually stoic face drawn with concern, while Gabriel had fed her spoonfuls of fruit ice. Noticing the towering figure at the threshold, Pandora had exclaimed groggily, "It's my watchdragon," and had demanded that he come closer to show her his bandaged arm. Before he had even reached the bed, however, she had fallen back to sleep.

Gabriel stayed at her bedside every possible minute, occasionally retreating to the moveable cot near the window for brief periods of slumber. He knew that Pandora's family members were eager to sit with her, and they probably found it annoying that he was so reluctant to leave the room and entrust her to anyone else. However, he stayed as much for his own sake as for hers. When he spent even a few minutes away from her, his anxiety kept doubling and redoubling until he expected to find her in the middle of a fatal hemorrhage by the time he returned.

He was perfectly aware that some of his anxiety derived from the ocean of guilt he was currently floundering in. It didn't matter if someone pointed out the ways in which it was not his fault—he could easily come up with just as many reasons to the contrary. Pandora had needed protection, and he hadn't provided it. Had he made different choices, she wouldn't be in a hospital bed with a surgically divided artery and a three-inch hole in her shoulder.

Dr. Gibson came to examine Pandora frequently, checking for fever or signs of suppuration, looking for any swelling of the arm or in the area above the clavicle, listening for compression in the lungs. She said Pandora appeared to be healing well. Barring any problems, she would be able to resume her usual activities in two weeks. However, she would still need to be careful for a few months. A hard jolt, such as the impact from a fall, could conceivably cause an aneurysm or hemorrhage.

Months of worry. Months of trying to keep Pandora still and quiet and safe.

The prospect of all that lay ahead of them, and the nightmares that tormented him every time he tried to sleep, and most of all Pandora's persistent confusion and lethargy, made him quiet and grim. Perversely, the kindness of friends and relations made him even surlier. Flower arrangements were a special irritant: they were delivered almost hourly at the clinic, where Dr. Gibson refused to allow them past the entrance lobby. They piled up in funereal abundance, making the air nauseatingly thick and sweet.

As the third evening approached, Gabriel looked up blearily as two people entered the room.

His parents.

The sight of them infused him with relief. At the same time, their presence unlatched all the wretched emotion he'd kept battened down until this moment. Disciplining his breathing, he stood awkwardly, his limbs stiff from spending hours on the hard chair. His father came to him first, pulling him close for a crushing hug and ruffling his hair before going to the bedside.

His mother was next, embracing him with her familiar tenderness and strength. She was the one he'd always gone to first whenever he'd done something wrong, knowing she would never condemn or criticize, even when he deserved it. She was a source of endless kindness, the one to whom he could entrust his worst thoughts and fears.

"I promised nothing would ever harm her," Gabriel said against her hair, his voice cracking.

Evie's gentle hands patted his back.

"I took my eyes off her when I shouldn't have," he went on. "Mrs. Black approached her after the play—I pulled the bitch aside, and I was too distracted to notice—" He stopped talking and cleared his throat harshly, trying not to choke on emotion.

Evie waited until he'd calmed himself before saying quietly, "You remember when I told you about the time your f-father was badly injured because of me."

"That wasn't because of you," Sebastian said irritably from the bedside. "Evie, have you harbored that absurd idea for all these years?"

"It's the most terrible feeling in the world," Evie murmured to Gabriel. "But it's not your fault, and trying to make it so won't help either of you. Dearest boy, are you listening to me?"

Keeping his face pressed against her hair, Gabriel shook his head.

"Pandora won't blame you for what happened," Evie told him, "any more than your father blamed me."

"Neither of you are to blame for anything," his father said, "except for annoying me with this nonsense. Obviously the only person to blame for this poor girl's injury is the woman who attempted to skewer her like a pinioned duck." He straightened the covers over Pandora, bent to kiss her forehead gently, and sat in the bedside chair. "My son . . . guilt, in proper measure, can be a useful emotion. However, when indulged to excess it becomes self-defeating, and even worse, tedious." Stretching out his long legs, he crossed them negligently. "There's no reason to tear yourself to pieces worrying about Pandora. She's going to make a full recovery."

"You're a doctor now?" Gabriel asked sardonically,

although some of the weight of grief and worry lifted at his father's confident pronouncement.

"I daresay I've seen enough illness and injuries in my time, stabbings included, to predict the outcome accurately. Besides, I know the spirit of this girl. She'll recover."

"I agree," Evie said firmly.

Letting out a shuddering sigh, Gabriel tightened his arms around her.

After a long moment, he heard his mother say ruefully, "Sometimes I miss the days when I could solve any of my children's problems with a nap and a biscuit."

"A nap and a biscuit wouldn't hurt this one at the moment," Sebastian commented dryly. "Gabriel, go find a proper bed and rest for a few hours. We'll watch over your little fox cub."

Chapter 23

IN THE WEEK AND a half since Pandora had returned home, she'd wondered more than once if they'd sent the wrong husband back from the clinic with her.

It wasn't that Gabriel was indifferent or cold . . . in fact, no man could have been more attentive. He insisted on taking care of her himself, seeing to her most intimate needs and doing everything humanly possible to ensure her comfort. He had changed her wound dressing, gave her sponge baths, read to her, and massaged her feet and legs for long, blissful intervals to improve her circulation.

He had insisted on feeding her, patiently spooning beef tea or fruit ices or blancmange into her mouth. Blancmange, incidentally, had turned out to be a revelation. Everything she thought she'd disliked before, its mildness, its whiteness, and lack of texture, turned out to be the best things about it. Although Pandora could easily have fed herself, Gabriel had refused to let her have the spoon. It had taken two full days before she'd managed to wrest it from him.

And flatware was the least of her concerns. Gabriel had once been the most charming man in the world, but now all his irreverent humor and playfulness had vanished. There was no more flirtation, no teasing and joking . . . only this unending quiet stoicism that was beginning to feel a bit grueling. She understood he had been deeply worried for her sake, and was concerned about potential setbacks to her recovery, but she missed the Gabriel of before. She missed the private energy of attraction and humor that used to connect them in an invisible current. And now that she was feeling better, the iron control he exerted over every minute of her day was beginning to make her feel a little hemmed in. Trapped, actually.

When she complained to Garrett Gibson, who visited daily to assess her progress, the doctor surprised her by taking Gabriel's side. "He experienced a great mental and emotional shock," Garrett explained. "In a way, he's been wounded, too, and needs time to recover. Invisible wounds can sometimes be as devastating as physical ones."

"But he will go back to the way he was?" Pandora asked hopefully.

"I expect so, for the most part. However, he's acquired an awareness of how tenuous life can be. A life-threatening illness tends to change our perspective on one particular thing."

"Blancmange?" Pandora guessed.

Garrett smiled. "Time."

Pandora gave a resigned sigh. "I'll try to be patient with him, but he's being cautious in the extreme. He won't let me read novels with adventure plots because he's afraid it will raise my blood pressure. He has everyone in the house tiptoeing and whispering so I won't be disturbed by noise. Every time someone visits, he hovers and watches the clock to make certain they don't overtire me. He won't even kiss me properly, only gives me dry little pecks as if I were his second-favorite great aunt."

"He may be overdoing it," Garrett conceded. "It's been two weeks, and you're doing well. There's no more need for pain medication, and your appetite has returned. I think you would benefit from some limited activity. Excessive bed rest can lead to weakened muscles and bones."

There was a knock at the bedroom door. "Come in," Pandora called out, and Gabriel entered the room.

"Good afternoon, Dr. Gibson." His gaze went to Pandora. "How is she?"

"Healing fast," Garrett said with quiet satisfaction. "No signs of aneurysm, hematoma, edema, or fever."

"When can I begin to go on outings?" Pandora asked.

"Starting tomorrow, I think limited outings would be acceptable. Perhaps you might start with something easy, such as visiting your sisters, or going to the tea room at Winterborne's."

Gabriel's expression turned thunderous. "You propose to let her *outside the house*? Exposing her to filthy public places swarming with germs, bacteria, vermin, street manure—"

"For heaven's sake," Pandora protested, "I'm not planning to run out and start rolling on the pavement."

"What about her wound?" Gabriel demanded.

"The wound has closed," Garrett said. "My lord, although your caution is understandable, Pandora can't be kept in a sterile environment forever."

"I think—" Pandora began, but her husband paid no attention.

"What if she falls? What if someone accidentally bumps into her? And what about the bastard who ordered the attack? Just because Mrs. O'Cairre is in custody doesn't mean Pandora is safe. He'll send someone else."

"I hadn't thought of that," Garrett admitted. "Obviously I can't speak to the issue of homicidal conspirators."

"Dragon will be with me," Pandora pointed out. "He'll protect me." When Gabriel didn't reply, only gave her a stone-faced glance, she said in the most reasonable tone she could muster, "I can't stay cooped up in the house for much longer. I'm far behind on my production schedule. If I could just go out every now and then—"

"I've already told Winterborne the board game won't be ready in time for Christmas," Gabriel said brusquely, coming to stand at the foot of the bed. "You'll have to come up with a new production schedule. Later, when your health permits."

Pandora stared at him in astonishment.

His control was going to extend to her business. He was going to decide when and how much she could work, and oblige her to ask his permission for whatever she wanted to do, all in the name of protecting her health. She felt her temper erupt.

"You had no right to do that," she cried. "It wasn't your decision to make!"

"It is when your health is at stake."

"Dr. Gibson just said I could go on limited outings."

"The first time you went out, you became mixed up with a group of radical political terrorists."

"That could have happened to anyone!"

His expression was unyielding. "But it happened to you."

"Are you saying it was my fault?" Pandora stared in astonishment at the cold-eyed stranger at the foot of her bed, who had changed from husband to enemy with bewildering suddenness.

"No, I'm saying—damn it—Pandora, calm down."

She was struggling to breathe, blinking against the rage that misted her vision in a hot red cloud. "How can I calm down when you're breaking your promises to me? *This is what I was afraid of.* This is what I told you I didn't want!"

His voice changed, becoming hushed and urgent. "Pandora, take a deep breath. Please. You'll work yourself into hysterics." He turned to Dr. Gibson with a quiet curse. "Can you give her something?"

"No," Pandora cried wrathfully. "He won't be satisfied until I'm kept sedated in the attic with an ankle manacled to the floor."

The physician regarded them thoughtfully, looking from one to the other as if watching a game of lawn tennis. She approached the bedside, reached into her leather doctor's bag, and pulled out a prescription pad and pencil. In a businesslike manner, she wrote a prescription, and gave it to Pandora.

Fuming, Pandora looked down at the slip of paper.

Take one overwrought husband and administer compulsory bed rest. Apply as many embraces and kisses as necessary until symptoms are relieved. Repeat as needed.

"You can't be serious," Pandora said, looking up at Garrett Gibson's composed face.

"I suggest you follow it to the letter."

Pandora scowled. "I'd rather have an enema."

The doctor turned away, but not before Pandora saw the flash of a grin. "I'll stop by tomorrow, as usual."

Both husband and wife remained silent until Garrett Gibson left the room and closed the door.

"Hand me the prescription," Gabriel said curtly. "I'll have Dragon take it to the apothecary."

"I'll tell him," Pandora replied through gritted teeth.

"Fine." He went to straighten the haphazard collection of items on the table near the bed, cups and tumblers, books, letters, pencils and blank paper, playing cards, and a little hand-bell that Pandora had yet to use because she was never left alone long enough to need someone.

She slanted a mutinous glance up at her husband. He wasn't overwrought, he was over*bearing.* But as she stared more closely at him, she saw the smudges of shadows beneath his eyes, and the lines of strain, and the tense set of his mouth. Gabriel looked tired and grim, restless beneath the surface. It occurred to her that, along with his constant worrying over her, two weeks of celibacy had not brought out the best in his character.

She thought of those brief, dry kisses he'd been giving her. How nice it would feel if he held her, really held her, and kissed her the way he used to. As if he loved her.

Love . . . he often used the word as an endearment. He'd demonstrated his feelings a thousand ways, but he'd never actually said those three simple words. As for her . . . she was the wallflower who'd somehow caught the handsomest man at the ball, the man everyone wanted. Obviously it wasn't fair for her to be the one to take the risk.

But someone had to.

As she watched while Gabriel sorted through the medicine spoons, she decided to take the bull by the horns. "You probably already know this," she said bluntly, "but I love you. In fact, I love you so much that I don't mind your monotonous handsomeness, your prejudice against certain root vegetables, or your strange preoccupation with spoon-feeding me. I'm never going to obey you. But I'm always going to love you."

The declaration wasn't exactly poetic, but it seemed to be what he'd needed to hear.

The spoons clattered on the table. In the next moment, he sat on the bed and gathered her against his chest. "Pandora," he said huskily, holding her against his violently thumping heart. "I love you more than I can bear. You're everything to me. You're the reason the earth turns and morning follows night. You're the meaning of primroses and why kissing was invented. You're the reason my heart beats. God help me, I'm not strong enough to survive without you. I need you too much . . . I need you . . ."

She turned her face to his. Here at last was her familiar husband, his mouth hot and hungering. The feel of his solid chest against hers brought the tips of her breasts to throbbing points. She tilted her head back luxuriously, and he feasted on the tender side of her neck, using his tongue, grazing with the edge of his teeth until she shivered with pleasure.

Breathing heavily, Gabriel lifted his head and held her, rocking her slightly. She could feel the struggle inside him, the violent longing and forced restraint.

As he moved to set her away from him, her arms tightened around his neck. "Stay in bed with me."

He swallowed audibly. "I can't, or I'll devour you whole. I won't be able to stop myself."

"The doctor said it's all right."

"I can't risk hurting you."

"Gabriel," she told him seriously, "if you don't make love to me, I'm going to run up and down the stairs while singing 'Sally In Our Alley' at the top of my lungs."

His eyes narrowed. "Try that, and I'll tie you to the bed."

Pandora smiled and nipped his chin, loving the slight scratchiness of his face. "Yes . . . let's do that."

Groaning, he began to pull away, but at that point she'd managed to slip a hand inside his trousers. They grappled, but it wasn't at all a fair fight because he was terrified of hurting her, and he was too wildly aroused to think straight.

"You'll be gentle," Pandora coaxed, unfastening buttons, pushing her hands inside his clothes. "You do everything, and I'll lie still. You won't hurt me. You see, this is the perfect way to keep me in bed."

He swore, desperately trying to restrain himself, but she could feel the heat rising in him, his resistance crumbling. She moved lower on the bed, her limbs sliding beneath his, and he gasped. With a primitive sound, he gripped the bodice of her nightdress and ripped it down the front. His head lowered over her breasts, his mouth closing over a nipple and pulling it inside, his tongue stroking and circling. Dreamily she lifted her hands to his head and slid them into his beautiful hair, sifting gold and amber through her fingers. He moved to her other breast, tugging rhythmically while his hands coasted over her body.

Oh, he was good at this, his touch sensitive and knowing, spreading thrills across her skin like a net of sparks. He touched between her legs, playing sweetly, his fingers sliding in with such teasing slowness that she moaned and arched in demand. The exquisite deep caress withdrew. He worked his hands beneath her bottom and tilted her upward, holding her like a chalice as he searched with his mouth. She sobbed, writhing softly as he lavished her with textures of silk, velvet, liquid fire, and gently rasping bristle. The muscles of her thighs contracted and relaxed helplessly, her body straining to take in sensation, while heat danced in her stomach and groin. She felt the tip of his tongue against the agonizingly sensitive peak of her sex, darting, tickling, bringing the rising pleasure to the edge of culmination.

There had been times when he'd kept her like this for hours, tormenting her with just enough stimulation to sustain the excitement, and delaying release until she begged for mercy. But now, to her vast relief, he didn't make her wait. She quivered in ecstasy while his hands gripped her bottom and lifted it more firmly against his mouth.

She lay relaxed in the afterglow, purring as his body covered hers. He nudged in slowly, the invasion satisfyingly hard and thick. Braced above her on his elbows, he held inside her without moving, his passion-drowsed eyes staring down into hers. She felt how taut and heavy his body was, how ready he was for completion. But he remained still, catching his breath whenever her inner muscles clamped on him.

"Tell me again," he eventually whispered, his eyes brilliant in the heightened color of his face.

"I love you," she said, and pulled his head down to hers. She felt his deep shudder as the release was pulled from him, the tide drawing back and rushing forward in abandoned waves.

ALTHOUGH THE SUBJECT of Pandora's board game business was not brought up again that night, she knew that Gabriel wouldn't stand in the way when she finally decided to resume her work. He wouldn't like her outside interests, would no doubt air his opinions about them, but he would gradually come to understand that the more he accepted her freedom, the easier it was for her to be close to him.

They were both aware that she meant too much for him to risk losing her affection. But she would never use his love as a whip hand over his head. Their marriage would be a partnership, just like their waltzing . . . not perfect, not always graceful, but they would find their way together.

Gabriel slept in her bed that night, and awakened the next morning looking much more like his usual self. He was all along her back, his long legs drawn up beneath hers, an arm slung loosely across her waist. She wriggled slightly in enjoyment. Reaching up, she searched for the beard-roughened texture of his jaw, and felt his lips press against her fingers.

"How do you feel?" he asked, his voice muffled.

"Quite well." Her adventurous hand crept downward, insinuating between their bodies until she had gripped the hard length of him, smooth hot velvet against her palm. "But just to be sure . . . you should take my temperature."

He chuckled and pried her hand away, rolling to the side of the bed. "Don't start that again, vixen. We have things to do today."

"Oh, that's right." She watched as he went to don a jacquard robe. "I'll be exceedingly busy. First I'll eat toast and then I'm planning to look at the wall for a while. After that, just for some variety, I'll probably lie back on pillows and stare at the ceiling—"

"What would you say to receiving a visitor?"

"Who?"

"Mr. Ransom, the detective. He's wanted to question you ever since you returned from the clinic, but I told him to wait until you were well enough."

"Oh." Pandora had mixed feelings, knowing the detective would ask her about her visit to the printer's works, as well as the night she was stabbed, and she wasn't exactly eager to relive either of those memories. On the other hand, if she could help in seeing that justice was served—and secure her own safety in the bargain—it would be worthwhile. Besides, it would be something to do. "Tell him to visit at his convenience," she said. "My schedule is quite flexible, other than my midmorning blancmange, which cannot be interrupted for any reason."

Chapter 24

PANDORA IMMEDIATELY LIKED Ethan Ransom, a good-looking young man with an air of quiet reserve and a sense of humor that was rarely permitted to surface. But there was an appealing hint of boyishness about him. It had something to do with the way he spoke, his middle-class accent carefully beveled and measured, like a serious schoolboy. Or perhaps it was the way his straight dark hair kept falling over his forehead.

"I'm from the secret service bureau," Ransom explained, as he sat in the parlor with Pandora and Gabriel. "We're part of the detective department, but we gather intelligence related to political matters and answer directly to the Home Office instead of the division superintendent." He hesitated, considering his words. "I'm not here in an official capacity. In fact, I would prefer to keep this visit confidential. My superiors would be displeased, to put it mildly, if they knew I was here. However, the lack of interest in Lady St. Vincent's attack, as well as Mrs. O'Cairre's death, has been . . . remarkable. I can't stand by and do nothing."

"Mrs. O'Cairre's death?" Pandora repeated, a sting of shock racing through her. "When did that happen? How?"

"A week ago." Ransom glanced from her to Gabriel. "You weren't told?"

Gabriel shook his head.

"Suicide, they claimed," Ransom said, with a twist of his mouth. "The coroner sent for a physician to perform an autopsy, but somehow the body was interred before it could be done. Now the coroner refuses to order it to be disinterred. That means no inquest. The department wants the entire matter swept under the rug." He surveyed them both cautiously before continuing. "At first I thought it was indifference or sheer incompetence, but now I believe it's more sinister than that. Secret Service has deliberately overlooked and destroyed evidence, and their interrogation of Mrs. O'Cairre was a useless mummery. I went to the detectives who'd been assigned to the interrogation and told them about Lady St. Vincent's visit to the printer's works. I also made certain they knew about the man she saw in the warehouse. They never asked Mrs. O'Cairre even one question about him."

"My wife was nearly murdered in front of the Haymarket, and they can't be bothered?" Gabriel asked with incredulous fury. "By God, I'll go to Scotland Yard and stir up a hornet's nest."

"You're welcome to try, my lord. But they'll only waste your time with jibber-jabber. They won't act. There's so much corruption throughout the department and the entire police district, it's impossible to know who to trust." Ransom paused. "I've been pursuing the investigation on my own."

"How can I help?" Gabriel asked.

"Actually, it's Lady St. Vincent's help that I need. Before I explain, you should know there's a stinger at the end of it."

Gabriel stared at him for a long, pensive moment. "Go on."

Reaching into his coat pocket, Ransom pulled out a small notebook with a few loose pages tucked inside. He extracted a slip of paper and showed it to Pandora. "Do you recognize this, my lady? It was in the bag of materials you brought from the printer's office."

"Yes, it's the little scrap I found at the printer's works. It looks like a sample of typographic lettering. It was the reason I followed Mrs. O'Cairre out to the warehouse. She'd dropped it, and I thought she might have need of it."

"These aren't typographic samples," Ransom said. "It's a cipher key. A combination of alphabet letters that are used to decipher coded messages."

Pandora's eyes widened with interest. "How exciting!"

That drew a quick smile from him. "Actually, in my world it's rather mundane. Everyone uses cipher messages—police and criminals. The department employs two full-time cryptographic experts to help unravel all the materials we acquire." He turned serious again. "Yesterday I came into possession of a coded telegram that couldn't be deciphered with the latest cipher key from our central office. But I tried this key"—he gestured with the slip of paper—"and it worked."

"What does it say?" Pandora asked.

"It was sent to a known leader of *Caipíní an Bháis,* the group of radicals Mrs. O'Cairre was connected with. It concerns a reception that will be held at the Guildhall tomorrow evening for the Prince of Wales." Pausing, he carefully tucked the cipher key back into the notebook. "The telegram was sent by someone in the Home Office."

"Good God," Gabriel said, his eyes widening. "How do you know that?"

"Usually, telegrams sent from the Home Office are written on blanks printed with a special number that allows them to be sent free of charge. It's called a frank number. It makes the telegram more liable to scrutiny, as the clerks in the telegraph office are instructed to make certain the privilege isn't being abused. A clerk saw a frank number on a coded message, which is against procedure, and passed it to me. It was a careless mistake for the sender not to have used an unidentified blank."

"Why in God's name would someone from the Home Office conspire with Irish anarchists?" Gabriel asked.

"There are ministers in Her Majesty's government who are fiercely opposed to the idea of Irish Home Rule. They know that if Irish conspirators commit an act of public violence, such as an assassination of the Prince, it would end any chance of Home Rule. There would be mass reprisals for Ireland, and the deportation of thousands from England, which is exactly what anti-Home Rulers want."

"What does this have to do with me?" Pandora asked.

Ransom frowned and leaned forward, tapping the fingertips of both hands together lightly. "My lady, I think the man you saw in the warehouse is going to be at the reception. I think he's from the Home Office. And now that Mrs. O'Cairre is dead, you're the only person we have who can identify him."

Gabriel replied before Pandora had a chance to react. His quiet voice contained the intensity of a shout. "Go to hell, Ransom. If you think I'll let you put my wife in danger, you're insane."

"All she would have to do is attend the reception

for a few minutes to see if he's there," Ransom said. "Once she points him out, you could whisk her away to safety."

"It is a limited outing, if you think about it," Pandora said to Gabriel reasonably.

Her husband gave her an incredulous glare. "Helping to foil assassination attempts against the Prince of Wales is not a bloody limited outing!"

"My lord," Ransom said, "if the conspiracy goes as far as I fear it might, Lady St. Vincent won't be safe until this man is identified and arrested. You'll have to guard her every minute, and keep her confined and out of public view indefinitely."

"I'll have no problem with that," Gabriel snapped.

"But I would," Pandora said softly. She met her husband's gaze, reading his anguished fury and gave him a faintly apologetic smile. "You know I would."

"You're not going to have your way on this," Gabriel informed her in a hard voice. "No matter what you say or do, it's not going to happen."

"WHO WOULD HAVE thought my first outing would be to see the Prince of Wales?" Pandora commented lightly as she descended from the carriage in front of the Guildhall.

"Who indeed?" came Gabriel's surly reply. He helped her down carefully, while Dragon made certain the skirts of her formal gown didn't brush the sides of the doorway. She was dressed in gleaming pink satin, the skirts embroidered lavishly with gold thread. A layer of gold-spangled gauze veiled the bodice and helped to conceal the small bandage over her wound.

She glanced at Dragon, who didn't look any happier about the situation than her husband.

Despite Dragon's brooding expression, he cut a fine figure in formal evening clothes, which had been purchased and altered with lightning speed at Winterborne's. It had been agreed that he would accompany Pandora and Gabriel inside the Guildhall and attract far less notice if he were dressed like the other men present.

"There's nothing to worry about," Pandora said with a confidence she didn't entirely feel. "We'll stroll into the Guildhall, I'll point out the man from the warehouse if he's here, and then we'll go back home."

"This is lunacy," Gabriel muttered.

Dragon kept silent, but his expression was one of complete agreement.

"As Mr. Ransom remarked," Pandora told Gabriel, "I'll be much safer when this collaborator is caught. And Mr. Ransom did agree to let you have five minutes alone with him, although heaven knows why you would want to talk to such a dreadful man."

"We won't be talking," Gabriel said curtly.

They crossed a paved limestone courtyard to the massive vaulted entranceway of the Guildhall, a magnificent stone civic hall built in the fifteenth century. Recent restorations had lent it the grace of Gothic spirit and detail, but it possessed a fanciful mixture of styles and ornamentation. The Guildhall was used for all manner of civic functions, including banquets and annual public meetings hosted by the Lord Mayor, and balls and receptions for royalty.

An enormous crowd had amassed in the courtyard, the glittering mass funneling into the entrance of the south porch.

Pandora regarded the gathering with amazement. "There must be two thousand guests here."

"Closer to three thousand," Gabriel said. "Damn it. If you're caught in a crush . . . if someone bangs into you . . ."

She clung to his arm. "I'll stay close to you."

In another minute, they saw Ethan Ransom approaching, lean and elegant in evening clothes. Pandora stared at him, struck by a sense of something familiar about him. The way he walked, the shape of his head. "How odd," she murmured.

"What is it?" Gabriel asked.

"I just had the sensation that I've experienced this before . . . as if I'm reliving something that's already happened." She made a face. "Dr. Gibson warned me to expect this for a few weeks, after having undergone amnesia."

Ransom reached them and bowed to Pandora. "Good evening. You're a vision, my lady."

She smiled and curtsied. "Mr. Ransom."

As they proceeded toward the entrance, Gabriel asked, "Shouldn't there be more uniformed officers for a crowd this size? So far I've only seen two."

"There should," Ransom said sardonically. "A spectacular lack of police presence, isn't it?" Glancing at the rows of mounted Coldstream guards and ceremonial honor guard officers, he commented, "No real weapons. But thank God there's plenty of gold braid, epaulets, medals, and shiny breast plates. If the anarchists attack, we can blind them with our sparkly decorations."

They entered the Guildhall and proceeded down a long, wide corridor that opened to the towering great hall. It was a breathtaking space, with a lofty oak roof comprised of intricate arched ribs, and elegant wall panels shaped like Gothic windows. A temporary wooden floor had been built over the stone floor for the event, to give the hall the appearance of an ancient baronial manor. The rectangular hall was divided into eight bays, with an orchestra playing at the west end, and a huge dais at the easternmost end. Imitation marble columns formed the sides of an arcade arch on the dais, with swaths of green cloth and an acre's worth of flowers spread lavishly all around it. A pair of heavy golden state chairs had been positioned at the front of the dais.

Pandora's uncertain gaze moved over the crowd. The hall was packed full of people, with more pouring in. Even if the man from the warehouse was here, how was she supposed to see him with so much happening all around her? Waltzing couples whirled in time to the exuberant orchestra music. People clustered in laughing, chatting groups. The high-pitched tone began in her ear, and she lifted a hand to tap it away.

Gabriel escorted her along the side of the hall. "Try to look at the room in sections," he said close to her good ear.

They moved slowly around the room, pausing often to exchange pleasantries with acquaintances. Gabriel introduced her to what seemed like a hundred people. Gabriel possessed an impressive recall for names and details, remembering to ask after someone's aunt who was in failing health, or about the progress of an elderly gentleman's written memoirs. The main topic of conversation, not surprisingly, was Pandora's experience at the Haymarket a fortnight ago. The assault, which was assumed to be an act of street thievery gone wrong, was pronounced shocking and abominable, and occasioned a great deal of sympathetic interest. Receiving so much attention made Pandora feel uncomfortable and shy, but Gabriel kept the conversation flowing smoothly.

The orchestra played beautifully, releasing music into the air as if it had wings, waltzes swooping and gliding and darting everywhere. The Mockingbird Waltz. The Fairy Wedding Waltz, the Evening Echoes Waltz. Another tune began, and after the first few strains, she and Gabriel glanced at each other as they recognized "Sally In Our Alley" played in waltz time. They both began to laugh.

Just over Gabriel's shoulder, at the eastern end of the Great Hall, Pandora caught a glimpse of a man with pale straw-colored hair, and her amusement vanished. Startled, she drew closer to Gabriel, half-hiding behind him, and peeked again. She recognized the broad, square face, the bunched chin, the pale complexion.

"You've seen him?" Gabriel asked.

Pandora nodded. "He just walked out from behind the dais." She took an extra breath before continuing. "Now he's headed along the north side of the room."

Gabriel turned to glance at the man, his eyes narrowed into bright slits.

Ransom joined them, wearing a social smile. "That's him?" he asked, his gaze flickering to the light-haired man and back.

Pandora nodded.

"That should be Mr. Nash Prescott," Ransom said quietly. "An Under Secretary at the Home Office. Occasionally I take orders from him."

Pandora glanced at the man again. He reached the door opposite the great hall's entrance, and went outside.

"He's leaving," Gabriel said.

"Damned if he is," Ransom muttered, and went after him, striding through the mass of waltzing couples and causing a few minor collisions.

"I wonder what he was doing behind the dais?" Pandora asked.

"I'll find out." Gently Gabriel turned her to face Dragon, who had approached them. "Watch over her," he told the other man. His gaze fell on a stone bench inserted deeply into one of the room's eight bays. "Pandora, go sit quietly over there for a few minutes."

"I'd rather—" she began, but he had already begun to walk away.

Pandora stared after him with a frown. "Well, this is anticlimactic," she said, while Dragon accompanied her to the stone bench. She heaved a sigh. "Back to sitting in corners."

Dragon didn't reply, only wandered restlessly around her.

Pandora watched the couples dancing, admiring their grace and quickness. She liked the way the abundant skirts swirled around the gentlemen's legs before whipping around in the opposite direction. A graceful woman tripped slightly on a patch of flooring just a few yards away, and her partner automatically compensated. It made Pandora feel slightly better about her own dancing. If an accomplished woman like that could make a mistake—

Her thoughts were interrupted as Dragon came to stand by the bench. He ran his hand lightly over some of the wall paneling, pushed on it, even gave it a knock or two.

"What are you looking for?" she asked, perplexed.

"Don't know." He continued to pace.

"Why don't you sit?"

"Can't."

"Why not?"

"I feel itchy."

"Dragon, I'm not unsympathetic, but footmen really shouldn't mention their personal—"

"Not that kind of itch. And I'm a bodyguard tonight, not a footman."

"You're right," Pandora said. "As a matter of fact, you look the perfect gentleman." She noticed another couple having difficulty on the same area of the floor. This time it was the gentleman who stumbled, as if his shoe had caught on the edge of a plank. "Perhaps some lovely woman will see you from across the room," Pandora continued, "and say to herself, 'who is that stranger with the dashing beard? I wish he would ask me to dance.'"

"I don't dance."

"Neither do I." More couples waltzed past them, Pandora frowned as she saw yet another woman trip. "Dragon, how difficult would it be to lift up one of these floor planks?"

"Not difficult. It's a temporary floor. But they won't like it if I rip it up during a dance."

"Perhaps when there's a lull in the dancing, you might help me look at something. I've seen three couples trip in the exact same place on the floor. Right over there. I'm sure it's only a badly laid plank. But now I understand what you mean about feeling itchy."

The strains of the waltz dwindled, and the orchestra struck up "God Save The Queen" to announce the Prince of Wales' arrival on the Guildhall grounds. As etiquette demanded, everyone stood in the room, arms at their sides, and sang along with the anthem.

Dragon, however, wasn't at all concerned about etiquette. He walked around and between the earnestly singing couples, staring down at the planks. Pandora went to join him. With her thin-soled slippers, she could feel a slight looseness in some of the boards . . . and a definite edge where one hadn't been installed properly.

"It's this one," she whispered, testing it with her foot. A few people shot affronted glances at her—it was very bad form not to sing the anthem.

Reaching into his formal evening coat, Dragon withdrew a slender, well-worn leather roll, shook out a sturdy metal pick, and knelt on the floor.

Four trumpeters entered the room, followed by a quartet of stewards with silver wands. The orchestra played as the Lord Mayor and Lady Mayoress proceeded to the dais, followed by city officers, aldermen, and members of the Common Council.

As Dragon pried at the edges of the plank, people around them began to protest.

"May I ask what you're doing?" one man demanded in outrage. "You're interfering with the Lord Mayor's speech, and furthermore—" He stopped as Dragon pulled up the board and set it aside.

Pandora looked down at the row of neat brass cylinders fitted into the space between the temporary floor and the original stone floor beneath. "What are those?" she asked Dragon, although she was afraid she already knew the answer. "I hope they're some kind of ventilation device."

"They are," Dragon muttered, pulling up another floor plank to reveal another row of gleaming cylinders. "They'll ventilate the roof right off the building."

"Bomb!" a man near them screamed. "The floor is lined with bombs!"

The music stopped, and chaos erupted inside the great hall. Earsplitting shrieks rent the air, while the crowd stampeded and surged toward the entrance and exit doors. As Pandora stood there, stunned, Dragon leapt up and pulled her into the lee of his body, shielding her from being trampled.

"Where is Lord St. Vincent?" she asked. "Can you see him?"

It was impossible to hear Dragon's reply above the roar.

As the fear-maddened crowd pushed, jostled, and elbowed its way toward the doors, Pandora huddled against him. In a minute she felt Gabriel's arms close around her, and she turned toward him blindly. Without a word, he picked her up and carried her to the side of the room, while Dragon blocked the people who pushed against them.

The three of them reached the shelter of an inset arch, and Gabriel lowered Pandora's feet to the ground. She clutched the lapels of his coat and looked up at him desperately.

"Gabriel, we have to leave here now."

"It's all right."

"It's not all right," she insisted. "There are bombs beneath the floor, lined up like sardines in a tin. A tin that's going to explode into a million pieces."

Reaching into his pocket, Gabriel pulled out a peculiar object . . . some kind of clockwork movement affixed to a small metal cartridge. "I found this beneath a loose plank behind the dais."

"What is that?"

"An alarm mechanism with a strike bar attached to a detonator cap. It was set to explode the charge."

"But it won't now?" Pandora asked worriedly.

"Not since I tore it off a row of cylinder bombs, by God." Gabriel glanced at Dragon. "The crowd is thinning near the north wall exit. Let's go. Make certain no one slams against her."

"I'm more worried about the bombs than being jostled," Pandora said, tugging at him impatiently. He kept an arm around her. With Dragon on her other side, they went through a doorway to a yard at the back of the hall that opened to Basinghall Street. Pandora felt weak with relief when they finally reached the cool open air. They stopped in the partial shelter of a bankruptcy court building.

Pandemonium reigned outside as a sea of humanity accumulated on the Guildhall grounds. People dashed every which way in panic. Mounted Coldstreams rode back and forth, while law enforcement vans, carriages, and horses arrived in a clamor. Whistle-shrills cut through the air as arriving police signaled to each other. Standing with her head against Gabriel's chest, Pandora felt the reverberations of his voice as he asked, "Did you lose Prescott?"

She turned to see Ethan Ransom standing there, looking the way she felt, tired but jangling, as if an electric current were making every muscle jump. Silently Dragon handed him the clockwork mechanism. Ransom turned the object over in his hands, examining it as he replied.

"I followed him along Gresham Street and cornered him at the General Railway Goods Depot. But before I was even in arm's reach, he—" Breaking off, Ransom shook his head helplessly, his face blank. "Strychnine pills," he said. "Took them right in front of me. I'm sorry, my lord, but you won't have your five minutes with him after all." He slid the clockwork mechanism into his pocket. "God knows how far this has gone, or who else in the Home Office and Detective Force might be involved. Prescott didn't act alone."

"What are you going to do?" Gabriel asked.

Ransom smiled without amusement. "I'm not sure yet. But whatever it is, I'll need to do it carefully."

"If there's any way I can help—" Gabriel began.

"No," Ransom interrupted, "it's better if we part company for good. Now that Prescott's dead, Lady St. Vincent is safe. The less you have to do with me, the better. Don't talk to anyone about the events of tonight. Don't mention my visit to your house."

"We'll never see you again?" Pandora asked, crestfallen.

A gleam of genuine warmth entered his eyes as he glanced at her. "Not if I can help it, my lady."

Ransom shook hands with Dragon, but hesitated as he turned to Gabriel. Usually men exchanged a handshake only if they were of similar rank.

Gabriel reached out and clasped his hand firmly. "Good luck, Ransom."

The detective responded with a short nod and began to leave.

"There's one thing I want to ask," Gabriel said.

Turning back to him, Ransom lifted his brows slightly.

Gabriel's stare was steady and speculative. "What connection do you have to the Ravenels?"

Astonished, Pandora looked from her husband to Ethan Ransom, who hesitated a bit longer than one might have expected before replying. "None at all. Why do you ask?"

"When I first met you," Gabriel said, "I thought your eyes were black. But they're dark blue, rimmed with black. I've only seen four people in my life with eyes that color, all of them Ravenels." He paused. "And now you."

Ransom responded with a dry laugh. "My father was a prison guard. My mother's profession is one I can't mention in polite company. I'm no Ravenel, my lord."

"WHAT DO YOU think will happen to Mr. Ransom?" Pandora asked during the carriage ride home. Dragon had elected to sit up top with the driver, leaving her in privacy with Gabriel. She cuddled in the crook of her husband's shoulder, while his warm hand stroked over her idly.

"He's in a difficult position," Gabriel said. "Accusing government officials of conspiring in terrorism plots with violent radicals generally isn't good for a man's health."

Pandora frowned in worry. "Gabriel . . ." She was forced to pause as an irresistible yawn overtook her. "Do you really think there's some connection between Mr. Ransom and my family?"

"It would be a strange coincidence," he admitted. "But there were moments now and then when I saw a hint of something familiar in one of his expressions or gestures."

"Yes, I noticed that too." She rubbed her eyes. "I liked him. Despite what he said, I still hope we'll see him again someday."

"We might." Gabriel pulled her into his lap, settling her comfortably. "Rest against me. Soon we'll be home, and I'll put you to bed."

"Only if you come to bed with me." She reached up to touch his lips with her fingertip, and tried to sound seductive. "I'll make it worth your while."

"I appreciate the thought," he said, sounding amused, "but you're already half-asleep."

"I'm not tired," Pandora insisted, feeling a surge of love for him, more searing emotion than her body could contain. He was her partner, lover, and husband—everything she hadn't known she'd always wanted. "My brain wants to stay awake."

"You can barely keep your eyes open," he mocked gently. "I'd rather wait until morning, when there's half a chance of mutual participation."

"I'll show you participation," she threatened. "I'll ravish you. I'll wear the flesh from your bones."

"Easy, little pirate." Gabriel smiled and smoothed her hair until she relaxed against him. "There's time enough for that. I'm yours tonight and forever, through joy, adversity, and the thousand natural shocks of life." His voice turned irresistibly soft, like raw velvet. "But for now all I want is to hold you, Pandora . . . my heart, my slow waltz, my sweet fate. Let me watch over your dreams tonight . . . and in the morning I'll worship you as you deserve. What do you say to that?"

Yes. Oh, yes. Worship sounded nice. Sleep sounded nice. Pandora was suddenly too tired to utter a word, her mind drifting into an agreeably warm, blanket-soft darkness, while his arms cradled her close. She felt him whisper against her bad ear, but this time she knew exactly what the words were . . . and she fell asleep with a faint smile.

December 6, 1877

"HOLD STILL," GARRETT GIBSON murmured, gently pulling at Pandora's earlobe as she positioned the tip of a steel auriscope tube in her ear. She squinted through an eyepiece into a microscopic magnifying lens, while Pandora sat with her head resting sideways on a leather table.

So far during the examination, they had discovered that Pandora's left ear could detect the ticking of a watch a half-inch away and a raised voice at six feet, although she couldn't hear a low voice at any distance.

Still holding the auriscope in Pandora's ear, Garrett reached for a pencil, and sketched a quick diagram. "The ear drum is called the tympanum," she murmured. "I can see the ragged perforation from the childhood injury, and some scarring from chronic inflammation. The tympanum is constantly replaced by the reproduction of cells, just like skin, so this type of perforation usually heals quickly. However, there are cases such as yours where it doesn't, especially when a severe infection accompanies the initial injury." Carefully she withdrew the tube, and Pandora sat up to face her.

"Is there anything that can be done?" Pandora asked.

"Since the condition has persisted for so many years,

I wouldn't expect to recover the hearing completely. However, I think we can bring about some substantial improvement, as well as drastically reducing or even eliminating the tinnitus and vertigo."

Pandora nearly quivered with excitement. "Truly?"

"We'll start you on a daily rinse of antiseptic solution in your ear to encourage healing. After a week of that, I'll have you come in for another appointment, and we'll apply nitrate of silver to the edges of the perforation, to stimulate growth of new tissue."

"How will you put it in there?"

"I'll melt a tiny drop of the silver nitrate to the tip of a silver wire, and apply it in seconds. It won't hurt at all. If for some reason this course of treatment doesn't prove as effective as I expect, I'll consult a colleague who is having some success at using collagen membrane patches to cover the perforated tympanum."

"If you could make any difference at all, it would be . . ." Pandora paused, searching for the right word. "It would be *magical*!"

Garrett smiled. "There's no such thing as magic, my lady. There's only skill and knowledge."

"Very well, I'll call it whatever you prefer." Pandora grinned at her. "But the result is the same."

After her appointment at the clinic had concluded, Pandora walked next door to Winterborne's, with Dragon following close behind her. It was Nicholas Day, when the store traditionally unveiled its annual Christmas tree under the soaring stained-glass dome over the central hall. People had traveled for miles to see the sixty-foot evergreen, every branch trimmed with magnificent figures and ornaments and swathed in glittering ribbons.

Cork Street was filled with throngs of Christmas shoppers laden with huge parcels and bags, and sticky children clutching cones of sugar-plums, macaroons, and other sweetmeats. Crowds massed around the department store's lavish display windows, one of them featuring an artist painting Christmas cards that were sold inside, another decorated with toy trains chugging around miniature tracks. One of the more popular windows featured delicacies and confections from the store's famed food hall, including a huge gingerbread carousel with a candy-paved roof, and gingerbread riders on gingerbread horses.

After they entered the store, Dragon took Pandora's cloak and gloves from her and retreated to a position near the corner. He had worn his livery, as he did whenever he felt a particular occasion called for the prestige of a liveried footman. Today, a week after Pandora's board game had been stocked in the department store, he had judged it necessary to don the hated blue and gold garments while she obtained her sales information from the toy department manager.

Feeling nervous pangs in her stomach, Pandora browsed among the displays. There was an eye-catching grocery store sized just for children, with drawers, counters, and cabinets, a real working scale, and artificial fruits and vegetables. Her gaze moved over china tea sets, doll houses, books, toy wagons, pop-guns, and dolls. A smile came to her lips as she watched a pair of little girls playing with a toy stove complete with miniature pots, pans, and utensils.

By next Christmas, Pandora had already planned to publish two new board games, a set of alphabet blocks painted with animals as well as letters, and a children's card game with a fairy tale theme. What she hadn't confided to anyone except Gabriel was her desire to try writing a children's book. Just a simple story, something lively and entertaining. Since she wasn't accomplished enough at sketching and painting to do the illustrations, she would have to find an artist—

Her attention was caught by the sight of a few uneasy children hovering near Dragon, clearly wanting access to a display of books behind him. He didn't move. Dragon knew next to nothing about children and seemed to regard them as nothing more than short, slovenly adults with poor depth perception. A small group had accumulated around him, three boys and two girls, none taller than his waist. They craned their necks, puzzled by the somewhat outlandish figure of the muscular footman garbed in blue velvet, with a beard, a scar, and a scowl on his face.

Pressing back a smile, Pandora approached the children, crouched beside them, and asked in a stagey whisper, "Do you know who that is?" They turned to face her with round-eyed curiosity. "He's Captain Dragon—the bravest, fiercest pirate who ever sailed the seven seas." As she saw the ripple of interest that ran through the group, she ignored Dragon's incredulous glare and added with relish, "He's been serenaded by mermaids, and he's battled a giant squid. He also had a pet whale who used to follow in the wake of his ship and beg for sea biscuits."

A boy glanced at Dragon's dark face with awe before asking Pandora, "Why is he dressed like a footman?"

"Seasick," Pandora confided regretfully. "All the time. He couldn't bear it any longer. So now he's a footman, and on his days off, he's a land pirate."

The children gathered cautiously around the stone-faced giant. "Do you have a wooden leg?" one of them asked.

"No," Dragon growled.

"Do you make people walk the plank?"

"No."

"What's your whale's name?"

Dragon looked exasperated. Before he could say a word, Pandora replied hastily, "Her name is Bubbles."

"*His* name," Dragon corrected, "is Splasher."

Highly entertained, Pandora retreated while the children continued to wring information from him . . . yes, he had once seen a mermaid with green hair, singing and sunning herself on a rock. As for buried treasure, well, if he had a chest of gold bullion hidden in a secret location, he certainly wasn't going to admit to it. Only chowder-headed pirates bragged about their loot. While Dragon kept the children entertained—or perhaps it was the other way around—Pandora decided it was time to find out about her sales.

Squaring her shoulders, she crossed to the other side of the towering Christmas tree . . . and stopped as she saw the long, lean form of her husband, half-sitting, half-leaning against a display table with his legs nonchalantly crossed at the ankles. Gabriel was all aristocratic ease and cool sensuality, the light of the overhead chandeliers seeming to strike sparks in the golden-bronze locks of his hair. His gaze fell upon her, and he smiled slightly, while his winter-blue eyes flickered with a quiet smolder.

From all the fluttering reactions and ecstatic whispering of the ladies shopping nearby, it was a wonder no one had fainted. Pandora approached him with a wry smile. "My lord?"

"I knew you'd be here after your doctor's appointment. And while I was waiting . . . I heard a rumor about a certain businesswoman whose entire stock of board games sold out in little more than a week."

Pandora blinked in confusion. "They're all gone? All five hundred?"

Gabriel stood and stepped away from the table, which was empty except for a placard on a small easel.

The board game of the season,
The Great Department Store Shopping Spree
will be back in stock soon

"I spoke with Winterborne just a few minutes ago," Gabriel continued. "It pains his mercantile heart not to be able to sell a product that's in such high demand. He wants more games as soon as your busy little factory can produce them."

Distractedly Pandora ran through some numbers in her head. "Blast. I'll have to hire more women, and appoint Ida as the manager."

"The lady's maid?"

"Yes, she's wanted the job for months, and I've resisted, but now it's unavoidable." Seeing his perplexity, Pandora explained, "Back in September I made a rather barbed comment about how much she likes telling me what to do, and how happy it would probably make her to have an entire crew of women to manage and supervise—and she *loved* the idea."

"Why is that a problem?"

Pandora gave him a long-suffering glance. "My hair is straight and slippery and never holds a curl. Ida's the only one who's ever been able to arrange it and make it stay. I never expected I'd have to choose between my appalling hair and my business."

Stepping closer to her, Gabriel nuzzled the upswept locks near her temple. "I love your hair," he murmured. "It's like midnight in my hands."

She twisted away with a stifled laugh. "No, don't be romantic in the middle of the toy department."

"It's not working?"

"It is, that's the problem."

Gabriel followed slowly as she skirted around the empty table. "What did Dr. Gibson say about your ear?"

Stopping exactly opposite him, Pandora grinned. "She says it will improve with the right treatment. No more ringing in my ear, or losing my balance, or being afraid of the dark."

Their gazes met in a moment of shared delight and triumph. Before Pandora could move, Gabriel had reached across the table and snatched her wrist, as fast as a striking leopard. "Come around to me," he murmured, tugging gently.

Flushing at the look in his eyes, Pandora tried to resist, her heart quickening pleasantly. "My lord," she begged in a whisper, "not in front of all these people."

His lips twitched. "Then find a corner where I can kiss you properly."

Pandora found herself wandering pink-cheeked through the crowd with her husband in tow. As they paused to allow some shoppers to cross in front of them, she heard his caressing voice behind her, close to her good ear. "No matter what happens, my love, you know you'll never have to be afraid of the dark. I'll always be there to keep you from falling."

As their fingers tangled together, Pandora reflected that as astute as Dr. Garrett Gibson was, she was wrong about something. There was magic in the world, and it was woven throughout each ordinary day, the same force that pulled the tides and drove the rhythm of a human heart.

Inspired by that thought, Pandora, Lady St. Vincent—a woman with admittedly poor impulse control—turned to kiss her husband right in the middle of the department store. And he—a gentleman obviously besotted by his wife—kissed her right back.

Author's Note

I LOVED HAVING THE opportunity to learn more about Victorian Era medicine and surgery while researching this book, mostly by reading medical journals, catalogues of surgical instruments, and textbooks on surgery, all from the 1870s (thanks, Google Books). Although some of the practices and procedures were just as primitive as I'd imagined, Victorian medicine turned out to be far more advanced than I'd expected. Starting around 1865, Sir Joseph Lister transformed surgery with sterile antiseptic surgery practices and became the father of modern medicine. Advances in anesthesia made it possible for surgeons to perform delicate and complex procedures, such as the one described in this book, which they'd never been able to attempt before. Physicians were able to use microscopes with powerful new lenses and draw from their accumulating knowledge of chemistry to accurately diagnose and treat conditions such as Helen's anemia.

The character of Pandora is my homage to the real-life board game designer Elizabeth Magie, who invented several games, including one called The Landlord Game in 1906. Charles Darrow eventually sold his version of the game to Parker Brothers and titled it Monopoly. For decades, Charles Darrow was given sole credit for creating Monopoly, but it wouldn't exist without Elizabeth Magie's role as the original inventor.

Gabriel's reference to "the thousand natural shocks" is from the "To be or not to be" soliloquy from Shakespeare's *Hamlet*. I think it's a perfect phrase to describe the normal challenges and conflicts we all face in life.

I've tried to make all the information regarding British women's property law in 1877 as accurate as possible. The notion of a married woman owning property or having a separate legal identity from her husband was resisted by society and the government for a painfully long time. A series of Married Women's Property Acts passed in 1870, 1882, and 1884 gradually allowed women to keep their own money and property instead of having it automatically go to their husbands.

Also it is true, as Pandora states, that Queen Victoria was against women's suffrage. As Victoria wrote in 1870, "I am most anxious to enlist everyone who can speak or write to join in checking this mad, wicked folly of 'Women's Rights', with all its attendant horrors, on which her poor feeble sex is bent, forgetting every sense of womanly feelings and propriety. Feminists ought to get a good whipping. Were woman to 'unsex' themselves by claiming equality with men, they would become the most hateful heathen and disgusting of beings and would surely perish without male protection."

More than ever, after having read so much about the incredible frustration and suffering of our sisters in the not-to-distant past, I cherish the rights they fought for—and won. Never discount your worth, my dear friends. Our opinions and our voices are valuable! The sparks you have inside will provide light for future generations, just as those wonderful women did for us.

Pandora's Favorite Blancmange

CONFESSION: I READ HISTORICAL romances for years without knowing what blancmange was. Now I do, and I'm sharing my hard-won (okay, it took ten minutes) knowledge with you.

Blancmange, the classic Victorian invalid-or-fancy-person's food, a French word meaning something white that you eat, is actually delightful. It's an amazingly delicate, light, pudding-like dessert, except you can't call it pudding because it's not made with eggs.

I sorted through a dozen period recipes, and my daughter and I tried the two we thought would work best. You can make blancmange with either gelatin or cornstarch, but we preferred the cornstarch, which is creamier. Also, use whole milk, or at least pour a splash of half and half into your other milk, because there is no more point to nonfat blancmange than there is to an egg white omelet.

Ingredients:

2 cups milk
½ cup sugar
¼ cup cornstarch
1 tsp. vanilla or almond extract (almond is more traditional)

Caramel syrup or fruit sauce

(You'll also need four teacups, small ½ cup bowls, or one of those molded silicone cupcake baking pans.)

Directions:

1. Pour 1 cup milk into a small saucepan and heat to a simmer (steaming with little bubbles at the edges).
2. In a separate bowl, mix the other cup of milk, the cornstarch, and the sugar, and whisk until smooth.
3. Pour the contents of the bowl into the saucepan, and turn the heat up to medium-high. Keep stirring with the whisk, or the mixture will burn on the bottom and your blancmange will no longer be blanc.
4. When the mixture really starts boiling (major bubbling action) keep stirring for 20 seconds, then remove from the heat. Pour into four teacups, or bowls, or silicone cupcake pan.
5. Chill in the fridge for at least six hours, and serve with a drizzle of sauce. (If you used a silicone cupcake pan, unmold the cute little blancmanges onto plates.)
6. Eat delicately while reading a romance novel.

My husband Greg ate four of these at one time because they're so light, and suggests that anyone with an actual appetite may want cookies on the side.

piatkus